PRAISE FOR *WHAT PASSES AS LOVE*

"In *What Passes as Love*, T..ntly . . .
written a powerful, thought-provoking, truly cinematic historical
novel that will have you turning pages well into the wee hours of the
morning. Her story is simply wonderful."

—Kimberla Lawson Roby, *New York Times* bestselling author of
Casting the First Stone

"Another triumphant work of art by the incredibly prolific Ms. Thomas.
What Passes as Love is a poetic, mesmerizing, deeply moving story that
will pull you in and not let go . . . long after you've put the book down.
A must-read by one of today's most exciting authors."
—Susan McMartin, author of *Understanding the Fall* and screenwriter
of *Mr. Church*

WHAT
PASSES
AS
LOVE

ALSO BY TRISHA R. THOMAS

WHAT PASSES AS LOVE

A NOVEL

TRISHA R. THOMAS

LAKE UNION
PUBLISHING

Text copyright © 2021 by Trisha R. Thomas
All rights reserved.

Published by Lake Union Publishing, Seattle

www.apub.com

Amazon, the Amazon logo, and Lake Union Publishing are trademarks of Amazon.com, Inc., or its affiliates.

ISBN-13: 9781542030601
ISBN-10: 1542030609

Cover design by Adrienne Krogh

Printed in the United States of America

Listen. You hear it?
Trees. Wind.
Pushing us to freedom.

Dahlia Holt

Don't think I didn't want to take Lizzy with me. Even if she was never mine to begin with. This is my story and the truth of what I learned along the way. Freedom is never free. It always comes with a price.

PROLOGUE

Vesterville Quarters

1850

The cabin is dark, way past resting hour. I stand in my bedgown listening to the heavy wagon roll against the gravel outside and come to a stop. I'm supposed to be asleep, resting for daybreak when I'll feed the chickens, grab the eggs, and run like crazy before those pink thorny feet chase me out the coop. I always sneak a few extra for Oleen, carefully tucking the eggs under the hay for later. The rest of the basket goes to the Holt house. I feed the hogs too, while Papa Sap stands close by, watching with a keen eye, his good eye. He lost the other when he was a boy.

Oleen tightens her grip. She gives me a jolt. "Get ya'self together, ya hear? This yo' chance. You goin' with him, Lewis Holt, Masta Holt, and that's that. This a good thing," she whispers.

Tears roll and catch in the back of my throat. I try to reach for Papa Sap's hand. He'll know what to do. He'll save me. Instead, I get another jolt from Oleen. "You stop it right now."

"Please, don't make me go. Who gon' feed the chickens? Who gon' fetch the eggs? I promise, Mama, I'll do better."

Her face tightens. Oleen hates when I call her *Mama*. Her own children, her real children, died, or were taken away, something she don't like to be reminded of. Cruel as it is and likely to break her spirit, I say it anyway. "Mama, I'll be good. Please."

Her eyes turn to water. Both of us crying, both of us hoping the other will give in. Both of us knowing it's too late.

The man steps inside, craning his neck, too tall to stand straight in our cabin. This is the first time I see him up close. Usually I see him only from a distance, perched on his horse, kicking up dust while he marches the edges of the wide fields. He doesn't look so scary now. He comes forward holding his hat. He kneels on one knee. "Now, girl, don't you cry. I'm taking you to a better place. I have two little girls just like you. You'll have Annabelle and Leslie to play with. You'll have a bed to sleep in. All your worries will be over."

With the man's hand resting heavily on my shoulder, I try to swallow back the tears so I don't drown.

"She is indeed exquisite," the man confirms to no one but himself.

"Mama, please," I beg one last time.

Oleen fed and raised me from before I could walk. Now she's letting me be whisked away like I never existed at all. Oleen, Papa Sap, and me are a family. Our dimly lit cabin barely holds the three of us with our arms linked together, forget about any space while lying down at night, seamless like the accordion Papa Sap plays on the Sabbath. Still, we belong together.

I twist my hand out of Oleen's grip. I scream. Even to my ears the shrill is as loud as anything my tiny body will allow.

"Come along now." Lewis Holt takes my hand.

I look up, plead one last time. Oleen puts a finger to her lips. *Enough. Go quietly.*

I'm lifted and plopped onto the back of the wagon. I hear footsteps rushing behind us.

"She can't go. You can't take her." Bo is my friend. He lives in the cabin next to ours. He must've heard my cries.

Oleen grabs him, takes ahold of his gangly arms as he struggles.

"Stop it, fore you get beat." She keeps a firm grip on Bo. Papa Sap comes to help hold him back. It takes the two of them to keep Bo from tearing after me.

"Why she gotta go? It ain't right." He wipes at his eyes, finally giving up.

Papa Sap clears his throat before answering. "You can't ask why if you want any peace. You just gotta let 'em go, son."

PART I

PART I

1

Bowman Carter

Bo saw the red thing coming toward him. Could've been a spirit float-ing, or an angry dust like one of those tiny tornados that kicked up when the heat came mixed with the winds and low clouds. The result was a whirl and spit of gravel landing in his throat and eyes. He braced himself, blinked, then squeezed his eyes shut. He gave it a second, waited. The red blur took shape. He could see her clearly now. It wasn't the wind, or dirt, but something—someone else.

Ever since Dahlia was taken to the Holt house, he wasn't supposed to talk to her. Not even look her way. He looked anyway. She was hard not to see. Even if he closed his eyes, erasing her like a gust of wind, the picture still hung there. By the time she was thirteen, she'd blossomed. If someone saw him looking, he'd be strapped good. He wanted to grow old like Papa Sap one day, so he only sneaked glances her way when no one else was around.

Oleen was the only one he couldn't fool. "She don't belong to us no more," she'd say before snatching his arm in the other direction. "She one of them now." *Them* being the Holt sisters, Annabelle and Leslie.

There were three of them with Dahlia thrown into the bunch. He'd worried about Dahlia. So he never stopped watching over her.

Like the day of the fire. He'd grown tall that summer after turning fifteen. He was up early, pushing the feed around for the hogs. Papa Sap had told him he was a man enough times that he believed it. When he saw the smoke carrying out the top window and flames licking the white wood, ready to swallow up the Holt place, he dropped everything and ran screaming, "Fire! Fire at the Vesterville."

By the time he got up the hill, Miss Rose, Master Holt, and the sisters were all standing and shivering outside watching the house glow. Women who kept the house in order stood idle in their nightgowns, grateful to have gotten out.

"Where's Dahlia?"

Miss Rose shook her head, concerned. She didn't know. Master Holt pointed up to the flames, at the top floor of the house. From his bloodshot eyes, leaning over in a coughing fit, Bo figured he'd barely gotten himself out, let alone helped anyone else escape.

None of them knew where Dahlia was.

He pushed past the watchers, ignoring the kitchen women who tried to nab at his sleeve. "Don't go in there, boy. It's too late."

Inside the house, the house he'd never set foot inside, was a haze of gray, thick smoke. Unsure which way to go, he screamed for Dahlia. "Where you at?"

He thought he heard her. The small voice came from upstairs. Smoke hovered over the stairs. He kept screaming her name two blind steps at a time. Down the hall, checking every door, he kept calling. Even when the smoke caught in his throat and burned, he moved from room to room calling out, "Dahlia?"

"I'm here," she barely coughed out. He found her in a big room filled with smoke. He saw her hand waving from where she peeked from underneath the bed. Fire ate up the wall behind it and was hungry for more. Black edges of curtains ran upward before disappearing altogether. The giant bed would be next.

He grabbed the pitcher from the water basin. The grip of the handle burned his palm but he held in his scream. He threw water on the floor. Scooped another until the floor was wet enough before going to his knees. He crawled low on his belly where the smoke was thin.

He grabbed her arm. She didn't want to come, afraid she'd catch fire. He was scared too, but more afraid of staying than going. He pulled the heavy quilt off the bed and draped it over their huddled heads. His arm stayed around her while they moved through the smoke and heat, ignoring the whine and creak of the house. They made it outside gasping for breath. The men from the quarters had formed a chain carrying buckets of well water up the hill. The house had already burned through to the legs once they were outside.

Miss Rose held her arms out for Dahlia to come to her. Bo stood there breathing heavy. He wiped his watering eyes and coughed out the burning in his chest. When Dahlia tried to look back at him, she was marched away. It wasn't just the quarters folks who wanted them to stay apart.

That was the closest he'd been to Dahlia. He could still feel her trembling beside him when he closed his eyes.

The house was resurrected that summer, out of bricks this time. It didn't stop him from knowing which window to find her in. He could still look up and see her prancing around.

Now, here she was just a few years later, good as new, wearing a fancy red dress. Her dark hair waved down one shoulder. Her gloved hands twirled a white lace parasol like she didn't have a care.

"Hey there, Bo." Her soft voice came with the scent of sweet berries. "Just playing pretend like when we was kiddies, that's all. Today is my birthday," she said. "I'm sixteen today."

"Happy birthday," he said, though his face surely showed concern. They had barely spoken to one another since the day of the fire. In those few years that passed, he'd been the driver taking the ladies into the city. In all those times, he'd never seen her wear anything but a plain cotton blouse and flat skirt. He'd heard about the red dress but hadn't seen it until now.

She could say she was only playing pretend all she wanted, but he could tell from the set of her jaw and the crisp tone of her words, she was somebody else. Long gone from the orphans they used to be.

Miss Rose arrived next, ready for their ride into the city. "Good morning, Bo." She was the ma'am of the house. Bo offered his hand and helped her climb into the carriage. Then Leslie. She gave him a wink. She gladly took his help. Not Annabelle, the oldest of the sisters. Bo backed away and gave her the space she needed to get in on her own accord.

Once the ladies were settled, he climbed up top, took his seat on the polished bench, and grabbed the reins of the horses. Papa Sap always told him this place was his throne. Here, he was in charge, looking out over the strong heads of the horses. He was the man leading the way.

"Ha . . . let's go." The horses started with an easy stride, their steps in rhythm, right along with the sound of Dahlia's voice in his ear. *Just playing pretend like when we was kiddies.* He worried about her. Seeing her like this broke his heart. Nothing good could come from her believing she was one of them. They'd make her see the truth one way or another.

2

Birth Book

I was six years old the day Lewis Holt came to take me away. It would be a few years later, when dusting Lewis Holt's office, that I'd find the thick journal sitting on his big, shiny desk, which smelled like fresh oak. I flipped open the pages and read each name with the birth date, their mamas' names, and the space for their father filled with the initials LH: Lewis Holt. All the way down it read the same way. The last line was my name, Dahlia Holt. I was right there with the others. I was their real sister. I didn't know it for sure until that day. It took everything I had not to rip the page out and carry it like a flag of freedom.

Lewis Holt had fathered thirteen children on this land called the Vesterville, and I was one of them. Acres upon acres used for growing crops, along with fifty-two slaves handed down to him from his daddy. After the senior Lewis Holt died, the family worth grew in accordance with the making of more bodies to do work or be sold for profit. Not that he'd understood his mission. Young Lewis Holt was only doing what a boy his age did. Beginning at age fourteen he'd had his first boy, Jeremiah, with a slave named Pearl. Then he had his second and third child by the time he was fifteen. At twenty, he had ten additional off-spring between a slave named Lucy and another named Ravena. Ravena was my mama. It was written right there in the book. Oleen used to say my mama was strong. I had no other description. I imagined strong being the most beautiful thing you could be. I wanted to be strong too.

There may have been more of us. I only knew about the names written in the birth journal. I knew how to read even before I was taken into the Vesterville. I was taught by Holt's mama, Mother Rose. I never asked if I could call her Mother Rose. It's what I heard from Holt and his daughters Annabelle and Leslie. Since I had learned I was his daughter too, that would make Mother Rose my grandmother. It was my right to call her by the same. But before, I'd addressed her as ma'am. Before that, she still called me Dahlia.

"Dahlia," she would call out, waving a hand. "Come on, here."

During that time, wherever I went, my friend Bo followed. He was a few years older than me. We'd sit with Mother Rose on the porch and she'd pass out figs dipped in sugar along with a soft pat on our heads. She read to us when no one else was around. She pointed to words for us to especially remember. Absolute. Happiness. Believe. She talked to us sweetly, saying we had the ability to be anything we wanted on her land: a carpenter, a farmer, or a seamstress.

When it was just me, she made me read on my own. The more words I got right, the more she smiled. Her skin folded hard against her eyes. "Well done, Dahlia."

Learning all those words is how I found out who I was.

I rushed out of Holt's study that day brimming with this information. I whispered about the names I saw to Miss Winnie, who worked in the kitchen. I liked her most of all since not having my Oleen anymore. She sometimes put plaits in my hair like Oleen used to do.

Winnie put her fingers to her lips to hush me. I wasn't to speak about this book to anyone. She told me she saw a book like that once. When she lived on another plantation not too far away. There were some who didn't get in those books, those who were buried before taking their first breath, and the ones who'd been born after their mamas were sold to other lands. She said I should be grateful to be in a book at all, to have a place to call home and a record of my existence. Here I was under the family roof, in a big house with warm beds and hot meals. If I knew what was good for me, I'd forget what else I saw.

I did my best to forget, but I kept thinking of those other names above mine. Some were scratched out. I could still see the first and last letters. I had an inkling of who was in that book right along with me.

I pressed Winnie a few days later, even after she'd warned me to stay silent. The questions kept coming at night. Why had Lewis Holt chosen me to come live in the Vesterville house, out of all his born children in the book? Had they been there before me and now they were grown and gone?

Winnie simply shook her head, refusing to partake in my foolishness. "Just be thankful for Mother Rose," she'd finally added to her silence. "Mother Rose loves you girls, and that's enough," is all she would say.

I thought back to how Mother Rose would watch me, sitting on the wide porch, rocking in her chair. She must've had it in her mind all along that I belonged with them. She'd watch Bo and me keenly behind those reading spectacles. Me and him holding hands, running through the tall grass under the blue sky with not a care in the world.

We must've looked like pure joy, a little fair-skinned girl splashed with freckles, holding the hand of a little boy the color of strong tea, oblivious to our fates. She must've found it hard to accept a girl-child who looked so much like her own, who was her own in a way, lost in a world of servitude. Each time she witnessed Bo and me touching hands, his fingers wrapped tightly around mine, she'd pull our wrists apart and say, "There, that's better." Black and white was all she saw. No in between. As much as she liked Bo, in her mind, he and I didn't belong together. And back then, we were always together. The truth was, I didn't fit in on either side, or anywhere for that matter.

I'd overheard the murmurings of folks in the quarters saying I was cursed. There was a birthmark, a brown river scratched into my skin from the base of my head to the end of my spine. It was like nothing they'd ever seen before. Never having seen the mark myself, I could only feel where the patch of skin began, different from the rest.

Mother Rose heard about the mark and the stories the house folk told. "A snake slithered underneath that gal's skin, ready to strike anyone who got too close. She cursed. Split and put back together again. That jagged line down the middle of her back is separating good and evil, she gon' have to choose," they would say.

Before I'd moved from the quarters into the Vesterville house, Bo and me used to sit with our scrawny legs dangling over the edge of the porch, eating figs. One day, Mother Rose untied my dress from the back. She traced the line with her finger before announcing, "Oh, little one, you just lost your wings, is all."

"Angels have wings," Bo said sharply. "She ain't no angel."

She smiled and tied the dress back in proper order. "Angels come in all shapes and sizes. She'll find her wings and be whole again."

I stayed angry with Bo for a long time for saying such a thing. If I was an angel and did have wings, all I had to do was find them. Whether he wanted to help me search or not, I'd find my wings. He'd be sorry when I did. I'd leave him and this place and fly right out of there.

After I'd been taken, it didn't seem right to be angry with Bo anymore. If anyone understood me, it was him. We both survived not having our mamas. His parents, Jeb and Mary Carter, died from the fever that raged through the quarters in 1849. Slaves were given the owner's surname, whether they were blood or not. Bowman Carter, my friend, was born on the Carter plantation. Once he told me about his daddy, remembering him as if he was still next to him. Sometimes he could still feel his arms around him right before going to sleep at night. I secretly wished I could feel a father's arms around me too. I felt bad for being jealous of this one thing Bo had that I didn't, a memory of his daddy, someone who truly loved him.

Seeing Bo from a distance, in his tattered overalls and with his skinny arms hanging idle with no hand to hold, made me ache for our time together. Our friendship, the way we'd been, left me lonely inside. I missed talking to him.

One day I saw him pulling a cart full of wood. He still wore his overalls, but now his ankles showed from growing in his sleep. I hadn't seen him up close for nearly a whole harvest season. No matter how many times I'd tried to get his attention, he'd marched in the other direction.

"Bo, I got some bread," I called out to him. I held a thick slice in front of his eyes. I took a bite. "Don't you want some?"

"No." He pretended to be busy staring off in the other direction.

"I got some jam too. Come on, sit with me."

"No. Sally and Oleen say they'll whip me good if I go near you."

So that was why he steered clear of me.

He ran off before I could talk him into seeing things my way. Sitting on the porch was no fun without Bo. I found a new place under an oak tree where the air was cool. I told myself he'd come around. I swiped the tears away and kept right on thinking myself into happy. I had my sisters, Annabelle and Leslie. Didn't matter that it was my job to fetch water and clean behind them, I was a real sister. My name was in the book. I saw it for myself. I laughed when they laughed, smiled when they saw fit, and quieted down when no one else was talking.

For a while, Mother Rose treated me the same as Annabelle and Leslie. She dressed us alike, almost identical to the porcelain dolls she kept on the mantel in the supper room. We wore white eyelet blouses and dark skirts with big bows tied at the front. Our shiny loose ringlets of hair framed our round faces. The only difference was, the sun warmed my skin while my older sisters' reddened in the light.

This all stopped when Lewis Holt pulled Mother Rose aside and gave her a stern talking-to. Our differences were to be recognized. Under no circumstances was I to be treated equally. If she kept up her collection of orphans, the house would be unmanageable. I was hurt when I overheard what Holt said. How were we so different? We were sisters, Annabelle, Leslie, and me. I didn't dare ask this question out loud, not when I was supposed to have never seen the birth book in the first place.

3

Red Dress

Thankfully, Mother Rose remained vigilant in making sure I was always within earshot while she imparted her wisdom on my sisters. I was more determined than ever to take in her teachings. I ironed the sheets, washed the floors, and emptied the basins listening to her lessons of grandeur. Where to place my hands at the table, the proper way to hold a teacup, and tidbits of the state's trivia for conversation at a supper party were all just a taste. Mother Rose would finish off with her declaration at the top of her voice, as if she were talking to me: "You have a purpose. There's more to life than being just pretty. Pretty things become ugly soon enough."

I believed her. I watched. I learned. I practiced when no one was around.

How do you do? Charmed, I'm sure. You're welcome. Do tell . . . Then a laugh as if I had not a care in the world. A delicate laugh, not like the hearty laughter that spilled out the time Annabelle wore the dress. I'd clasped my hand over my mouth, but the fit of giggles found their way into the high ceiling of the foyer. The echo bounced off the walls. Try as I might, I couldn't stop.

It was the dress making all the noise as Annabelle traipsed back and forth preparing to meet another potential suitor. She wore the red one made of woven silk. When she practiced her graceful walk, head high, gliding across the polished floor, she sounded like a steamboat chugging along.

"How dare you? Who do you think you are?" Annabelle's cheeks reddened. "Mother Rose—" she began to plead.

"I'm sorry. But the dress . . ." I struggled to stop giggling.

"Get it off me." Annabelle twisted and writhed to take the dress off. She attempted to lift it over her head instead of stepping out of it. Her arms and full bosom were caught in a snarl of stiff crinoline. Leslie helped as we pulled with all our might to free her.

The suitor and his family would arrive any minute, and here she was in the middle of the foyer in her lace corset and underslip. "Take it. Cut it to shreds. I never want to see it again," she huffed once she was free.

I stood cradling the dress too beautiful to destroy. Taking scissors to something so perfectly sewn would've been a waste. I was the one who'd sewn it. I respected the binding of thread to fabric, and the work it took measuring and molding until the fit was just right.

"You march upstairs this minute and mind your attitude, missy, or you won't see supper for a week," Mother Rose snapped. "Bring her another dress, one that doesn't sing like a swarm of bees."

"Yes, ma'am." I held back the tears. This was a first, Mother Rose being cross with me. I stomped up the stairs, as ordered, with the dress cradled in my arms.

For all the times Mother Rose pushed her granddaughters to be more than just pretties, her actions spoke otherwise. What she wanted was for them to garner husbands. To sit up straight, listen attentively, and wear a comely dress for a spectacular entrance. Since the quest began, Annabelle had met six potential suitors, and not one had a notion to take her as a wife. Pretty as she was on the outside, her steely disposition was no match for the young men who showed up hopeful and shy. From one to the next, Annabelle mocked and teased. *What are you, a mule or a man? Speak up.*

Inside Annabelle's room, I leaned against the door, grateful for having gotten the dress to safety. I held the crisp fabric against my body. Before I knew it, I was dancing around to a melody of my own making. I spun, then stopped abruptly when the door creaked open.

Winnie stood in disbelief. She was in charge of the house servants. She came inside and quietly shut the door behind her. "Gal, what you doing up here?" She stood with her heavy arms resting on her waist, shaking her head. Her job was to maintain order. She knew I was trouble the day I arrived at her hip. Too many questions, she'd said. She took me under her wing. The only way to keep a child such as myself under control was to keep her busy. Teaching me how to cut and sew was her way. "You ain't into mischief when yo' eyes and hands is busy," she'd said. I sewed the simplest things at first, a pillow, a sachet, the hem of a blanket, and—my favorite—doll dresses. Then there was the time I'd made a dress for myself. Winnie smacked me good that day, one strike hard across my face with a warning to never, ever take what didn't belong to me. "This here cloth belong to the girls and Mother Rose, you understand?" I rubbed the sting on my cheek and nodded that I understood.

That was then. What I understood had changed over the years. It wasn't stealing if someone else didn't want it. I snatched the dress away from my body.

"I'm getting another dress for Annabelle," I told her.

Winnie let out a heavy sigh. "Don't look that way to me. Nobody's got time to waste, child. You do what ya 'posed to do," she whispered. "Now hurry."

"Yes, ma'am."

Winnie waited. She wanted more than my word. She wanted to see for herself.

I moved across the room toward the armoire. Winnie closed the door with her disappointment lingering behind. Winnie's life had been spent working in big houses. She didn't like anyone upsetting the balance of things. She tried her best to teach me silence. It was delicate training to be seen and not heard. The very same as she was taught at a young age, and still here I was, bringing attention to myself.

When I no longer heard her in the hall, I rushed to the foot of Annabelle's bed.

The smell of sweet cedar rushed my nose as I raised the trunk open. I worked fast, setting the linens aside, carefully exposing the bottom platform.

I folded the stiff fabric of the red dress as small as I could, pushing it down before closing the latch. I intended to keep it safe from harm, right along with the other collectibles I'd taken for safekeeping. There was the lace parasol with a hole too small to notice, a stained handkerchief with the initials AH (Annabelle Holt) embroidered on the corner edge, a pair of worn leather slippers that pinched Leslie's toes, and a strand of Mother Rose's pearls with a broken clasp. "It takes more than a dress to make a young woman," Mother Rose would say before pulling one of her many necklaces from a carved jewelry box. I'd fixed the clasp. Mother Rose wouldn't miss one necklace when she had so many. All these things were bygones, things I was told to throw out at one time or another. No one would ever suspect I was harboring these odds and ends for my private use. Much later, I would look back and wonder, Had I known their purpose all along?

I returned to the foyer, where Annabelle remained in front of the mirror admiring herself. Even in her undergarments, she enjoyed her view. I carried a much more subdued dress, one with yellow eyeleted cotton and a dainty lace collar. One of the other house workers had sewn it. I wouldn't care, not nearly as much, if I was told to cut it into pieces. I slid the quieter, gentler dress over Annabelle's silky dark hair. The undermesh scratched both our arms. I stood behind her to bind the lace ties but stopped. My fingers wouldn't move. Annabelle and I stood nearly side by side in the long mirror. We were framed together in the ornate gold trim.

"Tighter. Your arms made of yarn? Pull," Annabelle demanded.

"I was just . . ." I waited for the feeling to pass. I stood in awe. Standing next to Annabelle, seeing our similarities staring back at me. What I saw barely allowed me to breathe. We had the same face, full and soft until it reached the small dip in our chin. The same dark, wavy hair and eyes.

"Why're you standing there like a mute? Pull it tighter. I need to look desirable, yet ladylike. This is the one. I can feel it." She smoothed her hands over the dress and the tiny circle of her waist before swaying side to side to test out the skirt's flow.

Leslie looked on with admiration. "Perfect dress, sister. It doesn't make even the slightest sound."

"Yes, stunning," Mother Rose agreed.

"Stunning," I said.

"Dahlia, are you in some kind of trance?" Leslie tugged the bulky sleeve of my smock. "Poor Dahlia has turned into a ghost." She laughed.

"You're excused, Dahlia," Mother Rose ordered.

I was grateful to be sent away where I'd have plenty of time alone. I rushed back to the wooden trunk. The dress was calling me. This time I stepped fully into the dress. I held it up with my arms wrapped around myself. I swept side to side, humming and circling in the center of the room, letting the dress make as much noise as it liked.

Hours must've passed but it felt like minutes. The bedroom door opened. I expected to see Winnie again and receive another scolding. But it was Annabelle, with Leslie just behind. Where had the time gone? I braced myself for the slap I hadn't yet received from earlier. Annabelle never would hit me in front of Mother Rose. But here, now . . .

"You look ridiculous," Annabelle said without much spirit. She was dulled by the evening's results. "Where do you think you're going, to a grand ball? Do you have a beau we don't know about?" She flounced on the bed in her quieter yellow dress. "Take it off."

"I think she looks adorable," Leslie offered.

"I'm sorry. I won't do it again." I stepped out of the red pile with my budding breast chilled by the cold. I scooped the dress up against my naked chest, fearing Annabelle would rip it apart and burn it.

"Oh, keep it. I wouldn't be caught dead in that monstrosity," Annabelle uttered.

Mine? I looked to Leslie to make sure she'd heard it too. I wasn't confused. All mine.

From sunup to sundown, I wore my red dress as I dusted, mopped, and polished the floors. It was still a bit too big for my frame, but I delighted in the swishing sound of a chugging train as I worked. The kitchen help and others accepted my new attire as folly, with a few snickers behind my back—until the dress accidentally slipped down low enough to reveal the mark. So, there it was. I was the cursed, the damned, the girl split between good and evil. The whispers became nervous gasps. They didn't want to find out if the myth was true, if I could strike someone mute or cold with a glare. Silence followed. No one said a word about the dress, except Lewis Holt, who'd taken notice. To him it wasn't all in good fun. It was disrespectful. A mockery of order.

"Why are you letting her run around like this, Mother? She's making us look like fools. Put her in proper clothes and keep her that way."

After a long while, I forgot about the red dress, right along with my missing wings. I'd been so busy being furious, so busy planning to be free of this place, I'd simply forgotten childish things. For months and then years, I'd barely remembered about the trunk where all my dreams had been put away. The dress, gloves, and pearl necklace were relegated to the attic, stocked away with all the other storage chests filled over time with cast-off dresses and outgrown treasures.

4

Day Trip

Our trip into the city fell on the day I turned sixteen, August twenty-fifth, just as it was written in the birth book. Once a month we traveled to the Hampton City harbor, mainly for textile shopping. These trips were my only reward, and I was joyous that this one coincided with my birthday. On Leslie's sixteenth birthday she'd received a pair of jade earrings. On Annabelle's sixteenth, she'd opened a box to a pair of French silk stockings Mother Rose had requested from a boutique in Hampton City.

Regardless of what Holt felt about my station, Mother Rose kept me in her light. Always with a hand pressed to my back. An occasional kiss at my temple. Warm words of encouragement. I could count on her to make this day special.

I arrived in the foyer searching for the box that would be mine. I wore a white pinafore over the front of my graying smock. I adjusted the bonnet over my hair and fooled around with the tied bow under my chin.

When Mother Rose arrived in the foyer, she saw the anticipation in my eyes. "What is it, Dahlia? Are you not feeling well?"

I searched over her shoulder, wondering if Winnie was close behind with my box. I felt the tears spring from my eyes before I could ask.

"Oh, dear, what is it?" Mother Rose touched my face with her gloved hands.

"I'm sixteen. This is my birthday. My sixteenth." I bit my lip, afraid to say more, to ask for more.

"My sweet, my darling," she whispered near my ear. "You are right. Today is your birthday. You should have something special. How could I have forgotten?" Her clear blue eyes turned apologetic. "Winnie," she called. Her voice echoed against the wood-paneled walls, though unnecessarily. Winnie was never further than a few steps away from Mother Rose.

"Yes, ma'am."

"Today is Dahlia's birthday. We'll have a celebration when we get back. Make one of those peach cakes."

"Yes, ma'am."

"Take her to the attic to find one of Annabelle's dresses, something pretty for her to wear. We can't have our birthday girl running around in this old smock. Not today."

"Yes, ma'am." Winnie led the way. Her labored steps creaked on the floorboards. She pulled the staircase down with her cane handle. She turned to face me. "Get on up there. Pick something. Be quick about it."

I climbed the stairs. I knew where the trunks were stacked. The first one I opened revealed my long-lost friend. I held it up to the light for inspection. The silk was still crisp. Taffeta was known to dull but the skirt fluffed and billowed as if it had been free all along, not cooped up in a case. I rushed to put it on. I filled out the bodice part nicely while the waist cinched just enough to breathe. My shoulders met the edge of the seams. I gathered the full skirt and moved carefully down the attic stairs, relishing in the brush of the fabric.

Winnie almost smiled when she saw me. "Let me close the back," she said. "You best keep your apron on over this." We went down to the foyer together. Winnie stood nervously behind me. Annabelle saw me first. She came closer, slowing her steps until she was sure she wasn't seeing things. She scoffed, but no words left her parted lips.

Leslie came down the stairs with a hard gallop at the landing. "Are we ready? What's taking so long? Oh my," she stammered, before looking to Annabelle to gauge her reaction.

Then came Mother Rose, who'd been patiently sitting in the parlor. She wobbled a bit on first sight, then cleared her throat. Her reaction was the only one I cared about. I waited to be sent upstairs to change. She could've easily decided against the idea in those few precious moments. *Keep her in proper clothes.* I held my breath, prepared for the disappointment.

It was Winnie who spoke up. "We got plenty more to choose from, Miss Rose."

"No, Winnie. She's fine. As a matter of fact, you can remove that pinafore. And the bonnet. Go on," Mother Rose said. They all stood in silence to watch as I proudly followed orders. I untied the apron and slowly pulled off the bonnet. Pins held my hair up at the sides. The rest fell smoothly against my back. A discernable breath came from Annabelle. Disagreement. Mother Rose ignored her. She straightened her wide-brimmed hat over her silver-streaked hair and proceeded out the door. "Ladies, shall we?"

Without a look back, I rushed out the door. On this day, I was a proper lady. Mother Rose was speaking to me when she said *ladies*. The word bounced through my chest.

As I got closer, I saw the worry on Bo's face. He stood regal in his fancy vest over a white starched shirt and cropped brown trousers. I only saw him on our day trips now, but each time he'd grown more handsome. He gave a modest nod of his head. He opened the carriage door and presented his hand for assistance. His grip tightened before quickly letting go. "Good day, Miss Dahlia," he said.

"Hey there, Bo. Just playing pretend like when we was kiddies, that's all. Today is my birthday."

"Happy birthday, Dahlia. Promise me you'll be safe."

"I promise." As if anything bad could happen on a day like this one.

5

Horse Trainer

Bo understood what it was like being different. He was treated like an outsider when he took the job from Old Ral in the horse barn. He no longer had to work in the fields and was free of shredded palms, calloused knuckles, and the sun beating on his back until dusk. Some would say he cheated. He got out of the backbreaking work on account of someone else's misery.

Old Ral, in this case, had taught him how to tend to the horses, how to dance with those big animals when Bo was no taller than a rail post. His job was to brush, feed, and water the horses daily. On a hotter day than usual, a rattler found its way into the barn. One of Master Holt's horses got bit. The venom didn't take long bringing the big animal to its knees. Someone was going to get the blame even if it was nobody's fault. A good horse met his end, and someone would be held by the collar for it. Old Ral pushed Bo behind him and took the blame.

Though Master Holt was the owner of the land and accompanying souls, he wasn't one for punishing or nasty business such as that. He left that up to the overseer's firm hand of judgment. That was Mister Dodd's job. He bound Old Ral to a tree with no food or water for days. By the time word got to Lewis Holt, Old Ral was a shriveled thing with the rope sagging where his rounded-out chest used to be. Holt untied him. "I'm sorry," he whispered to Old Ral.

Old Ral came away from it slow to rise. He'd lost his balance and some of his sight. Words caught in a stammer underneath the swelling of his tongue. Old Ral wasn't mad at nobody. Later, he gave his blessing for Bo to take over the horses all on his own. Even warned him about Annabelle. "D-Don't look her way," he stuttered from his tongue being too big. "Keep yo' head d-d-down and mind them horses."

Wearing a fancy vest and driving the Holt ladies into the city wasn't a bad way to spend his time. A few folks in the quarters called him *Judas*, as if it were his fault Old Ral got tied to that tree. He shut out the noise best he could. The hurt on his heart stuck around and ached fierce when anyone reminded him. Anyone who believed he was a betrayer wasn't likely to be his friend anyway. But it hurt. He and Dahlia were the same in that regard—not truly accepted where they stood. Not from either side.

That's why he felt a pinch of sadness for Dahlia. He'd heard plenty of stories of the goings-on in the Vesterville. One of those stories swept around the quarters like a brushfire on a windy day. Holt had doled too much attention on little Dahlia, asking how she was getting along and inviting her to sit with Annabelle and Leslie for his hand-puppet show. Holt realized Dahlia was the only one amused, so he focused his attention on her, using his puppet hand to squeeze the tip of her nose and make her gush with giggles. Later that evening, the way the house ladies told it, Dahlia brought Annabelle her tea that night and there was an unleashing. Annabelle threw the tea in her face. "You're not one of us," Annabelle screamed. "You're not his true daughter. You'll never be his true daughter. Father only brought you into this house to raise you as his bed wench, just like your mother and the others before her. That's all you'll ever be."

At the time, Bo wasn't old enough to know what a bed wench was or that sometimes a child was made from such a duty. But he understood mean spirits and knew the way Annabelle treated him every chance she got, watching, always ready to pounce since they were children. Any little misstep brought Annabelle's wrath.

Now, suddenly, he was supposed to believe Dahlia had been accepted into their fold, strolling out in that red dress like she'd been made queen of something. He knew he had no right to worry about her, or to judge her, for that matter. He was just as guilty for the way he turned his back on her long ago. He wished he hadn't listened to Oleen. He wished he'd tried harder to keep their bond. Kept some piece of her, something she could hold on to for times like this, to remember who she was and where she'd come from.

The trail of coaches ahead slowed to a crawl. The familiar slowing meant they'd arrived at Hampton City. The smell of rotting fish and salty air made him wipe his eyes. He pulled the reins for a complete stop and jumped off the coach. He put down the step stool.

"Ma'am." He put out a hand to help Mother Rose take her first step down.

"Thank you, Bo." She handed him a fig. "Excellent driving. We'll see you in a few hours."

"Yes, ma'am." He watched them leave. He couldn't take his eyes off Dahlia as she sashayed down the street with the rest of them. From behind, there was no difference between her and the two sisters, all three with their skirts full and parasols open. The looming swell came over him again, filled his chest with dread. He rubbed where the sharp pain rumbled in his gut. This day would end in misery, yet he was powerless to stop it.

6

Brothers

As we left the coach I spun around to wave at Bo, only to see him staring at me like I'd grown a squash for a head. I wasn't worried about
what he thought or didn't think of me. This was my day to celebrate.
Sixteen years alive. I was a lady now. The air smelled sweeter. The sky
looked bluer. I inhaled the fresh scent of plump, juicy peaches, plums,
and berries.

The harborside was filled with ladies and gents strolling, getting in
each other's way, bumping shoulders, and nodding hello and apologies,
and I walked eagerly in their company. Annabelle and Leslie glided
ahead while Mother Rose and I remained a few steps behind. Mother
Rose linked her arm in mine but kept a firm grip on her cane, not as a
crutch but a symbol of her influence. She'd shake the polished handle
at the shop owners to make her point. If she didn't get the price of her
choosing, she would not hesitate to move on.

We slowed as we approached the first stop. I was familiar with the
merchant's window. The same doll with a screaming painted black face,
sharp hideous teeth, and hair pointed to the sky sat in a mini rocking
chair, holding a wooden spoon. I didn't like that doll. She didn't look
anything like any of my folks in the quarters. The store was also filled
with pistols of various sizes displayed like art instead of weapons used

for killing. Larger weapons hung on the walls—swords, hatchets, and knives. Oddly, in the center of the store were delicate tea sets with tiny silver spoons for stirring. There were folded fine linens in brilliant colors. There were crystal figurines like the one Mother Rose was holding up for inspection.

I moved to her side. "I'm going to catch up with Annabelle and Leslie," I said, eager to leave. I couldn't bear to remain in that place a second longer.

"I'll be along shortly," Mother Rose said. "Don't speak to strangers."

I stepped out and greedily inhaled the salty air. I pushed my shoulders back and imagined this world through the eyes of a young lady simply out for a stroll in the city.

Annabelle and Leslie were ahead, their faces pressed against the Libby's Fine Laces and Textiles shop window. My attention turned to the scents and potions cart across the way. No one would notice I was missing until packages needed carrying. I had plenty of time while Mother Rose haggled over the price of her crystal bird. Annabelle and Leslie would touch every fabric by hand in Libby's Fine Laces. Annabelle was especially careful now. She no longer desired shiny satins and silks, what she called buffoon's attire. With each passing year, she increasingly favored heavy velvets and thick cottons. Having passed her twentieth year without a prospect of marriage had quieted her spirit and dulled her desire for fancy dresses.

"Can I help you, young lady? May I interest you in a scent?" The man's cheery voice came first, before he peeked from behind the mirror. He pushed a small brown bottle toward my face.

"No. No, thank you." I took a ragged breath and held it.

"Only the finest for a lovely girl such as yourself. Try it." He pushed a tiny bottle of scented oil under my nose.

"Why, thank you." I dabbed a small amount on my wrist the way I'd seen Annabelle do. I scrunched my nose.

The man laughed. "Not to your liking, huh? I have others."

The man confirmed what I'd prayed would be true. There was no judgment in his eyes. He didn't see a child or a house girl. I took several jubilant steps away before realizing I was on the other side of the street.

I hummed in a pitch too high, the only song I knew. Then the words came. *"Oh! Susanna, don't you cry for me . . ."* I sang the same chorus over and over, pausing to say "How do you do?" and "Good morning." I gave children pats on the head as they licked their Sunday creams.

"Aren't you adorable," their mothers greeted me in return. The elation in my heart could only be compared to . . . I had nothing to compare it to.

In my state of revelry, I'd strayed far past the main street. The stream of townspeople walking toward me made it difficult to get my bearings. I couldn't figure out where I'd gone.

That's when I noticed him, the young man staring at me from across the way. Smiling, even. I darted my eyes away. I peeked again; this time there were two of them. The older one with fair hair and handsome creases in his face parted his lips to say something to the other. He nudged the younger one with his elbow. Friends, I thought, until I saw the sly conspiratorial smile. Brothers, for sure. I held my breath as they approached. I considered turning and quickly walking off.

Before I could, the older one stood before me.

He took off his hat. "Hello. I take it you're new in town?" He pronounced his words carefully in a singsong sort of way, like visitors Mother Rose once had from England. Up close, the man's eyes were thinly brown, showing flecks of gold. He seemed harmless enough. "Ryland Ross." He reached out and took my gloved hand. "You're quite beautiful," he said before letting go.

"That would make two of us—noticing your beauty," the younger one interrupted. He was the opposite of his brother, dark hair and eyes, and yet there was still an overall resemblance between the two. "Timothy Ross, at your service. Pleased to make your acquaintance."

"My name's Dah—" I stopped myself. The song I'd been singing, "Oh! Susanna," came to mind. But it was the crystal bird with wide wings I'd left Mother Rose contemplating that shifted my decision. "Dove," I said, quickly scanning the ground around me, then seeing a basket of bright yellow lilies lying near my feet. "Lily Dove. Pleasure to make your acquaintance." I stepped a small distance away from both men, knowing Annabelle and Leslie weren't too far off. If Annabelle were to show up, she'd ruin everything and take no mercy in exposing me.

"Lily Dove. You'll have to excuse my brother. We're not all this forward," Timothy Ross said with a steady gaze.

"You make it sound like a clan. How many of you are there?" It was my best attempt at being jovial. Mother Rose always impressed upon her girls to be light, to glow in darkness. *Suitors will come like moths to a flame,* she'd say.

"We're not a tribe of savages, I assure you. When we see a beautiful young woman, we must speak our admiration." Ryland picked a long-stemmed rose from the nearby flower cart, inhaling gently before offering the flower. "For you."

There was obvious competition between the two, a game of sorts. The younger one showed a surge of confidence, pushing past his older brother. He picked a yellow lily from the bunch as his offering. "A lily for Lily. I'd love to accompany you for the rest of the afternoon."

Ryland huffed and chuckled. "Oh, really? Take it down a notch, brother."

"Why? I have no shame. You said yourself she was a beauty. I admit to being smitten by your loveliness, Lily Dove." Timothy's cheeks remained blotched with embarrassed redness. Though he pretended to be full of confidence, a shy cloak hung clumsily on his shoulders.

"I'm flattered," I said.

"My, my, you are elementary." Ryland narrowed his eyes with a smirk, staring back and forth at both of us.

"Elementary?" I asked.

"Pleasant," Timothy interjected. "He means you have a very pleasant air, a breath of fresh air, if you will."

"I think we should be leaving," Ryland announced with a suddenly stern tone. He leaned near his brother's ear. "It's time we let this young lady carry on with her afternoon. Good to meet you, Lily Dove."

"I'll stay with you for as long as you need me. A young lady should not be without a chaperon," Timothy said, ignoring his older brother's orders. His hands remained clasped behind his back. A lock of his dark hair fell over the side of his face.

I looked around for Mother Rose. I looked for my sisters before I smiled. "That won't be necessary."

"I insist," he said. "I absolutely insist."

7

Gone

"We should be going," Ryland announced, anxious. "We have important business to tend to, or have you forgotten, brother?"

"Then leave," Timothy said. His eyes landed on the black bag Ryland carried over his shoulder. "I insist on remaining in this lovely young woman's company for the rest of the afternoon. I'm sure you can handle what is left of the day, big brother. As they say, the devil is in the details."

"Fine, then. This will be your loss."

I lowered my lashes, confused. One minute Ryland Ross had been vying for my hand with flowers, and the next, he wanted nothing to do with me and wanted Timothy to leave with him.

"At the close of the day, I will be on the train, with or without you," he said. He walked off. He then looked back, meeting my eyes squarely.

"Shall we go?" Timothy asked. He was proud to be the victor. "A young lady in town alone. Your worries are over. It will be my honor to deliver you safely to your lodging."

I should've spoken up. I should've told him there was no lodging. I belonged in one place, and that was at Mother Rose's side. I wanted to end the charade and send Timothy off with his brother, but Ryland had already disappeared into the sea of hats and dark wool coats.

"You seem disappointed," Timothy said. "Should I have left instead of my brother?"

"No. I'm sorry. Not at all."

"Well then, shall we?" He propped his elbow out. I looped my arm through his.

What was I doing? If Mother Rose saw what was happening, she'd never forgive me.

"What is it?" His brown eyes sparkled. "You came to the city to shop, didn't you? Well, let's shop."

I looked around at all the faces coming and going. No one knew who I was or cared. Timothy was kind enough. He was hardly threatening. *Only for a moment,* I told myself. *I'll never have this chance again.*

We did exactly what he said we'd do: shop. Though I didn't dare step into one of those boutiques. Between looking over my shoulder and using the shop windows' reflection as a second pair of eyes, I tried to appear light as air. As I stood in front of one window after the other, he'd whisper things only I could hear. *"Ghastly. You wouldn't want to wear that. Maybe for a grandmother. Looks like a collar made of rat tails."* I found myself giggling, constantly smiling at what he might say next. After a while there was no need to pretend. I'd lost the blinding fear of being seen by Mother Rose or my sisters. I'd settled on one thing, which was that it was all perfectly worth it.

Those joyous moments of walking alongside Timothy with no destination were worth whatever punishment was in store for me. After a while, my feet sweltered and my ankles felt constrained in the lace-up boots I'd outgrown years earlier. We stopped and took a seat on a wooden bench overlooking the harbor. Never mind the dirt grazing my hem. I didn't mind. A lady such as myself would have someone to wash the stains, though of course that someone would be me.

I smiled at the thought, another me, at my hand and foot doing my bidding.

But quickly stopped smiling because there was no other me, only this one, and my time had run out. My mood changed as swiftly as the heavy clouds that had suddenly grown dark over the bay. A large ship passed slowly, letting out a trail of steam. Passengers waved with excitement as the ship grew distant from the harbor.

Timothy turned to face me. "I'm from England, a place very far from here, another country entirely. Are you familiar?"

What I knew of England, Mother Rose had spoken of as her grandmother's birthplace. I nodded for him to continue.

"My family moved here only a year ago to start anew. We have a nice home, a house large enough to start families of our own." His glossy eyes searched mine. The clouds overhead had turned the air suddenly cool and brought about a leaking spell. He moved a kerchief to his nose and patted gently at the moisture. "We're growing cotton, corn, and wheat. It used to be a tobacco farm. The soil is weak. The first crops haven't yielded a profit as of yet. If my brother and I fail, I fear we'll be back on that dreadful barge to sail twenty-one days and nights. It was a foul journey, one I never want to repeat. And now that I've met you, it makes my desire to stay even stronger." His hand covered mine briefly before I pulled away.

"That's a great deal of pressure." My throat turned dry. I blushed, genuinely overwhelmed by his words.

"I've told you about myself. You've told me nothing about yourself. Where are you from?" He took my hand again. I checked again for passersby before relaxing and leaving it in his possession.

I swallowed my fear and decided to try my hand at telling *Lily Dove*'s story. "I grew up here in Hampton. My mother died when I was very young. My father and grandmother raised me. Then it was only my grandmother and me, until recently." I peeked in his direction to see if he believed me.

"She's passed on as well, then?" he asked, seemingly hopeful. "So, you really have no one? You're all alone?"

I nodded yes. I wanted to end the conversation before my failings became apparent. There were endless questions and answers I wasn't prepared for. Next time, I told myself, my life would be perfectly reimagined. I stood abruptly and straightened the skirt of my dress. "It was a pleasure meeting you, Timothy Ross. But I must get back." The light mist in the air would turn into a drizzle. By now Mother Rose would be worried sick, demanding a search, shaking her cane at whomever was in listening distance. *Dahlia is missing.*

"Where must you go? I thought you were alone?" he asked again, needing to be sure. His hand gripped mine. "I'll escort you back to wherever it is you'd like to return to."

"No. Thank you." I pulled my hand away. I did a strange curtsey, a combination of what I'd seen Annabelle practice and my own interpretation with a half bend at the waist. "I'll be fine. It's best if I be—"

"Discreet," he answered for me.

"Yes. Discreet."

He followed closely as I began painfully walking. "I'll escort you as far as I can without being noticed. I promise not to compromise your good name, Lily Dove."

"I have to go back, alone. I'm sorry," I said, realizing I had no idea where I was marching off to. I turned and spun back in my original direction. I'd always walked behind Annabelle and Leslie, holding on to Mother Rose as if she needed my assistance when it was I who'd required her direction. All those many trips before when I'd followed along without noticing where I was being led now made me feel ridiculous.

So many streets had names that brought no recollection. The signs meant nothing. The rows of buildings painted in shades of ivory repeated each other. I couldn't tell one set of buildings from the other. One step off the beaten path and I'd fallen into a hole, lost, unable to figure out which direction would take me back to Mother Rose and Bo.

"Are you all right?" Timothy asked. Something in his demeanor seemed to take pleasure in me being lost. "I'm very familiar with the city. If you know the name of your destination, I can take you."

Just before panic closed in, a public coach passed with a carved plaque nailed to the side. "The Hotel De Forage," I sang out, reading the sign as the horses galloped past. The name was familiar. It must've been a place I'd seen many times.

"Hotel De Forage, I know it very well. Come along."

I followed one step behind, stopping every few feet, unsure, and growing more uncomfortable as he led me further, it seemed, away. I began to chastise myself at each step. He seemed kind. That is what I'd tell Mother Rose. I'd explain it was like those stories she would read aloud to us—me, Annabelle, and Leslie. Stories of mythical creatures, damsels and princes, castles and kings that I'd daydream about long after the story was told. I knew the tales were meant for my sisters, but I couldn't help but see myself galloping off into the sunset. I wanted the prince, the castle, and the magical basket of apples to feed the hungry.

Timothy, with his gentle mannerisms and square chin, was a perfect fit to place in the center of my dreams. And yet each step I traveled by his side made me afraid it would be my last. What if this prince turned out to be the death of me? I knew nothing of Timothy Ross. I had no proof he was a man of his word and would guide me where he'd promised.

Hotel De Forage, there it was, the building just steps ahead. A regally suited dark-skinned man with a tall black hat held the large red door open. He nodded as we approached. I slowed, afraid the man would see past my red dress and easy bearing and deny me entrance into the hotel. What if he could see the one drop of familiar blood, a silent kinship, flowing through our veins?

"It was a pleasure." Timothy spoke with his head low, as if his plan for greater purpose had failed. He put out his hand.

I only stared at it.

"I understand." His tone wavered slightly.

"Thank you, for everything." I turned to leave. I prayed I could slip back into my old life, back to Dahlia who'd wanted a taste of the forbidden. I'd smelled, tasted, and seen freedom; now it was time to step back into what was expected of me.

The doorman presented a wide berth between us to let me inside. Before I could cross the threshold, an alarm sounded, an incessant bell loud enough to vibrate the large hotel window where I still stood. My mouth went dry, and the river of skin down the center of my back came alive. The familiar tingling began as if I'd been lying in a thistle bush. I shrank back against the hotel wall. My stomach burned with sharp damning jabs. A rush of heat covered my cheeks. *Mother Rose sent the lawmen looking for me.*

Mother Rose would have no choice but to report me as a runaway. I'd be treated like a criminal, or worse, like a slave, dragged and beaten. I didn't want Timothy to see me that way. See me for who I truly was.

A sturdy lawman hurried past, carrying a large billy club. He yelled at us, "There's been an incident. Get inside." Two more lawmen ran past on the hunt. People began to rush through the middle of the street.

"You seem ill. What is it?" Timothy stayed at my side, unfazed by the chaos. "You should sit. Come, let's go inside."

"No. I can't go inside. I need to get back," I whispered.

"Get back where? We're here already, at the Hotel De Forage," he said over and above the noise. More people were moving as quickly as they could toward the edge of the city, where most of the carriages awaited. Bo and Mother Rose would be headed there too. I could simply blend in and move with the crowd.

My eyes watered gently, giving me fair warning. I was going to be ill.

Before I stumbled forward, Timothy wrapped his arm around my waist. "This way." He led me to a small space on the side of the brick building. He remained by my side as spasms racked my body until there was nothing left of my morning bread.

"I simply cannot leave you like this," he said, offering me his kerchief.

I desperately pressed the cloth to my forehead, afraid another wave of despair would break. I was at his mercy.

"Don't worry," he said. "I won't leave your side."

8

Lawmen

Bo sat up straight. Gunshots? Thunder? He checked the sky for clouds. The gray cast overhead wasn't dark enough to cause all this ruckus. A thud echoed from a distance, finding its way back to the outer edge of town. He pushed his hat away from his face to get a good look at the surroundings. Gunshots. He was sure of it. The horses swung their heads and stomped their hooves in the gravel. They didn't like a whole lot of noise.

He gathered the horses by their leather straps to let them know he was right there. "Take it easy, now. Everything gon' be all right."

"Boy, you see anyone running through here?" Before Bo could answer, a stab of pain swept up his back. The man dressed in all black, with a shiny badge pinned to his chest, had whacked him. "You hear me, boy? You see anybody run through here?"

"Sir, I'm waiting for my ladies. My ladies, sir, are shopping." His eyes watered from holding in a gasp. He dared not reach for the pain across his back.

"I didn't ask for all that lip."

This time the jab came to the center of his belly. He resisted the urge to fold. He gulped the air and kept standing. "I ain't see nothing, sir."

"You see something, you yell out," the man ordered before joining more lawmen as they ran up and down the street asking questions.

Other drivers knew to follow suit, heads and eyes straight. What had they seen? Anyone gallop past here? They let the lawmen poke at them with their sticks and ask questions, but they would keep their lips tight. Another lawman made his rounds, looking into the carriages to make sure no one was hiding.

After the lawmen moved on, Bo climbed up top to get a better look. Folks moved like a herd getting to safety. Hats and bonnets swarmed toward the waiting carriages. There was no sign of smoke or danger. No one was chasing them. They were just running. He spotted Annabelle, then Leslie and Miss Rose.

Annabelle reached the carriage first. "Where's Dahlia?" she asked, out of breath.

"She not here," Bo said, checking over the swarm of heads. He searched best he could. "I thought I saw her," he mumbled, then stopped himself from yelling *There she is.* The floating red thing could've been his mind playing tricks. The floating red thing wasn't alone. A man dressed dapper like Master Holt on a Sunday afternoon, close enough to be holding on. Afraid she might get away.

Annabelle rounded to the other side of the carriage, checking for herself. "I told you. I told you she's run off. Dahlia's not here," she confirmed to Mother Rose, who was a few steps behind.

Mother Rose had to take a beat to catch her breath. "What do you mean, she's not here?" She pulled out a soft linen to pat her face.

"Dahlia not here, ma'am. Been here the whole time." Bo pulled the curtain back to show there was no one inside.

"We have to find her." She cast a nervous look in the direction of the lawman who was circling back. "Over here. You," she yelled and flagged the lawman. "We can't leave," she announced. "We're missing our gal. She's wearing a red dress, my gal, she's fair skinned, long dark hair like my Annabelle here. Maybe you've seen her?"

Annabelle pouted at the comparison.

"You have to find her. Her name's Dahlia." Mother Rose faced the lawman. "Please. We can't leave without her."

"Sounds like a problem of ya' own," the lawman said over the ladies' heads. He used his polished stick to tap one of the horses on the back. "There was a bank robbery. We won't rest until this place is turned upside down. Best you move on."

"Let's go, Mother Rose," Annabelle whispered. "She's run off. You saw her dress—"

"Hush. Not now, Annabelle."

Bo took ahold of Mother Rose by her arm. "Ma'am, we better go."

She snatched her arm away. "No, thank you."

Bo wanted to find Dahlia. If he didn't bring her back unharmed, Master Holt would surely take it out on him. Then again, the horses were their only way home. He feared the lawman would take another swing at one of them. It would do none of them any good if one of the horses' legs got snapped. Mister Dodd would make sure he ended up just like Old Ral.

His mind spun. Was he really bartering in his mind over who was more valuable, the horses or Dahlia?

He whispered to Mother Rose, fighting off the tremor in his voice. "We got to clear out before he do something to the horses. We can circle back and look for Dahlia after the lawmen get on."

Mother Rose finally moved. Bo helped her into the narrow opening of the carriage. She plopped onto the padded bench and began to fan herself in panic. "We can't leave. Our gal is missing," Mother Rose hissed out the window to the lawman.

"Gal or no gal. You move this wagon, or I'll move it for you." The lawman rushed toward them.

Mother Rose made an unsteady leap down the step of the carriage. "You listen here. I am Rosetta Holt, mother of Lewis Holt the Second, a good friend of the governor. I will not be disrespected in this manner."

"I don't care who you are. You'll do what I say." The lawman's slits for eyes matched his tight line of a mouth. "I got one job, to clear the streets, and I'll do whatever it takes to make it so." He lifted his stick to come down on Mother Rose.

Bo put himself between them and snatched the stick.

The lawman looked up at Bo and tried to pretend he wasn't frightened for his life. "You stay away from me. I'll have you shot."

"Mother Rose, get in here right now," Annabelle screamed. It took both sisters to pull her into the carriage.

Bo threw the lawman's stick and hopped onto the coach. He snapped the reins. The lawman stuck the whistle, his only weapon, in his mouth and blew for help.

Bo kept hearing that whistle the whole way home. His heart thudded against his chest. He'd left Dahlia behind. The whistle may as well have been her voice in his ear. *I'm sorry, Dahlia. I got no choice.*

The horses moved with urgency, as if they understood Bo's life was at stake. They ran fast and hard away from the city.

9

After

Bo turned down the private path of the Vesterville. His mouth stayed dry with fear that the lawmen were on his trail. There were only a handful of plantations in the area where they might search. There were bigger problems than Bo and a kindly old lady, but you never knew what drove a man.

"When we get home, Daddy will send out the patrollers. Someone will find Dahlia and bring her back to the house," Annabelle said to appease Mother Rose. Then she addressed Bo. "She won't get away with this. This is all your doing. Neither of you will get away with this."

His doing?

Bo tried not to let it settle over him. This wasn't the time to plead his truth. Sweat dripped from his pits and down his back. He wiped what he could from his neck, leaving him swatting gnats and stingers who wanted a piece of his sticky, sweet skin. He could barely hear the rest of Annabelle's rant the whole way back. Whatever Dahlia had gone and done, he hoped she'd decided on her own. The picture of that man around the red floating thing came to mind again. He couldn't make out if she was struggling or scared.

"I'm telling Daddy you helped Dahlia escape," Annabelle announced as soon as the coach pulled to a stop. She marched off to find her daddy. She couldn't wait to start telling her story.

Bo made his way to the porch. He stood straight, not allowing his eyes to blink. He waited.

"The two of them had this planned all along, Daddy." Annabelle came stomping her way back. She stopped with her finger pointed just shy of touching Bo's nose. "Did you really think you were going to get away with it?"

"All right, now. That's enough," Master Holt snapped. He stepped between them and took a firm grip on Annabelle's shoulder. "This is no way for a young lady to behave. You stand back now." Holt had been dragged from his study on a perfectly good afternoon when he'd planned to smoke his cigar in peace, one of his finest cigars he'd kept in a wooden box for when the women of the house left him alone for the day. Now it was going to waste, dying out in his left hand. "I need to know what happened. Bo, look at me."

Bo dared not fix his mouth to say a thing against Annabelle. But how could he say the truth without calling her a liar? They wouldn't believe him no matter what he said, truth or not.

"Speak, Bo. You tell me right now what happened."

Mother Rose and Leslie had been slow getting up the porch steps. Now they stood idle, wanting answers too. How had this day gone so terribly wrong?

The hot smell of Holt's whiskey and tobacco filled the space, making Bo's eyes water. "What happened to Dahlia out there?" Holt asked again.

Bo remembered when Master Holt used to tower over him. Seemed he was the biggest man in the world. Now all Bo saw was the shiny top of his balding head as he carried on back and forth with his questioning. "You know where she is? Did she tell you where she was going?"

Bo straightened his shoulders and lifted his head. "No, sir. I didn't want to leave her, sir," he said, keeping his lids low and voice steady. "The city shut down. Lawmen say something about a bank robbery. Dahlia could still be out there, scared and alone, but the lawman say if we don't clear the street he'll hurt the horses . . ."

"You think she run off or not?" Holt asked, wanting a yes or no answer. The sound of crickets chirping filled in the space.

Eventually Bo answered. "No, sir. I think . . . a white man took her. He held her by the arm."

"Why didn't you say something?"

"They was too far off. Wasn't much anybody could do, with all the people being pushed out of the city." He was too far away to see faces, frightened or happy. No way he could tell for sure. They could've been any white man and woman out for the afternoon.

"I told y'all to watch out for them slave poachers," Holt belted as if he'd known it all along. "Damn it, now look what happened. They steal your property right from under your nose. How many times did I warn you? Mother, why'd you let her out of your sight? You know them slave robbers will kill to get their hands on a young one like Dahlia."

"Wasn't no slave poachers," Annabelle said. "She ran off. You should've seen how she was dressed. Bo and Dahlia had this planned from the very moment she put that spectacle of a dress on. She pinned her hair the night before, then hid it under her bonnet. I'm telling you, she ran off and Bo helped her. I can feel it. She's out there laughing at us."

"Oh—so what I'm hearing is, you see her wearing this fancy dress and nobody said nothing? That's what you're telling me? What you got to say for yourself, Mother? Now she's gone." Holt shook his head in disbelief.

Mother Rose had taken a seat on her favorite rocker. She fanned herself and looked out toward the fields, unfazed by her son's rant.

Annabelle was different. She didn't like the finger pointed at her. She fumed in silence, waiting for her chance to speak again.

"I warned y'all, and nobody listened," Holt went on, determined to get some answers. "You should've stayed till you found her. I don't understand how you could leave her out there."

"We had to leave, Daddy," Leslie blurted. "There was talk about a bank robbery. Lawmen made us clear the streets or else they'd hurt Bo and the horses."

Annabelle faced Bo with renewed anger. "Doesn't matter. Doesn't matter about the lawmen or none of it. You're a liar. Lying to my daddy's face. You and Dahlia thick as twine. Always have been. I saw the way you two looked at each other. The two of you always having your heads together, plotting and planning. How long you been planning this, huh?"

Bo swallowed the dry ball in his throat. "Thick as twine when we was young. Not now. I don't know what she up to now, living with y'all—" He stopped himself from finishing, *living with y'all—drive anybody out they right mind.*

"Daddy, you have to believe me. He helped her get away."

"If she was up to something, I don't know. I swear, Masta, sir." It was hard to keep his voice from wavering. Bo was angry now, standing there with his knees shaking and sweat running down his back. He'd said all he could say. He'd told the truth.

"All right then, get on with your day, Bo. Go on, get," Holt ordered with a hand swipe at the air.

"Thank ya, Masta, sir."

Annabelle stomped her boots, shaking the birchwood porch he'd helped build a couple of years back. He couldn't guarantee its sturdiness. He was a horseman, not a carpenter.

"It's not right, him getting away with this," Annabelle pleaded one last time.

Bo looked in her direction, but only for a second. He didn't want her to see the satisfaction in his eyes. He was free to go, and there wasn't nothing she could do about it.

"I wish she'd taken you with her," she shouted after him.

Me too.

He wished Dahlia had grabbed his hand and said, "Come on, Bo, we leavin' this place."

He made his way to the coach. He grabbed the reins of the horses and rode slowly, every so often looking over his shoulder. He whispered praise to the animals as they walked the small distance to the barn. No doubt the screeching of that girl made them just as scared and turned around as he was.

The barn was dark when he pulled up. He released the carriage straps and led the horses behind the latched gate. He could hear the music. Papa Sap pressing his accordion. That meant the festivities had begun. Saturday evenings were the start of the resting time, the one day out of the week when folks in the quarters could relax. He couldn't wait to get a bowl of yam soup and sweet cornbread.

Between Annabelle's accusations and the lawmen in the city, he had much to be grateful for. He'd survived. He could only hope the same for Dahlia. If she walked off into the sunset having planned it all, so be it. No white man would harm her, thinking she was one of their own, her wearing that big fancy red dress like she was going to a party, and fitting in right nicely, he might add. She looked like any gal in the city strolling around. That man wasn't a poacher or slave patroller. Bo liked to think, or hope, it was just a fella who'd found a young woman in need of help. He wanted to believe she was safe. It was the only way he could live with himself.

10

Lily Dove

I awakened with a jolt, thrown with the train's movement to and fro. I was well rested despite having dreamt of Annabelle slapping me across the face. I touched the skin on my cheek where the imaginary hand had struck. I realized it was warm from resting against Timothy's shoulder. The brash wool of his jacket must've reddened my cheek. He'd said the trip wouldn't be long. I, having never ridden on a train before, could only guess how fast we were traveling or in what direction.

We rolled along the tracks with no hope of stopping. I didn't complain that my ears rang from the churning noise of the engine. My stomach lurched with every screech of the car as it leaned into the curves.

"You had a rough episode," Timothy said next to my ear. He took my hand. "You're feeling better now?"

I nodded. "Yes. Much better."

"Thank goodness. You had me worried."

Ryland coughed where he sat across from us, peeking up briefly from the edge of his newspaper. Since we'd met up at the train station, a silent line of disapproval had replaced his smug grin.

I'd started out sullen too, thinking of Mother Rose scouring the town streets looking for me, believing I'd been kidnapped by the poachers Holt constantly warned us about. He made the same announcement each time we prepared to leave for the city. "Keep an eye on Dahlia and Bo. Those slave traders will steal your property right from under your nose."

There was no need to worry anymore. I wished I could get word to Mother Rose that I was safe. Slave thieves weren't a concern because I was no longer anyone's slave. Timothy and Ryland Ross believed I was Lily Dove.

Free. Freedom. The words floated over my head, soothing me along with the rocking motion of the train. At first, the thought sent shivers over my entire body. Thinking about it, even now, shook me to my core. But the way Timothy held my hand and asked me if I wanted to come with him, where it was safe, made me believe it was possible.

I could've said no and found my way back to the carriage. I could've gone back to the life I understood, where I knew my place. Or . . .

I tried to slow my breathing, the smell of burning coal igniting the urge to be ill again. I was already living with the embarrassment of having spilled the contents of my stomach on Timothy's shoes. I didn't want it to happen again, this time in front of Ryland.

I spent the rest of the train ride listening to Timothy talk about his mother, Tilda Ross, a woman of distinction. On this new soil, he explained, she was unsure of her place. She'd yet to establish her ground, roaming the halls aimlessly in her too-large mansion, annoyed by the smallest inconvenience. Yet it had been her idea to move and start over, leaving her circle of friends, whom she never liked much anyway. She would not be in her best mood, he warned. Of course, it would be a shock, bringing home a young lady he'd barely known a full day. It would be a bit unsettling at first, he said, but she would come to understand how impossible it was to leave a defenseless young lady in distress.

I hoped he was right.

"She'll inquire about lineage. Are there any links to royalty? Perhaps your father was a prince or a duke?" Timothy asked.

"No dukes. I've heard there might be a king. My great-grandmother was from England," I offered. "Like you."

Ryland chuckled, shook his head, cleared his throat, and then returned to his solemn expression.

Timothy saw this and decided to take a more serious tone. "I should let you know, at one time our family was considered one of the richest families in Lancashire, England. We owned cotton mills until weakened by the industrial crippling of our country." He turned his head away, as if there was a painful memory attached. "I don't think my mum will ever give up hope that the Ross family name will be of relevance again."

This was their new life and Timothy was starting on bad footing, taking on an orphaned girl, a stray cat.

I, on the other hand, had been reborn. There was no bad footing, only one step in front of the other. As fearful as I was giddy, as lost as I was found, I couldn't wait to see what new adventure awaited me.

When we reached our stop, it was dusk, with dew in the corners of the windows. Once the sun began to set in the evenings, the cold became unbearable. After all the time spent on the train, nothing had changed. The trees were the same; the sky and smells were the same. I shivered and fought off the uncertainty. There was one big difference: I would take my first real breath of freedom.

We stepped off the train car and walked a short distance in the gravel. Timothy put his coat around my shoulders.

"Need a ride?" A man standing at the station's edge walked beside Ryland at his pace. "Plenty of room for the three of ya."

Ryland nodded. Timothy and I followed the short distance to his coach. The driver demanded his payment up front, and Timothy gave the man a large bill pulled from a folded leather case. I'd only seen Master Holt and Mother Rose sign their names on notes as payment. Timothy saw me staring and shook his head, as if questioning how I'd managed to get through life before him. If only he knew.

The driver reached out and took Timothy's satchel. He went to take Ryland's heavy bag, only to have it yanked from his grasp.

"I got it," Ryland sneered. His mood went even further into gloomy silence once we'd piled onto the coach.

The wheels dipped in and out of holes on the path. I let my mind drift to the Holt plantation. I melted into memories of running through the fields with Bo. I'd cherish my time from the past so I'd never forget where I'd come from. I knew right then I would never go back to Hampton City. I didn't offer this to Timothy when he spoke of going back to the city for my things. We'd go after the chaos had cleared, he said. I stayed silent. I couldn't go back. The punishment might be more than I could handle. I'd seen what happened to runaways. A man had run off but was found. The overseer made sure he never ran again. His toes had been chopped off. We'd heard his cries from the pain for days.

"Here we are," Timothy said when the coach stopped outside a grand gated entrance.

I gasped. "This is your home? It's lovely, Timothy," I said as calmly as my beating heart would allow. The mansion before me was something out of a picture book. I only stared straight ahead, avoiding images of the fields. I didn't want to see anything beyond the pink roses climbing up the wide trellis over the porch. Large pillars framed the entrance. Shiny green shutters flanked every window. Expansive white stairs led up to the magnificent front entrance. Two doors with brass knobs looked like the entrance to heaven.

"Lily, it can be your home too." Timothy spoke hurriedly, as if the chance was fleeting. He checked over his shoulder. "I know—I know what you're thinking. But how is it any different than if someone had introduced us for arrangement? I sense you are a good person. I'm a good person. Why not? Let me introduce you to my mum as my betrothed? Please, I don't see the harm, do you?"

"Betrothed?" I shook my head, confused.

"Too late to turn back now," Ryland said as he pushed between us, carrying his heavy bag. This was the first time he'd spoken directly to me since our travels. He bounded ahead, taking the steps two at a time.

Timothy looked, once again, hurriedly toward the grand porch, as if his life depended on my answer.

"Of course, Timothy. Yes," I answered. This was the good fortune I deserved. Wasn't this what I'd asked for, to be on equal footing with my sisters? I could be loved just as easily. I could be the princess in the storybooks Mother Rose read, with the birds chirping and the leaves fluttering on the trees. I could be Timothy's betrothed. I pictured my sisters' faces in shock and then anger that I'd been chosen by someone—first.

Tilda Ross appeared with a burst of energy. Her dark hair tinged with gray was swept in a chignon, showing off her angular features. Delighted in her sons' return, she opened her slim arms in welcome. Ryland put down his satchel and hugged her fully. He whispered something in her ear to make her smile, only briefly. She was a delicate figure against Ryland's embrace, yet there was no doubt of who was in charge of this family.

Her attention turned to Timothy. Her eyes narrowed for inspection. "My sweet boy, whom have you brought to join us?" She remained on the landing like a queen on her throne.

"This is Lily Dove." Timothy took my elbow and escorted me up the stairs. He smiled uncomfortably before giving her a hug. "She will be staying with us, Mum."

"Is that so?"

"Lily is my future bride. You've made it no secret that you were anxious for me to marry. Well, I've found her. This is the young lady I will make my wife. Isn't she beautiful? Since we've met, we haven't been able to part company." He took ahold of my hand.

"Magical," Ryland chimed. "Love at first sight."

"Pleased to make your acquaintance, Missus Ross." I could say no more. No matter how much I'd practiced *I am Lily Dove* in my head, this was far more than batting my lashes and singing winsome melodies. This was far more than making up a story about a girl who'd lost her beloved mother and father and was raised by her grandmother.

She lifted her chin and made a quick but graceful appraisal. Head to toe, she scanned for whatever faults she might find. Time seemed to stop while she made her assessment.

"Yes, quite beautiful." The edges of her eyes crinkled into sharp, fine lines. "Please, come inside. You must be exhausted from your trip." She finally exhaled. Her questioning gaze couldn't be stifled, and she clearly wondered whether her son had made a complete fool of himself.

We followed her inside and were met by a young man with brown skin and straight black hair. His baroque jacket over a white lace-collared shirt was regal, unlike his tattered pants. He kept his gaze downward until Timothy entered. A smile rose on his full cheeks. "Welcome, Timothy, sir."

"Hello, Pico. This is Lily Dove. She will be staying with us."

"As his *betrothed*," Ryland added. The smirk returned.

"Pico is my personal assistant. Anything you need, anything at all, ask him."

I nodded. "Hello, Pico. Pleased to meet you."

"Luggage, madam?" Pico asked in the very same accent as the rest of Timothy's family. He'd come with them from England. He was a mysterious mix of dark skin and shiny black straight hair. His dark eyes shifted in my direction and searched near my feet then rose again, landing on my face.

"She has arrived without luggage," Timothy said to answer his question.

"She has you," Ryland quipped. "Considering, baby brother, that you are one big bag of tricks."

Timothy found no humor in what he'd said. His cheeks brightened with redness before facing Pico. "Her luggage will be sent along later."

"Not even a satchel. How is that possible, for a young lady to have not even a personal valise?" Tilda Ross interjected. Of all the possible reasons to find suspicion, this one thing alarmed her. Before she could get an answer, a woman with pearl skin and rosy cheeks came rushing toward Ryland.

"You're back, my darling. And who do we have here?" Her red hair fit the spark of energy she'd brought into the foyer. She had an accent as well, but it sounded more chipper than the others, nearly singing every word.

Ryland placed a kiss on the young woman's cheek. "This is Lily Dove, Timothy's betrothed," he said, maintaining his stance of finding humor in the situation.

"How wonderful! And welcome. I'm Maggie, Ryland's wife. Are you hungry? You look absolutely famished."

I didn't answer. I was too busy mulling over the announcement of Ryland having a wife, wondering why he'd pursued me at the beginning right along with Timothy, pretending they were in competition for my attention. Here I'd thought my choosing Timothy over him had caused his animosity when all the while he had a *Maggie* at home waiting for him. I had much to learn about the ways of men.

"It's nice to make your acquaintance," I finally answered, putting out my gloved hand for a delicate shake.

I followed Tilda down a dark hallway, eventually to a dining room with a long shiny table and huge chairs squeezed side by side. Timothy was at my heel. He took his coat away from my shoulders. Before he could lay it over one of the tall chairs, Pico took it from him. He stayed close to Timothy, anticipating his every move.

"The inquisition won't take long. I need to speak privately with Mum," Timothy whispered in my ear. He pulled out a heavy chair for me.

"I'll be fine," I assured him.

He placed a kiss on top of my head before leaving for the next room. I could see Timothy pacing past the wide opening. I closed my eyes to hear better, a skill I'd learned in the Vesterville.

"Do you know anything about her? You just bring someone home that you know nothing about?"

"Mum, she was in dire need, lost and alone. The city was called to evacuate. She has no family. I couldn't leave her alone. And once we started talking, I realized how fate must've wanted us to meet. She's enchanting, full of life. Gentle and loving. You'll see, Mum. Just as I did. This is all meant to be."

"However you explain it, it makes no sense. I've constantly introduced you to proper young women. All turned away. Young ladies from prosperous families. Why? Suddenly, you've found the one seemingly penniless girl who has no family and she's the one?"

Pico came to the wide entrance and pulled the glass doors closed. Timothy's voice was muffled but still easily understood.

"All I'm asking is that you give her a chance."

"I demand to know who this Lily Dove is. Where she comes from. Surely she didn't just fall out of the sky."

"Perhaps she did, Mum. Perhaps she fell out of the sky and into my arms. I have no interest in sending her back."

The silence from Tilda Ross glided like a hot swirl of wind around my ears. The buzz was maddening. I fought the urge to rise from the chair and run out of the room. If she felt this strongly, she'd seek and find a way to expose my falsehoods.

"If you insist on being suspicious, I will have no choice but to take Lily and leave. I will leave," he said, clearly knowing the outcome.

"I believe you," she said with a quick change in attitude. "I'm just concerned there may be more to her story."

"And I'm telling you it doesn't matter." Timothy wasn't backing down.

He entered the dining parlor with Pico not far behind. He touched my shoulder. "I'll leave you two alone for a moment, to get to know each other while I speak to Ryland." He looked over his shoulder at his mother through the doorway, a silent warning. She nodded pleasantly as if she hadn't just demanded I be sent back to the sky.

Timothy had prepared me on the train ride. I knew the questions his mother would ask. Where had I been born? Who were my parents? Was I a member of any social clubs?

I was born to Ferdinand and Mary Dove in Hampton, Virginia. I'd made up the names from reading the stories from the back of Ryland's newspaper. *I attended the School of Etiquette.* This one was Timothy's answer. It sounded lovely. He knew I was concealing my background, and he didn't care. In fact, it made him more fascinated. "You are all mine, then," he'd said, grinning. "No one else can lay claim to you, my Lily Dove."

When Tilda returned, she sat across from me. I used the tiny spoon to stir my tea, then laid it back down on the right side of the saucer. I was impressed with myself.

Tilda studied every bat of my lashes and every tilt of my head. I was prepared to go on with my tall tale with tidbits I'd overheard about Annabelle's suitors and now found useful. I explained how *my* family once owned a tobacco plantation. The sale to neighboring landowners left a small inheritance, enough for travel and a bit of shopping here and there. All *my* family had died off, and now there was only me. Lily Dove, that is.

Tilda wasn't fully thrilled or fascinated by my tragic tale. Not the way Timothy had been. Tilda instead focused on the business at hand. Her dull expression remained. "I'm sorry you have no family. So young. Very unfortunate."

"Yes, well, I've learned to survive."

"On the kindness of strangers, no doubt." She leaned back in her chair. "Do you love my son?"

I wasn't prepared for the question. Love wasn't something I understood. Caring, understanding, sacrifice, and obedience, these commands I had a thorough knowledge of.

"I'm not sure," I answered without having to lie.

"An honest answer," she said with a quaint smile and a raise of her brow. "Love comes in time. We won't let the lack of family get in the way of a celebration. The guest list will be a bit scant is all." She bordered on excitement, a far leap from her earlier derision.

Did this mean I'd passed the inspection? "Yes. I don't mind at all. A small celebration will be fine."

"I'll send out the invitations to my dearest friends. There'll be plenty enough in attendance."

For a moment my stomach plunged. Then I remembered. I calmly blinked and tried not to let on what Timothy had told me. Tilda Ross had no friends here in this new land called home. She had no one to inquire about Lily Dove's whereabouts or who knew what. I would be safe here, far away from anyone who would know me.

A kitchen servant entered carrying a tray. Her brown hands moved swiftly, pouring tea and placing a plate of small round breads on the table. A slow panic rose in my throat. I kept my head turned. I wondered if I'd always feel this way around *my own*, afraid they would see through my thin veil of pretense.

"Eat, dear," Tilda said sweetly. "Poor thing. You look like you haven't eaten in months."

Maggie entered the dining hall and smiled politely. "Well, now she has us. No shortage of goodies to eat around here."

11

Missus

Tall, polished posts stood guard at each corner of the large, spacious bed where I stared straight ahead, awake, in my very own room. I counted seventeen days having passed in my new home. Timothy and I rarely saw each other. Briefly, during supper, we sat across from one another listening to Tilda's stories of her grand English home that she'd loved before coming here. Before crickets ate her azaleas, before the moist heat of summer saturated her brocade draperies, before ladies refused to understand their place in the world. I learned more about my new family every day. Maggie was from Ireland. Pico was born in a place called India but was practically raised in the Ross home.

Morning was also when I'd awaken, panicked. Knowing all that I could know, being well-spoken, none of it would stop the patrollers or bounty hunters from knocking on the Ross door at any minute holding a WANTED notice with my picture and the name Dahlia Holt printed underneath.

I was a runaway. No different than the men and women working the fields here on the Ross land. As much as I tried to not see them, I had to face the truth. This Ross family, they were slave owners too. Was there no ending, no place to be safe? Why did I think it would be different?

The panic made me wonder if it wasn't too late to go back home to Vesterville—not the house, but the quarters with Oleen and Papa Sap, where I was truly wanted.

It was the drip-drip of water coming from the shiny pipe over the basin that reminded me of home. This miraculous thing that only required the turn of a latch to make water flow sent my heart and mind back to the quarters. The porcelain faucet dripped all day into the night, reminding me of those rainy days in the quarters when we'd slept with buckets at our heads and feet, me waking up tightly pressed against Oleen's back knowing what my day entailed. In the tiny cabin, if we slept too hard from exhaustion the buckets would overflow.

The rainwater would spill onto the floorboards, causing us to wake sopping wet. Oleen would snap us into action, rolling up the cots. She'd tie them high to the wall. We'd get the heavy cotton mops and begin pushing the water back until Bo, Papa Sap, and the others got bushels of hay to dry up what we could.

There was something to be said about having a purpose. I liked knowing what to do, how to do it. Even in the Vesterville, there too was method to Winnie's madness. There was no mystery as to what she expected from a day's work. From sunup to sundown, I knew what to do and how. If I leaned outside her rules, I knew how to fall back into rhythm without missing a step.

There was no order, no rhythm, here at the Ross mansion. So much space to be free and yet I was lost, floating in nothingness. The panic sometimes made me unable to breathe in my new home. I feared I'd be swallowed whole by the long hallways and wide half-moon entries.

How could I miss everyone and yet be equally afraid of returning?

I went about the ritual of forcing myself out of bed. I stood at the basin. The water came streaming out of the pipe. As much as I wanted to have purpose, I didn't miss fetching the water in pails and carrying it up the stairs for Annabelle and Leslie.

I pumped more water until the basin was filled. I pushed my hands in the cool water before splashing my cheeks. I stared at myself in the oval mirror, ashamed. Who was I to have this life while others were toiling in misery? I observed how my face had grown even thinner since I'd arrived at the Ross home. Though Maggie promised I'd be full and happy with breads and tea cakes, most mornings I barely ate at all, afraid of being judged by Tilda. She watched me all the time. The way I picked up my bread, or held a fork or cup, was of great interest to her.

I heard a knock at the door and grabbed a clean linen to pat my face. There were tears and I couldn't have explained why. "Just a minute."

The door opened without anyone waiting for my permission. Cleo, who had been assigned as my house aide, entered. Her warm brown skin had escaped the rigors of sun. Her dark eyes stayed lowered. I tried to ignore the feeling of kinship. I kept my eyes low as well and away from hers, not sure if she could see my lips fuller than most, or my cheekbones high and proud, or the depth of my constant soul searching. I didn't know how long we could avoid each other.

"You need help this morning, Miss Lily?" She stood patiently just inside the doorway. Tilda had sent her to move me along. It was obvious I wanted nothing to do with morning tea. The ritual of sitting across from Tilda every morning had grown tedious.

Cleo took the borrowed housedress of Tilda's from the foot of the bed and pulled it over my arms.

"Timothy promised we'd go shopping for a wardrobe as soon as things quieted around the house." I spoke as if she cared to listen. She lifted my hair from being captured in the collar, smoothing it out with her fingers.

She nodded politely then remained standing in the middle of the floor. She must've been under strict orders to not return without me. I wouldn't make things difficult for her. I made my way downstairs.

I entered the room with lightness. "Hello, Tilda. Good morning, Maggie."

"Good morning," Tilda sang over her cup before taking a sip. "You nearly missed tea, having slept so long. We have arrangements to discuss." She paused to look up. "How are you, dear? You look a bit piqued."

"I'm fine," I answered. "Just getting used to my new home." I poured a cup of tea.

"Yes. Well, these parties don't plan themselves," Tilda said.

She'd been busy giving orders to the staff about building an arbor and fussing over details. I observed her mannerisms. The way she gracefully folded her arms one over the other and tilted her head in thought. Nothing was good enough, and though she tried to hide it, I could tell she was thrilled with all the wedding planning, even if she still didn't approve of me, a young woman not of her choosing.

"Meeting new people isn't easy. I am the same way," Maggie added.

She startled me. I hoped Maggie hadn't noticed my studying of Tilda. It was the way I learned, watching.

"Maggie, you have such lovely penmanship. I'll need help with the guest invitations." Tilda placed a long list on the table. "This is the guest list. The invitations will be sent out on crème paper, written with gold script."

I plopped down in shock. *The list.* Who were all of these people? Timothy had said she knew very few, and yet here there was an entire list. I scanned quickly for the names of Mother Rose or Lewis Holt. The train ride from the city of Hampton felt so far away. Surely there'd be no names I recognized. How far had we traveled, really? I had no indication. Not really. Had we gone north or south? East or west?

"Would you like me to read the invitation to you?" Tilda enunciated loudly.

"I can read," I said, then felt my cheeks burn. It wasn't the proper response. I picked up the note card.

You are cordially invited to witness the union of
Mr. Timothy Ross and Miss Lily Dove
Saturday October 6th at 2 o'clock in the afternoon in
the garden.

"We must go shopping for the dress," Maggie said. "Libby's Fine Laces and Textiles has the most beautiful lace."

"No," I said too quickly with my mouth dry. I was all too familiar with Libby's Fine Laces and Textiles. The last time I'd seen my sisters, they'd been standing there in the window, browsing for new cloth. I could never go back to the harbor. Never. "I'm sure I can borrow something. Something blue," I said, not sure where I'd heard the term. "It would be an honor to wear one of your dresses, Missus Ross."

"I'm sure I have something. Yes. Yes, I do," Tilda said to herself. "I'll have Cleo fetch a few for you to choose from. Cleo can sew in the waistline. But dear, sweet dear, you will have to eat. We don't want our guests to think we've captured you and held you without food."

"Yes. I'm sorry. I haven't had much of an appetite."

Timothy arrived as I said this last. "Maybe we should have the kitchen prepare something Lily might like." He pressed his lips to his mother's cheek. "Good morning, Mum."

"Yes. If I knew what that something might be. Lily hasn't offered much in the way of sharing. We know so little about her."

Timothy reached over Maggie and grabbed a piece of toast. "Let's ask her, shall we? Lily, what do you like to eat?"

I looked at him shyly, recalling our time in Hampton City.

He winked. "Anything at all. Your wish will be granted."

I had to think of my favorites. Eating in the Vesterville had been uneventful. But there'd been the meals prepared for Annabelle's suitors. Those special evenings when duck was served with warm mint and berry jam brought a sensation over my tongue. The parts of the duck left over were fatty and slick with grease. It didn't stop the flavorful enjoyment for the kitchen help. I took pleasure in those nights.

"Duck with mint jam," I said, "is one of my favorites."

Timothy clapped his hands together. "Then duck it is. I do believe this mystery is solved. I have pressing business to tend to, ladies. Enjoy your tea."

12

Hunter

Bo pushed the pitchfork into the hay and lifted his worth in weight to move it to a new pile. He worked diligently while trying not to worry about Dahlia. The stories going around the quarters changed daily. How Dahlia magically flew away. How the mark down her back opened up with wings and she'd flown off like a dragon to her cursed brethren. How people ever got any work done thinking about nonsense day in and day out baffled him.

The sound of a horse's arrival made him take a break. Outside the barn a thick-necked man sat on his horse waiting for someone to come and greet him.

"Hello? Anybody here?" the man called out.

This man came from a distance; Bo gathered, from the bowed head of his horse, a long ride without a minute of rest.

"Sir?" Bo approached gently.

The man finally slung his heavy boot over one side to step down. "I'm here to see Lewis Holt."

"You in the right place. Can I get your horse some water?"

"Him and me both," he said.

"Yes, sir." Bo took the reins of his horse. "Master Holt right inside," he said, pointing to the entrance of the house.

"John Browder, that you?" Holt appeared on the porch. In the short time Dahlia had been gone, Holt had thinned. His loose shirt held dark spills and sweat stains. The Vesterville facade seemed to have dulled as well. Paint peeled away from the pillars. The porch weighed to one side more than the other. It might've been that way all along and Bo just now noticed.

"That's right, friend. I rode straight here when I got your telegram. Good to see you. It's been a while."

Holt stepped down from the porch for a heavy handshake and shoulder pat. "You're the best man for the job. Thank you for coming."

Browder let a hand fall on the pistol belted on his hip. "Haven't lost one yet. I get results."

"Good. What I need to hear. Her name's Dahlia. She's belonged to me since her birth. Some filthy poachers took her in the city. I don't want her harmed. Just found and brought back."

"I'll do my best."

"No. I said, I don't want her harmed, and I mean it," Holt snapped. His mood had thinned as well. He could be heard yelling from the furthest corner of the house all hours of the day and night. When he wasn't causing a skirmish, he was silent and drunk.

John Browder scratched his chin and chuckled. "She must mean a lot to you."

"She's my . . . my property. Stolen from me," he slurred. "I want her back. I swear, this is the worst way to feel, helpless and taken for a fool. I don't know what to believe—if she run off from me or was taken," he said, appearing somewhat embarrassed.

"No harm will come to her. You'll get your chance for answers, one way or another. Why don't we settle up on terms? The sooner I get started, the more likely I'll find her."

"How fast? I'll double your asking if you find her in three weeks' time."

Again, the scruffy chin scratching and chuckle. John Browder shook his head. "Three weeks? Holt, I'll be lucky to get a hint of her direction in a month or two."

"I'll triple your rate." Holt had already put out his hand for a shake. "Please, I'm depending on you."

"I'll need the first half up front."

Holt noticed Bo still standing there holding the man's horse reins. "You get this horse watered and ready. Mister Browder's got important work ahead."

"Yessir," Bo said. He led the horse away. Eavesdropping on the two men had left him shaken. He pushed water onto his face before tying the horse near the trough. Three weeks. That's how long the man would take to find Dahlia. Unharmed. That's what Holt requested. No harm should come to her, he'd said, but Bo could tell from the man's eyes he'd have no cares if he broke that promise. Dahlia was in danger.

He wanted to tell someone what he'd heard. Oleen might listen. She might also turn her back to him. The messenger of bad news wasn't welcome. The womenfolk in the quarters had enough to pray for. There was only so much time left to care for the young and old after a long day in the fields. Still, no one went without a kind word.

Illness was cured with broth and shrubs. Despair was fought with chants and prayer. It could also be the place where belief turned to suspicion.

Bo saw it in their eyes. It wasn't like the women to turn their heads when they saw him coming. Until now. They blamed him. Whether Dahlia ran off, magically flew away as they suspected, or was kidnapped, he should've stopped her from leaving or saved her all the same. These women, who never much cared for Dahlia, acted like he'd committed the greatest sin. Now they suddenly cared, when they'd all abandoned her long ago.

Oleen was the only one he wished didn't feel that way. He felt Oleen's loss, maybe even more so. When he came close there was blame in her eyes. He'd let her down. He could see it in the way her mouth twitched like she wanted to say something. Instead, she turned her back to finish the washing or cooking until he walked away.

This time he stayed at her side. "Holt is sending a bounty hunter after Dahlia," he whispered.

Oleen's lips clamped shut.

"I'm scared for her. That man looked like a killer. He won't care about bringing her back alive."

"What do you care?" Oleen hissed. "You left her out there."

"Why would I do that? I cared about her more than anybody. All of them was afraid to look her way. I was the only one watching out for her."

She didn't move. Her eyes shut but her hands stayed moving as she rubbed the laundry against the washboard. She wanted him to go away.

"Don't you think I feel bad enough?" he said.

A single tear crept down her cheek.

"If I could bring her back, I would. Don't you know that?"

Oleen nodded her head. Her body quaked a little. "I don't want to hear no more about Dahlia. She gone. There ain't nothing we can do."

13

Truth

Bo tended the horses and stayed out of everybody's way. He wanted to keep his ears and eyes open for any news of the bounty hunter. If John Browder found Dahlia, Bo wanted to know about it. When he came around the Vesterville house he didn't make a sound. He watched and listened. Annabelle kept her scowl, Leslie did her polite nodding, and Mother Rose offered figs dipped in the small sugar tin she kept in her bag just like when he was a boy. Most days, Holt milled about the property, but by evening he was drunken and silly, his anger buried under glossy eyes and silence.

That's why Bo didn't believe a word of it when someone said he was being sold. The first he heard of it, he was manning the wagon for loading cotton bales. He went from row to row picking up the full bundles. Ezekiel tossed his bag up, then walked around the side with a rough hand extended. "You a good man, Bowman. Don't let anybody tell you different."

"Ah, thanks, Ezekiel," Bo said, grateful for the unexpected praise. Then there were two more men taking the time to reach out with kindness. It went on like that. He finally asked one of the men what was happening.

"We heard you was being sold, Bo."

No. He shook his head. "Nah, sir. You heard wrong." It didn't stop there. From the Vesterville to the wide fields, every warm body felt the need to pray on sight. Well-meaning hands reached out and touched Bo's head or squeezed his shoulders, or lithe arms twisted around his back for a final goodbye.

"You being taken, Bo. That's what they saying. We gon' miss ya," Sally sobbed against his chest.

He wasted no time finding Oleen. She'd know what was going on. Oleen's eyes watered before he was close enough to catch her hands.

"None of this could be true," he told her. "I was just with Holt. He ain't said nothing about selling me."

"You gon' be a'ight. You strong," Oleen said in return. Wet droplets filled her eyes until they flowed past her cheeks.

He slid one of her tears away. "Holt would never sell me, Oleen. This my home. Nobody else gon' care for the horses like me. He needs me. He ain't never sold nobody no way."

Most of them had been born and would be buried on the Vesterville land. Bo hadn't been born there, instead arriving in his mother's arms, swaddled in rags. And by the hand of grace, he had no plans on leaving any other way. He'd speak to Holt come morning and clear up the noise the ladies were spouting.

The next day, he tightened the straps on his boots and trudged up the trail muddy from night rain, straight to the house. Bo planned to get over there first thing and say his piece and make Holt see reason.

Holt was waiting for Bo along with another man holding a rope. Bo stopped and turned the other way. Maybe he could run.

"Bo, come on over here," Holt called.

His voice scratched at Bo's neck, leaving prickly heat running over his face and ears. He turned slowly to face Holt and the other man. It was like Bo had walked straight into his own grave. He didn't bother trying to plead or fight. No matter how many times he'd told Holt it wasn't him who helped Dahlia run off, Annabelle's story won. There was nothing more he could say.

Papa Sap stood at the edge of the fence as the wagon rolled past. He fixed his lips to say something but turned his head instead. Bo could still hear Papa Sap from that night Dahlia was taken from the quarters. *"You can't ask why if you want any peace. You just gotta let 'em go."*

The wagon ride was slow and long. They stopped in a clearing with other wagons lined on the side of the path. Bo searched the oak trees for rope, a natural assumption. The branches only held leaves. A man dressed in his Sunday best stood on a square landing built with steps. Across the grass, tattered Negro men and women didn't bother looking up when one of them was ushered up the stairs and led to stand in the center.

One after the other, the auction man read their sortings from a book. The white men gathered for purchase and raised their hands until a price was reached. When it was Bo's turn, he looked out at every pale eye upon him. He told himself it was better than being tied from a tree. Whatever happened, he would survive.

The man read aloud. "This one here is a horseman, skills not likely held by many. Good breeder, strong legs, good back, and thick genitalia."

Bo closed his eyes while a tear slid down. He prayed and yet there he remained, going to the highest bidder. No band of angels was swooping down to save him. He was on his own.

The image of Mary came to him, not the one from the Bible, but his mother. Mary Carter had turned ill and passed on before he was old enough to remember what she looked like, but right then and there, her face came to him. Her coal-dark eyes and jutted chin looked down on him like he was a baby in a cradle, and then she smiled.

He knew her smell, her touch. He closed his eyes to feel it all.

Hush now, baby.

"Sold," the auctioneer yelled, slamming down his gavel.

The man who bought him for one hundred and fifty dollars had no intentions of keeping him. Bo was led to a wagon and connected to the other men and women already attached on one long rope. None of them spoke to one another. The waft of misery had its own language. They were wholesale mules destined to be separated. There was no need to exchange hope or names.

During the course of the day, they ended up with more bodies squeezed into the small wagon. Once it became too heavy for the mal-nourished horses to pull anymore, Bo and the other men were forced to walk. The women stayed on the wagon.

As the sun beat down on Bo's head, he could hear Papa Sap's voice. "Believe me, son, things can always be worse."

Bo had no idea where he'd end up. Only a rare few plantations in the area could afford more slaves. Bo knew about the dire woes of the landowners from driving Master Holt around for visits. He most likely would end up at Master Evers's, where his folks barely had enough to eat, or the Davis place, where he kept families tied up, tethered to each other at night so no one could run off.

At this point any of them would do. He wanted it to be over sooner rather than later. Traveling by foot was dangerous with rattlers on the road, which made the trip longer than it needed to be as he and the others constantly looked down to watch every step.

Bo was lucky to have solid boots from his days of horse tending. The rest of them wore soles too thin for any good. He didn't dare take his boots off at rest, to eat, not even to sleep, knowing they'd end up on someone else's feet by sunrise.

They stopped on the side of the road and made a fire for cooking.

"Eat up, boy. You're my prime stock. There's extra there for you." The trader handed Bo a larger scoop of corn mash. Bo ignored the angry stares from the others. He was familiar with being singled out, set apart. Even though they were all going to the same place in the end, the backbiting would start. He took the food. He knew better than to turn down the "extra," whatever that meant. It wasn't enough. In the morning, he'd be starving again as if he'd eaten nothing at all.

There were eight men now. He'd overheard the trader tell his driver he had a specific place he wanted to take Bo. The trader could get more for him than all the rest put together. He was a horse trainer, a breeder, and worth so much more. The thought scared Bo, to be dragged around on foot to God knew where just because the trader wanted as much for him as possible. He looked around at the others, knowing a few wouldn't make the trip and it would be all his fault. They'd blame him in the end.

14

Ceremony

Only six weeks had passed since that fateful day I met Timothy. It felt like a lifetime had passed. The constant fear of being found out. Holding my breath, awaiting the moment Tilda said, *Enough with this farce—Lily Dove, you do not belong here.*

There was no need to fear the worst. The marital ceremony was an hour away. The tick of the clock's hands on the mantel moved forward to my destiny. This was not what a bride should feel. I stood in front of a long mirror, wearing a dress borrowed from Tilda. Cleo had sewn in the sides and taken up the sleeves. I would've given anything to pick out my own lace and satin, to sew the dress myself, but knew it was a skill I should not have if I were truly from a wealthy family. Lily Dove would not know how to sew a gown or make a veil of tulle. Dahlia Holt would. Besides, I could never go back to the Hampton City square, to Libby's Fine Laces and Textiles. I could never show my face there again.

I welcomed the sound of the harpist playing. The calm melody traveled through the open window of my room. The sun warmed the fall sky. Guests milled about near a beautiful white arbor decorated with roses. Nothing could have been lovelier. I should've been satisfied and grateful. Instead, there was a lonesome howl buzzing throughout the room. I caught myself wishing Mother Rose was at my side to place a strand of pearls around my neck. To offer words of wisdom. I wished for Oleen's knotted hands holding mine. This was the day I should've been surrounded by the people I loved and who loved me. I had no one.

The knock came. Cleo entered. "They ready for you, Miss Lily."

I picked up the wreath of white roses and placed it on my head.

"Let me help you." Cleo straightened it, then handed me the bouquet. I sniffed the white buds mixed with lavender and rosemary.

"You about to be Missus Timothy Ross. Smile," Cleo said with her own pleasant example. Her curved lips went into a full grin. "You beautiful, Miss Lily."

It only took Cleo making this declaration to push the tears that had threatened to fall all morning. "I can't. I can't do this," I said, sobbing.

Cleo sighed before rushing to get a linen handkerchief. She delicately blotted my tears. She did the unthinkable and wrapped her arms around me. "This yo' wedding day. You can't be sad."

Another knock came, and this time it was Pico. "The madam says, please come now." His crisp white shirt and bow tie were part of the uniform all of the menservants were wearing for the ceremony. Tilda wanted all hands at the ready to serve her mystery guests.

"We'll be down in a spell," Cleo snapped at Pico. "Just tell 'em she comin'."

I paused to make sure Pico had gone. "I have no one," I stammered. "I miss my—"

Cleo shook her head for me not to speak. She gripped my shoulders. "You have a good life here. You take it."

Her words were like hearing Oleen all over again, telling me to go to live with Master Holt and his daughters. It was best. A better life. The same thing was happening all over again. As much as I didn't want to go live with Lewis Holt and his family, it was true, a better life was found. I had Mother Rose, who taught me how to read and write. She gave me the heart to live valiantly. I learned how to smile when my heart bled inside. I was well practiced at staying silent even when I wanted to scream. So much of a good life, a better life.

I let the last tear fall. I took in a long, shaky breath, then blew out the rest of my fear.

"That a girl," Cleo said, prompting me to go first out the door. She lifted the tulle as she followed behind.

I walked out, head held high, ready to become a wife to Timothy Ross.

The ceremony was rushed. I heard the words "till death do you part" and caught my breath before tears broke. "You are man and wife," the man in a black suit and white banded collar announced as his spindly fingers gripped a Bible he hadn't bothered to open.

Now I was a wife, a woman who would lie under her husband. Timothy leaned forward and brushed his mouth against mine, my first kiss.

Timothy looped his arm in mine. We walked down a narrow path of rose petals.

Afterward, the crowd stood around with their wine glasses filled. I pointed around, inquiring who this or that person was. None of the guests were Timothy's friends or family. I know because I asked and Timothy answered, "Surely I do not know. This is my mother's creation. The process of being well received is very important to her."

The men leered too closely, with yellowed teeth and foul breath. "Congratulations." The ladies wore half smiles and offered good wishes devoid of true emotion. The entire day felt like a charade as guests danced to music played by a quartet dressed in dapper black suits and bow ties. Distinguished, proud Negro men holding violins and bows astonished me. All the while as I watched, I wondered if they were free men, able to walk out the door and into their own homes with wives and children waiting. I'd heard about entire towns filled with independent souls, free Negroes. If that was possible, I thought . . . if that was possible, I wouldn't have to pretend.

I fought the urge to clap at the end of each triumphant song, instead keeping my hands to my sides, ignoring their talents, like the rest of the guests.

"May I have this dance?" Ryland stood in front of me with his hand out. "It's customary that the bride and groom have the first dance, but since my brother seems to have disappeared, I'd be honored to take his place," he said with a bowed head.

I wondered how long Ryland had been watching me from a distance, if he'd seen me admiring the quartet, and what my face was saying. I searched briefly for Timothy before I placed my hand in his. I moved a beat slower to follow his footsteps. The music wasn't what I was listening to. Ryland's breath in my ear turned to words.

"You look beautiful. My brother is a lucky man."

"Thank you. And here I thought you didn't like me at all," I said with forced confidence.

"You and I are going to be spending a lot of time together. We should like one another, don't you think?" His cheek brushed against mine.

The patch of skin down the center of my back tightened. My breath became shallow and my face warmed, forcing me to pull away before the music ended. I stepped further back, putting distance between us. I knew this was wrong, the way he'd touched me, the way I felt in return. "I'm feeling a bit light-headed."

He adjusted his striped ascot as if feeling the same sudden heat. "Understandable. It's been an overwhelming day. Maybe you should take a moment for yourself. Go lie down. Rest a spell. It's going to be a long evening." His light eyes brightened. "Would you like me to escort you?"

"No. No, thank you."

"Off you go, then. I'm sure no one will notice you're missing. I'll cover for you," he whispered.

I searched around to excuse myself but Timothy was nowhere to be seen. No sign of Tilda, either, who was probably somewhere ordering the staff around.

I was grateful to slip away unnoticed. I moved through the throng of guests and made my way up the stairs. As I rounded the corner of the hallway, Pico bolted out of nowhere, ramming into my shoulder. He was holding his arms close to his exposed chest where his shirt was undone. Three buttons pulled loose. He was shivering. Maybe he was ill. I'd only seen him an hour or so earlier and he'd been fine. Now his dark, smooth skin glowed with moisture as if he were coming down with a fever.

"Pardon, Miss Lily," he mumbled.

I rubbed my shoulder where we'd met bone to bone. He did the same briefly, then went back to shivering. I moved toward him.

"Pico, are you all right?" I reached for his shoulder, to comfort him, but I was mostly concerned about his state of mind. His eyes darted off, then back to the ground. "Pico?"

I stopped questioning what I saw as my attention turned to Timothy through the bedroom doorway. He scampered to put his foot through his pant leg, hurriedly bouncing, keeping his balance. His shirttails hung over his bareness.

I looked back at Pico. I placed a hand on the wall to keep myself steady.

I backed away, sliding against the wall, and held my breath. This was why my newly married husband couldn't be found to have our first dance. I turned in the opposite direction, not sure where I was going. Back to the party? To my room?

I was off balance. For a second or two I teetered, until I felt a firm grip holding me up. I shook the hand off my arm.

"I thought you might need assistance." It was Ryland. "You didn't look well when you left the party." Ryland looked away. His gaze slid in the direction of Timothy's room, where the door was now closed. He knew exactly what he'd find in that direction.

"This is why you suggested I go lie down. You wanted me to find him. Why would you do that, Ryland?"

"I'm not sure what you're going on about, Lily." He stepped too close and slid his hand across my cheek, then down to my shoulder. "I know this is difficult. But I'm here for you."

I knocked his hand away.

He'd known. This explained his strange behavior in the city. His strange humor suggesting his brother was a bag of tricks. When he'd introduced me to Maggie, he'd fought the urge to laugh in my face. *Love at first sight,* he'd teased. *Too late now.*

"Let me help you," he offered, again touching my arm.

I slipped past him. "Stay away from me."

I rushed inside my room and closed the door, turning the key until I heard the lock click in place. I didn't have the strength to wedge the chair against the door. I fell face first into the bed and held my breath, hoping to black out from the madness. This place was madness.

This explained why Timothy had been in such a hurry to scoop me up, the wayward girl he'd found with no family to speak of. He'd found the perfect young lady to stop the questioning and nagging about finding a wife.

In the quarters at Vesterville there'd been two young boys who'd been found together naked, embracing each other. The quarters folk said it was an abomination, a sin from the Bible. Oleen made me cover my eyes any time they walked by. I felt their pain. I understood when they were called names and teased, no different than me being taunted about the scar splitting me in two. I hated how they were shunned and treated. Shamed for being with a person of their choosing.

Pico's sad eyes came to mind. I wondered if he was forced or if he was with Timothy out of choice. Either way, I recognized his hopelessness.

I snatched the crown of roses from my head and threw it to the ground. Embarrassment wrapped its hot arms around my skin. Here I thought I'd fooled everyone, Timothy and his family, and all the while the farce was on me.

Did they all know? Maggie? And Tilda? Were they all in on it?

I wasn't sure how long I lay there before the knock came.

"Please open the door, Lily. Let me talk to you." It was Timothy who spoke from the other side. "I'm sure you're confused. Ryland told me about you being upset, about what you thought you saw."

"Go away. Just leave."

"Lily, we still have guests. I'm worried about you." He knocked again. The knob shook easily before stopping, and then I heard the sound of his boots slowly walking away.

I continued to lie there wondering how I'd let myself be tricked this way. Had I really believed I'd been so charming and irresistible that a polished man such as he would want to bring me home to meet his mother—after one afternoon?

The more I thought about it, the more I understood I had no right to be angry with Timothy. Only with myself. Timothy was no more than a pretender, no different than I. We were trying to survive the best way we knew how. Pretending. Lying. Suffering in silence.

I remained in my room the rest of the day. The wedding guests took their time leaving. I listened to the steady click of horse carriages winding down the path.

"Miss Lily," Cleo whispered at the closed door.

She didn't wait for an answer before somehow letting herself in. I was sure the door had been locked. "You need some tea." It wasn't a question. She came inside with a tray, placing it at the bedside. She poured the brewed tea in a pink flowered cup and held the sugar bowl, waiting for instruction on how many lumps of sugar.

Having someone do for me the very things I used to do for others made me uncomfortable. No matter how many times I told myself I deserved to be treated with dignity, this felt wrong. The murky voice in my head whispered, *You are nothing but fodder for this family. For Timothy. For Ryland and Tilda. Oh, how they must laugh. You are nothing but a fraud.*

I took the sugar. Two lumps, just like Annabelle used to do.

"Would you like me to call you missus now?" she asked, still looking down. "Now that you a married lady, missus is the proper calling."

"You can call me whatever you like."

She glanced in my direction. "Is there anything else I can do for you?"

"Yes. Throw this out." I gathered the dress borrowed from Tilda and placed it in Cleo's arms.

"Have a fine evening, Miss Lily." Cleo quietly closed the door behind her.

As soon as she was gone I tied a silk robe around my waist, then moved to the window. I peeked from behind the curtains, tea in hand, watching as Tilda said her goodbyes to a few guests who'd lingered, each feigning interest in what the other had to say. This was the life I'd asked for, what I'd wanted to be a part of. I would have to play pretend better than I'd ever played before.

That night, Timothy chose to sleep in his room while I stayed in mine. There was no marriage celebration. No first night together. I was relieved to be alone.

The only person not satisfied with the sleeping arrangement was Tilda. The very next morning she spoke abruptly. "A man and his wife must share a marital bed. Whatever is the point of marriage if not that?"

"That's not necessary." I sat with my shoulders back, ready for battle.

"Of course it's necessary," she said.

"Did you ask Timothy about me moving into his room?"

Tilda took note of my obvious discomfort. "I understand your youth may not offer a clear understanding of what is required as a wife, but there's nothing to be afraid of. Maggie and Ryland are getting along splendidly. Maybe you should speak with her to put your mind at ease about what is expected of you."

"Isn't it a lovely morning? Did I hear my name?" Maggie's angelic voice entered the parlor before she did. Her sun-torched hair framed her pale skin and flushed cheeks. She poured herself tea before joining us at the table.

"Good morning," I said, relieved to change the subject.

"How's it feel to be a missus?" she asked. Maggie may have genuinely not known I was only a figurine, a doll like one of the porcelain beauties Mother Rose liked to collect.

"Not much different," I answered honestly. I took a bite of the small biscuit on my plate.

Maggie smiled hesitantly, looking between the two of us, realizing she'd entered a tense conversation. "Discussing wifely obligations, are ya? Not all that exciting. I'll tell you what is: I've learned a new quilting stitch. I plan to get four rows on my blanket by late afternoon."

"A blanket speaks of good news. Is there a child forthcoming?" Tilda asked.

"You never know. Nothing like planning ahead. What about you, Lily, what are yer plans today?" Maggie's light lashes fanned over her curious eyes.

"I don't have any just yet."

"I have a suggestion," Tilda interrupted. "Gardening. There's a wide square of sunshine on the grounds that would make a lovely garden.

I can have the area cleared for you. You can grow whatever you like. Roses. Lilies. Maybe something delicious like berries."

Maggie pursed her lips in delicious anticipation. "Umm. Berries."

"I appreciate the suggestion." I rose from my chair.

"Where are you going?" Tilda was only getting started. She hadn't dispensed all of her marital notes.

"To my room."

"To gather your things, I hope. My dear sister, Gertrude, will be arriving tomorrow. She will be staying in the room, your old room." She made her meaning clear with a raise of her brow. She then turned her attention to Maggie and smiled pleasantly. "I can't wait to see the blanket you're working on."

I went back to my room and took one last look around. It was the only space I'd ever known as my own, however so briefly. Now it was gone.

"Knock, knock," Timothy said to announce his entry. He'd given up with his explanations. He took a seat on the edge of the neatly made bed already prepared for the new guest. "Looks like we've been ordered to unite our loins," he quipped.

I faced him. "Your mother making this kind of decision doesn't bother you?"

"I've learned to let Mum think she's in charge. Then I do as I please." He leaned back on his elbow and crossed his legs for comfort.

"I noticed."

"Oh, come now. Pico and I were having a harmless row. Yes, he's in our employ, but we've also been friends since childhood. I don't understand why you're committed to believing something sinister was going on." Timothy ran his fingers through his loose hair. "I chose you as my bride. I was taken by your independence, Lily, and now it seems you're using all that wayward thinking against me."

84

I cleared my throat and turned away from him. "Timothy"—I shook my head to try and find the right words—"I don't think we should be . . ."

He let out an exhausted sigh as if we'd spoken on this subject one hundred times before. He stood up and took my hand. "I have no intention of making you do anything you're not inclined to do. I won't take advantage of you, if you promise not to take advantage of me. How about that? One day at a time, aye?"

I did my best to look him in the eye. "Why me, Timothy? In the city, when we met, why me?"

"We have better things to do than hash over the day we met. My aunt Gertrude will arrive tomorrow. The woman's very existence is about making everyone else feel small. I should prepare you."

"I'll be fine," I scoffed. I'd had plenty of preparation in that regard. I faced the room. "Your mother told me to gather my things, but nothing in here is mine. I have nothing." And that was the truth of it. Where would I go if I left? What would I do? Go back to Vesterville in shame. My choice was simple.

Timothy grabbed the heavy gold clock. "Ah, this looks like yours. And these." He gripped several books in his hand, stacking them against his chest. "Oh, and this gem. You don't want to forget this." He slid a set of candlesticks under his arms. "Maybe we should take the entire bed? We'll push it side by side and Mum will never be the wiser. And these." He grabbed two pillows. "Aunt Gertrude can sleep flat on her back."

His charm and good cheer offered a glimpse of the man I'd met that day in the city. I'd wanted to hold contempt for Timothy, for his secrets and dishonesty, but having disdain for him would only make me more ashamed of myself, for my own dishonesty, my own lies.

Timothy and I each carried a stack of books. He took the candlesticks and feather-stuffed pillows while I followed him a few yards down the hall.

I'd only seen the inside of Timothy's room from the hallway, a brief peek when I was only focused on seeing him uncovered and exposed. It was nearly a replica of the room we'd just left, except brighter with the curtains pulled aside, letting in full sunlight. The same bed with tall posts, a painting of a sailing boat on an ocean, and an enormous oak bookcase furnished the large space. He placed our book bounty on his desk, making the stack appear immediately out of place.

"Well, here we are. Welcome to my abode." He swung the armoire doors open to reveal clothing on wood hangers. "Your dresses were already brought here."

Disappointment shrouded my brief excitement. "They're not my dresses."

"They're yours now." He pulled on one of the drab dresses Tilda had probably thrown out long before I'd arrived. "This will be fine for supper tomorrow evening. Perfect for meeting Aunt Gertrude. She appreciates moderation." He kissed my forehead.

I would learn to appreciate the delicate foundation of lies our life was built on.

Our silence on important matters would come in handy.

15

Mercy

Bo closed his eyes and fell into a deep, exhausted sleep on the cool ground. He was a child, a boy again, holding hands with Dahlia. They were running across a field of high grass, laughing because they'd hidden from whoever was calling their names. Him, grinning, ducking behind the beginnings of straw, unable to stay quiet. Her, telling him to *shhh*, but unable to stop her own giggling. Her laugh. God, he loved her laugh.

"Run," he told her, leading the way. Not more than a few feet away he was stopped by what he saw. His feet took root in the ground. There was a man lying in the field, flies buzzing around his torn face. They both stopped, seized with fear. Dahlia screamed. Bo covered her eyes with one hand and pulled her away with the other. The man rose up with his bloodied, eaten face, his outstretched hands grabbing at both of them. *You won't get away.*

Bo sat up with his heart in his throat. The moan of pain that had awakened him was coming from somewhere else. It wasn't just the eaten-face man in his dreams. This one was just a few feet away. He'd been badly beaten. The rest of them stirred out of their only rest to the brightness of the moon. They listened but were unable to help him.

The man's old master had beaten him badly before putting him out for auction. He still wore the bloodied shirt torn in lines with each severe lash he'd received. Infection had set in on the open gashes. The rotted blood in his veins could have been cooled with enough water, something the trader wouldn't be willing to part with. If Bo could find wild mint growing nearby, he could put it on the wounds. Tied to the rope with the others, he'd never get far enough to forage.

He listened to the man's ramblings asking for mercy in the darkness. That mercy would only come in death.

"I say we put him out of his misery," one of the others whispered.

"Don't you dare touch him," Bo whispered back. "He gotta right to live, like any of us." He shut out the suffering man's howl. When it was time for a man's death, only God would know. Killing only brought about more pain. He could never do it, kill a man, not unless the man tried to kill him first.

Bo put his hands over his ears and tried to close out the sound. Before long he stopped hearing the moans.

Come daylight, the man lay stiff, his mouth caught in mid-wail before death had slipped in while the others slept. At least that's what Bo chose to believe. He eyed the others, wondering if any of them had played a role in the man's quick reach to the other side. A hand over his face was all it would've taken.

The trader untied a few of them to drag the body into the brush of trees. Flies immediately found a new home against the body's rotting scars. Bo wiped his mouth to fight the urge to heave. The only thing left in his stomach was the ache of sadness. "All right, time to move," the trader called out, already perched on his horse.

A day later Bo was breathing fire. It was him hacking and howling in the middle of the night. A heavy weight pressed on his chest. He coughed good and hard to push out the smothering feeling only to have it come right back again. He'd never been sick in the quarters. Here and now, he felt one step away from giving up breathing altogether. It hurt to move, leaving him on the ground while the others were ready to stand and take their morning piss. They had to go where they stood.

Bo lay with his eyes closed, waiting for the worst.

"Come on, man. Get yo' feet under ya." Those big hands yanking Bo up from under his arms belonged to the big red one with brown dots all over his face. They never exchanged names, but Bo called him Red on account of his red coiled hair and onion-colored skin.

He let Bo rest against his shoulder while he relieved himself. Bo followed suit, grateful not to wet himself and have to wear it throughout the day. His throat hurt too much to say thank you.

They moved together to the burnt hash cooked in a rush. Bo took a sip of the ladle of water passed around and nearly cried out from the pain of swallowing. He didn't stand a chance of eating the half-cooked cornmeal.

"You gotta eat something," Red ordered. "You ain't gon' make it without something in your belly."

He forced one bite. It hurt like hell when the food rolled down, so much he had to cradle his chest. "Come on, one mo' scoop," Red ordered. "That-a-boy," he whispered. "You gon' be all right."

Bo ate through the pain because he didn't want to die, not just yet.

Voices and footsteps scrambled in the early-morning darkness. Bo peeked first before moving, before lifting his head to wonder what was happening. He lay still, watching the big boots kick dirt around him. It took a mighty will, but he sat up to see what all the fuss was about.

"All of ya, on your feet." Two white men roused the womenfolk.

"I told you. I have the purchase papers," the trader announced. "Ain't no stolen property here."

"Don't mean nothing. If you bought stolen property it's still a crime," the man called out.

Bo couldn't see him, but he was sure he recognized the voice. John Browder, the man Holt hired to find Dahlia, was here.

Wherever *here* was. There'd been so many different auctions, stopping for two or three days and then on to the next, that Bo couldn't keep track. It all felt like one big circle. He recognized the locations, the same white men who'd showed up looking for a bargain. Two for the price of one, three for the price of two. Conroy McVee, the trader, refused to make any deals. He was a businessman. This was his living, selling off folks like livestock.

"Hold on now. I'll get them up. Don't hurt none of them," McVee pleaded.

"Take down your shirts. Turn around," John Browder ordered the women. The sun was rising through the trees, offering enough light for his inspection. Scars from their past, healed over, appeared in various shapes and angles. Browder walked past each of them, checking their backs closely. "What's your name?" he asked the youngest.

"Sesalie," she answered, tired but not afraid.

"I got her papers right here," McVee said.

John Browder pushed the purchase papers out of his face. "See this," he said, holding up his proof. "There's a reward out for Dahlia Holt. More money than I ever seen. People are looking. If you see her, know of her whereabouts, you'll be wise to return her first before somebody puts a hole in your head." He put his fingers to the trader's head with a thud.

John Browder and his men gathered up and rode away. The women shuddered, grateful to be where they were because it could always be worse than the last.

The yellowed paper rested on the ground with a boot print. Bo saw the big letters spelled out. REWARD. He'd learned to read a little right alongside Dahlia when Miss Rose was giving out her lessons.

Here was the reward notice. The sketch was Annabelle, with only the name changed. He'd heard Master Holt tell Browder to use the small portrait of his eldest for the sketch because Dahlia and Annabelle looked enough alike.

"Give me that," the trader said, snatching the notice from Bo's hand. "Y'all see what happens when you run. A man like that will surely make you pay."

McVee stamped out the fire. He'd had his fill of being sneaked up on. He told his trusty driver, no more fires. That meant no more corn mash. He wasn't a thief but there were men who were. He didn't want anyone stealing his property. He wasn't a rich owner. He couldn't afford to hire some bounty hunter to find his lost property. What he lost would be gone forever. So the lot of them would travel in the day and sit in cold darkness at night.

16

Belles

"Well, if it isn't the belle of the ball," Ryland said between sips from his amber-filled glass. "Glad you could join us, baby brother."

"You know how we belles are. Can't make our appearance without proper diligence." Timothy smoothed a hand over his freshly shaven chin, then introduced me to his aunt Gertrude. She wore a frilly white blouse with layers flowering up to her chin, making her look like a bowl of frothy whipped cream. This alone made me instantly take a liking to her. She had a sense of style unlike any woman I'd ever seen.

I'd worked hard to avoid Ryland, and yet somehow my seat at the table had landed directly across from him. I didn't like it.

"Lily," Ryland called across the table. "I thought you southerners were big on etiquette. Being late is just plain rude, y'all," he finished, with an exaggerated drawl of his words. He surveyed the rest of the table to see if everyone else enjoyed his humor as much as he did.

Timothy spoke up for me. "Forgive our tardiness. We were busy making each other smile." This swiped the usual smirk from Ryland's face. A tinge of uncertainty replaced it as he must have wondered if Timothy could be undone so easily. If the thing he knew about his brother could be altered.

I reached over and let my hand rest on Timothy's. Ryland dropped his eyes to watch this small act of solidarity, as I knew he would.

"Are we done yet?" Aunt Gertrude asked. She sat at the far end of the table observing the strained interaction of her nephews. She snapped her lips together after taking a sip of her wine, bored with the banter. "Can we get back to the subject of my finances being wasted on this infertile land?" she asked with a frail wave. "You, Timothy, are you the one in charge of the books?"

Timothy's jaw pinched on the sides. "Yes. I thought we'd save the discussion for after supper."

"Enough with the diversions," Aunt Gertrude spat. Everyone jumped at the sound of her bony hand hitting the table. Maggie, Tilda, and even Ryland flinched, perhaps afraid she'd broken something in her own body. She turned calmly to Timothy. "Do you want to tell me why I have yet to see a return? You and your brother have been so busy acquiring bedmates that little work is getting done. I loaned the money as an investment, not for charity."

Timothy stayed quiet before announcing to Aunt Gertrude, "This is Lily. She is not a bedmate. She is my wife."

Maggie didn't seem to be offended by the name calling. Neither was Ryland. I was proud of Timothy for speaking up. I reached under the table and gave his hand a squeeze.

"I apologize for my use of an old term, Lily." She gave a proper pause before returning to her mood. "Good to see everyone so happy and satisfied with their lives. Now, pay attention," she continued. "Four seasons have passed, and we still have no profitable crops. I thought this soil was the land of plenty, or at the very least a few bushels of corn. Is this what I was promised? No. I think not."

"We're breaking even, something many cannot claim," Timothy answered with confidence.

"Breaking even? We should be doing more than breaking even. You have bedmates to feed, don't you?"

There was that word again. As much as I respected Aunt Gertrude's outgoing revelry, I winced each time she said it. I fought off the sound of Annabelle's voice in my ear. Bedmate. Bedwench. *Wench.* What was the difference?

"Breaking even is not what I was promised." Aunt Gertrude slurped her wine, letting a drop fall on her white blouse. The stain spread, turning into a bright pink circle. "I would like the return on my investment before I die, which is highly unlikely at this rate. Don't think I didn't see the many horses you purchased. Did you need six horses? Are there six of you?"

Ryland cleared his throat. "Horses are a fine investment, Aunt Gertrude. Breeding is more profitable than farming, in fact."

"So, you and your brother didn't need a thousand acres or this house. All you needed was a stable and six horses. Why didn't anyone tell me?" She rested her wrinkled hands on the table.

"Gertrude, please, that's enough," Tilda said. "Let's have supper. You and the boys can discuss the accounting afterward."

"After supper, then. This will be resolved." Aunt Gertrude went back to sipping her wine.

Cleo entered from the kitchen, carrying a carafe. "Pardon, miss." She leaned over, grazing my shoulder to pour. She then made her rounds to the rest of the table. After all the glasses were filled, Ryland tapped his spoon delicately on the side of his.

"I think the time is appropriate to make an announcement."

Aunt Gertrude blew out a hoarse sigh. "I'm breathless with anticipation."

Ryland reached for Maggie's hand. He cleared his throat. "We will have the first heir on our new land. We are with child."

"This is wonderful." Tilda could hardly contain her joy. "You are an angel, my dear. My first grandchild. You're sure?"

"Yes. I'm sorry I didn't tell you when you inquired about the blanket. I wanted to tell Ryland first." Maggie gazed at him longingly. "I couldn't wait to share the news with all of you."

"Congratulations, brother." Timothy raised his glass, genuinely happy for them.

"Maggie, you are my blessing," Tilda sang. "You've made me so happy."

Dread filled my throat. The more everyone cheered and smiled, the further I disappeared into a blur. I lifted my glass with a weak hand, unsure if it would remain there or crash to the plate below. "Congratulations, Maggie."

A child required consummation. I hadn't thought of this. Bodies were required to touch. The matter of children, the next step in a union, had obviously been overlooked in Timothy's masterful plan. There was more involved than acquiring a wife for appearances' sake. The thought of having a child scared me.

"Wonderful. More mouths to feed," Aunt Gertrude snapped. She wiped the corners of her downturned lips and tossed her napkin on the table. "I have no intention of continuing as the interloper in the very home I have provided. When you are ready to discuss business instead of planting your damn fertile seeds, I'll be in the library." She moved ever so slowly to her feet.

Ryland rose from his chair and followed Aunt Gertrude. Timothy eventually went too. Maggie, Tilda, and I were left alone. We could chatter about whether there would be a boy or girl, and plans of the future.

"To the addition to our family," Tilda said with a raised glass.

"Cheers." I raised the poured glass of wine, making a point of finishing it all. Before coming here, I'd never tasted wine. The lightness made me giddy and joyful all at once. Thoughts of Timothy and me, unions and babies, became far off.

Cleo returned with more. Without thinking, I reached out and touched her hand. "You are too kind. Thank you, Cleo."

Tilda gasped. Maggie blinked nervously. Cleo fled the scene as if the moon had been set ablaze.

I finished pouring the wine, filling the glasses myself. "Here's to bedmates and wenches."

Tilda stood up. "I think I'll retire for the evening. Lily, perhaps you should do the same."

"Perhaps I will, or perhaps I won't," I said, madness stirring inside me.

Tilda and Maggie looked at one another. Maggie tried to match Tilda's stern expression but lost the fight. She let the smile, then the laughter, come out. "Perhaps I will, or perhaps I won't, have another glass of wine as well." She sipped. "To bedmates," she chimed.

"Cheers," I said, ignoring Tilda's disdain.

Timothy slipped into our room later that evening, trying not to wake me. He sat on the edge of the bed, staring straight ahead at nothing.

My head swam. When I closed my eyes, I imagined I was on a giant boat the way Timothy described traveling endlessly on the blue ocean. I would never let wine touch my lips again.

"I was worried about you." I forced myself up on my elbows.

"I'm sorry to interrupt your sleep." His mood was somber. He began taking off his coat and unbuttoning his vest, then became frustrated that he'd forgotten to remove his cuff links before attempting to pull his hands through. "My God, will anything ever go accordingly?"

I reached to turn the oil lamp higher so he could see instead of wrestling with himself.

"No. Don't. I'm fine," he said, embarrassed.

"What did your aunt Gertrude have to say?"

"I'm sure you can guess. Threats." Timothy's voice cracked in defeat. "In a few days, I'll have to leave for the city to secure more workers. Attend one of those ghastly auctions. I don't know how long I'll be gone." With his shirt off, he bent over and struggled to remove his boots next. His tense narrow shoulders revealed the extent of his worry. His labored breath filled the room with the scent of alcohol. "I must meet with bankers after that. I will not depend on Aunt Gertrude for my livelihood. The woman is unstable."

"We should talk about this tomorrow when you're feeling better." I didn't want to think about Aunt Gertrude. I wished the entire evening could be banished from my memory.

I stroked the dark waves of Timothy's hair, one last effort to calm him down.

"What are you doing?" He stood up.

"I thought . . ."

"You thought you'd make my aunt Gertrude be right and turn yourself into a bedmate?" he spat.

"No. That's not what . . . I didn't mean to—"

He sloppily slapped his hands to his face. "No. I'm sorry, I didn't mean any of that, Lily," he said with the flicker of lamplight reflecting in his eyes. "I do sincerely care for you. I'm sure you understand."

But I didn't understand. I couldn't figure out what I was supposed to do. As his wife, so far, I had done nothing but sit by his side and nod pleasantly at supper.

"What is it that you want from me, Timothy? I'm here but I'm not here. I'm just as invisible as I was . . ." I bit my lip to silence myself from saying what I was thinking. I was nothing more than how I'd started. Dahlia Holt or *Lily Dove*, neither of us held a place here. Neither of us was important to anyone.

I had no power to influence my husband to feel better with a gentle nudge or a soft touch. No power to reason with him.

He left me alone to descend further into heartache. I shook from the sudden chill. I wrapped a blanket around my shivering body. I went to the window, which offered a dark sky. The moon shed light on the acres of trees and dense low shrubs. Dogs howled in the distance, then barked. This sound meant somewhere in the woods there was a search happening. Someone had escaped and would risk life and limb to be free.

The morning brightness pushed past the closed shutters, past the closed lids of my eyes. There was no escaping the bright yellow sun in the room. I turned over to the empty side of the bed and tried to fight the immediate memory of sadness. Even with the sun flooding the room, it wouldn't warm until far past noon. I pushed the covers away, stepping into slippers at the foot of the bed. I wrapped a morning coat around my shoulders and tried to tread lightly, without making the floor creak from the cold.

Timothy's desk was clear except for the inkwell and quill resting in the center. I wondered what he wrote with his feathered quill. I pulled open one small drawer at a time. There were cuff links, stray buttons, and an array of copper coins.

I slid into the wide oak chair and leaned back, absorbing its power. That's when I saw the journal, red with a burgundy ribbon sticking out to mark his page. It was just like the one I'd seen of Master Holt's, the book that identified his slaves and many offspring. I grabbed it, expecting but hoping not to see the same thing. Maybe it was an accounting of what he owed Aunt Gertrude. I was hungry to know anything I could about the man I'd married. I flipped it open to the page he'd last visited. His handwriting was impeccably neat and rhythmic. Each word and letter flowed into the next with barely a space.

I read it aloud. "Each time I think of your hand in mine I am transported to a place where I surrender heart and soul. With your love, I am free."

I read the date on the poetic note. I couldn't help but feel a pinch of envy. This powerful statement of love had been written days before we'd met. Maybe written for Pico. I turned the page. A separate paper fell. It was heavy and parched at the edges.

Notice of Auction. It was a list of names. Slaves for sale, descriptions and prices. People were like livestock. I covered my mouth, squeezed my eyes closed, and hoped the scream was only in my head. Timothy had this list long before Aunt Gertrude had arrived. More slaves, he'd said, were required. He'd already planned to purchase them, apparently.

I wished I could explain how more hands and backs bent over wouldn't help make his land profitable. I couldn't tell him what I'd learned growing up at the hip of Papa Sap. How he'd survey the land with just a handful of dirt to his lips, sniffing first before sticking his tongue in for a taste. Mostly he'd smile brightly, missing all but the bottom two of his teeth, and smack his lips to the taste. If the soil wasn't right, his face would screw up in a tight frown and he'd spit the biting acid out of his mouth. After a stretch of his long body upward he'd prop his hands on his thin sides, considering what to do next. Papa Sap never asked for permission. He simply went out and found what was needed—cattle dung, dry grass, pigs' piss, or the bones of slaughtered animals, which he'd learned to store in the back of the barn in a large heap. Once an odor started to seep into the air, he'd pile it into sacks and carry it out to the land to spread and mix with the old dirt.

Within weeks, new seedlings would reach for the sun, green and vibrant, ready to grow new leaves every day. But that had nothing to do with the number of hands you had or the amount of backs bent.

I went down the list, reading the names on the auction list. There were so many. But then again, one was too many.

Bowman Carter. A horseman, skills not likely held by many. Good breeder, strong legs, good back, and thick genitalia.

I stared, waiting for the name to change into something else. *Bo.* This couldn't be true. Shock raced through my veins. I shook my head no. This was Holt and Annabelle's doing. They must've accused Bo of helping me run off. This was his punishment. *I did this.*

I was unable to move, even when I heard voices and footsteps coming. It took a moment before I closed the journal and shoved the list into my robe pocket. I put the journal back with shaking hands. I knew what I had to do. I was determined to make Timothy listen to me. I wouldn't take no for an answer.

PART II

17

The Wylie

The trader held up a hand, the sign for the driver to slow the wagon. The driver gently tugged the reins. The tired horses were grateful to stop. This was Bo's new home. Because . . . *dead or alive, I'm never leaving.* Like the famished horses, he couldn't take another step even if he wanted to.

The gate made of iron had a giant sign above it. *The Wylie,* with a gold circle around it. Any place with a gate that large was a place of means. As tired as he was, a shift of hope came calling. Poor owners were in no position to house and feed others. Here, at least he stood a chance. Food. Water. Maybe a warm place to sleep.

"Get this gate open," the trader barked. The wagon driver was an owned man like the rest of them, and yet he possessed a whip belted at his side. He jumped down, his heavy boots too large for his feet, and unlocked the loop of chains holding the men together. He pushed Red forward, away from the rest of the group—one of the few who still had good legs after the trip. After Red pushed the gate open, the driver tied Red back up, got on his perch, and started the caravan moving again.

Slow steps marched in line through the wide entrance. This land felt different, with plentiful shade from tall oak trees and a cool breeze. The trees had broad, hardy branches from every angle. They continued one after the other, blocking out the sun and sky, an endless line of giant monsters waiting to get their hands on him. The hovering mass didn't stop until they reached the very steps of a house bigger than any one family needed. It was the size of its own small town, with windows high and low.

A well-dressed man rushed down the stairs off his grand porch. Bo dropped his head and lowered his gaze.

The trader introduced himself. "Conroy McVee, purveyor of quality human resources, at your service."

Bo had heard the same introduction a number of times from the trader. "Special delivery, sir," he'd say before removing his hat with a nod as if he were bringing flowers instead of broken spirits.

"Why are you at my doorstep with this business? Take them to the quarters."

"Sir, when you pay me the balance, you are free to have your property placed wherever you'd like. My job is to deliver the goods. I believe this order is cash on delivery." McVee handed over his paperwork.

"It looks like you're a few short. I have word of four females and four males."

"All of them didn't quite make it. Part of the attrition process. Saves you from taking on the weak ones. Better to lose them on the way. I deducted their worth from the balance. It's all right there. Now, if you don't mind, we should settle up." McVee wanted to get paid for the bodies while they were still alive. With every second that passed, the risk was high he'd lose another sellable soul. Bo's ears rang, right along with the spinning going on in his head, making him sure he'd be the next soul lost. He wished Conroy McVee would settle his business and let him go die in peace, preferably without heavy shackles cuffed around his waist.

"I'll pay after I've had a thorough inspection." The fair-haired man talked in a singsong sort of way, no match for the down and dirty McVee.

"Well then, inspect away."

"So then, if you'll lead them to the quarters, to my overseer, we can begin."

"No one's taking another step till I get my pay. You want to test me? There's no shortage of takers of fine stock."

Bo listened to Conroy McVee tell his lies. There were no other takers, not for the prices he was asking. They'd circled around the same five plantations for the last six days. There was only one man who'd offered the trader the price he wanted to hear. That man had wanted them delivered in a timely fashion, and now they were here, being held up by a standoff.

"Fine then," the new owner conceded. He pulled out a leather billfold.

Conroy McVee slipped off his horse to level ground. His boots plodded on the clay dirt. Signatures and money were exchanged. The sounds of moans and sighs of relief followed. They were all on their last breath.

"Now, move them to the quarters," the new owner ordered.

"Your highness," McVee mocked with a cluck of his tongue. He half bent at his knees, then sent a brown glob of spittle that landed where Bo was barely standing. "You imports think the world evolves around you. Well, it don't. We got rules of business conduct here." He pulled himself up on his horse.

The fair-haired owner let out a teasing laugh. "Obviously, you have no record of your history, no idea where you come from. The world does absolutely revolve around me. Now do as I say and move these men. If they die, they're worthless to me."

Bo proved the new owner right by dropping to his knees. Since the chain connected to the others held him from falling properly, he hung there, tilted over. No amount of extra food or water could've fixed the wear and tear on his mind and what was left of his body. He'd fought off fever, drowning lungs, and his throat on fire. He struggled to get back on his feet, then heaved what little was left in his belly, bitter drops of clear, vile liquid. His head felt pressed in a blacksmith's vise. The other men by his side did their best not to go down with him, knowing it'd cost them all a severe punishment.

"Get up," his friend Red warned. "You know you 'bout to get the whip." Red tried to pull him up as he'd done so many times before. Bo's knees were too shaky, and Red had nothing left to give.

The sound of the whip whizzed near Bo's ear, a warning. Bo doubted he'd feel the sting with his body already on fire. If anything, he was ready to meet the other side. Heaven was what he'd been promised. It had to be better than this.

Before the second attempt of the wagon driver's whip, a voice sang over the hollow air in his ears.

"Stop. Don't you dare strike him."

His blurry eyes opened. He saw a white woman coming toward him. As she got closer, Bo was sure he was seeing things. "Dah . . ."

"Shhh, drink." She held a bucket of water and a ladle. With gentle hands, the woman held the ladle while his mouth shook with desperation. Water never tasted so good running past his cracked lips, down his chin and throat, gathering and unfolding what life was left in him.

"What are you doing? Get back inside. How dare you embarrass me this way?" The new owner knocked the ladle from her hand before Bo could get his fill. The bucket hit the ground. Water splashed and pooled around Bo's knees, turning the ground into a muddy paradise. Coolness surrounded him, if only for a minute.

"Get up or so help me," the wagon driver ordered. The lash of the whip followed quickly.

"Stop it!" The woman's scream echoed through the trees and back again. "I will not stand here and watch these people die."

"Fine. What you do with them now is your business," Conroy McVee huffed.

The new owner tried to speak to the woman calmly. "Get back inside, Lily. You are putting yourself in danger. I will handle this."

Lily. It's not Dahlia.

"Let go of me." But her voice wrapped around Bo like a soft blanket. For the first time, Bo believed that someone up above cared about him. When she was done, the new owner grabbed her again, this time not so gently, and hurried her off.

I heard the rumble of a slow wagon. Men on foot were connected behind. Bedraggled bodies unable to take another step. It took a second to realize what I was seeing.

I ran to the kitchen, scrambling for a bucket to get water. I ran past Cleo, who'd offered to fetch whatever I might need. *No. This is something I have to do.* There was no time. The men and women were parched and worn to the depths of despair. I gave them sips of water. Before I knew it, I was standing in front of Bo. It was him. *Bo . . .*

It was the grip at my arm that stopped me from calling his name, thank goodness, bringing me to my senses.

Ryland began to drag me away. I fought, spilling the full bucket at Bo's feet. I fought while Ryland dragged me to the top of the porch steps and then gave me a sharp shove through the front door. I landed on all fours.

"What's happening? What did you do, Lily?" Maggie asked. She stood horrified where I'd landed at her feet.

"Keep her inside," Ryland hissed. "She's utterly lost her mind." He trotted off to where the slaves remained. To where Bo remained, chained and nearly dying from thirst.

"Did you see what just happened? You ask me, what did I do?" I stood and could barely catch my breath. I rubbed the wringing pain in my hands and wrists from having landed hard. "Your husband dragged me here like some rag doll and threw me to the ground, and you want to know what I did?" I paced for a second with my mouth covered, afraid of what I might say. My heart was pounding. As angry as I was, my thoughts stayed with Bo, seeing him in chains.

"Ryland is a very gentle man," Maggie stammered while keeping her distance. "He . . . he would never hurt you or anyone."

"He had no right to put his hands on me," I shouted. My knees began to sting. I'd fallen hard, but still I knew the pain was laughable compared to what Bo had been through. I swallowed my silly concerns, ready to get out and try again. Bo needed water. They all needed water.

Maggie moved in front of the doorway, blocking me from going back outside. "Wait, Lily. I'm sorry. You're right, he shouldn't have treated you that way. But you can't go out there." She took my hand. "Let me get a cool rag. You're bleeding." She turned to call out to Cleo for a wet towel.

Cleo was standing there, a witness to it all. She understood the truth about me. She'd seen it all along, but now truly saw the depth behind my dark eyes and underneath my sun-hued skin. I looked around, unable to figure out how to do what I needed to do without putting everything at stake. I couldn't leave Bo out there for another second.

"Where are you going?" Maggie asked, walking beside me, blocking my way further. "What are you planning to do? Just wait, please. Calm down," she said, touching my arm, doing her best to keep me from taking the dangerous step outside.

"Don't touch me." I took a deep breath, realizing from the look on Maggie's face that I'd revealed too much. My throat rang with the pain of silence. I spun around and faced the hall, then the door again.

I forced a gentle tone. "I'm sorry. I shouldn't have taken it out on you. Please. I'm fine." I swallowed my fury and blinked away the loss and frustration and replaced them with calm. A lady of the house had every right to speak up and demand decency. I would have to do things differently, that's all, quietly. I stepped away and headed to my room.

"Where are you going?"

"Maggie, I'm fine. I'm . . . fine."

18

Miss Lily

I hadn't slept. I'd tossed and turned in fitful spurts. My head pounded with urgency. My thoughts stayed with Bo. Was he all right? He'd barely survived. I hadn't wanted to believe Bo would be blamed for my running off. I'd wanted to believe in the decency of Lewis Holt.

I'd been proven wrong. Bowman Carter for sale, his skills listed, a purchase price for his worth.

Thank goodness I'd heard enough of Ryland and Timothy's conversations about their need for a horse trainer. Ryland had difficulty maintaining his riding schedule without a horse worker. And wasn't it written right there on the auction list? *A horseman, skills not likely held by many.* I made Timothy listen to me. I talked until I ran out of breath. I kept on with the idea. "Wouldn't it be lovely to purchase a horse trainer as an offering to Ryland, to show appreciation for all his dedication to the new land? A gift always brings people closer." I'd talked about it at sunrise and sunset. "You and Ryland need to be stronger together right now, in light of your difficulties with the land. A united front for Aunt Gertrude," I'd said. "A horse trainer could do just the trick." I kept up the tickle under his skin until it was Timothy saying the very same words like a tune he couldn't get out of his head. *I will buy a horse trainer for Ryland as a gift.*

Then there'd been the next step of making him remember the auction notice. The list tucked away in his journal.

"Isn't there a list of some kind? An auction list must have a horse trainer." The suggestion became a seed neatly planted and sowed. Timothy nodded his agreement, and a few weeks later Bowman Carter landed at my feet. In chains, but he was here, and wasn't that all that mattered?

The knock at the door came. I knew the door would open with or without my permission. Cleo stood with folded linens in her arms.

"Miss Tilda wants you down for tea." Pico stood close behind, holding linens. Did that mean Timothy was back? He'd been scarce around the house, around me, and this time had been gone for days. When Timothy was gone, so was Pico.

"Is Timothy here?"

"Miss Tilda would like to see you in the parlor," Cleo repeated dutifully. She wasn't in the mood for forced pleasantries. She put the linens on the shelf in the armoire. Pico handed her the second set, and she placed those neatly on the next shelf.

"Tell Miss Tilda I'll be down soon."

She turned to walk out.

"Cleo, can I speak with you?"

Pico stayed by her side.

"Go on, I'll be out in a minute," Cleo told her trusty assistant. He left and closed the door. She stayed but kept her eyes lowered.

"Cleo, you can look at me."

She faced me. Our eyes met long enough to know I was right. There was a pinch of fear.

"I'm sorry if I've done anything to offend you," I said.

"You haven't offended me. I been told to mind my place, is all." She'd been warned about my display of gratitude the other day.

110

"I shouldn't have been so forward in front of the others. I'm new to all of this. I promise from now on I will keep proper distance around them." I eyed her closely to see if "the others" meant anything to her.

"That was a nice thing you did, giving them water. Mistress of the house don't usually do that kind of thing. From now on, I think you should be more careful," she said in a tone meant for secrecy.

And now I was sure. This was her warning for my own good.

"I will. Thank you, Cleo."

I approached Tilda where she sat on the veranda.

"Good, you're here." She motioned to the chair across from her. "Sit. Please. We have much to discuss." Tilda lifted a silver bell and shook it lightly to have more tea brought in. "So, where shall we begin? I think with an apology," she said, answering her own question. She stared off into the distance for a second or two trying to figure out what she apparently hadn't given much thought to before now. "Ryland should've handled things much differently, and I'd like to apologize for his behavior."

Nattie, one of the women who worked in the kitchen, came behind Tilda with a tray of tea. She cut her eyes in my direction but only briefly.

Tilda excused her and poured the tea herself. She handed me the cup as a pleasant offering. She appeared tired and a bit unsettled. Her hair was swept into a braid over one shoulder. Her bland gray dress was open at the neck instead of the usual—fully buttoned to the end with a bow tied at the top. She kept herself neat, but her appearance today felt rushed and untidy.

"I understand how restless you must feel while Timothy is away on business. The misunderstanding between you and Ryland may have been avoided had you been more occupied."

"He had no right to shove me." My voice shook.

"To my understanding, Ryland did not shove you. You tripped while he was escorting you inside."

The image of what had actually transpired—him dragging me up the stairs and shoving me—rose firmly in my mind. "He may not have swung his fist, but he inflicted harm. He intended to inflict harm." I could feel the child rising up inside of me, the little girl who could never make anyone listen. I'd been hurt so many times by Annabelle. She'd slapped, pinched, or thrown anything she could reach at will, and I'd had no say and she, no consequence. I wanted to be heard. I wasn't afraid. I wouldn't back down about what Ryland had done.

"He was trying to protect you, dear girl. Slaves are very dangerous."

"How are they dangerous? How did I need protecting from someone in chains? All I wanted to do was give them water before they collapsed and died at our doorstep." I paused, hoping Tilda would see that I was right.

"I understand." She nodded. "But these are not men and women, at least not the kind you and I are familiar with. They are incapable of reason. When you approach them without supervision, you are putting yourself in harm's way. Until they're trained—"

My hand shook until the cup fell and shattered. The porcelain only broke in a few pieces. A leaf, a flower, and a tiny painted bird had parted ways. Tilda raised her bell and shook it.

"We'll have that cleaned up right away. Don't you worry." Tilda's eyes landed on my bruised wrist before looking away. "Can I make a suggestion? Leave the dealings of the property to Ryland. That's his side of things. Timothy, as you know, is better suited to commerce and negotiating agreements. Everyone has his or her place. I know it's difficult. I understand you have a great deal of time on your hands. Perhaps gardening, as I suggested before. It will keep you occupied until . . . well, God willing, a baby is born. A child will fill your heart, and your time." Tilda continued but her words could no longer be heard over the shouting in my head.

There will be no child. I pray never to bring a child into this nightmarish world.

". . . Let me know what I can do to make you feel better. I want you to be happy."

"I appreciate your kindness, Tilda. Thank you," I uttered, ready for our time to be over.

She, too, was growing impatient. I could see the way her regal nose flared, then relaxed. She expected more than what I was giving her. Each time she tried to reach inside, gain a teeny bit of insight as to who I was, how I came to be, she came up empty-handed.

"Dear, we're all family now. I simply want you to know that you belong and are accepted. I can see what Timothy saw in you. You're a lovely young woman. Why, I'm sure you've heard all the praise. Those luminous eyes, your flawless skin, and your hair—what I'd do to have your hair, so shiny and bountiful. Men write sonnets about a delicate beauty such as yourself. I think what Timothy really adores about you is your innocence, though now I'm finding you aren't so innocent after all, are you, dear?"

Before I could answer, or ask what she meant, she continued.

"You must understand, moving to this forsaken America was my sons' grand plan. I agreed for one reason: to keep them ambitious. A ripe and healthy ambition is what makes a man a man. There is nothing worse than young men with no goals or passion. In England, they'd lost faith in the future. There was deterioration in the streets and in the hearts of the young and old.

"The British social order was collapsing as some people started forgetting their proper place in the world. I'd hoped the boys could start anew and find a calling here. Leaving was easy and a satisfying excuse for why the banks had sent men into our home to carry off our most prized art and furnishings. I don't know if Timothy shared with you about their father, my husband. Seibel Ross died an untimely death. We lost our home. It wasn't his fault, of course. My husband was a great man."

Timothy had told me she hated his father for leaving them destitute. In public, for her sons' sake, Tilda only evoked fond memories and stuck to her story of loyalty and devotion. But when the doors and windows were latched, Timothy said, she cursed his very name. Seibel Ross had shot himself in the head. Timothy had wept when he told me. How he'd walked into his father's study and found him slumped over his desk in a pool of blood. He could not forgive himself for not being able to save his father, though what could a child have done? He'd cried endlessly and dreamt about it for even longer.

"Ryland and Timothy are my only reason for existing," Tilda said, looking off, barely remembering I was there. "Oh, my boys. Ryland was a handful, always getting into mischief. As he grew into a man, his focus turned sharp and determined. He would come to blows with the other boys if they teased Timothy for being small or not wanting to get himself filthy in the mud on those countless dreary days. Ironically, I worried about Timothy's behavior far more than Ryland's.

"Timothy was unpredictable. One wrong attempt at pressing him and he acted like a boar forced to come out of hiding. From his slight features and delicate tone, one would never guess about his short temper. Those constantly varying moods kept me from delving too deeply into what was bothering him. In my best estimate, I guessed he needed a companion. He never showed interest in anyone. Timothy needed someone who could soothe his heart with a kind touch or smile.

"As soon as we settled into our new home here in America, I joined the League of Quaker Women and a Literary Friends group, determined to get a firsthand look at their daughters. Unfortunately, the young ladies in the area showed themselves to be vapid, losing Timothy's attention after the first hello." She paused and actually faced me.

"It is no wonder his attention would be piqued by someone such as yourself. You have a curiosity about you, grand opinions. Evident in your need to be heard. The way you refused to back down about the treatment of the slaves. Your outspokenness is to be admired regardless of how you'd put yourself in harm's way. From here on out, I will make sure your forwardness is not stifled. It's the very thing Timothy loves about you."

Nattie made an unsteady return, nearly slipping on the wet puddle of tea. She began picking up the broken cup with a shaky hand, placing the pieces in her apron.

"What I'm saying is, you make Timothy happy. My son deserves to be happy, and I'll do anything within my power to make it so."

I sat forward and took a long inhale, looking for the strength to finally confess about my lie, our lie. Timothy and I, we would not be the happy couple she described. Confessing and taking the consequences would relieve me of sitting any longer listening to her counsel. I swallowed and waited for the right way to break it to her. *Your son does not love me, nor do I love him.* I clasped a hand over my uneasy stomach.

"Oh, for heaven's sake," Tilda said under her breath with a swat of her hand. "These flying things are impossible." She shifted back to a smile, beaming. "I am here for you," she said. "Whenever you need to talk, I will listen. For now, maybe you should rest, relax for a spell." She waved her hand in the air. Flies. Wayward young women. Both had been a nuisance to her morning tea.

19

Ross Manor

I stared at the brass clock hands pushing toward two o'clock. I was determined to get to the quarters this afternoon to check on Bo, but hadn't figured out how. I didn't want to arouse suspicion.

"Master Timothy is home," Cleo said. She wore a colorful scarf over her head, making her copper-penny cheeks glow. "You asked me before and he wasn't. But now he is." By her expression, I might've needed a bath and a bit of prayer.

"Thank you, Cleo." I paused. "I know I promised I wouldn't ask anything inappropriate of you, at least not in public. But this is private. The new arrivals, are they all right? Are they all . . . alive?" I didn't know how else to ask.

She nodded. "Yes, ma'am, they all right." She placed a serving tray on the side table. She walked over and opened the curtains wide. She pushed the window open. "How about some fresh air? It'll do you good." She offered half a smile.

She left the room and closed the door behind her. I jumped up when I heard voices coming through the open window. Timothy's voice. I looked out to see him ordering men around. The old gate was coming down. The land the Wylie family had lost to the bank would no longer bear their name. The Ross name was replacing the Wylie.

A group of men every shade of black, brown, and white held the heavy metal steady as fire sparked and singed it into place. Timothy stood with Ryland, proud of their new declaration. Ross Manor was now official.

I worked diligently to become presentable. I bathed and combed my hair. I donned a flat gray dress from the wardrobe Tilda had passed on.

Before long the excitement of the new gate had come and gone. The only sound in the house came from the veranda. A breeze swept past me as I stepped outside.

Timothy sat at the white iron table with his quill and journal open. He closed it when he saw me approach.

I had so much to say and yet my words stayed carefully placed, like fine crystal afraid that even the tiniest movement would shatter the balance. I stood contemplating how to start. I didn't need Cleo's silent warnings to know the dangers of being overly passionate about the lives of men and women who shouldn't have mattered, but did. It was a line I was fully aware of crossing, showing interest and care when I should've been looking the other way, ignoring their suffering.

"They were chained together worse than a herd of animals," I blurted to Timothy in lieu of a greeting. "I do not—how is this acceptable?"

"Lily, I was told you weren't feeling well. I'm glad to see you up and about."

"Timothy," I said firmly, "I cannot live here with you, with your family, if you are to treat people this way."

"Every well-cared-for home needs servants, Lily," he recited, as if he'd known what was coming. As if Tilda had already prefaced my grievances. "I made the purchase, remember, specifically at your request. Instead of one horse trainer, the ingrate of a trader made me buy the whole lot. I cannot control how they are delivered." He leaned back in his chair.

"It's just that . . . I was shocked at their treatment. And when I tried to give them water . . . Ryland. I couldn't stand by and watch men die without water. You said this would be our home. I won't let anyone be mistreated this way—in our home, my home." I swallowed the stone of truth lodged in my throat. *The whole lot* were my people, my Bo. I swiped a tear before it rolled over my cheek.

"They are no good to us weak and hungry, Lily. I will of course make sure they are well fed and watered. We want them in good spirits." He stood up and pulled a chair for me to join him. "No one is being mistreated. Is this new for you? Are you telling me that your family did not own property, slaves?" he asked, genuinely wanting to know. "Surely you've witnessed worse, having lived here all of your life. This country is known for maltreatment and torture, spanning decades. That, I assure you, we do not do in England."

"But Pico is a . . ."

His eyes narrowed. "An indentured servant. He is not a slave."

"I understand." I changed my approach. "You said you'd be sure they're 'well fed and watered.' They're people. Not animals."

"What exactly would you have me do?" He leaned forward. "Tell me. Is this more about a simple row between you and Ryland?"

"This isn't about Ryland."

"Then let me explain something to you," he said, his voice raised. "My family came here to be on equal ground. Why would we arrive and not expect the same rewards as the other American landowners? Slavery was abolished in England years before I was even born," he announced proudly. "This is *your* country's tradition. We are only partaking in what is duly ours to have. We have only one more season to yield a profitable crop. Ryland and I have to come up with a plan to increase our yield. The best we can do is acquire more labor. The dirt must be tilled, seeds planted, and crops harvested, just that simple. To do that, you need backs bent over, with hands and feet working the land. Who else would you have do such work? Can we be done with this subject, Lily?"

My required silence made me ache. I inhaled and released the stirring against my chest.

"Ryland and I have to succeed. I can't go back—we can't go back to England. My father died there because of misery and failure. I won't have the same happen to me. I won't die penniless."

I shook my head. "You can at least treat them like human beings, not animals," I cried. I wiped the tears but only more came.

After a pause, Timothy reached out and calmly took my hand. "This is what I love about you, Lily, your compassion. You care about everyone and every living thing." He looked on with pity. "I hope you will forgive Ryland for his bad judgment. He means no harm. Perhaps if he'd known it was all your idea, to seek out a horse breeder for his stable, he wouldn't have been so harsh. He would be thanking you instead."

"Yes. My idea." I looked away, only to catch Tilda staring at me from the foyer. She came forward with her tea but stopped, realizing we were in the middle of a conversation she did not want to be a part of.

"Mum really has your best interest at heart." Timothy followed my stare past him. "She wasn't taking sides," he said sweetly, kissing my hand. "Everything will be fine. You've gotten yourself all worked up. Calm yourself, Lily. Enjoy what's in front of you."

20

Home

It was sundown when Bo awakened in a heap of himself. His mouth bone dry, making it difficult to swallow. A woman in the darkness used her arms to prop his head high enough to take one or two sips of water without choking. She was strong, considering he was deadweight, unable to move anything but his eyelids.

"Took you a few days to break that fever. Come on now, drink. Thought we'd lost you," the woman said from above his head. She dipped a rag in the water before placing the fresh moistness on his cheeks and dried lips. "Must've been a long trip. Where'd you come from?"

Bo wasn't ready to answer questions. He'd witnessed enough incoming new stock at the Vesterville to already know the questions he wasn't in any shape to answer. The inquiries were meant to help find a displaced loved one: a boy separated from his mama, a man taken from his wife, a friend never to be seen again. A familiar name could jog the memory. Any small nugget of information could offer a bit of hope that he or she was still alive out there.

What plantation had he come from? Who were his folks? What had he done to get himself sold?

The best he could do was say his name at barely a whisper. "Bowman Carter."

"Welcome to the Wylie, Bowman Carter," the woman said sweetly. "My name is Ruby. We're all kind of new here. This land was closed and dried up from too much tobacco farming. These new folks got big ideas to get the earth moving again."

Bo took in as many faces as he could before his blurry eyes closed on him. Besides, none of the people standing there was her. Did he really believe she'd been real? He thought he'd seen a white woman but when she was closer, a touch away, his mouth had formed to say *Dahlia*.

Dahlia would be long gone from this place, or any place that had to do with slave business. Unless she'd been captured, sold, and brought here too. Bo shook the image out of his mind: her hands holding the ladle. Her telling him to hush, to drink.

"Everybody, give him some space. Can't you see he's worn out?" A high, sweet voice came closer. He opened his eyes to see a woman. She had a wide face and a red rag tied around her head. Her big eyes shined in the darkness. Her skin was smooth like tree sap, catching what little light was in the room. She leaned forward, holding a platter made of wood. "Bowman Carter, would you like something to eat?"

"Yes, ma'am."

"Don't you 'ma'am' me. My name's Essie. I do most of the cooking around here." From where he sat, he couldn't see what was on the platter, but it smelled like home. Her face came close enough to see she was young and pretty.

Ruby remained by his side and helped pull him up as far as he could go, shaky and weak. He rested against her, grateful she wasn't going anywhere. "You looking for your friend? The big red fella? He been asking about you. I told him we'd let him know when you was awake."

"This here is fried yam. Watch it now, might be hot," Essie said, making her way closer. "Ruby, why you hovering? Let him eat some if he wants to."

"Well, you don't gotta choke him trying to shove yo' food down his throat," Ruby snapped. The two women were having a showdown of sorts.

"We got plenty. Don't you worry, Bowman Carter," Essie said, ignoring the one named Ruby. She rested the wood platter on her hip. He reached up and took a big piece of the yam. He could've cried like a baby on the first taste. He took a second piece before she could move on.

"Bo," he said between chews. "Everybody calls me Bo."

"Nice to know. Everybody calls me Essie," she said, touching the knot of her head wrap with her free hand.

"Essie here has five children," Ruby added to the introduction. "Why don't you bring 'em over to meet Mr. Bowman Carter, Essie?"

"Maybe I will," she offered. "Go on, take another piece, Bo." She waited for him to take as much as he liked.

"Essie, I think he's had enough."

"Essie, Essie, Essie," Essie said, mimicking Ruby. "It's just a name, but it's mine." She walked off and Bo was still watching, whether for her food or her sass he wasn't quite sure.

"All right, now, let me show you where your sleeping space is," Ruby practically purred in his ear. "This gon' be home."

A week later, Bo started out in the cornfield. He chopped too close with the swing blade, leaving mangled cobs on the ground and making his work twice as hard. By early afternoon, the overseer, a ragged man with badly broken teeth, approached, sitting on his mule. Even though Bo feared a whipping for going too slow, he was grateful for a reason to stand upright from the backbreaking work.

"Follow me," the overseer ordered. Bo carried his sack full of ruined cornhusks past the tall grasses to the end of the row, while the others watched. "Drop your bag," the man yelled over his shoulder.

Bo gladly let go of the heavy bag and kept walking. He followed, his breathing heavy from keeping pace with the mule. The man on the mule kept on talking. Fear clouded Bo's hearing. Did the man say something about horses? The closer they got to the wide-plank building up ahead, the surer Bo became. Yes, horses. The overseer led him straight to the biggest barn he'd ever seen. He wasn't going to die today.

"Clean this place up and keep it that way." The overseer pointed out the order of things.

There were six horses, each with its own quarters, water trough, and feed basket tacked to the fencing. Bo introduced himself, giving each horse face-to-face time and an easy pat, and then went right to work. He swept the grounds out quickly and filled the watering trough with a few trips back and forth to the well.

He took the horses out one at a time, holding their reins and pulling them for a short walk. The overseer had made it clear he was to never ride them, ever. After walking them for a couple of laps each, Bo was tired, not quite back to his physical peak. Then he wondered what to do with the rest of his daylight hours. He didn't dare sit. Being caught idle was an invitation to lashings, that much he knew regardless of the status of things. Ruby had said these new owners were a different kind. They didn't talk the same or act the same. In Bo's estimation, didn't matter where they started, they all ended up the same. Just like Lewis Holt's betrayal. All those years of smiling and being full of trust and look where it got him. He shook the images out of his head, of the men who hated the color of his skin but loved having him around. For the time being he was alive. *Best to be grateful.*

He forced another round of walks with the horses, talking to them the whole way. Telling the horses about growing up at the Vesterville, about Dahlia and seeing her every time he closed his eyes. But then he'd seen her awake, standing right in front of him. He'd been close to death, that was the only explanation. She appeared before him. A dying man's last vision. The sooner he convinced himself of that, the quicker he could call this place home.

The sun setting over the rise of land let him know his day was done. The quarters would be filled with famished folks. Essie would be whipping something up with rations of corn and pig scraps. The girl was a miracle worker, making a full meal out of nothing but the innards of the pig, snout to tail.

She made it no secret she wanted Bo's attention, bringing him food before the rest of the folks and talking like a purring kitten. He had no plans to show his hand. He knew better than to take a liking to a lady. Caring for someone who'd never be yours only ripped out a man's heart. He'd seen way too many souls plucked like ripe fruit from a tree by the masters, then brought back a shell of themselves, nothing left to give. It was best not to get attached.

In this new world, Bo awakened looking forward to the workdays. He took in the blue sky while he walked fast to the seat house. He liked to go first before there was a line of ten or more.

"Look who's up nice and early this morning." The man they called Preach squatted next to Bo with his bony knees hiked close to his chest. He said he had no recollection of his born name. Everyone had always called him Preach on account of his timely quotes from the good Bible. But since not many of them could read, most wouldn't know if he was making stuff up or reading the words as they were written. He looked to Bo. "So, how you liking your new home, young sir?"

Bo wasn't one for having conversations with his pants down. "Just fine," he answered quickly.

"Guess so, seeing as how you're already doing clean work. You ain't spent one full day out in that field, and you already got you a fancy white shirt, long and ready for tucking into fancy dungarees. Yes, sir, you a regular houseboy in training, but I ain't got no malice in my heart.

No, sir. Proverbs 12:24 says the hand of the diligent will rule while the slothful will be put to forced labor." Preach took a short pause to finish what he had come to do. "So, I guess we the slothful, huh? While you been working extra, the rest of us ain't doing much of nothing. Ain't no other way to explain it, huh?" He cinched his pants with a tattered rope he used as a belt. "You live righteous and the Lord will provide. I'll be seeing you around, young sir."

Bo gave Preach a nod. The separation of those who worked in the house and those who remained under the hot sun wasn't anything new. Bo had landed somewhere in the middle, and yet he always ended up as an outsider.

There was no denying he worked hard, getting his hands plenty dirty. He knew how to skin an animal, butcher it up, and smoke it too, but he wasn't the cook. He knew how to cut wood, nail in planks, and paint solid strokes, but he wasn't a carpenter. He knew how to do things, necessary things. Wasn't his fault if he'd avoided the drudgery of the fields. Whatever he did, he did it to the best of his know-how. He also knew when to stay quiet and let a man clear the misery off his chest. No point in worrying about what he couldn't help.

He made his way to the horse barn, hoping to get there before the new owner, who liked his morning rides. Berth was the master's favorite mare. The master rode her, then brought her back to be watered and stroked all over again.

Where Bo came from, horses tilled the soil, pulled the wagons, and carried the overseers. Here, that work was left to the mules. Every so often, Bo took some care with the mules, offering them a stroke of the brush and a bucket of fresh hay. Even with all the goodies fed to the horses, there was plenty left over.

He worked quickly, raking hay, growing the pile with each stroke. The new master liked a clear path under his feet, not a single stray clipping.

The metal gate pulled open. Master Ryland stood in his long morning coat, pulling on his gloves. "There she is." He stroked Berth, then led her out by the reins.

Bo moved ahead and opened the gate fully. "Have a good ride, masta-sir."

Master Ryland hadn't said a word to Bo, not directly, since Bo had started in the barn. He'd nodded once in agreement when Bo said it was a good day to ride. Other than that, it was best to keep the chitchat down.

He watched as Master Ryland rode away.

21

The Stable

He'd been working for two weeks in the stable, or what he called the great barn. Greater than any place he'd ever seen for horses or even mankind. The high rafters and the spacious stalls for each horse left him feeling small and alone in a huge space. The time alone meant too much thinking.

He pushed a finger into his ear to stop a buzzy noise. A tick had maybe found its way inside and was driving him insane. Then he stopped and listened more closely.

"Bo," the small voice called out again. "It's me, Bo."

He turned around to see no one. But there was a scent. A woman. Only a certain kind of woman would smell this way. Soap and flower petals.

"It's me, Bo."

He stayed in one spot, afraid to breathe. Dahlia stood before him. She stepped closer. Her skin had grown paler. Bo fought the urge to rush forward, to pull her into his arms. He still wasn't sure she was real. "Dah—"

"Lily, Bo. Call me Miss Lily," she whispered. "I'm Missus Ross. I'm a mistress of the house. I'm married to Timothy Ross. I couldn't believe

Master Holt sold you. It was because of me," she said, talking faster than he could follow. "I'm so, so sorry, Bo."

She came toward him. He stepped back. Then again. He put up his hands. "Stop." He swallowed, afraid. "You can't be here."

"Listen to me. I'm going to request you as my aide. I will have a garden that needs tending. You can still work the horses, but this way, I'll have a chance to see you so we can talk. You have to listen to me. This place is no different than the Vesterville. No different at all."

He could only hold it in for so long. He closed his eyes. "Get out. You and me can't be seen together, ever," he whispered, now moving toward her. He leaned in close so she understood with certainty. "Go."

She tried to plead with him. "I never thought Master Holt would blame you. I was only pretending. I didn't mean to go through with leaving. Next thing I knew, I was on a train headed to a new life. None of it was worth having if you were going to be hurt. Then I saw a list of slaves going to auction. I couldn't believe it was you on that list." She seemed to push back the urge to cry. "What did they do to you out there, Bo?"

"What you think they done?" He paused, not willing to be as bitter as he felt. He wanted to tell her to be worried about herself. Not him. There was a man out there looking for her. John Browder. Bo wouldn't forget his name, his voice, and those steely empty eyes. The man was a killer. But she looked like she had burden enough to carry.

"Can't you stop being angry for one minute to hear what I'm telling you?"

"I'm not angry. I'm scared," he said. "I'm scared for you."

"You don't need to be scared for me. No one knows who I am."

Bo let out a sigh. He had to tell her. If he didn't and the bounty hunter came sneaking up on her, he'd never forgive himself. "There's a man, a bounty hunter with a sketch on a WANTED paper. Holt used a picture of Annabelle to have a WANTED paper made, but it's your name on it. The bounty hunter takes it around with him, checking all the women slaves."

"Good thing I'm not a slave then," she whispered.

"This place ain't too far from where we started. I should know. I walked every step of it. If you in here trying to talk to me, they gon' find out about you. Is that what you want?" He walked toward her. She moved, almost afraid of him. *Good. Be afraid.*

When she was back far enough, he grabbed the handle of the gate to close it. "Don't come back here," he whispered without looking up. He didn't know if the earth was listening, but someone was. Someone was always listening. No place was safe. Rain began to spatter on the roof with a steady beat. The large metal doors shook from the wind. A storm was on the rise, which meant Master Ryland would turn back from his ride sooner than later.

Drops of rain landed at her feet, on her face. She wiped away the moisture. Some of it was tears. "Bo. I know you got hurt. But you'll be safe now."

He closed the gate before she said more. He didn't want to hear nothing about Dahlia's next great escape. There had to be joy somewhere. If he could stay out of trouble, keep a clean stable, and turn a blind eye to whatever trouble she was cooking up next, maybe, just maybe, he could have a long life in one place.

"Bo, please don't be mad at me forever," she said through the metal between them. There was no point. Bo had made up his mind. Just like when they were children. He'd been good at it then, turning her invisible, a dart of his eyes in the other direction. It wasn't safe.

"Come on out," Bo said, already knowing who would come to the surface. He pushed his shoulders back and tried to come out of the haze he'd been in with Dahlia. The wind and rain whipped and howled. He'd known someone else was inside the great-sized barn. He knew the sounds of the horses' breathing like his own. But this was different. There'd been another body struggling to stay quiet while taking in and letting out precious breaths.

"You messing in dangerous waters." Essie revealed herself. She held a basket filled with scraps meant for the horses. He'd noticed the missing stash a few times before. The carrots, apples, and turnips would eventually end up in one of her soups. What was considered scraps and horse feed was something the quarters weren't allowed to have. Her big eyes blinked innocently in the darkness.

"Essie, how long you been hiding in here?" His heart was beating in his ears.

"Long enough. How you be friends with a white woman?"

"Kindness don't come in colors," he replied, something he'd heard Papa Sap say, though if Dahlia really were a white woman, the only thing she'd want to do was run in the other direction. "She the lady of the house," he said, pretending to not much care about what Essie thought she'd heard. What if she told what she saw? Who would she tell? No one would believe her anyway, he told himself. Friends with a white woman. No such thing. He shook his head at the notion.

Essie inched closer. "You get caught talking to her kind and your only friend gon' be Jesus or the devil."

"Her kind?" This Essie, her skin coloring not much different from Dahlia's, had been fooled. Bo wondered how she couldn't see. He'd always been told kin could see one another. For good or bad, they recognized ancestors in the blood. Bo nodded his head. "You right. Guess it'd be best if you not tell, then. I'd appreciate if you kept what you seen and heard to ya'self, Essie. You don't tell my secret, I won't tell yours." Bo nodded toward her basket. Her bounty was considered stealing in the eyes of an overseer.

"You a good man, Bowman Carter." Essie made a faint swipe across her lips to prove her silence. "I just hate to see you getting a case of trouble for nothing. I've seen it before. Just a side glance, barely looking in some white lady's direction, and half the skin on your back get whipped off." Essie's hand came to rest on Bo's shoulder. "You like her kind, is that it?"

"Essie, you should probably get somewhere dry and safe before this storm carries you away."

Her bright, round eyes lowered from the rejection. She gathered the rest of her evening bounty, pulled her wrap around her shoulders, and then backed away in a few slow steps. She headed out the way she'd come, awakening the locusts with each step. The high-pitched noise of their wings rubbing together was talking at him. They said, *A wife is what you need in this world. Essie's a good woman. She'll take care of you.*

He knew it to be true. But he didn't want to think about that right now. If this was going to be his home, he'd have to keep his focus on simple things. The stable. The horses. And keeping Dahlia away.

22

Path

The walk back to the house took far less time than the walk to the barn. Bo's rejection carried me forward like a brisk, harsh wind rushing at my back. He had every right to be angry with me. I'd expected as much. But we had each other now, just like when we were little, two ragamuffins running around. I smiled remembering those times. I'd make him remember too.

Up ahead I saw the enormous house, with dark, full clouds surrounding each corner high and low. The drizzle of rain kept my eyes batting open and closed. I thought I saw something move ahead of me. An amber light flared. Nothing but the long inhale of a cigar could've caused this shot of brightness. I stopped and focused.

Ryland's face came into view through the mist. "Out for a stroll, Lily?" He approached, tilting his head slightly. The scent of whiskey and cigar hung in the moist air. The smoke billowed as he puffed.

I tried to move past him. He slid into my way. "Coming from the quarters. Still worried about the new additions, I'm gathering. I thought you were done with all that unnecessary concern."

"I am. I just wanted to check on them. We southerners are hospitable, if nothing else."

"Very sweet." He leaned in near my face, grazing my chin with his forefinger. "Why are you here, Lily Dove?" He nodded toward the horse tied to a nearby tree. "Can I give you a ride the rest of the way? You'll get dreadfully wet."

"No. Thank you. I can walk."

He turned up his flask and took a long drink. Something felt off about Ryland. I tried to look unbothered. "We should make amends. Maggie and Timothy would want that."

"Yes. We all would want that."

He stepped aside. I moved, grateful to be free.

Ryland mounted his horse and trailed behind me. I carefully navigated the wet path, willing my legs to stay strong and keep moving as the ground became slicker.

Panic closed in when he sidled alongside me. "I saw you first," he whispered. "I saw you first, Lily Dove. You realize I'm the one who found you, and yet you've never said a polite thank-you." He pulled to a stop in front of me. The large horse blocked my path.

He climbed down. He slowly wrapped the horse's reins around a sturdy branch.

I didn't want to give him the satisfaction of seeing me afraid. Though afraid is exactly what I felt.

"What do you want, Ryland?" I held my breath.

"What do I want?" he asked. "I suppose that's an important start." He leaned toward me.

I was unsteady on my feet, not sure which way to run. Or even if I should. The ground was entirely wet and slippery. I couldn't stand there and let him do what he intended to do.

I took off, bolting forward only to trip on the hem of my skirt. He caught me by the back of my collar. The grip choked me—until the buttons on my bodice gave way. I went down, face first. I rested for a moment before the blurriness cleared and the air came back.

"Lily . . ."

"Don't you dare touch me." I stood shakily. Pellets of rain landed on my face. I forced my steps away, not turning back. I ran to the house, sloshing in the moist ground, not caring if I fell again. I simply wanted to get away.

At the house, out of breath, I found Cleo in the kitchen. The others stopped what they were doing and stared, confused at the mistress of the house coming into the kitchen, disturbing their sanctum.

Cleo put down a plate and towel and rushed to my side. "Miss Lily, what's happened?"

"I fell. I tripped," I lied, staring down at the mud covering the hem of my skirt. The front bodice had ripped with the buttons. I stood dripping wet on the cleaned floor.

"Go on up. I'll be right there. Go on, I'll be along in a minute," Cleo repeated when I was slow to move.

The others got back to work. One of them whispered, thinking I couldn't hear, "What kind of trouble she got? Where my tea, where my bath, fetch me mo' wine."

A jumble of snickering followed.

"Stop it. Womenfolk got problems," Cleo said. "No matter who, or what, they are."

I moved quickly through the foyer and up the stairs. I reached my room, peeled off my clothes, and climbed into the cool tub, shivering while I waited for Cleo.

It wasn't long before she came inside carrying a tin bucket of heated water. She poured the warm stream, barely filling the bottom of the tub. She left and came back with more. When the tub was filled enough, she sat by my side.

Cleo hummed, stroking a wet towel over my shoulders. When she stopped, it was only to catch her breath and begin again. She dipped the rag in water, then sprinkled small drops of scented sweet oil before rubbing my skin with a soothing touch. She traced the scar down my spine ever so gently, as if it were something she understood. As if it were normal to be torn down the middle and put back together again. She didn't ask, or flinch from fear. This wasn't the first time she'd seen it. And never once had she asked where it came from.

"I was born in North Carolina," she said. "I was only ten years old when I got pulled in to work the house." She paused for a moment. "Miss Lily, I don't know where you come from, but I do know, ain't no going back. We can never go back. This here is home now, for me, for you, until it's not no more."

That's when the dam broke. A flood of tears pushed past my ability to stay silent. For all that Cleo had been through, for every chained soul taken without permission, I let out a prayer. I covered my face with my hands, ashamed to be broken by "a simple row with Ryland," as Timothy would call it if I tried to complain. I'd hardly been touched, nothing like the savage way Cleo and others had been treated all their lives.

Cleo encircled her arms around my shoulders. We rocked side to side. "You're freer than any of us will ever be, Miss Lily. You gon' be safe. We protect our own," she said, putting her head to mine.

Not everyone had the ability to see, I was learning. It took a special kind of sight. Those women in the kitchen had no idea who I truly was, and I was grateful. But Cleo knew. She understood my danger of being found out.

The water had grown cold. "Miss Lily, you should get out now. Lay yourself down and rest."

She helped me out and wrapped a wide blanket around my shoulders as the rattling chill spread over my skin.

I saw you first, Lily Dove.

There was so much Mother Rose hadn't prepared me for. Becoming a wife to a suitable husband was the only important thing on her list. She forgot to teach me how to be invisible. To be safe in silence. It was too late now. As Cleo had said, I could never go back to who and what I was before.

I was numb, devoid of emotion. I sat up in bed against the soft pillows. The crackle of the dying fire gave off a gold glow. I stared at the peaceful, warmed light.

"There you are." Timothy came into the room. His shoulders sank. "It's good to be home. I've had no luck. The bankers all feel the same. Our land isn't worth the investment. Seems I get close, and then I'm back at the beginning." He pulled his ascot loose. He'd spent the day traveling. Too tired to notice the redness around my neck or the knot growing on my chin where I'd fallen. The light from the fire wasn't enough even to see I'd been crying.

"Is it so bad to be helped by your aunt Gertrude? Why must anything change? If she's keeping you afloat, you shouldn't feel like the boat is sinking." It was the best bolstering up I could do. I was intensely worried about my own survival, and Bo, here all alone. How awful he must feel not having Sally, Oleen, or Papa Sap.

Timothy leaned toward me. "Well, that's a fine example. Yes, the boat is sinking," he said. "You see, Aunt Gertrude has already shorted us our payments. It's only the beginning. She means to see us suffer. You've met her. Have you any doubt what she's capable of? I'm leaving at dawn. I have one more banker who has agreed to speak with me in Hampton City."

"But you just got back. How many days will you be gone?" Desperation spilled from my throat. "You can't leave me here with—" The inability to say his name stopped me from finishing.

"What . . . who . . . my mother? Ryland? Oh, he's harmless. All bark and no bite. What has he done this time? Tell me what happened."

"Nothing. It's nothing."

"Dear Lily, you know I wouldn't leave you if I didn't have to. These are very volatile times. It's up to me to save this family. Once I've done this, there's an opportunity I didn't want to speak of just yet, but all right, I'm going to tell you but don't breathe a word. There's a group of landowners who've asked that I be their representative. There has to be someone in Washington to keep our best interests protected. It's called a lobbyist. It comes with a wage and housing. That way you can be with me all the time."

"When? When can we go?" I held my breath and closed my eyes. This was how Bo and I would leave this place. He would be my personal assistant, my aide, my driver. I was so busy making plans in my head as he continued on, I wasn't listening to the rest.

". . . As I said, I still have matters to deal with here. Getting our financial dealings secure is first priority. After that, I must get Ryland up to speed. He's not the most business minded. I can't be sure when I can take you with me, but I promise it will be soon." He touched my shoulders and peered closely into my eyes. He pushed my hair away from my face. "Are you all right? Should I call Cleo?"

"No. I'm fine." I bit my lip to silence myself. "I'm fine."

"You see, this makes it all that much clearer. We should take as much time as we need before getting you on the road. The trip to Washington will be long, yet so beautiful. I promise it will be worth the wait."

I swallowed the emotional ball in the back of my throat. Joy, hope, anticipation. I could soon be free of this place. I didn't want to wait.

Timothy placed a kiss on my forehead. "Don't worry," he said. "I promise to give you the life you deserve."

23

Peace

Essie squeezed herself into the small space where Bo slept. In the months since she and he shared secrets from the great barn, she'd found her way next to him at night. The cabins were bigger at the Wylie, now called the Ross. The quarters were spread over green hills with plenty of space in between. A trickling stream could be heard beyond the trees but couldn't be seen. Peaceful. The sun came up over the trees and birds chirped just in case it wasn't enough to get the morning started.

"You were moaning and yelling like the devil was chasing you," Essie whispered in the gray dawn while waiting for the sun to fully rise. Her soft hand glided over his gritty chin. Bo hadn't found a sharp blade to shave with. He didn't want to take a chance on dull steel taking a chunk out of his tender neck skin.

"I'll be fine. Go on now, tend to your own," he whispered, nodding toward Essie's huddled brood in the corner, sleeping soundly. Essie had birthed all five babies way too young, and yet he sadly understood how landowners and overseers started in on the girl folk early. Now her children were growing up fast and exhausted from the rigors of living. Being a child meant something different for them.

Bo shifted to turn away. Essie wouldn't be thwarted so easily. Her hand moved down to rest on his bare chest. "I'll stay right here. Gon' be sunup anyway," she purred. She pressed herself against the curve of his back. With her heart beating against his body, it was only a few deep breaths before the rhythm put him back to sleep.

The next time he awakened, it was because a happy hen had strolled in and pecked at his ear.

"Essie," he hissed under his breath, though she was gone. The cabin was empty except for him and the hen.

He rushed out, skipping his morning rituals, and got to the barn. Being late was sacrilege. Getting Berth ready for Master Ryland's ride was all he had to do in the morning, and he was late.

He heard the gate sliding open before he'd gotten the girl saddled up. Panic shook through his body. He turned around, ready to make his apologies and to plead his case. Instead, he was met by blinding sunlight and a small shadowy figure, the overseer's son. This one was second in command.

"Follow me, boy," the small boy-man said.

"Sir, I need to finish this for Master Ryland's ride."

"Then be quick about it."

Bo worked his hands over the buckles underneath Berth. That's when he felt the weight under her belly. He was meant to take care of the horses as well as breeding them. Getting Berth bred was a fine accomplishment, but he didn't have time to cheer or slap himself on the back for a job well done.

"Bring your rake and hoe."

Bo sighed with relief. "Yessir." As they walked, he was keenly aware of every sound. In the distance, sparrows sang and nipped at each other. When they stopped, there she was: Dahlia.

Overseer Junior left them alone with one order. "This is Missus Ross. Do whatever she says do."

"Dah . . . Ma'am . . . Lily." Bo strung the names together until he'd run out of things to call her. "You tell me what you want out here, and I can do it," he said nice and loud.

"I can't just stand by while you do all the work," she offered, but in a whisper.

"That's what a missus would do," he whispered right back. "Why you got me out here? You can't be around me. You understand what I'm telling you?"

"Bo. I told you. I brought you here to be close to me, to be safe."

He turned his attention to the thick greenery that needed clearing. He grabbed his rake and started turning the dirt over. "Like I said, go on back to your house. Worry about being Missus Ross."

"No. I want us to be free together. You deserve to be free too, Bo. And I'm going to make sure you're free. Just like me."

Bo shook his head. "Just like you, huh?" He looked up at the sky to wonder what he'd done wrong to deserve this. Why did he have to care so much about what she said, what she did? He took in the innocence of her notions. She meant well. "Let's just take it one day at a time."

24

Garden

I watched Bo work in silence. When he was finished turning over the dirt, he left. He simply turned around and walked off, forgetting his rake in a rush to be free of me.

I picked up the long, rugged tool and winced when a splinter slipped into my palm. I picked at the tiny source of pain, making it hurt more. I didn't care. I pushed and stabbed at the tiny wood chip too stubborn to budge, just like Bo too hardheaded to understand I was trying to help him.

The way he said things sometimes dug right into my heart.

I listened to the birds a short distance away. Bitter chirping, fighting and fussing in their way. Like family. A mother chastising her baby birds. Baby birds hungry to be first. Didn't make them love each other any less. I missed my family, all of them, Oleen to Mother Rose. I wanted to make everything the way it was, offer penance for ruining the life Bo had, give him back everything we used to have. Oleen. Sally. Every day, I thought about our life before here. Had it been so bad?

Here, it seemed no better. I was still unable to speak or think without caution. Still afraid of doing or saying the wrong thing. But instead of a slap across my face from Annabelle, I feared Tilda's peering eyes or

Ryland's unwanted attention. All the thoughts rumbling in my head stopped entirely when I heard footsteps behind me.

I turned around, anticipating the sight of Bo. He'd come back. He was ready to listen.

I was wrong.

Ryland stood at the edge of the square of dirt. I pulled the rake close as if it were my protector. I felt the stab of another splinter but ignored the pain. I swallowed my fear. But there was the tingling. I hated the tingling, the sharp tug up my back. I didn't know exactly what it meant. The mark that left so many fearful of me made me fearful as well. When the tingling started, I had the awareness of a feral animal, hearing, seeing, and anticipating danger. I wasn't sure what I was capable of—if I had to protect myself.

And here he was. "Haven't you learned your lesson?" I pointed to the faint scratches nearly healed on Ryland's neck. Though I hadn't done it on purpose. When he'd tried to stop me from falling, I'd reached back because his grip was choking me. My nails had bitten into his skin. I'd take the credit if it would help. "I've warned you to stay away from me."

"Yes. Indeed, I've been warned." He touched his neck. "But I'm not here to cause any harm to you. I wanted to apologize. I get incredibly rude after one too many drinks." Ryland kicked the dirt around with his boot. "With Timothy gone, I wanted you to know you are safe and in good hands."

"I would prefer not to be in anyone's hands." My grip tightened around the rake. The sharp teeth were a kiss away from my face. Ryland noticed my fierce grip as well.

He chuckled.

From the corner of my eye, I saw movement coming toward us. Ryland and I both turned our attention to the laughter coming from the green hillside. Maggie and Tilda slowly appeared over the rise. Ryland plopped down on a garden bench as if he had not a care in the world. I changed too, into a calmer face. I put up a hand and waved as they strolled in our direction. I put on my best face, smiled brightly. I smoothed my hands over my apron, not realizing the split skin where I'd picked was still bleeding. The smear of red across the white bib caught Tilda's attention.

"What have you done to yourself, Lily? Ryland, you're sitting here without offering a helping hand?" Tilda asked. "You need to wrap that, dear."

Ryland tilted his head, confused. "I offered but she refused," he lied easily. He stayed in his seat on the bench with a casual leg slung over the other.

"Oh, Lily, your garden has begun. What will you plant?" Maggie plopped down next to Ryland, wearing the same heavy dull dress, the only one that fit her growing belly. The dark wells under her eyes called attention to the puffiness of her face.

"Looks like nothing but more dirt to me," Tilda said.

"I'm just getting started."

"Perhaps her personal aide, Bowman, will move things along quickly," Ryland said. "I've given him permission to leave his duties at the stables to help Lily for as long as she needs."

"Working alone with a slave?" Tilda interjected.

"Fret not, Mum. He's harmless. I like the chap," Ryland said. "Timothy asked me to look out for Lily and her every need. This was one favor he'd specifically asked of me, I assume by special request from Lily herself. So I made it happen. Someone should be thanking me," Ryland said in my direction.

"Oh my, a kick," Maggie announced. Her hands rested on her growing belly. "Do you want to feel, darling?"

"Of course." Ryland gently leaned in her direction.

"Aw . . . there. You feel her? Amazing, aye? It's going to be a girl. A girl for me," Maggie sang. "Lily, would you like to feel?" she asked.

Ryland glanced in my direction. My skin chilled. I set the rake down but shook my head no. It was best for everyone.

"Lily, please do," Ryland offered. "Come." He patted, offering space on the bench.

"No. My hands are filthy and I have a cut." I held them up for proof. "I wouldn't want to pass this grime onto your baby."

"Ridiculous. You can't pass anything along just by touching someone," Maggie declared.

She was wrong. I'd seen as much. The way hands could be laid on someone to heal could easily work the opposite and destroy a spirit or soul. Hate traveled. Misery spread like a fever burning everything in its path. I didn't want an innocent child's welfare to weigh on my heart. And there was that thing again, the tingling of discord moving down my back.

"Touch. It's good luck. Maybe a baby for you," Maggie announced as if all she had to do was make the request from the sky above. She flagged a plump, pale hand. Her ring finger was void, too large to hold the gold band from Ryland she'd proudly shown with their initials engraved. "Come. Please. You must feel."

My hand stretched toward her, already trembling with regret. Ryland reached out and secured my wrist, finishing what I could not. My hand landed on the roundness of her stomach, which felt no more like a living thing to me than a rock sitting in the middle of a road.

"It feels hard," was all I could say. The same moment I was ready to pull away, Ryland's hand covered mine, keeping it there. Then I felt a pointy roll shifting underneath my touch, an elbow, maybe a knee, doing its best to move away from the pressure.

"You feel her? Isn't it amazing? It's going to be a girl, I just know it." Happy Maggie. Joyful Maggie. And why shouldn't she be? She'd been protected, shielded from the ugliness of the world. She hadn't had to look over her shoulder and wonder when the bounty hunter would land at her doorstep pronouncing her a runaway. She hadn't had to worry about one brother coveting his brother's wife.

The three of them left together. I stayed, expecting to feel relief. I stayed long past the sun setting. The air turned cool around me. I ignored the clouds' rumble. I refused to go into the house. I wasn't hungry or thirsty. I didn't need to relieve myself, or at least I fought the urge. I wanted to stay in the garden rolling the clay soil over and over in my hands. I moved from one corner to the next spreading the dirt, waiting for the answers. What was I capable of? What was my freedom worth? What was I willing to do, and how far was I willing to go, to keep it?

Sweat dripped from my brow. Moistness hit my arms and trailed down my wrists. Neither the drizzle of rain nor hard work was making me wet. My tears, sick and heavy, tumbled down with the weight of pretending.

25

Commons

"Cat got yo' tongue?" The bench creaked with the weight of Red when he sat down next to Bo.

Now that Bo had learned his real name was Dover, he should've used it. But instead he still called him Red. And Red answered to it quite easily. Inside the commons where supper was served, they naturally found each other for sitting over a hot meal and catching up on the day's happenings.

"I bet I know what got your craw," Red said with a sly grin.

"Oh yeah?" Bo truly didn't know what he was talking about. He'd been thinking about Dahlia all day. Her and her highfalutin ideas. Freedom. Had she not learned a thing?

"She in a family way," Red said loud enough to be heard over the scratch music coming from the far corner. "You work fast, my friend. You scared, right? First one always make you scared."

"What?" Bo followed Red's nod toward Essie.

Essie?

Bo stared at her with new eyes. She moved gracefully, doling out rations of beans. Her skirt cinched at the waist with an apron over it showed a slight rise, a fist-size knot, like Berth with her new baby inside.

"Drink up. This'll take the edge off," Red said, handing over his mason jar full of crushed berries. "Nothing to be scared of."

Bo took a long sip of the drink offered. Red's skill was making elixir from berries or anything he could squeeze into a jar and let sit in a warm place. The first taste went straight to Bo's head. Floating, his thoughts and worries seemed to slow.

Red laid a heavy hand on his shoulder. "Essie's a good woman. You a lucky man."

"Dover, what you two talking about?" Ruby came and took a seat on Red's strong leg. She wrapped her arms around his neck. She smiled and revealed a happy space between her teeth. "Who lucky around here?"

"You listening to men talk, woman? Mind yourself, you hear?" He nuzzled at the center of her full bosom. "But if you have to know . . . I'm the one lucky."

"Yeah, you are." Ruby grinned harder. "We should be getting on to sleep now, don't you think?" she said near his ear.

Red didn't waste another second. He and Ruby walked in step out of the commons. They'd get some alone time before the rest of the cots were full for the night.

Bo turned his attention back to Essie. Right then, she caught him looking. She smiled and nodded. Red had assumed it was his. He and Essie hadn't been close like that. He could only wish to have a family one day. One day wasn't now. It wasn't like he and Dahlia would ever have a chance in this lifetime.

Essie came over and rested a hand on his shoulder. She slid onto the bench beside him. She pushed a platter of sizzled pig skins toward him. He picked one and slid it into his mouth. It was like a month of Sundays all at once, since that was normally the day they had the heavy meal. Bo licked the salt off his fingers. "Essie. Umph. Thank you," he said.

"I want more than a thank-you, Bo. I'm done here. You want to go for a walk with me?" Her open palm slid over his thigh. "You should let me wash that shirt of yours. Get all that mud off. I'll let it dry by the fire. Come morning it'll be good and clean. Come with me," she whispered in his ear, leaving a bit of a kiss behind.

Bo closed his eyes and tried to think of something tragic—too late. The tightening of his pants had made the decision for him. Her hand gripped the center of his bulk. She used the empty platter as a shield so no one could see what was going on.

"Come with me, Bo." Essie got up first.

Bo saw old Preach looking their way. But it was the eyes of Abel, a big man who pretty much kept to himself, that gave Bo pause. He slowed, thinking twice about going off with Essie. She coaxed him with another kiss around his ear. After her warm breath left a wave of heat all over him, he let the worry slide away. He ignored Abel, Preach, or anyone else looking his way.

Essie led him away from the commune of good food and shared stories to a place where he could stop listening altogether. He didn't want to hear the big voice in his head. He didn't want to care or think about right or wrong, loss or pain. This was the only life he knew, would ever know, until death came.

He followed her out by the hand.

Under the clear black sky, Essie kissed him, hungry, eager, full of heat. He couldn't help but kiss her back the same way, as if it were his first time, because it was his first real kiss. Her mouth was warm and open like a freshwater spring inviting him in. He pushed her hand down to show her how to squeeze him the same way he did to himself on those nights when he couldn't sleep . . . most nights.

She knew what to do, how to wrap her palm over the base of his fullness. Before he could reach his peak and drown out the roar in his head, she let go. She lifted her dress, all the skin of her thighs exposed. She pushed him down to the ground, then slid on top of him with a swiftness. She sank low, swallowing up every part of his manhood. In that moment, he decided that death wasn't the only freedom.

"Essie . . ."

She put a finger to his lips. "Shhh, we okay. Keep going," she said with more kisses, this time on his fluttering lids. He forced himself out, then back again, harder, faster, until his heart raced.

The cool, firm ground underneath him turned hollow, cracking and splitting, until he felt swallowed up. He opened his eyes after the trembling stopped. The dark sky above was filled with tiny dots of light. A calm blanketed him, making it hard to move a muscle, let alone get up. Essie kissed him again, this time like a child in need of love.

He wanted to get up, go back to where he had been before it all happened. Essie had a completely different idea, practically curling herself underneath him.

Bo couldn't think of anything to say. Surely he should, at a time like this. "I never seen the sky so bright before."

"Maybe 'cause you never seen it after having your eyes roll around in your head." She giggled. "I had to put my hand over your mouth, the way you was hollering at the moon. Boy oh boy, there's some kind of wolf inside you, Bowman Carter."

"I guess we should get up off this cold ground."

"I don't want to. I rather you hold me like this forever." Essie took his hand and pressed it to her lips. "My name is Esmelda Lane. My mama named me. I belonged to a good family in Tennessee. Then they lost everything from the tainted tobacco farming, disease ate the plants and soil. They had to sell off all they property. I been owned by three different folks since then. Came here only a year ago. I'm lucky the Ross people let me keep my babies. Most would've divided us up. You have any children left behind?"

"No." He grunted at the impossibility.

"So, I'm your first?"

Bo stayed quiet.

"I knew it," she said, assuming. "I could tell. Well, now you won't be able to go without. You'll need me again and again." She announced this as fact. "Best we accept it as our duty to each other, just easier that way."

The way she said "duty" felt like an anvil weight on Bo's chest. He didn't need any more assigned tasks. Between the horse barn and Dahlia's demands, he had all the work he needed.

"We best be getting back," he said, trying to rise before she could pull him back down. She had a lot of strength in that small body of hers. And he was in no position to protest. It happened again. The trembling of his body against hers went a little longer this time. But his heart raced with relief and joy all the same.

Afterward he helped her to her feet. The heavy sack of her dress fell over her legs without a single bit of proof of what they'd just done. She adjusted her apron over the small bulge of her belly. He battled with himself whether to mention her circumstance, not sure it was his place to ask.

The man who'd lain with her would be back, whether one of their own or one of the Ross masters. If Bo was beholden to the sweet touch of her body, he'd be nothing but a possum caught in a trap waiting for his slaughter. He wouldn't see it coming. He'd be wise to walk away and never let it happen again.

26

Telegram

Timothy sent a telegram announcing he was bringing home a gentle-man named Mr. Harold Yates, the man who'd offered him the job in Washington. I held the note in my nervous hands. We were to have supper together when he arrived. The date on the message was from a week earlier. Meaning Timothy could arrive any day.

I paused to take a look at myself in the vanity mirror over the washbasin. The specks and shards weren't only ingrained on the mirror. It was me. I was a stone's throw away from a beggar in the street. My face was smudged with dirt. My hair in need of washing. Now, excite-ment poured over me. I would meet Mr. Yates. Timothy and I would leave and take Bo with us. Ryland wouldn't win at whatever game he was playing. His constant work at unsettling me would be done and dismantled.

For now, I pushed through the dresses Tilda had passed on to me. I had a mind to rush to Maggie and ask for one of hers. She wouldn't need them anytime soon. She was getting late with the child growing and stretching her in every direction.

As I went off to find Maggie, there he was. "Timothy." I threw my arms around him. "You're here," I sang. I needed his presence. I needed him to keep his promise to take me to Washington.

Timothy was taken aback and cautiously peeled my hands from around his neck. He glanced in the direction where Pico stood beside him holding a stack of brown-wrapped packages. "I have a surprise for you," he said as he stepped past me into our room. Pico followed.

"You're really here." I did my best to push at the hair hanging over my eyes. Regardless of what I'd felt about him, he was my only semblance of the life I'd boasted about. Telling Bo I was a free woman, Missus Lily Ross. And yet, it meant nothing without Timothy's existence. Alone, I was nothing more than Tilda's undertaking and for Ryland a ball of yarn to bat about like a cat at play.

"Don't mind me. I saw your telegram. I promise I will be ready to meet Mr. Yates." I clasped my hands together to contain my joy.

"I have no doubt. You are beautiful without even trying."

Pico stood proudly awaiting acknowledgment for his role to begin. He nervously placed the boxes on the floor. He opened the first one with shaking hands and pulled out a billowy new dress made of cotton and lace. Then another, and two more after that, and he laid them out one by one on the bed.

"Thank you, thank you, Timothy." I clasped my hands to my face. I pressed the beginning of tears. Happy tears were a first for me in the Ross home.

"I can't take all of the credit. Pico has a keen eye and accompanied me while shopping. Washington has wonderful dress boutiques. You're going to love it there, darling."

"So we're still going?" I asked, hopeful.

"Of course."

Pico pulled out the last dress, a red one, reminding me of my old favorite when I'd arrived. I'd made sure Cleo took that dress away so no one could ever say Dahlia Holt had been here.

"This one," I let out with zeal. I swallowed the memories and made room for what would make me anew. "Go," I ordered, but Timothy didn't budge. "I can manage myself. I want to try it on. Thank you, Pico. They're beautiful."

Pico nodded before leaving. I wasted no time heading to change.

"But there's more." Timothy held up a pair of black satin slippers. "I had to guess your size."

"Oh, Timothy. Thank you." I ducked behind the wardrobe panel and worked, quickly stepping into the dress.

"Let me at least lace up the back," Timothy called out.

"Yes, of course." I appeared in the new dress, excited. I spun around for Timothy to hook and lace the back. "How much did all of this cost? You didn't have to—"

"What's this?" he gasped, seeing the mark on my back for the first time. "How . . . oh my, how did this happen? Did someone hurt you, Lily?"

I swung around. "It's nothing really."

"My God, it looks terribly painful." He looked aghast. "Are you hurt all over?" he asked. His eyes searched.

"No. It's just my back. It doesn't hurt at all, honestly. I forget sometimes that it's even there. I'm sorry to have startled you. I was born with it. A birthmark." I took a step back, not sure if he would try further examination. I truly had forgotten. Being giddy over the new dresses, I'd dropped all the fear and shame I normally kept close at hand. Since we'd never consummated our marriage, there had never been a reason to disrobe in front of him.

"Maybe you should remain here. Rest," Timothy advised as if I'd just contracted a deadly illness. His eyes searched my face, neck, and whatever he could see of my skin.

"I wouldn't dare miss the chance to meet your guest, Mr. Yates, the chairman of the Farmers Alliance." I'd memorized as many details from the note as I could.

"Lily." He wasn't convinced.

"Timothy, this mark has haunted me all my life. I was teased by the other children. I've been called witch, devil child, the cursed one. There was no end to their cruelty. I was different from the others, but really not so different at all. If anyone should understand—" I paused, knowing I was visiting dangerous terrain. If anyone should understand being different it would be he, I wanted to say. But we never talked about this truth between us, both of us being kind enough to live in silence.

"Please, I'm fine. I won't miss the supper, or a chance to wear this dress," I uttered, deciding for him. "I will meet Mr. Yates and we will leave here. Please," I said at barely more than a whisper.

He heard me. He understood. He held out his arms. "Let me help you."

I cautiously turned my back to him.

He touched my shoulder. "I'm sorry I behaved that way, Lily. I never want you to feel the way you were treated when you were a child." He took his time with the hook and binding in the back. He finished and rested his hands on my shoulders. "We are more alike than I could have ever imagined. Sometimes our marks and scars are just hidden."

We arrived at the dining parlor and were greeted by a line of serving staff outfitted in white tailcoats, black trousers, and bow ties, with their gloved hands clasped at their sides and ready for service. I noticed Bo right away. He was freshly shaven. His skin was moist and smooth, his dress shirt buttoned to his neck and topped with a perfectly straight bow tie. He kept his square chin forward and his eyes straight.

For this evening, Tilda wanted to make a good impression on our guest of honor, Mr. Yates. She had ordered Cleo to choose extra field workers to have on staff. Those who were quick on their feet, stood straight, and had steady hands were brought into the home for the dinner party. It was also Cleo's responsibility to have them spiffed and polished for the occasion.

"You've met my brother, Ryland, and his wife, Maggie. And my lovely mum, Tilda," Timothy said to Mr. Yates, who stood as we entered the room. "And this is my wife, Lily."

"Timothy talks about you all the time. What a lovely pair you are." Mr. Yates leaned forward and took my hand. His full white mustache and beard left little of his mouth to be seen when he spoke.

"It's a pleasure to meet you, Mr. Yates," I said, genuinely thrilled to be in his company. Before Timothy could pull out a chair for me, I graciously placed my hand on the seat next to Tilda. My only other choice would've been next to Ryland, and that could not happen.

Tilda nodded toward him with a smile. "Now that we're all here, a toast to Mr. Yates for traveling all this way to dine with us this evening. It really is a pleasure to meet you." She raised her glass, her wrist adorned with pearls.

"You have a beautiful home, and one of the largest estates I've seen. Crops are going to be very profitable. You should be very proud of your son."

"Sons. None of this would be possible without both my sons. Being a widow and all, I'm dependent on my boys for just about everything." She batted her eyes with ladylike affection. "You are a welcome breath of fresh air. It has been daunting living out here without civilization. Luckily, I have my boys, and their wonderful wives who are like daughters to me."

Timothy glanced nervously at his mother before turning his attention to Mr. Yates. "You've met everyone, and now I think it would be the perfect time for you to tell my family what this prestigious visit is all about."

Mr. Yates took his time before beginning, clearing his throat. "I am here from the National Farmers Alliance. Our sole purpose is to protect the financial interests of plantation owners who've invested their blood, sweat, and tears into the soil of this great land. Not all of us in the

Northern colonies believe in Washington, those Congress dilettantes, looking to tax our earnings from our hard work. We won't even go into the errant dismantling of our property base. How are we to stay afloat without the workers?"

"You mean slaves," I said almost at a whisper. I heard myself speak and wished I hadn't. Tilda's eyes darted toward Timothy, as if this was something she'd warned him about ahead of time.

"Well, young lady, I guess you don't like to beat around the bush. Yes. There are landowners who depend on their slaves. We have just as much at stake as the South. Every president before this one has owned slaves. That's no secret. This Lincoln fella is the hypocrite, if you ask me. He has decided he's above it all. Well nay, I say." He slapped his large hand on the table.

Even Tilda jumped, having not expected the theatrics.

"Now, he's out to take away our liberties as businessmen who've supplied this nation with food and tobacco. With that said, we need a watchdog over their activities. Nothing combats chaos like organization. Your son Timothy is our choice to remain in Washington to have an ever-vigilant voice in our favor. As our spokesman, he'll make sure our interests are protected behind those closed doors. This young man is quite the charmer. Who can resist his easy persuasion?"

"So this job will have you staying in Washington full time?" Tilda asked, surmising the important part, ignoring all of Mr. Yates's fairy dusting. Her son would be gone. That's all she heard of the conversation.

"Yes, Mum. Staying in Washington is required," Timothy began before being cut off by the sound of Ryland clinking his glass with a spoon. It was the beginning of another one of his magical toasts.

"Well, I'm impressed. May my brother find peace and happiness in his new venture. May he use his gift of gab toward a grand purpose and to find the answers of this life he truly seeks. I wish you success, brother."

For a moment, Timothy looked disturbed, having assumed there was a barb in there somewhere. This time, Ryland had said nothing insulting, which was a first. He usually took any chance to tease his younger brother. I couldn't help but think the "gift" of the horse trainer had actually done some good for their relationship.

Tilda picked up the bell that seemed to follow her everywhere and shook it excessively. "We can begin serving supper now," she said to the staff lined up as if the loud clanging wasn't signal enough. The bustle of too many people moving at once filled the space.

A strong, distinct arm reached over to set down a silver tray. "May I pour?" the server asked in the reserved dialect of a gentleman. *Bo.* I almost smiled but knew better with Tilda, and now Ryland, too, watching my every move.

"Yes, please do," I said without a hint of interest. When Bo moved to the other side of the table, I risked glancing in his direction. I saw the look on his face as he stood there, his dark eyes smoldering with suspicion. He watched with an unsettling sense of intrigue. He didn't understand the world I'd created. He didn't trust it. He was right not to do so. Best he not end up like me. The duality ate at my soul. The talk of keeping the slave-run plantations in good standing made my skin burn.

"Tell me, Mr. Yates, when will you be taking my dear brother off to his new duties?" Ryland asked. The question was a reasonable one.

"As soon as possible would be my choice, but I understand time is needed to teach you a few things, like his side of the business here," Mr. Yates offered.

The pendulum on the large brass clock on the mantel swung, and the click of the time moving forward made it obvious that Ryland was putting thought into responding. The silence was awkward. Timothy stayed quiet, knowing better than to attract attention when his brother was antagonized. He waited.

We all waited.

"So that's what you've been doing, teaching me everything. That's odd, considering I've taught my baby brother everything he knows," Ryland joked. Tame. Again, concerning.

Mr. Yates's hearty laughter replaced the nervous silence, offering the rest of us relief.

Timothy chimed in after a few good-natured chuckles. "I assure you, sir, I will be in my position as soon as the books are squared away. I admit my brother is a great teacher of many things, but accounting ledgers are not his cup of tea. I'd say by the end of the month I can take the position."

Tilda cleared her throat. "And how often do you plan to return?"

Timothy ran a hand through his dark hair. His cheeks blew out to give him time to make the right answer. "Mum, it's going to take a while to get acclimated. I'm sure once I get settled, I can visit. As for now, I'm not sure of a schedule." His response was enough to keep Tilda from running out of the room screaming, and me satisfied that I would have distance from Ryland soon enough. I leaned in a little closer to Timothy to show my full support, then pulled away when I felt Bo's eyes on me.

"Well, I expect you won't completely abandon us. I've taught my boys better than to ignore their mother."

Timothy rose from his seat and walked to his mother's side. He wrapped an arm around her shoulder. "I can never ignore you, Mum. You will always be first in my life."

I held my smile in place, feeling the sting of his vow. Ryland watched for even the slightest hint of discomfort. I wouldn't give him the satisfaction. My mouth twitched slightly as I couldn't hold the false smile in place. "We will visit, and expect you to visit us," I said, looking at Tilda. "I hear the capital is lovely in the spring." I glanced up to see the one person who knew my tell. Bo stood regal and straight in his serving attire, with his gloved hands at his side, waiting for the next course. His eyes shifted away immediately. He understood this to mean I was leaving once again, leaving him. But he was wrong. This time we would be leaving together.

"Well now," Mr. Yates said. Timothy cleared his throat. "Enough business. Let's enjoy this good food, shall we?"

27

The Kitchen

Essie frowned at Bo. "Seem like every time I turn around, you grinning like a huckster. You a clown now? That it?" She ran a rag around the center of a plate and then handed it to Bo.

Bo didn't answer. He wasn't listening while he dipped the shiny plate in the clean basin of water to rinse. The water swirled in motion.

Ruby took the plate from his hands. "And when exactly was the last time you seen a huckster or a clown, Miss Essie?" Her thick body leaned past Bo and handed the plate back to Essie. "This one's not clean."

Bo couldn't help the smiling thing. He tried to stifle the urge, but he couldn't. The grin on his face came from thinking about Dahlia sitting there, fooling them all, and them not even knowing it. That girl was full of gumption. He hated to admit it, the simple truth, but she fit in just fine. Seeing her this way, fitting into her new world, was far better than worrying, waiting for the sky to fall. If that bounty hunter came around here, he'd never know who she was. Not in her pretty dress and with hair pinned up.

"I know what he got on his mind: her," Essie said out of nowhere.

Well, here she go. He knew it was coming. She'd been watching him watch Dahlia all night, with a none-too-pleased look on her face. Essie recognized her from spying in the barn, overhearing the two of them talking.

"Who's *her*? Who you talking about?" Ruby's turn to hold up the wash line. She shoved a hand on her wide hip, determined to get to the bottom of this.

"Miss Lily," Essie said reluctantly. It was too late to try and walk it back. Ruby wasn't going to stop asking *who, who*, like an owl. "She the young one sitting in there all prim and proper."

"We gon' talk about this later," Bo hissed at Essie. He was finally paying attention. "We don't need to go around starting trouble for other folks," he said, though he knew it was too late.

Cleo entered with a tray stacked with platters. "Shhh. Why y'all talking so loud? Keep your voices down." She was the leader. She knew how to read, reporting back to the quarters with news of their town and neighboring counties, who, what, and how folks were doing.

Dahlia was sort of the same way. Knowing how to read would do that to you, he guessed. *Now look at her, sitting at the big table, at the big house, in her big britches.*

"She not one of us. I don't care nothing about her." Essie faced her audience. "That gal out there—Bo know her from another plantation. They friends."

"That's enough," Cleo snapped. "I need y'all to finish cleaning this kitchen fore y'all get put out to the—"

"—quarters. Well, guess what, we all going back to the quarters anyway," Ruby teased. "Now I want to know about the gal. Who is she?"

"Her name is Miss Lily. Go on, peek out there and see. All she do is smile and bat her eyes," Essie said.

"Missus Lily, to you," Cleo whispered. "Stop spreading tales and finish cleaning in here."

"Nah, nah, I want the dirt. She got eyes for our Bo?" Ruby asked. "What'd you see, Essie? She trying to get our Bo hanged?" She looked up at Bo, her cherub face studying him intensely. "Don't be foolish now. You know better."

"All right, stop it, y'all." Cleo grabbed a towel. "I guess I have to do these dishes myself. Go on back to the quarters. All of ya. See if I have you out here again. To think I was gon' let y'all take all the stuffing and meat back to the quarters."

Ruby elbowed her way back in the wash line. "Stop being so hot collared. Me and Essie trying to save Bo from himself. Don't you care?"

"Bo don't need saving," Cleo blurted. "That gal Negro too." She put her hand to her lips. She'd said it out loud. It was the truth that nobody else should've known.

Bo licked his lips and couldn't think of a thing to say except "Y'all need to stop talking about something you don't know nothing about."

Ruby slapped a hand to her head. "That woman out there a Negress? Shut your mouth. She done slipped through." Her hand came down in judgment, slapping at the edge of a porcelain platter, sending it flying. The crash to the floor was loud enough to be heard in the parlor.

Cleo put a finger up to her lips. No one breathed while they waited for someone to come see what all the commotion was about.

After a pause, they all let out their collective breaths. Cleo went on. "Please don't tell what I say. Miss Lily helpless, like any one of us. Don't matter about her supposed to being white. Don't matter at all." Cleo shook her head in pity. "You see, Master Timothy don't know she like us, but Master Ryland, I think he knows. He all fawning over Miss Lily and acting like he got a right to touch her. She came in dress torn, face scraped. It was Master Ryland. Why else he do her like that?"

"I seen plenty of white ladies get pushed around by they menfolk. Don't have to be no slave for that," Ruby remarked. "I've seen it with my own eyes."

Cleo shook her head. "Don't matter. She one of us. We gotta help protect her," Cleo announced. "That's all there is to it."

"She's nothing like *us*," Essie said. She pointed her finger close to Bo's nose. "If you ever talk to her again, you might as well be wishing for your own death, and you gon' take her along with you." She went back to washing the plates, her shoulders rolling soft and relaxed with each stroke of the rag as if she hadn't stirred up all this trouble. She was content in her new power of knowing the truth while Bo was coming undone.

Hearing what Cleo said about Dahlia . . . Lily not having a say, not having a choice, was all wrong. She was a white man's wife. If what Cleo said was true, she was fighting off Master Ryland like any one of the ladies in the quarters would. No different.

"You not smiling no more?" Essie asked quietly, striking the final blow at Bo.

"All right, that's enough, Essie. Can't you see he's feeling some kind of way about his friend?" Ruby sidled up to Bo. "It's all right, Bo. Don't you pay no mind to this mean ole cat."

"I gotta get out of here." Bo pushed off his jacket, pulled at his tie, and tossed them on the ground. "I'm done with this."

"Stop this foolishness. What're you doing?" Cleo picked up what he'd thrown down one piece at a time, holding on to it for dear life. But he wasn't through. Shoes. Shirt. Pants. He kicked everything out of his way, standing there, free and loose.

"Where my clothes? I'm leaving," he announced.

The ladies gawked at his bare chest as if they'd never seen one before. Ruby covered her mouth, giggling. ". . . Umph. Honey."

Cleo carried everything over to Bo and shoved the clothes back in his hands. "You may not care about yo'self, but think about the rest of us, Bo. Please. Don't let nobody walk in here and see you like this."

"See? See what I mean?" Essie snickered. "I told you, you gon' get killed over that woman. Can't even control yo'self."

Bo slid behind the middle pantry to put the bare minimum back on, the shirt and pants. He wanted nothing more to do with this house, these Ross people's kitchen, or anything else. He kept his back to the women. He didn't understand what made Essie act this mean and petty.

The best he could hope for was that the Ross brothers didn't find out the truth about Dahlia. Gossip flew faster than a hawk peering on fresh prey. Hopefully the grapevine never traveled past the quarters. Cleo and Ruby would never talk that way to the masters and missuses of the house. Essie he wasn't so sure about.

He returned to the kitchen fully dressed except for letting his tie lie loose around his neck. He stayed silent and refused to even look in Essie's direction.

"If I knew y'all were up here in this big ole house having this much fun, I'd'a come sooner. I'm missing the good stuff down there in the quarters." Ruby kneeled over to pick up the pieces of the broken platter.

Cleo raised her apron bib for Ruby to stack the pieces there. "I hope Miss Tilda don't see one of her plates missing. She going to think one of us stole it."

"Oh please, she got plenty of plates. And when she ever gon' be in this kitchen to ever know?" Ruby chided. "I bet she ain't washed a plate in her life."

The heavy doors to the dining room fanned open. Nattie's eyes spoke before her words. "There's a man here. He saying he want to see all the womenfolk. He holding paper. Reward paper. He want to see all the women's backside. Miss Tilda told me to come in here and wait," she whispered.

Cleo stopped what she was doing. "Wait right here."

"What's this about?" Ruby asked.

Bo closed his eyes. This couldn't have happened at a worse time. Not now while Essie was still steaming about Dahlia. She might see the sketch. She might add it up who "Miss Lily" really was. Bo quieted the thoughts in his head. He was getting ahead of himself. *Calm.*

Just as quickly as she left, Cleo came right back in. "We got to go line up outside. Just the women. We not gon' say a word, you hear?" she said, mostly to Essie. "Not a word."

"What? You think that Negress is who they looking for?" Ruby asked. Before she could get her answer, Cleo hustled the ladies out through the back door.

The women left the kitchen together, hesitant. They waited at the top of the porch stairs, holding the banister for support.

Bo followed them out. It was John Browder. He stood holding a lamp, with a paper in his hand.

The mistress of the house could be heard, agitated. "This is unnecessary. How dare you accuse us, my family, of stealing? We are from Lancashire. We are not of your depraved community."

The man picked the youngest out of the kitchen staff and told them to line up in front. Essie was part of this group. They were ordered to unbutton their tops and let the fabric fall to their shoulders.

He was looking for the scar. The mark on Dahlia's back. John Browder had finally come to the right place.

"No more. Enough," the mistress yelled. She flipped open her fan and waved frantically. "Can't you do something?" she asked her son, Master Ryland, who tried to calm her.

He pulled her close. "Mum, let the man do this and be done. There's no cause for concern. There are no stolen slaves here," he said loud and clear. "We have nothing to hide."

Master Timothy and the man who'd come for supper were nowhere to be seen. What could they do against John Browder and his rifle-carrying clan anyway? The guns gleamed in the moonlight, strung over their backs. They could do what they pleased.

John Browder held up the paper with the picture next to Essie's face, then told her to turn around. He yanked her white shirt down all the way, exposing her breasts to the night air. He did the same to Ruby, though she looked nothing like the sketch he held in his hand.

"This is maddening. What in the world are you looking for?" Master Ryland asked.

"Never you mind," John Browder snapped. "Do not interfere or I'll assume you have something to hide."

When he was done, John Browder faced Master Ryland. "Please accept my apologies," he said in his booming voice. "When there's a theft, it's a crime against all hardworking citizens. If you ever endure such a crime, please remember me. John Browder at your service."

A second horseman pulled over the hill. He shook his head, letting his boss know their search of the quarters was unsuccessful as well.

John Browder handed the paper to Master Ryland. "There's a reward, a thousand dollars. Highest payout for a slave I've ever seen. Good evening, gentlemen, ma'am," he said before mounting his horse and riding out the open gate.

"What's the point of having a gate if anyone can come on your land?" the mistress yelled. "Get everyone back inside. How dare this man? How dare he?"

Dahlia wasn't outside. He bet she was watching. He hoped now she understood and believed him. There was no safe place.

28

Women

My head pounded with fear. I'd sneaked off the minute I heard about the bounty hunter and his men searching the premises. As soon as everyone began to file out of the dining parlor, I went the opposite way, up the stairs and straight to my room. I didn't bother locking the door. I listened for the heavy footsteps of a man, any man. Whoever came would have only one reason, and that was to take me back to the Vesterville.

If I were found out, a locked door wouldn't save me. I kept my head pressed against the door, still listening. After no one came and I heard the sound of horses galloping away, I could breathe relief. I still paced the floor. I still wondered what had happened to Cleo and the others, if anyone was harmed.

Staggering steps and the voice of a drunken Timothy came toward the room. I ran and quickly stationed myself in the bed.

He would know the truth about me now. He'd seen the mark on my back, which I had no doubt the bounty hunter knew about and was looking for. The truly telling sign of who I really was. I turned to my side and pretended to be asleep. Timothy crawled from the edge of the bed to lie down fully clothed.

I braced myself. He curled himself behind me. "Darling Lily." His hand rested on my shoulder. "Are you awake?" he slurred in the darkness. Timothy rarely drank.

I turned and faced him. I waited. I was prepared to apologize for lying to him.

"I've thought about things. Maybe, perhaps, it might be better if I didn't force you to remain with me."

"What?" I shuddered. "What is this about?"

He removed the hand that had rested on my shoulder. "Ryland . . ." Timothy said in that exhausted way he did when he talked about his brother. "Ryland and I had a chat. He's wise in this regard. Women. He knows a thing or two. Things I don't understand. He thinks I am doing you harm, a disservice, by keeping you as my beloved," he slurred. "I don't want to keep you from finding love, true love," he whispered in the darkness.

"I don't need—I don't need anything but you. Timothy, what happened out there? A man showed up requesting the slaves line up for inspection, correct? What happened after that?" I asked. I took ahold of Timothy's chin to stop him from nodding to sleep. "Did someone, anyone, get hurt? Did that man threaten anyone?"

"You deserve love, Lily."

I was hardly concerned about love when all I wanted was freedom. I pushed my forehead against his. "Timothy, please. Tell me what happened. Just tell me what happened."

"Something terrible happened this evening. A slave patroller interrogated Mum about stealing a female. Our family, accused of stealing a slave. Mum was humiliated. It reminded me of what a dangerous world we live in. I felt bad for the slaves to be treated that way, stripped down in front of everyone without a shred of dignity. And I thought of you. I thought how you've been trying to tell me that they're human beings. Real people who deserve so much more. Well, I spoke about this with Ryland after Mr. Yates retired for the evening. Just Ryland and I." He rolled over. He stared at the ceiling.

"We spoke of you as well, Lily. Ryland made me see that you're a woman in need of love. You're so beautiful, Lily. You need to be touched. You need love. And children." He turned his back to me, curled himself tighter into a ball. "I can't give you these necessary things. We all simply need love," he said before closing his eyes.

The faint breath, then a clogged inhale, and he was deep asleep.

I lay still, unable to grasp how my relief at not being found out could so easily be replaced with a new fear.

What was Ryland up to now?

You deserve love, Lily.

Only when morning came did it hit me. The bed was empty where Timothy had slept.

I tried not to assume anything, but wouldn't be sure until I searched the library. I told myself he wouldn't go off to Washington without me. I prayed as I tiptoed down the hall.

The house was eerily quiet. I wanted to search for Timothy and yet didn't want to chance seeing Cleo. I was too ashamed to see her or anyone after what they'd been through, having to stand in the night air with their tops down while men searched for a mark that was mine. Cleo would know without a doubt I was the runaway the men were searching for.

I slipped inside the library. Just as I'd thought, there sitting on the wide oak desk was a folded note with my name on the front. I knew what it said before opening it.

> *Dearest Lily,*
> *I've gone, but only for a short while.*
>> *I have an urgent meeting with Mr. Yates.*
>> *When I return, we will discuss our future.*
>> *For now, rest easy and be assured that I am thinking of you.*
>> *Timothy*

I pressed the letter against my chest. This was Ryland's doing. *A woman needs love.* As if he would know a thing about that. Convincing Timothy there was no hope between us, making him believe there was no future with me. Ryland's convenient words of advice were his attempt to convince Timothy to leave me here alone. To leave me, period. And it worked. I had no one to protect me against him.

I didn't want to think about what grand scheme Ryland had set in motion.

I grabbed the ink jar and quill from the desk. I had one thing on my mind. If Timothy wouldn't take me away from this place, I'd figure out a way to make it happen on my own.

My hand shook as I turned the knob of the room at the end of the hall. I pushed the door open. This room was on the farthest side of the house. I'd stumbled upon it once out of confusion. The endless hallways and doors made it difficult to keep my bearing in the beginning when I'd first arrived. This room was used for storage, relics of the Ross family's past life. Sealed crates as well as furnishings were stacked wide and high. Large oil paintings of oceans and villages from a far-off place had never been hung.

A beautiful white bassinet that I imagined had held both Timothy and Ryland sat next to a rocking chair and a set of folded blankets. All would be used for Maggie's baby soon and then one day passed to the next Ross heir. I pushed the blankets aside and took a seat. A small window offered enough light to see. I sat down with the ink and quill carefully, trying not to spill it.

I used a box as my station and began to practice writing. It'd been a while since I'd put quill to paper. The lessons from Mother Rose were a long time before. Every letter connected to the next. *Long, flowing lines, lift, and begin again,* she'd say.

If only my hand would stop shaking. Each word was more unrecognizable than the last. My chest felt heavy, as if I had to force myself to breathe. I had to get it right.

I put the quill down and checked my work. The F in *freedom* looked like a P. It would not pass for an authentic document. I needed more stationery.

I went to stand and knocked over the ink jar. It landed first on my skirt, then on the floor with a heavy thud. I stumbled back, knocking over a few crates. I fell to my knees and tried to blot the black smear from the floorboard and save what little ink was left in the jar.

I heard the door creak open. I hoped it was Cleo.

"And here Mum thought it was vermin." The familiar ring of contempt sent a shiver down my back. "I thought a ghost, but this is far better. You." Ryland came fully inside and closed the door behind him. The distance was hardly more than a step between us. I held my breath before attempting to move past him.

He stood firm to face me. His brown eyes seemed even thinner than usual, dull and unfeeling. "I've missed you, Lily. Seems we can't find any time alone these days." He looked around, taking notice of the black stain on the floor and my skirt. The smell of stale whiskey on his breath filled the stuffy room.

I spoke carefully, forming my words as if he'd have trouble understanding. "I was working on a letter to my . . . dear friends. I miss them dearly."

He stepped closer. "Your friends? Who exactly would that be, the Holts of Vesterville near Hampton City?"

The shock of him knowing where I'd come from became a latent fear compared to his hand on my cheek. I tried to turn my face away. He took a firm hold of my face, bringing it to meet his. "I wish you understood how much I care about you. From the day we met, I wanted to protect you."

I grabbed his wrist, leaving fingerprints of dark ink on his skin. "Ryland, don't do this." My eyes peered into his. I searched for a moment. I'd seen a small glimpse of decency before. In the beginning, when we'd first met, he had cared.

"Ryland, you can't . . . don't do this."

He seemed to reconsider, then followed through with a kiss that took what was left of my breath. I attempted to scratch at his face. He took my arms one at a time, capturing them in a binding hold behind my back. His mouth remained on mine. My head swam as I fought for air.

Floating. No. I was being carried, my feet barely skimming the ground. I pulled my arms free and used both hands to push against his chest.

"Don't fight me," he whispered.

We crashed into the rocking chair. I tried to scream, only to have the air knocked out of me as I fell backward and he landed on top of me.

I cried out again, desperate. In my ears, my voice sounded loud and defiant, but I knew it was no more than moans and whimpers of fear. My feet kicked against the wood floor. His heavy boots struggled to keep control of my legs. I refused to stay still. The burn of his hand pulled my wrists together while the other hand worked havoc between my thighs. The weight of him, the heaviness, closed out my air. *Breathe. Fight.* And then there was stillness. His weight collapsed on top of me. His body even heavier.

Two hands gripped the sides of his shoulders. Once he was rolled over, Cleo stood over me, panicked and scared. I saw a steel bucket off to the side. A tiny tinge of blood smudged on the bottom edge.

"C'mon, Miss Lily, help me stand him up." Cleo jerked my arms forward until my body followed.

"Is he dead?"

"I barely hit him. He was already full of drink from last night, then some more this morning. It's a wonder he made it up the stairs to come after you in the first place. I found this in his room." She pulled out the notice, the flyer the bounty hunter had left behind. Ryland had circled my description and written *Lily.* I took it from Cleo and tore it into pieces.

"Go on," she said. "You better leave before he wakes up."

"What are you going to do?" I huffed, out of breath.

Cleo tried to prop him up on her shoulder. "I've found him stooped over plenty, Miss Lily. Go. Everything gon' be fine."

"But he'll remember. He'll know I had something to do with that knot growing on his head. He'll know." I looked around, panicked.

"Nah, he'll wake up and won't remember a thing. We got to move him now. Miss Tilda and Miss Maggie out on the porch having their tea."

I swallowed the dry ball of anxiousness in my throat and forced myself to see straight. I quickly grabbed the tattered practice paper covered with my scribble and shoved it into my fist. I helped lift Ryland, using my full body under his other armpit. We dragged him past the boxes and out to the hallway. Once we were sure no one was around, we staggered with each step until we could push him through the door of his room. He hit the floor face first.

"All right," Cleo whispered. "You go on to your room and get your-self cleaned up." She dashed off, leaving me to move at my own pace.

I stayed behind, still dazed from what had just happened. My body ached from fighting with every possible limb. I sat on my knees next to Ryland's listless body. His breathing was labored, as if he was fighting in his dream. I leaned over him thinking long and hard before stopping myself from slapping him hard across the face. What would it mean if he wouldn't know I'd done it?

"You're a horrible person, Ryland Ross. You will be punished. I swear you will."

He stirred with a bit of drool pooling down the side of his mouth. I jumped back, afraid he was coming to.

My hand snagged on the loop of a black strap. I pulled to get free, dragging the weight attached. It was the satchel Ryland had carried on our train ride. I snatched it open and pulled out a second bag. This one had writing printed on the side.

Central Bank of Virginia.

I pulled the heavy weight toward me and swung the flap open. Stacks of banded papers filled the bag. Filled it to the rim. One by one, I pulled out the banded stacks, seemingly endless, tearing off one band and fanning the papers out.

I knew enough of their value to know that stacks this large could buy anything. It was surely enough to buy out Aunt Gertrude, to end Timothy's worry about finding investors. So why hadn't they used it? All this time Ryland was holding it and hiding it for himself. Why?

I dragged the bag closer for a full inspection and a heavy pistol fell out. I didn't dare touch it. I'd never seen a gun like this, not up close.

It was the paper notes I was interested in. I studied the paper bills. Big scripted letters arched across the top, *Virginia Treasury Note,* with the amount, the number 20, printed in each corner. There was a bright red stamp with a set of numbers underneath, different on every bill, along with the drawn picture of a stoic man on one end and a woman on the other.

"What're you doing?" Cleo's brown skin was now nearly crimson. Of all the acts she'd witnessed and heard, this was the tipping point. "You stealing from this man?" she asked, shaking her head. "Leave now. Just go."

"I'm not the thief," I said under my breath as I stood. "Ryland must've stolen this money." It all began to come together. "I was there. I saw the entire town shut down because there was a robbery. It was him."

"I don't care how he got what he got. None of my business to mind, or yours. Now go."

I backed out holding one of the stacks behind me while Cleo tended to Ryland.

I rushed back to my room and closed the door. I understood now. That day when the lawmen were running through the town streets, I thought they were looking for me. The runaway. Later, I'd heard people on the train muttering about a bank robbery. We'd left the city in a rush right along with hordes of others on the train. The lawmen had cornered off every block. While Timothy and I sat on a quiet bench talking about our hopes and dreams, Ryland was robbing a bank. Or possibly they'd robbed it together long before they'd approached me. I'd seen the black bag hanging from Ryland's shoulder.

I still couldn't figure out why Timothy continued to plead distress about Aunt Gertrude and needing capital. This was capital. Maybe he truly did not know. More of Ryland being Ryland, letting his brother flail about looking for financial rescue. I gripped the small amount I'd taken. I shoved books around on the mantel until I found a space to hide it.

As far as I was concerned, I'd earned my share. What was worse was that Timothy could never know how I'd stumbled upon the money. He could never know why I'd been in Ryland's room, on his floor cursing him to hell. If I told Timothy about Ryland attacking me, Ryland would tell Timothy the truth about *Dahlia Holt's* mark.

"Miss Lily, water," Cleo offered through the closed door, speaking louder than usual in case Tilda or Maggie was within earshot. This time I had locked it properly. The handle shook as she tested it. "Miss Lily, may I come in?"

"No. I'm fine, Cleo," I called out. I wasn't sure if she had pity for me or wanted to make sure we both had our stories straight. Or, better yet, wanted to make sure none of the notes were missing.

I opened the door wide enough to take the cup of water with a trembling hand.

The worried look on Cleo's face had become a mainstay. It was indeed pity staring back at me. "Thank you, Cleo."

"Miss Lily, please, I'm begging you. If you took anything, you got to give it to me, now," she whispered. "I'll put it back like it never happened."

I opened the door wide enough for her to come in. She stood rigid with her hands nervously rolling into each other. She wasn't there to negotiate. The line had been crossed. I had put her in a dangerous place.

"Cleo, he'll never know. Trust me, he'll never know it's missing, because he stole that money from a bank. He's the thief, not me. I know what I'm talking about. I was there. I know what he did. Having that money is my only proof. I need to keep it for safety, for my own protection. I'm going to tell him I took it. You don't have to worry about being accused. I promise, Cleo. You aren't in any danger."

Cleo shook her head and closed her eyes in a silent prayer. "Lawd, lawd, lawd. I should've listened to Essie. I should've listened to her. What she said about you is true. You ain't nothing but a pot of mess waiting to be stirred. Anybody dealing with you gon' get trouble coming they way."

"Essie? Who is—" It didn't matter. Whoever this person was and whatever she'd said about me meant nothing. I only cared about leaving this place, and the paper notes were my way. I stood firm. "You saw what he was about to do to me. He's a despicable man."

"Don't matter. They all bad. You can't fight 'em. All you can do is protect yo'self. Once you go messing with a white man's money, they turn a different kind of ugly, something you don't want to see."

I wasn't giving it back. It was all I had to fight against Ryland. A fair exchange, one secret for another. "I swear, Cleo. I swear on everything, I will not let you be accused."

"You're just a whole heap of trouble, Miss Lily. You better watch yourself." She left in a huff, slamming the door behind her.

29

Deal

I'd kept myself in my room with the door locked for some days after. At least I'd thought the door was locked. I'd awakened to see Tilda. Her somber expression and dark gray dress buttoned to her neck made me wonder if someone had died.

Timothy.

I blinked a few times to get my focus. "What's happened? Why are you here?" I breathed out in a panic. My eyes shifted to the mantel, my hiding place, undisturbed.

"You're awake. Good." Her thin lips turned up then quickly fell back to a flat line. "Cleo said you refused to come down for tea. I refuse to let this go on." She sat in the chair facing the bed. A set of keys hung from her hand. So much for the usefulness of the lock on the door.

"I've called for a doctor, someone to give you a thorough examination. I've seen situations such as yours. A young woman can be very lonely during her husband's absence. It happened to many young women whose husbands were off fighting wars for England. A malaise would set in. Some would harm themselves, or others." She raised an eyebrow.

"Tilda, I'm fine. I'm much better now." I sat up to prove my malaise had passed. I'd needed the few days to rest after the ambush from

Ryland. Not to mention the emotional toll. "A doctor's visit isn't necessary," I told her.

"I beg to differ. As I sat here, you were in a full state of delirium, jumping and battling demons under your closed lids. You called out for Rose. Mother Rose." She waited for my response. "Other names were a bit different—Papa Sap, Oleen, Winnie," she listed, as if she'd written them all down. "Friends you left behind, perhaps?"

"Yes, my grandmother, my tutor, and the others who served our home. I remember them fondly."

"But you were an only child, correct?"

"Yes."

"Why wouldn't you want these good friends to be invited to the wedding?"

I'd avoided this question when she made her list for invitations. But now she'd asked outright.

"My family friends wouldn't have understood. I left unexpectedly."

Tilda sighed. "I think it's for the best. A specialist who examines in matters of the mind, dear. There's no need to suffer." She stood and gave my hand a pat. "The physician is coming from a renowned treatment center. I've seen this type of thing often. Women are more susceptible to malaise. You've been so tired and sad, it could only get worse if something isn't done about it. Timothy will thank us later. You can continue to rest until the doctor arrives tomorrow."

"I absolutely refuse. Tilda, I won't be examined. There is nothing wrong with me." I couldn't let it happen. The mark down the center of my back was my only true connection to Dahlia Holt. Even a physician of the mind might demand a full examination. The bounty hunter had left the notice behind after the search of each and every slave. No doubt it was posted in every town in this region and the next. My description—fair-skinned slave, sixteen years of age, jagged scar down her back like a brown river—would not easily be forgotten, especially by a doctor. At some point, he would remember the notice. I would be apprehended.

"There's no shame in needing help. We're only human, after all." Tilda wrapped her shawl around her and faced the door. She'd said her piece and that was the end of it.

I stood and grabbed my robe. "Maybe I'd feel better if you would stop coming into my room without permission. Maybe if I wasn't always being stalked by Ryland. Has he told you anything about that?"

The key dangled from her hand as if I were her possession. "You see, this is what I'm concerned about. This paranoia, continually thinking everyone is out to get you. We are a family, dear. We only have your best interest at heart. Ryland told me you are the one who attacked him. Or don't you remember? He said he heard you crying. You'd been spending time in the storage room, desperately lonely. He offered you a shoulder to lean on, and you attacked him. He has the lump on the back of his head to prove it."

Astonishment swept over me.

"He didn't want to tell me. I insisted he tell me what transpired between you two. From the scratches on his face, it's clear you were having some sort of spell."

"I was having a spell?" I couldn't stop myself from repeating her words.

"Yes. So now you understand. We can't have this kind of thing happen again." She closed the door before I could respond.

I had to end this nonsense of being seen by the physician. I dressed and made my way to where I knew Ryland would be having his breakfast tea before his ride. He saw me, put down his cup, and sat up straight. I saw fear, if only briefly, that made him sit up at attention.

"You realize we're alone," he said. His eyes were bloodshot and tired. The scruffy beard was badly in need of trimming. His riding coat hung unevenly on his shoulders.

"I'm glad we're alone," I said confidently. I held eye contact with him, gripping the back of a chair. "I didn't come to fight with you, Ryland." I took the seat across from him, but not close enough that he could reach out and touch me.

He touched the back of his head. "Yes, you are quite the adversary."

I was happy to know he thought it was me who'd clobbered him over the head. Cleo was free and clear.

He rested his head in his hands as if the weight of the day had already taken a toll. "What do you want, Lily?" He forced a grin, pronouncing *Lily* with a roll of his tongue.

I lowered my voice. "I know what you did, the bank robbery in the city that day when I met you and Timothy. I have proof." The recognition on his face was all that I needed. "Does Timothy know you have the money? Or did you lie to him?"

"Seems we both have something to hide, don't we?"

"I'm not afraid of you. I don't care what you think you know about me."

"Yes. So noted." He squinted as if the knot on his head were still making him dizzy.

"Your mother wants me to see a specialist for the mind, a physician." My voice wavered slightly. "I realize how I must look to her. But I want to assure her that I'm over my difficulties."

"Mum is quick to make assumptions, but she's usually correct in her assessments." He let out a trifling laugh. He leaned closer. "She thinks a prescription of some sort will fix you." His grin remained.

"Well, now we know I don't need fixing." I pushed one of the notes in front of him. "I will not be seeing a mind doctor."

Silence followed. He understood my meaning. I hadn't calculated what should take place from this point on. I presumed this was all that needed to be said. "I would hate for your mum to find out what you've done. Of all the things you're capable of, robbing a bank might shock her. It would crush her heart to be disgraced not only in England, but now in America. I also don't think prison is a place you want to be. And there's Timothy. You've had the ability to help him save this place all along. Does he know what you're hiding under your bed?"

He sipped his tea. I could see he wanted to look unbothered, but his grin became strained. "I suppose I could tell her to call this ridiculous examination off. Maybe I'll explain how you've become settled and are now happy to accept your circumstances."

"Yes. We might all be happy if we accepted our circumstances," I said, feeling some kind of new power. I wouldn't turn away. I faced him and tried not to blink.

"I will never be happy with our circumstances, Lily. You are young. Maybe that makes you fearless. But I'm wiser. Remember that." He shoved his chair aside and marched off. I listened gleefully as he rushed up the stairs to check his bounty.

The air in the dining room turned thick. I was afraid I'd never be able to breathe without this unsettled feeling again. I was in a constant state of panic. The cloud movement outside drained the light out of the room. A storm was coming. Darkness rolled in, settling deep around the edges. It was the circle being drawn around me and growing closer.

If I stepped or stumbled too close to the edge, I would be eaten alive. It was a risk I had to take if I was going to survive. If I was going to save Bo and not make what Cleo said be true, I had to risk it all, including meeting Ryland eye to eye, a dagger for a dagger. If he wanted a fight, I would be a worthy opponent until my last breath. I wasn't afraid anymore.

30

Handshake

Bo liked being in her garden because even when she wasn't there, it still felt like she was. She had that way about her. Her scent, her voice, her smile connecting to him.

But then Master Ryland showed up. The man before him seemed to feel the same way, often hovering behind every step Dahlia made.

"So, Bo, how goes it?"

"Masta Ryland, sir. Goes fine." Bo pushed the gate closed on the garden and looped the hook so it couldn't be nudged open. He'd built the wood-and-mesh gate to keep the rabbits and vermin away.

"We haven't had a chance to chat. My morning rides are always in such a rush. You've done a fine job here." Master Ryland looked around, surveying the handiwork, and extended his hand in greeting.

"Thank ya, masta-sir." Bo brushed the dirt off his hands. This would be the first time he'd ever shaken a white man's hand. The hand was not nearly as soft or feathery as he'd expected.

Firm, weathered, and stronger, Master Ryland's grip wasn't the kind a white man was supposed to have who didn't work all day. The touch turned into a strength of wills. Neither of them knew when to let go.

"Keep up the good work, Bo," Master Ryland finally said, releasing his hand.

"Yessir, will do." Bo didn't let himself breathe until he'd put a good distance between them. Even after that, he listened for Master Ryland to come running up on him. He didn't trust him. He knew the story from Cleo in the house kitchen. Dahlia . . . Miss Lily being torn between two brothers in the Ross house.

The stillness followed him. His chest pushed out in his effort not to show fear. He would have to stay alert even when he was sleeping. Master Ryland had made that trip special, just for him. A handshake for a black man? What did Master Ryland know?

He didn't like feeling afraid. But he was.

"Essie, did you tell anybody about Miss Lily? You know, about what was said in the kitchen?" he asked as they lay on the cot. In the distance, a scream carried in the night air and chilled him to the bone. A woman bringing a child into the world was like no other animal. He'd stood by plenty of times while fillies, calves, piglets, even goats left their mother's wombs. It happened most times with ease. The release of the greasy fawns, then the natural search for a mama's teat.

But a woman howled. She searched for relief, sometimes praying for her own stillness, to be rid of the pain.

Since Bo had been there, Ruby had brought three children to the arms of wailing mamas.

"Since when it so hard to push out a baby?" Essie whispered near his ear, ignoring his question. The cot they shared was no choice of his own.

Whether or not she was mean to him all day, there she'd be at nightfall, right up under his wing.

"Essie, did you tell anybody?"

She squeezed closer. "I pushed out five babies. I ain't ever screamed like that. Bo, I betta tell you something."

"What?" He braced himself. He knew it; she'd told. Master Ryland knew . . .

"I just wanted to tell you, I love you. I'm happy when we together."

"Essie, I need sleep," he said, frustrated. If she wasn't going to answer his question, wasn't any need to keep talking.

"Yeah. When you need something else, don't come looking my way," she said, scowling. Even if he couldn't see the frown, the knit of her brow, he felt it.

The screaming and sobbing went on. There was a paste the womenfolk used at the Vesterville. Papa Sap taught him how to make the foul-smelling concoction. The nasty stuff was what he put on the gal horses to make them hungry for mating. Turns out it worked on real gals too. The baby catchers in the quarters spread the paste thick on the insides and out, making their flower petals push wide and strong during birth. Bo had made a batch as soon as he got the job in the barn. If he wasn't afraid of getting buckshot in his back, he'd run down and get that gal some relief. Being caught outside the quarters after dark meant only one thing: runaway. Bo wasn't sure if the Ross place put out rope traps after dark. If a gun wasn't pointed at you, a rope could haul you up to the sky with one wrong step.

A collective sigh moved through the cabin when the wailing stopped.

"Oh, thank the heaven above," whispered Essie.

Bo closed his eyes, grateful too for the silence.

Come morning, he walked slowly to the barn. He did everything too slow. He yawned in between breathing and fought to keep his eyes open while sweeping the dung out of the stalls.

Roosters squawked in the distance. Morning dew mixed with heat made the hay dust thick in the air. From the corner of his eye he saw something bigger than dust. He turned around but didn't see what was coming.

The slam against his head came with a thud, like the thwack of metal to metal.

Unfortunately, Bo was only a man. He hit the ground facedown.

Later that night, Essie was the one who found him in one of the horse stalls. She whispered his name and shook at his shoulders. Her hands squeezed, pinched, and smacked until she got the results she wanted.

He gasped.

"You alive?" she asked. "You been here all night." Essie yelled over his limp body, "Dover, over here! I found him."

Footsteps scooted close to Bo's head. A shovel kicked out of the way.

Red's voice came as a welcome salve. "Who did this? Bo, can you hear me, Bo?" Red rolled Bo's shoulders so his body had no choice but to follow. He pushed him to sit up. Bo still hadn't opened his eyes.

Pain shook from the back to the front of his head.

"I knew something was wrong. He didn't come for supper," Essie huffed. It took both sets of hands pressing, pushing, and pulling to sit him forward. And still, even then, Bo slumped in the other direction.

"Bo, come on, now. Wake up." Red was a bit more gentle. He didn't pinch and punch like Essie. He touched Bo's chin. "Listen up, here. You got to wake up."

"I'm okay," Bo whispered. He took in a ragged breath. His ears rang. He opened his eyes to prove no one had to slap him out of it, then closed them just as quickly. The air spun too fast. He was a whirling ribbon tied to a windmill. Every time he opened his lids, the spinning started up again. He grabbed at his head for it to stop.

"Who did this?" Essie asked. "I bet it was one of them masters. This 'cause you messing with that Lily gal. I told you this was gon' happen."

Bo couldn't guess who'd hit him. He barely knew where he was.

"Come on. We gotta get him back," Red whispered. "Sun come up and we all ain't on the count, there gon' be trouble."

Bo was in no state to argue. He wanted to tell them to leave him there. It'd be safer if they sneaked back to the quarters the way they came. Dragging him along would only bring attention. The overseer or his son would be on watch.

Red wouldn't have listened anyway. He and Essie each took an arm and hoisted him up.

"I can walk." Bo swallowed the pain with each step. "Watch out for rope traps."

Whoever did this wanted to take Bo down a notch or two. A man wasn't a man until he'd gotten back up. Bo ignored the dizzy whirl. If he kept his eyes wide the whole way, he wouldn't see the spinning. He'd keep his eyes open from now on. Next time he'd see whoever did this coming.

31

Namesake

Murmuring could be heard through the floorboards. From Tilda's tone of apology, I knew the specialist had arrived. I assumed the rumblings back and forth were about his having traveled all this way for nothing. I pressed my face hard against the uneven paneling on the bedroom floor. Nervous heat spread over my neck and down my back. I raised my hair off my shoulders and fanned myself. I hadn't thought about what excuse Ryland would give to his mother for calling off the examination. I didn't care how or what he had to say. No one was coming into this room.

I tested the knob for the hundredth time, it seemed, making sure it was locked. Not that it mattered. But with the high-back chair pushed underneath the brass fixture, I had assurance no one was entering through this door.

The voices moved, then stopped altogether. When they began again, it was through the open window. I peeked out to see Tilda walking alongside a tall, gangly man. They sat in the courtyard only a few feet away. The doctor would stay for tea. Tilda's pitch rose with contentment. She was happy to have a guest, even one whose travel and services she had to pay for.

A knock came, and then a note appeared underneath the door. I went over and picked it up. The scent of Ryland escaped each corner of the paper as I read.

L, You have nothing to fear. I will personally
escort the doctor back to Hampton City.
Ryland

I stared at the note and let the victory sink in. I had Ryland right where I wanted him. Peace of mind felt glorious, though I had no idea how long it would last.

I went to the mantel and checked on the stash I'd put away. It wasn't the safest place. Cleo busied herself dusting there. I'd panicked yesterday after returning to my room when I saw her, back hunched over, where she sat in the corner. I thought she'd found it. When I moved closer, I could see she was holding a book in her lap before she noticed me. She snapped it closed and jumped to her feet as if I were untrustworthy. As if I would tell someone. Reading was against the law for our kind. At the time, I clenched my mouth shut so to not speak. As badly as I wanted to tell her she was welcome to enjoy one of the books, any of the books, I was more angry that she thought so little of me.

She quietly placed the book on the mantel and rushed out the door. We still weren't on good terms. She had avoided me as much as possible since our disagreement over the stack of notes.

As much as I wanted to be in Cleo's grace, I couldn't give up this one thing granting me power over Ryland.

I hoped the dining hour with Tilda and Maggie would be less stressful. I planned to be on my best behavior. If I could smooth Tilda's feathers, all the better. She was only doing what a mother should do, take her child's side. If only we'd all been so lucky as to have someone fighting our battles, protecting us at all times.

I prepared myself in one of the dresses Timothy had given me, not an easy feat without Cleo at my side. She kept her distance. I kept my silence.

I made it downstairs after a second and third change of mind. I joined Tilda and Maggie, coming in the middle of a stilted conversation about how the cold, dry weather was painful to the touch. Their daffodil skin was drying out. I knew better than to interject with a real concern or care. We were dolls sitting around the table at a tea party, not much different. We weren't supposed to be interested in the harvest or crop yield. We were to ignore the cries at night that escaped in the wind and knocked at our door.

But I knew. I'd heard from the kitchen staff that someone named Mabel had a difficult childbirth. That her baby hadn't survived.

I sat with my hands folded over my lap, grateful when Cleo entered carrying the soup tureen. She moved slowly as she ladled steaming potato soup into the flowered bowls. She wouldn't look at me.

"Smells delicious," I said, meant as a compliment to Cleo for her hard work, but it was Tilda who said, "Thank you."

"Wine," Tilda demanded, waiting for Cleo to pour some while she was clearly juggling the soup.

"Yes, ma'am," Cleo said, calmly putting the soup ladle down. She went around pouring wine.

"Hear, hear," Maggie replied as a thank-you. She held up her glass before taking a long swig. She emptied her glass, then held it out again.

Cleo tilted the decanter until the dark Bordeaux reached the rim of Maggie's glass. I thought I saw Cleo fight a smile.

Tilda's shoulders tensed. "That's very expensive. There's no need to pour abundantly," she admonished Cleo.

"We can be sure that it won't go to waste." Maggie's full cheeks were paler than usual. She toasted the air. "Helps me sleep." After a full gulp, she belched, giddy. "There goes my Irish blood showing," she chided herself.

I was glad it wasn't me being the rebel for once. If Maggie was happy, we all should be. We didn't want to put undue strain on her. She wasn't looking well these days. Her skin had a bluish tint, as if she were frightfully cold all the time.

"Oh my," she said. "I wouldn't mind another taste." She used both hands to grip her heavy goblet, extending it for another pour.

"Perhaps you should eat your meal before you have another taste," Tilda said.

"Maggie, have you thought of a name for your little one?" I asked, diverting the attention from her empty glass.

"Oh yes. I have." Maggie beamed. "Henrietta, after my grandmother, if it's a girl. And Bartholomew if it's a boy, after my grandfather." Her shiny gums gleamed with her smile.

"I like the name Henrietta. And Bartholomew, very regal."

Tilda cleared her throat. "Namesakes are so burdensome. Henrietta . . . seems heavy, such a cross to bear. What's wrong with something lighter, happier, like Jane or Mary? How about Elizabeth—you can call her Beth or Lizzy? Those are sweet names, light and joyful. Truly, you don't want a young child saddled with a grandparent's name, do you?"

"Perhaps, if it's a boy, she should name him Mr. Darcy, like in the book I've been reading. It's one of yours, *Pride and Prejudice*." After using the book as a hiding place for the paper notes I'd taken from Ryland, I'd decided to actually delve into the pages. I'd read the entire book, cover to cover, while sequestered in my room.

"I don't like being made fun of. It's obvious you have contempt for me, and I honestly do not understand why."

"What? No . . . I didn't mean to make fun of anyone. I just . . . I'm sorry."

"Some people are so ungrateful," Tilda added tersely.

I cringed when I heard this. I'd heard it many times before and understood the way Annabelle had used it against me. Because I deserved so little, I should be happy for whatever scraps of joy came my way. "You're right. Thank you for your kindness, Tilda. I should be more grateful."

"When have I ever treated you poorly?" Tilda continued, unsatisfied. "I've done nothing but try and help you adjust to your new home while you sulk in your room for days at a time. I'd like to hear examples of how terribly I've treated you. Was my welcoming you into my home, a perfect stranger with no verifiable ties to a single person in this county or the next, lacking? Perhaps it was the beautiful garden I provided for you? Or maybe it was the awful way I've given you my full attention every time you've needed someone to listen to your grief. Pray tell?"

"Tilda, you are perfectly right—"

"Please, let me hear what's lurking in your heart. You're dying to speak honestly. It's only us ladies here. Say what's on your mind." Tilda flattened her hands on the table, ready to get to the bottom of my silent accusations.

"Fine. If it were really the case that we were allowed to say what was on our minds, I'd begin with how many times you've made excuses for Ryland," I said, the words rushing out of my mouth in anger. "Maybe if just once you'd listened to me, you wouldn't have assumed I needed examining or punished me for my sulking. If just once you'd taught your son about respect, he wouldn't have believed it was acceptable to take anything he wanted, including his brother's wife."

Tilda's hand clasped the table linen. "How dare you make these accusations when Ryland is not here to defend himself? Obviously you've had too much wine this evening."

"I haven't had a single drop of wine, Tilda. I'm telling you what's on my mind, as you asked." A soft clearing of the throat drove me to look at Maggie. Her horrified expression, very near tears, snapped me out of my anger. "Maggie, I'm so, so sorry. I didn't mean to . . ."

"We should not be talking about this." Maggie spoke meekly. She'd lost what little warmth the wine had provided to her hands and cheeks and now looked ghostly blank. She put a hand to her forehead. "I'm feeling a headache coming on, I'm afraid."

"Maggie. I shouldn't have said those things. Let me help you to your room so you can lie down."

"Please. I'm fine," she said, attempting to stand.

Cleo had returned to the dining room carrying a covered silver platter. She stopped before reaching the table, staring down. I followed her line of sight to the floor. I watched as a tiny pool of liquid gathered underneath Maggie's seat.

"Oh, Maggie." I rushed to help her.

"Yes, I've made a mess," she said, following that with a hysterical giggle.

"It's too soon," Tilda announced. She went to the other side of the table to see what all the fuss was about. Once she saw the real proof, she was beside herself. "The midwife isn't to arrive for several weeks. Look at me. Are you truly having this child?" she asked, both hands wrapped around Maggie's shoulders.

"We have to get her somewhere comfortable." I took hold of Maggie's limp arm. Her skin was cold and clammy. Tilda attempted to take the other. She was impossible to move, like a heavy damp rug.

Cleo stood still, holding her silver tray full of food. Eventually, she set everything down and took over for Tilda. Maggie moaned as we walked with her. Tilda couldn't stop staring at the spot left on her baroque chair. "Look at this. Cleo, this must be tended to."

"Tilda," I snapped. "We have to get Maggie somewhere to lie down."

"Of course," Tilda said. She waved her arms for us to follow her to the library. "This way."

Cleo summoned the strength, grunting the whole way, to help carry Maggie down the hall. I didn't understand where my strength was coming from either, but I managed to do my part, halfway dragging

Maggie while Tilda led the way. The library was the nearest room. The wing of the house was dark.

Tilda cleared the way, moving small chairs from the path to a long chaise. She then turned. "Wait, no. Here," she said, pointing to the wood floor, the only area with no fabric covering.

"She won't be comfortable there."

"Well, I won't have this chaise ruined like the chair. It's completely ruined. I bought it in France for a great deal of money."

I ignored Tilda. We continued toward the long sofa.

"What're you doing?" Tilda asked, anxiously rolling her hands together.

We sat Maggie down. Cleo lifted her feet and stretched her out. I picked up the pillows and placed a couple behind Maggie's head.

Cleo put a hand over Maggie's forehead. "She's burning up. I should get Ruby. She know all about bringing babies into the world."

"Who is Ruby?" Tilda kept wringing her hands into each other. "We need the midwife. She can't have a child without the midwife."

"Go get her, Cleo. Hurry." I turned to Tilda. "The baby is coming."

"But a slave? I don't want a slave to be the first hands laid on my grandchild."

Maggie chuckled with delirium, which quickly turned to a whimpering moan, then a cry and gasping for air. Her long howl of pain made me feel it just as well. I gripped my stomach. "We don't have a choice." I eased Maggie's legs and feet up in a folded position, ignoring Tilda's woeful grunts about the French brocade on her irreplaceable sofa.

"At least put this under her," Tilda ordered. She held a patchwork quilt in her arms, just as beautiful as any of her French tapestries as far as I was concerned. I understood the immense work put into such a work of art. Quilting meant love, a family, someone who cared enough to stitch each piece together.

"Towels would be better. Rags, cloths, anything," I said.

Tilda remained standing over me. "Use it. It's nothing but a rag. It will at least protect my sofa."

I gently tucked the blanket underneath Maggie's bottom half. I thought about my mother, the one who gave birth to me. The only gift she left, the only memory I had of her, was a quilt, one that I had left behind at the Vesterville. Blocks of bright blues, reds, pinks, and greens, all from scraps of beautiful dresses she'd sewn over time, were used to make a quilt for when I was born.

Maybe this quilt was a blessing, exactly what we all needed to bring Maggie's baby into the world.

"Oh God," Maggie screamed, bearing down.

"I can't believe this is happening. My grandchild is coming. Ryland isn't here. We have no midwife." Tilda paced, finally accepting the inevitable. "We were supposed to have one more month to prepare. This is too soon. This isn't right. Is this Ruby person coming? Does she understand how to birth a white child? We need certain provisions."

"Tilda, please calm down. Children are children. We're . . . we're all born the same. Maggie will be fine." I eased her back to stand near the door. "If you want to be helpful, get the staff to make some hot water. We also need some light."

"Of all the days Ryland has to be gone," Tilda rambled.

She came back from her assigned tasks too quickly, wringing her hands and pacing to and fro. "What if this slave woman doesn't know what she's doing?"

"The baby is coming. I can feel it," Maggie said between howls. "If I die, please name him Henrietta."

"You mean *her*. We can't have a boy called Henrietta, can we?" I smiled and pushed a stray hair away from her face. "You're going to be fine. Next time the pain comes, push. Don't try to hold on. Push and scream all you want."

I'd been present at enough births back at the Vesterville—always a bit squeamish, watching from a distance. Quite different from delivering a baby with my bare hands. In fact, my hands were shaking. I steadied myself, trying to breathe right along with Maggie. I could do this. We could do this.

"We need another blanket. Something to wrap over her. Tilda, can you find a blanket?" I turned to see why Tilda was not responding with her usual rant. She sat with her face buried in her hands.

She stood in place. "Cleo!" she screamed. "Where is she? Cleo, get me a blanket."

"Cleo's gone to get Ruby, remember?" I got up and grabbed Tilda's shaking hands. "Sit with Maggie. I'll go."

I left Tilda at Maggie's side.

I rounded the corner and was halfway up the stairs when I heard Tilda wailing louder than Maggie.

The third door on the left. Down the hall. Turn. I rushed, trying not to think the worst. Another yell of pain sailed up the stairs.

I grabbed as many blankets and towels as I could stack in my arms. I walked carefully, unable to see over the pile. I kept my head barreled sideways. I saw light coming from Tilda's room. Her door usually remained closed. A lamp glowed at her desk. I salivated at the chance of a rare glimpse into her private world, especially when she'd spent so much time trespassing into mine.

The gas lamp flickered gently, illuminating her desk and papers.

This wasn't the time. But I saw a letter opened, splayed underneath the light. I nudged in closer, leaned in and saw it was a telegram. For a few seconds, I thought, hoped, it was a note from Timothy.

I read the first line aloud. "The new President of the Union threatens to end slavery."

I dropped everything in my arms, picked up the paper, and read as much as I could understand, what felt like the most important words. *"Morally end slavery for the decency of the Union."* The words rang like sweet music. I read it again to be sure. Did this mean the misery would end? The telegram had come from Timothy, something Tilda should've shared. Ending slavery was the most important part of the message. I swallowed back the hope. Maggie's painful wail pushed through the walls, shaking me from my revelry. It wasn't time to celebrate just yet. I picked up the towels and linens and rushed out of Tilda's room, worried about Maggie but elated. The possibility of freedom for everyone, especially for Bo, carried me like I'd finally found my wings.

I arrived back in the library out of breath. There were three more ladies in the room, kitchen and house staff, who had wrangled together towels and water. The first quilt had soaked through. Hands worked together, lifting Maggie slightly to push more towels underneath her. She didn't look well. She'd been pale all evening, and now she was shivering uncontrollably.

The woman named Ruby had arrived, commanding everyone to action. "Good. Get those blankets around her shoulders. Somebody turn up the oil. Why's it so dark in here? I need to see what I'm doing." She looked around, taking a survey of all that was required. "I need a needle and some thread in case she gets tore up down there."

"I'll get it," Cleo volunteered.

"What should I do?" I asked the new leader.

"Keep her calm. What's her name?"

"Maggie. Miss Maggie," I said to correct myself, knowing Tilda was watching and listening to everything from where she sat, frightened, in the dark corner.

"Okay. Tell Miss Maggie everything's going to be just fine," Ruby said. "Keep her breathing and talking best you can. You might want to get her a little chug of the heavy stuff. You know white women don't know nothing about a little pain." Ruby chuckled innocently with her explanation, but before she could finish, Tilda appeared like a gust of wind.

Ruby didn't see her coming. The slap landed across Ruby's face, then a second and third, like Tilda was fighting for her life. Ruby put up her hands to defend herself. I pulled Tilda away.

"Did you hear what she said?" Tilda huffed. "How dare you speak that way? You will be dealt with when my sons return." She pressed forward.

I stayed between them.

Ruby rubbed her cheek with narrowed eyes. Tilda looked equally full of disgust and rage. The two women stayed locked in a silent battle. I stood frozen. Ruby spoke that way because she knew about me. She knew, and thought she was among friends, comrades. *We. Us. Them.* She hadn't seen Tilda sitting in the corner, silent with fret over her ridiculous possessions and textiles.

"Ruby's all we have. You can't interfere. Maggie needs her help."

"I will have her whipped and hung from the highest tree," Tilda rasped. "Did you hear what she said, the blasphemy? To defile our name," she blustered. "I'm beyond . . . I'm just . . ."

I touched her arm. "Tilda, she's here to help. Let her help."

"But did you hear what she said? I will have her skinned alive. You will not recognize yourself," she hissed loudly over my shoulder to Ruby.

I swallowed. "Yes. Can we focus on Maggie? We should be praying for the safe delivery of this baby, your grandchild."

Ruby had gone back to helping Maggie. "Push, you can do it," she told her just as gently as she'd started.

I continued to speak calmly to Tilda. "Maggie can hear everything around her. Our disagreement, the stress of our bickering, now this— she can't take much more."

"You're blaming me?" Tilda asked incredulously. "This, all of this, is my fault?"

There was no end. My own anger began to surge. "Why don't you go wait in your room until the birth is over?"

"I will not leave her alone with my grandchild."

My patience had grown short. "I will stay with Maggie. Go wait in your room or in the dining parlor." My hands wanted to shake her. Instead I reached out and hugged her. "Please, Tilda. I will watch over

Maggie." There was the telegram upstairs. There was freedom waiting. I would not let Tilda ruin everything.

She stepped back, albeit hesitantly. "Fine. I want to know the instant the baby arrives. Not one hair on Maggie or this baby's head shall be harmed or so help me."

The room felt calmer the minute she'd left. Ruby got back to work, doing her best to soothe the mother and unborn child. I rushed to Maggie's side and took her hand. "Maggie, I'm here. Only a little longer."

Her eyes barely opened. "I'm so tired," she murmured.

I looked to Ruby, concerned.

"Baby turned sideways," Ruby whispered, still afraid Tilda would jump out of nowhere. "Might take some doing to get it facing the right way. Babies can't come out like that."

Ruby instructed one of the ladies to place a few of the towels in the warm water and then wring them out and place them around Maggie's swollen belly. "Sometimes just the heat alone make a baby want to crawl out of there."

Cleo returned with fresh water and more towels, having missed the Tilda incident. I looked to her, not feeling as confident about Ruby as I had been.

"I'm worried," I told Cleo.

She darted her eyes in the other direction. "Ruby deliver babies all the time. She knows what she's doing."

"But the last baby, Mabel's baby . . ." I blinked. I'd heard about the baby dying in the quarters. Life's ebbs and flows made it down the grapevine, which clearly was how Ruby knew the truth about me. *Us. Them.* Maybe it was Cleo's revenge on me. I'd put her in jeopardy by taking the money from Ryland's room. Or she'd spilled the secret accidentally. Trying to keep a secret was like holding water with both hands. It would eventually leak. It was only a matter of time before everyone knew about the Negro slave girl masquerading as white, living in the big house with her husband and his family. Everyone, including Tilda, would eventually know. It would all make sense for her the moment she found out. *Ah yes, a fraud. I knew something wasn't right about that girl,* she'd say.

I looked past the nervous bustle of women trying to deliver Maggie's baby and considered taking flight. Every minute I sat still, I imagined the plume of truth spreading over the quarters on the Ross land, rolling out like a large, heavy black cloud bursting with rain, spilling my lies. I imagined Tilda sending a telegram to Timothy, telling him his wife was a fraud, an impostor who'd stolen his trust. He must come home immediately to decide what to do with her. My heart fluttered with fear until Maggie's grip squeezed hard. She sounded like a cat suffering in heat.

"I think I can get something that'll help," I announced, already up and moving before Ruby or Cleo could ask questions. I rushed out and headed straight to the quarters to find Bo.

32

Salve

The sun had long set. Bo would be in his cabin. Finding which one was my only problem.

I walked the trail with the lamp swinging in front of me. The cast of light was barely enough, since I'd only gone this way once before, to the stables. The quarters were the other direction from the crossroad.

I needed the salve. Wild raspberry leaves, horse urine, and cow's milk was fermented into a powerful concoction for birthing a mare or calf. I told myself it would work. It had to work, to save Maggie. I practiced under my breath. *"I know you have it, Bo. I swear, I will never ask another thing of you again."*

When I reached the row of cabins, I had no choice but to knock on one door at a time until someone could tell me where Bo was. Knowing the quarters folks knew the truth about me, I wasn't afraid. I was used to both treatments, being either shunned or feared. It didn't matter. All I wanted to do was help Maggie and her baby, and now Ruby. Because as Tilda had said, if harm came to either one of them, Ruby would pay dearly.

Bo knew how to make the salve, and I'd guessed it was the first thing he'd done once he started working with the horses. Breeding livestock was a priceless skill on a big plantation. The more animals roaming the land, the more that land was worth.

I knocked on the first cabin door. It slowly creaked open. I stood still and tried to look as if I had a right to know.

"Where's Bo?" I said.

A hand pushed out and pointed. "Last cabin on the edge." The man I couldn't see slowly closed the door.

I made my way down the dirt path. A door opened for a peek, then closed quickly. I was out of breath again at the last cabin. Voices were heard, then stopped abruptly. I knocked. "I'm looking for Bo," I said to the door barely hanging on hinges. "Please, I need to speak with Bowman Carter."

A young woman not much older than myself pushed the door forward. "Why?" she asked. There was contempt in her eyes. She knew who I was. I knew this look.

"I need to speak with him. Is he in here?"

Shuffled sounds came up behind her. "Dah . . . Miss Lily." Bo blinked hard like the moonlight was in his eyes.

"You don't need to be up." The young woman snapped at Bo like he was a child. "Go lay down."

"Bo, I need the salve," I said quickly before the gatekeeper could pull the door closed. I pulled my shawl around my shoulders to fight off the shivering. I was shaking from fear and exhaustion. But I straightened my stance. "I can't wait, Bo. I need it now," I said, knowing the young woman was close behind, watching and listening.

His large chest and arms expanded, blocking out the woman entirely. He stepped out and held on to the beam of the small landing for support.

"What happened to you?" I asked, reaching out to help him stay straight.

He grabbed his head. "I'm not sure. I woke up with a crack in my head."

"Are you all right?"

"You with child?" he asked, realizing finally what I'd asked for. It was a risk to use the extract made for a big animal on a small woman.

For some, that was precisely the point. Having the baby expelled was far less painful than having the life stolen from her arms once it was born. Sold, and never to be seen again.

"It's not for me. Master Ryland's wife, Miss Maggie, she's not releasing. The baby is twisted inside her," I explained with patience, though I wanted to scream, *I need the salve.* There was no time for reasoning or answers.

He tried to shake his head no. Even the smallest movement made him cringe in pain. He shut his eyes. "Too dangerous, Dah . . . Miss Lily. If something happens to that woman and her child, you the one they gon' blame," he whispered.

"Either way, something's going to happen to the baby or the mother or both. I have to help, Bo. Tell me where it is. I'll get it myself. I don't have much time."

The gatekeeper stepped outside. The moonlight captured enough of her face to show her concern. "Don't you dare," she said. She'd been listening, of course.

"I'll be right back, Essie. It's okay," Bo told her.

"You in no condition to go anywhere."

Bo was already down the porch step. She stayed, watching with disapproval.

I followed behind Bo while he took his time walking to the stable. He moved slowly, as if each step caused him pain.

When we got inside, his strong arms reached the highest plank of a shelf to grab a canning jar. From behind, I saw the raised hill on the back of his head.

"Bo, how'd this happen?" I came closer. This was what had caused him to move so slowly. He'd been hit with something to make the lump and gash on the back of his head.

He turned around and handed me the glass filled with the brown paste. "Don't use too much." His hand kept ahold of the jar. "Papa Sap used to tell me, you got to have something valuable, worth keeping you around for. When you got no worth, you just another mouth to feed, and they bound to sell you. This stuff here is magic but I guess it wasn't enough, 'cause the first thing Master Holt did was put me on the auction block. I hope it saves them and you too. 'Cause if it don't, and something goes wrong . . ."

For a moment, I wanted to tell him about the telegram I'd read in Tilda's room. But talk of freedom would only make him feel sorry for me. I could see it in his eyes. There was pity.

"I'll be careful. I know what it can do. We just need to get that baby out of her. She's not going to make it if she has to keep going on like this."

The distance between him and me grew further as we stood there.

His eyes shimmered with light. He was afraid for me. Seemed I did nothing but bring him grief. He leaned forward and took ahold of my shoulders. He hugged me slow and easy. This moment in his arms ended too soon. I wanted to stay there and be held. "Bo," I stammered.

"Go," he said. "Be careful. Be safe."

I rushed back to the Ross house. Every step, each movement closer made me question if I was doing the right thing. If something happened to Maggie after I used the salve, Tilda would blame me. There was no doubt in my mind. I couldn't very well walk off, disappear as I did in Hampton City. There was no parting train with a young man willing to whisk me away. All my talk of leaving meant nothing. I truly hadn't the first clue as to where I'd go, or how. There was no easy escape.

And there was Bo to think about. Someone had attacked him. No matter what, if I had to leave, he had to come with me.

I hurried back into the library and pushed the jar into Ruby's hand. "It makes the baby come faster."

Ruby refused to touch it, knowing from the putrid smell what I had in my hands. "No, ma'am. That stuff might kill her."

"Just use a little. A tiny amount rubbed on her womb will make it easier to turn the baby around and get the baby out of her. If you don't, they're both going to die, and you know it."

She nervously rubbed her hands down the front of her apron. "If something happens to this lady, they gon' try to kill me, not you. I ain't using your witch magic."

I leaned in close. "Ruby, she can't go on like this much longer. And after what Miss Tilda heard you say, you're going to be blamed anyway. Better to keep her alive."

The voice of reason that could turn the tide was Cleo, but she turned her back and focused her attention on Maggie. She soothed her forehead and neck with the wet cloth. I certainly couldn't blame her for wanting to stay out of this decision. She'd seen for herself, everything I touched brought about havoc. *A mess,* she'd said. Wherever I went, disarray and trouble followed.

If trouble came from taking risks, this was one I was willing to take. Maggie's chest rose and fell in shallow huffs.

"Fine . . . I'll do it myself. I won't let her die." I sat at the edge of the couch between Maggie's open knees, holding the brown paste in my hand.

Cleo spoke up. "Wait. Look at her. She's too weak. If something goes wrong—"

"Then what?" I snapped at Cleo. "The baby can't stay inside her much longer or they'll both die."

Ruby snatched the small jar. "All right, I'll do it. Damn it to hell. If something happens to her, you better speak up for me, ya hear? Both of you," Ruby said, waiting until Cleo and I agreed.

I gave a nod with grateful tears budding. "Hurry."

Cleo shook her head. "What if she still die?" she asked, truly expecting an answer to a perfectly good question. "What then?"

"We can't think about that. We have to get the baby out now." I moved out of Ruby's way to let her work.

After a brief pause, Ruby's hands disappeared between Maggie's thighs. Cleo and I touched hands, both praying silently. The women behind us did the same.

Maggie simply lay still. No more torturous screams. Only murmurs and faint short breaths. At half past the hour, we were inclined to believe the salve had not worked. Perhaps it had lost its potency sitting on Bo's warm shelf.

I paced, looking down at Maggie drenched in her own fluids. Then Maggie screamed, "It's coming. Oh God, it's coming." Her eyes flew wide open. Where she got the last burst of energy would always be a mystery, except that maybe she knew it was the last chance to save her baby. She grunted and pushed while Ruby's hand slid inside to guide the head of the baby.

"You got it. Keep pushing," Ruby ordered. "Keep on, child. Push."

Maggie obeyed. After another long, hard breath, she bore down, and the tiny thing slipped out as easily as if she'd never been stuck. "A girl," Ruby said, before putting her finger in the baby's mouth until she choked and coughed out liquid. Ruby wrapped her small pink body and handed her to me.

The warmth and weight of her released what I'd tried to hold in. Tears. "Cleo, go get Miss Tilda. Tell her she has a beautiful granddaughter down here waiting to meet her."

Ruby hummed proudly while her hands still worked, cutting the cord and pulling out the afterbirth. She worked steadily like a trained master at her craft, no longer doubtful of her standing. When Maggie was clean and wrapped, she leaned in close. "You did good, Miss Maggie. You ready to hold your little one?" The answer didn't come.

Maggie remained still, listless, her mouth hanging open. The will to fight had left her body. I held her child and closed my eyes. Was it that day in the garden, when my hand landed on her stomach? Had I done this? *No, Maggie. Please.*

"Miss Maggie, wake up," Ruby pleaded. She pressed her palms on Maggie's chest, looking for a heartbeat, then leaned into her face to listen for a sound of life. "She dead. Now what?"

Bo slept uneasily most nights, so it took barely a whisper to wake him. This time, voices making plans in the darkness made him open his eyes. A glint of moonlight resting on two women near the tiny cutout of a window showed their heads pressed together, them talking in rushed gaps. Then to make sure no one else was listening, they stopped talking altogether. Bo had already heard the important part. A string of words he knew all too well.

"I'm leaving. Tonight."

"You can't. They gon' find you."

Nobody wanted to leave their people, the only family they'd ever known. It was safer to cling together and weather whatever storm was gathering. Bo sat up. Essie waved him over. He took careful steps with his bare feet. He was still fighting off the spinning circles in his head. When he reached the two women, Essie grabbed his arm and led him outside. The damp night air was welcome compared to the hot, cramped quarters. He already knew there was some recklessness going on, the likes of which he had no plans to be involved in.

Ruby's large eyes welled with glossy tears. She was weary and tired. Last he'd heard, she was up to the big house helping deliver Master Ryland's child. The exhaustion in her eyes said things hadn't gone well. *The salve.*

"What's happening?" Bo asked.

She shook her head, unable to repeat what she and Essie had been whispering about. Essie spoke for her. "She got to leave before Master Ryland get back. His wife dead. Miss Tilda mad and can't wait till Master Ryland get back to have Ruby hung."

"Hung?" Bo repeated.

"The missus think I killed that woman. Purposeful or not, she blame me. Death come with childbirth all the time," Ruby pleaded, as if Bo was the judge and master and could change anything at all. "It's not my fault. If I hadn't used that clay Miss Lily gave me, they both be dead. I helped her best I could and saved the baby. At least I saved the baby."

Now Bo wished he'd stayed in his cot, kept his eyes and ears closed. As soon as he heard "that clay," he knew trouble lay ahead for Dahlia, and then back to him.

"That woman . . . what she really mad at . . ." She shook her head, ashamed. "I said something I shouldn't have said. I thought we was alone, me, Cleo, Miss Lily. Seeing's how she Negro, I thought we was safe. But here come that crazy lady jumping out of the dark like a ghost, smacking me across the mouth, screaming like a banshee. She heard me."

Essie gave Bo a pinch, doing her best to cause harm, but her fingers were too numb from picking harvest all day, with not enough strength left to do anything but fuss. "See, look now, she got Ruby running. I knew she was bad news. I told you."

"Where you running to, Ruby?" Bo asked, already knowing she didn't have an answer. "There's nowhere to go."

Ruby's round eyes grew big and frightened. "You think I'ma stay here and wait to die? I rather go out there and starve to death than have them do God knows what to me."

There were stories. Even if a runner never came back, never got caught, no one really knew if they'd survived. There was the one thing heard over and again, how if a slave was caught, the lesson was more severe than if they'd stayed in the first place. Cutting off one limb where they'd never be able to walk, let alone run off again. There was no limit of creative ways to torture a child of God. Fear was crippling enough.

"Slave hunters. They'll do worse to you than Master Ryland," Essie said.

"I'ma take my chances. I'm more worried about his mama than him. That woman likely to slit my throat herself she so mad."

Essie threw her arms around Ruby's soft shoulders. "I'm so sorry. You don't deserve this."

"Wait. Listen. We should talk to Red," Bo said, trying to buy some time. He knew how harsh it was outside the gates.

"Dover can't help me," Ruby said. "Nobody can help me." She took ahold of Essie's hands. "I'ma be fine. I already feel the air carrying me right out of here, freedom making me light as a feather."

Essie shook her head, not believing a word of Ruby's faith and big talk. She handed Ruby the food she'd saved for her children. Ruby took the canteen and satchel. She backed away one step at a time before rushing into the darkness till they couldn't see her anymore.

"She gon' die out there." Essie shifted her attention to Bo, looking up at him with some kind of measuring in her eyes. "Guess there's nothing left to do but pray for her now."

"Wait." Bo reached out and stopped her before she could go back inside. "What Ruby say in front of the lady—what come of it?"

"It would serve her right if everybody knew the truth about her," Essie barked before going back inside the cabin. Even Essie had to duck a bit to get inside the quarters. The entry reminded Bo of a raccoon hole. Just the thought of stepping through into the black hole made his throat thick, him hardly able to breathe. Maybe Ruby had the right idea, to just leave, find freedom, even if it meant she died trying.

He awakened at dawn, wishing the talk of Ruby running was all a dream. But seeing the cot empty where she would normally be, wrapped head to toe in her rough burlap blanket to protect herself from the mosquitos at night, made him realize it was real. She was gone. He hoped she had made it as far as the trees, where it was easy to slip into the richness of the groves. No one would be looking for her till late morning, after they counted heads. He closed his eyes again. "Please keep her safe," he whispered.

Bodies began to stir with the rising sun. He could guess Essie wouldn't be bringing him a fried egg this morning. They'd come so far in their strange union. He agreed to just about everything she asked and she fed and nourished him as reward. Now Essie was back to being angry. He knew because she hadn't slept next to him.

He wanted to tell Essie this wasn't his fault in the first place. And maybe if she hadn't started all that trouble in the kitchen, Dahlia's secret would've been locked away. No one would've been talking to "Miss Lily" like that. Ruby wouldn't have been thinking she was among her kinfolk where she could speak freely.

Whether he pointed out Essie's part in all this or not, she was going to blame him. The salve or Ruby's loose lips; either way, she'd lost her friend. Though half the time they acted like they couldn't stand each other. *Friend* wasn't enough. She'd lost her sister. Bo understood. He was worried about Ruby too. Just as much, he worried for Dahlia's safety. He could only guess what Ruby had said in front of the mistress of the house. Essie wouldn't tell him. He'd have to make his way to the garden and see if Dahlia had the same calling to meet him there.

He hoped the lady of the house was too busy thinking about her new grandbaby to worry about secrets. He feared those mistresses of the house more than those masters. They were a sneaky bunch. You wouldn't see them coming like the masters and overseers. Dahlia would be so busy trying to blend in and smooth feathers, she'd be blindsided.

Essie passed Bo on her way to the outhouse, leading two of her boys by their shoulders. When they tried to speak to him, she shoved their heads in the other direction. Bo went about his morning. He struggled to do menial things. Filling the buckets and carrying them up the hill to the stable took twice as long. Pouring the water into the metal troughs left him panting. He had two more trips to make before each one was filled. He moved as fast as he could, hoping to get over to the garden and catch Dahlia there. With everything that had gone on in the night, he guessed she'd want to talk. But it would be him doing the talking.

If her offer was still alive and well, he was willing to leave, he'd go. All they needed was a firm plan. It wasn't safe to stay anymore, not for Dahlia, and not for him if the Ross family found out where the salve came from.

After the troughs were filled, he began the ritual of leading the horses out. While they got a cool drink, he cleaned out their stalls.

He stopped. He wouldn't be sneaked up on again. "Hey, who's there?" He listened for where the noise was coming from while taking a firm grip on the pitchfork.

"Anybody there?" he asked, though it sounded like an animal.

Not likely a polecat would answer, or a fox for that matter, which were the only things he could think small enough to slip under the wall slats.

He used both hands and aimed the fork at the corner, toward the sound. Before he took a healthy stab, he heard another moan, the human kind. He thought it could be Dahlia, and fear caught in his throat. He dropped the shed tool and crawled low on his knees, peering into the dark space.

He saw legs sprawled out. "Ruby?"

Her head tilted forward, eyes shut. "Hey there, Bo," she said like it was a mellow Sunday morning.

He touched her face and attempted to lift her head.

"Copperhead bit me right there on the ankle." She coughed. "I snatched his neck, yanked him off. Hurts. Gee-zus, it hurts."

He saw the swelling, the black and blue punctures in her skin. The snake had got her good.

He hurried out, scooped some of the water he'd just poured for the horses into the bucket. He rushed back, went down on his knees, and crawled into the small space with Ruby.

"Drink." Bo held the water to her mouth. She sipped but dribbled most of it down her chin. He used what was left to pour over her wound.

"Best to leave me here to die. No sense in getting yo'self in trouble too."

"If you was gon' die, you already be dead." He pulled at the hem of her dress until a thin strip tore apart. He wrapped her leg tight, ignoring her groans of pain. "We'll get you to the quarters."

"No. I can't go back there, Bo."

"Ruby, you can't stay here. You need somebody to look after you." He let out a long sigh. "I told you this was a bad idea. At least in the quarters, nobody can accuse you of running away."

Ruby's big eyes weren't so big anymore, all puffy and nearly closed like she'd been in a fight. "I'm scared, Bo."

"Me too. Been scared all my life. Makes you tired." He lifted her with a full grunt and carried her. She cried the whole way, part tears from pain and part from fear. Nothing he understood more.

He got Ruby safely to the quarters. She needed rest and water. That would keep her well enough until the women came back and forced some broth down her throat. Bo stood and stretched from having carried the weight of Ruby on one side of his body. He jumped, startled when he heard the squeak of the door pushing open. It was the overseer's son, probably sent to look for Ruby after the count.

"Morning, sir," Bo said, taking a moment to nod for respect.

"You forget where you s'posed to be?" He looked past Bo to Ruby shivering in her cot. "What's wrong with her?"

"A snakebite. Been making sure she don't go into shock or nothing."

The young overseer barely looked in Ruby's direction. "Come with me."

Bo followed, grateful the overseer wasn't thinking about Ruby, at least not yet. They walked at a steady pace toward the mansion. Bo had plans of his own to get to the garden early as possible. He certainly didn't need an escort. But then after a while, they took a new direction.

That's when Bo got scared. He'd never been on this side of the property, the outer edge where grassy hills ran far past where the sun went down. The good green land spanned as far as his eye could see. Looked like land that could be used for more crops if you asked Bo. He always saw a use for things no matter how big or small.

"Right here," the overseer said, handing him a shovel. "Dig a deep hole about yea wide and this long," he said, measuring himself with his arms.

Bo got the hint. Somebody was being buried, and it wasn't someone from the quarters. They surely weren't offered a hilly green side of the meadow as a final resting place. And then for a quick second he thought, *Dear God, not Dahlia.*

"Make it neat. Keep the dirt in one pile. They want Miss Maggie put in the ground today, so work fast."

Of course. It was for the lady who'd died having her baby, rest her soul. Bo started digging, hitting the dense clay, relieved and saddened at the same time. This wouldn't be the day he spoke to Dahlia about leaving. He'd be digging till sundown.

PART III

33

Lizzy

Tilda tried to wait until Ryland and Timothy returned before burying Maggie. She wanted a proper memorial with family by her side. Ryland had not returned from Hampton City. Timothy, on the other hand, could've remained gone for weeks.

With the smell of Maggie's blanketed body moving throughout the house, Tilda relented and said it was time for the burial.

I wore a dark dress with every suffocating button closed past my neck and a hat with mesh covering my face. I waved a lace fan back and forth to no avail. After we stood for a quiet moment, I placed a bouquet of wildflowers on the high mound of dirt. I said a prayer, along with a silent apology.

Not because of the salve, or pouring her too much wine, or the disruption of bickering with Tilda at supper. No. I was convinced it was my rage toward Ryland. The power released with the touch of my hand that day in the garden. I'd caused this.

"Bless her, O Lord, in heaven, as you have done on earth." Tilda placed her flowers next to mine. Her face was unreadable except for the blinking of her misty eyes. "We should get back. Looks like it may rain," was all she said afterward.

Despite our differences, we walked back arm in arm, holding each other in silence. Tilda must've felt guilty too for the way she'd handled Maggie's last hours. Her tears flowed. Mine had come in the night, enough to fill a river. Now I had no more tears to give. I only wanted to do right by Maggie's little girl. I had very little faith that Ryland would be a doting father. Tilda would be a distant grandmother from across the table at teatime.

I understood what it was like to be raised as an orphan, to only be cared for and not truly loved. I didn't want that to happen to her.

The sky darkened before we reached the pathway leading to the house. The thunder and lightning were a welcome change. The spring days had made it difficult to breathe and sleep at nightfall. We reached the back entrance. Once inside, Tilda and I separated, wordless and tense, our hostility toward each other reignited with the slam of the door. We were back to the way things were.

Cleo was slowly moving her mop back and forth in the library where she'd been cleaning for days behind the childbirth, emptying buckets of red and filling them with clear water. She leaned over to squeeze out the excess and started again.

I tossed the hat Tilda had given me to wear to the side table. I used the white floral pitcher and poured a cup of water in an agitated state. I started to offer Cleo my help, then stopped myself. I'd made enough trouble for everyone. I turned and went up the stairs. I could feel Cleo watching from the hall.

I pushed open the door to the nursery. I eased into the room slowly and moved with delicate steps so as not to disturb the baby's feeding time. I'd set up the bassinet using blankets I'd found in the storage room, along with folded cloths Cleo had cut and made into the baby's nappies. Tilda had been in no condition to make arrangements for the new baby.

The first wet nurse assigned was Mabel from the quarters, who'd lost her own baby days earlier. Having milk ready to give, she was chosen immediately, but her sadness prevented the letdown. She couldn't feed another woman's child. Her body wouldn't allow it.

Another young woman showed up a day later. I remembered her as *the gatekeeper* attempting to block me from seeing Bo at the quarters the night I'd come for the salve.

Now her animosity toward me had intensified. What had I expected? I was the mistress and she was the wet nurse who'd been summoned away from her own children. When she arrived to replace Mabel, I introduced myself.

"Hello, my name is Miss Lily. I don't believe we were properly introduced."

She frowned and narrowed her eyes. She knew the truth about me, the same as Ruby. I had to make her understand that treating me any way other than the mistress of the house was dangerous, for both of us.

"Essie," she answered, not bothering to offer anything more. There'd been three others lined up in front of the big house after Mabel was dismissed. All three, filled with fresh new milk, could've done the wet nursing just fine. But it was Essie who was chosen, whose name Cleo called out as if it were some kind of honor.

"I don't care nothing about being in the big house with these folks. My little James still need me. He still nursing. I can't be here nursing somebody else's child," Essie had nearly yelled at Cleo.

I listened to their exchange, waiting for some kind of hint as to what was going on at the quarters. I was eavesdropping for answers about Ruby. Since Cleo refused to linger anywhere close to me, I was barred from the grapevine, no longer privy to the community that wasn't my own. And that day, Essie had nothing else to add except to wish she hadn't been chosen to serve *these folks*.

Too late. I remembered Ryland saying the very same to me, *too late*, when I'd arrived at their doorstep. No turning back now. Life was set in motion. Maggie was gone and the baby needed feeding, with fate having brought us together.

"I'll keep her for a bit," I said, holding out my arms for the baby. "I'll keep her while you go to your own children, Essie." I said her name in hopes she'd feel appreciated, but her face remained full of disdain.

"Thank you, but I'm fine." She pulled the sleeping child's mouth away from suckling. She closed her cotton blouse over her breast and buttoned the top, then got up and bounced the baby gently in her arms. She made an effort to look engaged, but her mind was certainly elsewhere.

"You have a boy still nursing, correct? James? You can go, be with him. I won't tell. If anyone comes, I'll cover for you," I repeated, unsure of my tone. I wasn't trying to sound demanding or give orders. I wanted her to trust me.

"Will you, now?" she questioned, looking me directly in the eye. This clear sign of disregard was the exact thing I was afraid of. If Tilda saw her even glance in my direction this way, someone would pay.

"Essie, you can trust me."

"Like Ruby," she huffed and turned her narrow back against me. "I'll be just fine." Her voice echoed off the wall.

"I will cover for you, Essie. Go see your son." Her stomach was raised underneath her skirt. From the looks of things, she'd recently given birth, or there might've been another on the way.

Essie wavered, facing me. "What if she get cranky?"

"I'll keep her content." I came to her side, eased the swaddled child from her arms, and took her into mine. "It'll be all right."

It took a moment before she fully dropped her guard. "Okay. She fed already. Just keep her warm."

"I will." I held my breath, waiting for her to move toward the door. Instead she rushed to the large armoire, opened it, and gathered a handful of biscuits she'd collected from the morning tray. She left, but I heard her stop at the top of the stairs, checking to make sure no one would see her, then taking each step softly down the rest of the way.

Once Essie was gone, I pressed my lips lightly to the baby's soft cheek and smoothed a hand over the barely visible tuft of hair on her head. I hummed, then sang, "Oh sweet Henrietta, do not cry for me." I sang softly, replacing the name with the one her mother had wanted, though Tilda had made it clear her name was Elizabeth, Lizzy for short. Maggie's wishes were an afterthought.

I sat in the white seat with painted flowers and began rocking gently. I owed Maggie the decency of protecting her child. For the first few hours after her birth, I wondered if the baby was next, watching over her to make sure she was still breathing. When I could no longer keep my eyes open, I asked Cleo to take over. We would protect her in shifts.

Turns out the little one was strong. She stirred and stretched her tiny limbs, opening her mouth wide with a yawn. I had no right taking joyful pride in caring for another woman's child when I'd had a hand in her death. Yet I relished the baby's warmth close to my heart. I inhaled her. I closed my eyes to hear better her tiny breaths.

"Yes, my sweet, I will protect you." This must've been what motherhood felt like, what I feared the most—loving someone so much I'd forget about the greater plan, getting away from here.

"Well, isn't this a sight." Ryland stood at the door of the nursery, his face weathered from the ride.

He came closer to where I sat in the rocking chair. I held the baby a bit tighter, then put my finger to my lips to indicate she was sleeping.

Ryland still wore his riding gloves. He reached to pull the blanket back for a closer inspection. "Can I hold her?" he asked, as if he didn't have a right to hold his own daughter. He pulled off his gloves. What looked like emotion welled in his watering eyes.

I rose with the child close in my arms. I motioned for him to take the seat.

"You don't have to get up," he said.

"It's okay. She likes the chair, the rocking motion. Sit." The baby's little hands stayed balled near her face, the way she slept in between feedings. She arched her back but remained asleep.

After a shaking breath, he calmed enough to sit down. Admiration swept over his face, and there it was again, the slight budding of tears. I forced myself to look away, taking in his boots, the clay dirt on the cuffs of his pant legs.

"I never held a baby before." He rocked back and forth, his weight making the chair creak every time he leaned back. He stopped, sensing the noise might wake the baby—or worse, that he'd break the antique chair. "I should've been here when she was born. Maggie might still be alive had I been here," he said, as if he could've changed the course of events at his whim. He kept his gaze on his daughter. "Mum tells me you helped bring her into the world." A long inhale followed, then he let out another shaky sigh. "Thank you."

For a second, I had to fight off the urge to laugh. His sincerity was bordering on ludicrous. I wanted to believe he had a gentle, caring side, and yet feared having any compassion would make me look silly and gullible.

He'd made me touch Maggie's stomach, hadn't he?

"Yes. It was a difficult birth." I took a step back. "I'll let you stay with . . . Lizzy." I had to force myself to say *Lizzy* if I wanted to keep peace with Tilda.

"No. Please stay." His lowly demeanor continued to be out of character, the way he persisted in staring at his daughter with genuine gratitude as if he knew she was the only thing good he'd ever done. "Mum says the woman brought from the quarters to take care of Maggie failed and may be responsible for her death. You were there, is this true?"

"If she'd failed, you wouldn't have a daughter to hold right now. Maggie wasn't well. We all did everything we could for her." As I stood in front of him, I felt light-headed remembering Maggie's difficulty, the blood, her screams, hearing her wails of suffering one minute, then touching her limp wrists the next. I moved to the chair near the window. A slight breeze gave me a chance to recuperate.

I knew the story Tilda had already told. I needed to tell him what had really happened. "When Maggie came to supper, her energy was low. She drank wine. She barely ate. Not long after, her water broke, and she could barely keep her head up. We carried her to the study. Ruby was called from the quarters. She's had experience delivering babies. Lizzy was turned, twisted sideways. Ruby did everything she could as quickly as possible.

"Maggie lost what was left of her fight. Her heart gave out," I said to him, as much as for myself to understand.

He still wouldn't look up.

"Ruby saved your daughter's life."

He appeared to not hear what I was saying. "I can't believe I have a child, a daughter."

"Yes, you have a beautiful daughter. She doesn't need the shame or guilt for one more loss of life. She is the goodness of you and Maggie."

I finally saw a glimpse of understanding. *Please don't harm Ruby.* The glistening in his eyes released. He wiped the tear away with the back of his hand. "Take her. I have to deal with Mum."

I moved swiftly to take Lizzy, relieved to have her warmth back in my arms. Ryland remained in front of me. He kissed the baby's forehead. Briefly, we caught each other's eyes.

"I will take care of her," I said, as close to a promise as I'd ever come.

"Thank you." He nodded.

34

Tea Cakes

"Hey, there." Essie popped up out of nowhere. Bo was jumpy at the littlest noise since he'd been clocked over the head with his own shovel. The shovel he found with his blood on it. He'd wanted to say something about the baby she was carrying, coming along six months or so from the looks of it, but knew it wouldn't end well. For now, he wanted to get through his days without anybody being clobbered, bit, or dead.

He gave Berth a pat as if she'd been the one in need of calming. Her shiny dark eyes questioned the interruption. "There, there, girl." Bo continued to stroke the horse, ignoring Essie.

"Brought you something." Essie put out a closed fist and waited for him to take the bait. When he didn't, she opened her palm to reveal a small biscuit, flat and dry.

Bo turned up his nose. "Looks like something Berth would like. Huh, girl? Want a smashed biscuit?"

"Just taste it," Essie said, smiling with full cheeks and bright eyes. "It's a tea cake. That's what they eating up there—breads, cakes, anything sweet."

"Guess that's what you been eating too," he said quietly, posing a question without a question. His eyes fell to her belly. It was time to talk about it. She'd plumped up since taking on wet nurse duties. Eating and nursing. Her cheeks had rounded. Her breasts were nearly bursting through her buttoned top.

"Oh, Bo, now you knew this was gonna happen. Didn't yo' mama teach you about mating? Just like these animals of yours." She rubbed in a full-circle motion. "I hope it's a girl. I already got five boys. A girl would be nice. But then, who'd want to bring a girl into a land where she gets poked and prodded with no say?"

"We all got that problem," he said, taking a bite of the tea cake, unable to taste the sweetness she'd promised. "Thank you." He gave the rest to Berth, which she licked out of his hand.

"You're welcome." Essie wrapped her arms around him from behind. "I got some time . . . I mean if we hurry," she whispered.

Bo looked around, over his shoulder. "Not a good idea, Essie. It's broad daylight."

She nodded toward the stable. "We done it there before." Her hands rummaged around his belt, expertly pulling the buckle loose without the need of sight. He was proud of his belt and didn't particularly want anyone else touching it. He grabbed her hand.

"It's still dangerous. Somebody might come this time of the day."

She turned Bo to face her. Her strength still surprised him. She put her arms around his neck and planted a firm kiss on his mouth. "I want you, Bo. Don't you want me back?"

"Essie, I'm saying, not here. Ain't you supposed to be watching the baby up at the big house?" He'd missed her cooking the last few days but not her unpredictability. Her mood swings had landed on his head with a punch or smack or two. Even now he could see she was only seconds away from exploding into meanness.

Her cheeks began to burn red. Her coal-black eyes watered slowly, looking up at him. "I bet if I was your precious Miss Lily, you'd be all over me right now." She shoved him in the chest, pushing him against the firm body of Berth, triggering a high step from the horse and a snort of her nose.

"It's okay, girl." Bo turned and gave her muscular neckline a soft rub. "This one's got a filly growing inside her. Master Ryland will have my head if anything happens to her. You okay, girl?" He stroked her some more, determined to avoid Essie's peering eyes.

"I hope you know she ain't nothing better than me. She just a Negro whore pretending to be a white woman."

"Essie, why you keep bringing up Miss Lily? She ain't got nothing to do with us. Let it go, all right? This is not the time." Bo faced her and could see this was something she planned to get off her chest. She had plenty more to say.

"I know you think she's some grand dame. She ain't no better than me, none of us."

"Stop it, Essie." Bo's chest burned heavy.

She folded her arms over her chest, ready for battle. She wanted him to say something. He knew better than to show any interest. He kept quiet. "You care so much about her . . . well, guess what? You better do right by me, or I swear I'll tell Miss Tilda. After what she done to Ruby, I'll tell anybody who'll listen what she is and what she ain't."

He was tired of her waving threats over him. Just about then the ache in his head started again. The pounding came and shook him hard. "Essie. Just stop."

"You stop!" she screamed. "You stop acting like you don't care nothing about me. We having a baby, Bo. Me and you. Don't you care?"

"I do care. I swear, I do," Bo said, putting out a gentle hand to touch her cheek, trying his best to find the goodness, or whatever had drawn him in in the first place. Now he listened for the mating call, wishing for those nights when he closed his eyes, engulfed in her warmth, seeking what little hope he could find in her arms, the good times he liked to remember. This other side mostly scared him.

"No. You don't care. She all you want to think about. You think they won't listen to me? Miss Tilda don't like her much anyway. She'll be happy to hear what I got to say 'cause what happened to Ruby and Miss Maggie is all her fault."

This was what their time together had come to, threats against Dahlia. Around the same time as he was imagining how to get away from her talking, she threw her arms around him.

"I'm sorry, Bo. I don't know why I get like this. I can't help it sometimes. You make me mad as a wild fox in a henhouse." She forced a pleasant smile.

His dry mouth couldn't find any words. She reared back to get a direct view of his emotions. He swallowed hard, forcing a wave of moisture to coat his tongue. *She's waiting. Not much time before she takes back all her sorry and turns mean again. Say something . . . nice.*

"Essie, we are important to each other. No one else matters," he blurted.

She beamed with acceptance but wanted more.

"I don't want nothing bad to happen to neither of us. Doing dangerous things puts us both at risk. If you tell on Miss Lily, I'll be in trouble too." He could feel himself reaching deep down, searching his soul, scrambling around like he'd just found a bag of new tricks.

Now the words came easy. "You and me, one day, we gon' have our own house on our own land, a place to raise our babies," he said. Is this what he'd come to? Being nothing but a liar, making up a life, storytelling, just like Dahlia? He gave Essie a pat, no different from how he cared for Berth and the other horses. Then he quickly remembered a full embrace was much better. *Pats are for horses,* he told himself. "Essie, we'll be all right. Next time you come, I'll figure out a safe place for us to be alone together."

"Oh, Bo, you're right." All her heat and prickly thorns were clipped down to the nub. She nodded approval, still holding on to him. "I'm so happy. I'll come back tomorrow when we can spend more time together."

"All right, then." He gently unwrapped her arms from his torso. "You go be with your littlest one." Bo wondered why she had so much time on her hands lately, with her duties for the newborn in the mansion.

"I'll be here tomorrow. I have plenty of time to do whatever I want."

"How?" He couldn't help it. He figured he had a small chance to ask while she was regretful. "How you got so much free time?"

She turned her eyes sideways toward him in a scorched-earth kind of way. "What does it matter? Why you keep asking me *why?* I said I could be here tomorrow. You don't want me to come, is that it?"

"Nah, it's just that I don't want you losing your house position, not over tending to me. You wouldn't get all those fancy breads, and Lord knows you don't want to be back on that crop line."

Essie blinked a rare moment of understanding. "Yep, you right about that."

"So, is there something you want to tell me? You know you can trust me. Something going on in the big house? Why you got all this time to yourself?"

She looked down for a moment and rubbed her belly. "Miss Lily obsessed with that baby."

Had he known it was that easy, he would've said all the right things earlier. "Obsessed?"

"Full up. Ain't nothing else on her mind. She can't help herself. Your Miss Lily needs to always be holding that baby. Guess she can't have none of her own. So I get time for myself," she answered with a pleasant tone.

Full up . . . with the baby. Bo was somewhat relieved. He'd thought she was in some kind of danger.

"So, tomorrow then?" Essie asked with the sweetness of a new kitty. She'd found a sudden interest in the ground, watching the hem of her skirt sweeping the dirt as she swayed side to side.

"Tomorrow. Yeah. Be here late morning, after Master Ryland gone on his ride." Bo couldn't very well say no. He didn't know if Master Ryland was coming or not. He hadn't shown up in a long day or two. But Essie would keep coming back. What could he do? What would he say or do to stop Essie from becoming *full up* with him? He'd have to figure it out. It couldn't become a ritual, her showing up.

Master Ryland could've been coming over that ridge anytime. Not that owners minded when slaves coupled up. Meant more property for them, no different from breeding horses. A fresh crop of new babies to grow up and put to work or sell for a profit. That was fine, but the coupling had to be done on the slave's own time.

And besides, anybody could see, Essie was already showing with child. Masters or overseers wouldn't be too pleased if he and Essie were caught coupling for the pleasure of it.

Bo dropped his head in relief once she was gone, resting against Berth's thick rib cage. The horse sputtered and gave her silky mane a shake, not willing to be leaned on. She had her own problems. Bo picked up the brush out of the bucket and began to wash her down. He swallowed hard, trying to push away the disgust he felt for being two-faced with Essie. He wished he felt the way Essie wanted him to instead of having to lie, pretending just to keep her calm and quiet. Soothing her with strokes, no different than brushing on Berth here, so she wouldn't ruin Dahlia's world completely.

"Everything's going to be all right, girl. We don't always get to choose our kin. Sometimes we got to go along to get along," he told Berth. Yet he didn't mean it. More double-talk. The more he lied to himself, the less he was sure about anything.

35

Persuasion

Silent tension blanketed the mansion by the time Essie returned from her visit to the quarters. I looked up to see her out of breath.

"Whew. My little James nearly took every bit of life out of me. He hadn't eaten all day." Essie plopped down on the cot where she slept beside the bassinet. "Being here in the big house might not be too bad after all. I can stay here all day, escape the harvesting time, then see my babies with fresh rolls in the evenings." She cut her eyes to me. "You all right with that?" she asked, as if we'd made some kind of arrangement I wasn't aware of.

"I . . . I'm not sure."

"My boys liked those fancy breads." She was still out of breath from rushing back. Her stilted tone had greatly softened from earlier. It was something different now. Frustration had been replaced with opportunity.

"I'm sure we can work something out." I remained in the rocking chair, holding the baby. She'd grown restless, hungry, and tired all at the same time. Essie's arrival was perfect timing. "She's ready for her feeding."

"I can't feed her. I told you I got nothing left. It's gon' take me a minute," she said, struggling to rise from the too-low position of her cot. It took a minute, but she came forward with open arms. "Here, give her to me. You been holding her the whole time?" she asked. "She ain't gon' break if you put her down."

"It's all right, really. I enjoy holding her. I'll wait till you're ready to nurse."

I wanted to ask about Ruby but didn't want to tread in dangerous territory and ruin Essie's good mood.

"Holding her'll help bring the milk down." She held out her arms, waiting for the passing of the child.

There was a light knock at the door before Cleo's bright yellow head covering made an appearance. "Miss Lily, Miss Tilda wants to see you. She's waiting on the veranda out front."

"Thank you, Cleo. Let her know I'll be there soon."

"I think you best come now." Cleo stepped inside and closed the door. She sidled next to me, nearly on her knees. Her crisp white apron smelled of laundry and cornstarch. "They got Ruby down there," she whispered. "Asking her questions. She ain't told about the salve, but I don't know how much longer she can keep quiet. She in a bad way."

Essie squeezed in closer to get in the mix. "What's happening?" She lowered Lizzy on one hip, clearly paying no attention to how she held her.

"They got Ruby down there," Cleo told her. "Miss Tilda trying to get her to confess to doing something bad to Miss Maggie."

"Why can't they leave her be?" Essie snapped. "Bad enough she was bit by a snake and nearly died. She can hardly see straight."

"Bit by a snake?"

"Yeah, you wouldn't know nothing about that." Essie paced, holding the child. She walked to the window and peered over the open edge. "I swear, if they do something to Ruby—" She looked down at the baby.

"Give her to me," I said. The way Essie was talking scared me. "I'll take her with me."

"Why we gotta be whipped and treated like animals? Do we look like animals? Do we?" she asked, waiting for a real answer. She held on to the swathed baby. "You supposed to be one of them, why they treat us this way?"

Cleo grabbed Essie, pulling her away from the window with both hands. She lowered her voice to a steady, soothing whisper. "They might hear you. Things are already bad for Ruby. It could be me next, or any one of us. Give me the baby," she ordered.

Essie handed the baby over to Cleo. "Why can't they just leave us alone? None of us done nothing to nobody. We do what they ask. I left my own babies to be here to take care of they child. No sacrifice is enough? I don't understand why they can't leave us alone." She sat down in the rocking chair.

"Everything is going to be all right, Essie. Miss Lily is going to fix everything."

"Ruby saved that baby's life. I know she didn't mean nobody no harm. You the one gave her that voodoo clay. You gon' tell 'em 'bout that while you fixing everythang?" Essie mocked, rolling her eyes.

Cleo was tired of playing nice. She yanked Essie's collar. "You calm down. You hear? We got no time for this." She turned to me. "I'll stay with Essie. Just go. We'll be fine."

I was hesitant about leaving. I took a moment to gather myself. "All right, I'm going to talk to Miss Tilda. I'll straighten this all out."

"Oh yeah? We'll see about that," Essie chirped as the door closed behind me.

I went slowly down the hall, waiting to see if any sounds close to tragic came from the room. Not until I was sure Cleo had full control of Essie and the situation did I head toward the stairs. The oak banister held me steady as my mind rambled. Ryland and I had an understanding. It was Miss Tilda I'd be speaking to this time, my personal testimony in a trial for which she was the judge and jury.

I slowed, stopping at the bottom of the last curved stair, meditating on Essie's question. *You the one gave her that voodoo clay. You gon' tell 'em 'bout that?*

The clouds had parted, allowing the sun to make a full appearance before it disappeared over the ridge. The highly polished floors reflected a dagger of light, making me squint as I approached the open doors to the veranda. This was where Tilda was perched during most days. A cool breeze found its way to this side of the property in the late afternoon.

When I adjusted to the light, a shadowy figure came into focus. Outside, Ruby was standing unsteadily. Her eyes were swollen, barely open. Beside her was the overseer, a scruffily dressed man using one arm to effortlessly keep her from toppling over. The man's face was sun worn, dark and leathery. His tattered hat covered a mesh of reddish hair coated with a week's worth of grime and sweat. When Ruby leaned too far, the man gave her a good yank. She did her best to stay upright, at least for a while.

Tilda's shrill voice sent a jolt through me. "For goodness' sake, why can't she stand?"

Ruby's ankle was wrapped with a strip of fabric from the hem of her dress. She hopped lightly each time she forgot and leaned on the wrong leg.

"She got a snakebite," the overseer responded. "She all right."

I forced myself to make the seemingly ever-growing distance to the door. What if Ruby had already told them about the salve? Or worse, what if she'd told Tilda the truth about me? She had nothing to lose at this point. No matter what, I couldn't let her take the blame.

Tilda sat on a chair, holding her bifocals between two fingers as if she were only taking a break between chapters of the book on her lap rather than taking stock of a woman's fate of life or death.

Ryland leaned against the rail in the farthest corner of the veranda. He puffed on a cigar, then addressed me when I made my appearance. "This is the woman who delivered my child?" he asked, hollow and empty, hardly the man I'd felt sorry for earlier.

"Yes. This is Ruby. She did a fine job as the midwife." I didn't look in Ruby's direction, hoping to not incite any emotions in her. Emotions meant losing control, saying the wrong thing.

Tilda scoffed. Her chin pushed toward me. "May I remind you, Maggie is no longer with us because of this ungrateful thing."

I turned to Ryland, only to see his back. He faced the distance of the land as if bored in the moment. A puff of smoke left his breath from his cigar. I turned to Tilda. "She did everything she could. You knew it was a difficult delivery. The baby was turned sideways. Eventually, Ruby turned her about. Maggie had lost too much of herself by then." I'd said it enough times in my head. Now it felt practiced and unemotional even though it was true.

Ruby moaned with her head down, as if remembering the tragic scene. "I took good care of her," she mumbled out loud. "I helped her."

"That is an understatement. You helped her die," Tilda yelled at Ruby. "You showed immediate disdain, and then you took your sweet time allowing my poor Maggie to bleed to death."

"I'm sorry, Tilda, but that's just not the case. There is only one version of events, considering that I was there and you were not," I announced.

Tilda visibly flinched. "Of course I was there. I would never leave Maggie's side before my grandchild was born." She turned toward Ryland to plead her case. He found more interest in his cigar.

Tilda's hands clutched at the square arms of her chair. "I will not be made out to be a liar. This woman is responsible, and that is all."

"No one is sorrier than me that Maggie's gone," I said. "For her sake, we should move on and stop bickering. But if you have to blame someone, you can blame me, for whatever relief that will bring you."

Ryland shifted, growing weary with the process. He took a deep inhale of his cigar. "Mum, I can handle things from here."

"Please do so. Get this *Ruby* out of my sight for good."

Before he could say more, I walked toward him. "Ryland." I reached out, letting my desperate hand linger on the sleeve of his jacket. "Thank you for your understanding."

The piercing gaze he returned was an announcement of the balance shifting between us. It was now in his favor. My side of favors and secrets had overlapped his. Ruby's life was now included. A deal was a deal, and yet I had no idea to what I'd just agreed.

He moved past me. "All right then, we all have better things to do. This matter has taken enough of our time. Maggie is gone. Hurting someone else is not going to bring her back, Mum." He planted a kind but dismissive kiss on Tilda's forehead.

"You'll take her word over mine?" she huffed.

"Take her back to the quarters," Ryland ordered the overseer. "Make sure she gets plenty of water and no work till she's healed."

The overseer helped Ruby climb onto the back of the wagon. She scooted the best she could against the frame and plopped down with exhaustion. She lifted her puffy lids in my direction. I could not look away. *Ruby.* The overseer snapped the reins for the horse to move. Ruby was at least strong enough to hold on to the edge of the wagon.

Tilda rocked back and forth in her anger. The sun quickly retired behind the clouds, as if knowing its duty had been served. The sky darkened instantly, making the house dim as well.

Ryland entered the house and made it all too clear he expected me to follow him into the dining parlor.

"Thank you, Ryland. Can we let this rest now?" I asked gently. "Nothing will happen to Ruby? She won't be sold or punished in the middle of the night? Please." I knew the word of one man could not stop the complicity that happened behind closed doors.

But I had to try.

"You have my word. We all should be treated with some kind of decency, wouldn't you agree?"

"Yes."

He smiled slightly. "I hope I've proven there's no need for you to be afraid of me anymore."

I took a long, unsteady breath. "I'm not afraid of you," I lied. "Not anymore."

"Good." He picked up his gloves and turned to leave, then turned back to say one more thing. "And thank you for taking care of Lizzy."

I rushed back to the nursery. I gathered myself before going inside. I went straight to the bassinette to check on Lizzy. She slept soundly.

"What happened to Ruby?" Cleo rose from where she'd been curled in the corner keeping watch over Essie.

Essie stood up. "So? I want to hear this. What they say?"

"The overseer took Ruby back to the quarters. Master Ryland promised nothing would happen to her," I said, trying to keep my voice from shaking. I wanted them to believe me, as much as I wanted to believe Ryland.

36

Silence

Essie and Cleo resigned themselves to silence around me. Cleo brought clean linens and moved about so as not to bring attention to herself. They made it a point to address me only when necessary, responding with "Yes, miss," or "No, miss."

I couldn't take the silence any longer. Other than little Lizzy hearing the songs I sang to her, no one could see or hear me. Once again, invisible. After a few days of skulking about, I wanted to speak to someone. Cooing to baby Lizzy didn't count.

I took the steps down the back staircase the house servants used. I went that way avoiding the middle landing that creaked. I made it to the bottom and dashed out the side door into the night air.

The music and voices let me know I was headed in the right direction. It was supper hour on a Sunday, the only time when folks weren't exhausted from a week of field labor. Sheets of plank wood resting on raw pine posts covered the communal area.

Bo didn't see me at first. He must've felt me, though. He looked up while sitting at a long table with the other men, turning slightly as if someone had called his name. He rose, taking his bowl with him. He walked to the edge before a step down was required.

There he stood, looking out into the darkness, continuing his meal. He scooped beans and gravy to his mouth in a slow and steady rhythm. I was still too afraid to show myself, waiting behind the shadow of a large willow tree. I surveyed the area, making sure no one had his or her eye on him. Besides a few men in the corner throwing dice and others at a table with a card game, betting with nothing but rocks as winnings, there was no one who would take notice. In the back, someone with the gift of music strummed a banjo while children clapped along.

They had a community, friends, family, the type of belonging I ached for. While I watched their ease and comfort with one another, I wished to be a part of their whole instead of constantly feeling empty inside. Thinking about the past week of death and isolation only made my heart heavier. Tears flowed without warning. I mourned the loss of Maggie, but it was another kind of sadness I now realized. A different kind of loss made me weep. I pressed my sleeve to my face and used my hands to fan away the proof of my misery.

"Bo, over here," I whispered, then pushed myself back under the shadow, away from the moonlight.

He hesitated for a second, looking around to make sure no one was watching as he stepped off the landing. "Come for supper?" he asked before taking another scoop of his beans.

"I came to see how Ruby's doing. No one will talk to me in the house. I came to see for myself."

Bo looked over his shoulder to where everyone remained lively, talking and eating. He turned to look distinctly at the corner space where a small group of ladies sat.

I recognized Ruby sitting, staring off into nowhere. "I'm thankful she's doing good, at least better than the last time I saw her."

"So far. I wished you never would've asked me for that salve," he blurted.

I bit the inside of my cheek to stop a tremble from embarrassment. All at once my throat closed. My lips went parched. This wasn't what I expected. "I knew the salve would save the baby," I stuttered. "Maggie was already too far gone to be saved. We did what we could." I'd told this story. I didn't think I'd have to say it again to Bo. I'd come here for solace, friendship, and a soft place to land.

He took a step closer so his voice wouldn't carry. "Your foolhardy decisions make me scared. When are you going to figure out how dangerous this game is you playing? One minute you're telling me you got to run, leave this place to save your life, and the next you want to be the hero at the risk of telling on yourself, on me, on Ruby. She was so sure they was coming after her, she tried to run away. She went out there and got bit by a snake. She could've died."

I stayed silent.

Bo spoke up again, shaking me from contemplation. "You better hope they don't come back for her a second time. If they do, she's in no position to keep secrets, you understand. That snakebite left her mind half of itself. Don't mean she won't remember the events of that night."

"I understand."

"Do you? Are you done messing in folks' lives?"

"Maggie dying had nothing to do with that salve. The way things happened just happened." I rushed my words. "Miss Tilda wanting to hurt Ruby, making her scared enough to run off in the woods and get bit by a snake, had nothing to do with me, or the salve, or even with her daughter-in-law dying—Miss Tilda, she was . . ." I wiped the spittle that seeped from my bitterness. "She was angry because Ruby came through that door talking loud about white women—*and you know how they are, hee-hee, don't like no pain*—and Miss Tilda sat right there and heard every word. I had to beg her not to do something crazy right then. If Ruby hadn't come in there acting like we were best friends when I'd never laid eyes on her before in my life, none of this would've happened. You know who's to blame?" I continued. "Whoever felt the need to tell the truth about me. So now all of you down here know I'm just one big joke." My voice grew hoarse. "You can stop pointing the finger at me.

I got enough stuff to be sorry about. I don't need you telling me how wrong and ridiculous I am."

"Everything is connected," he said. "Don't you see that? One thing touches another in ways you don't even know."

How right he was. I was hurting. Cleo, Tilda, and now Bo saw the worst in me. Everything and everyone I touched seemed to turn to ash.

I did not need Bo to tell me about consequences. From sunup to moon's passing, I took fault for every single thing that happened around me. I sniffed back a choke of sobs threatening to come no matter how hard I fought. Things certainly worked out one way or another. That was for sure.

"Dahlia, I'm scared for you, that's all. You know I never mean to say things to hurt your feelings. I'm just trying to get you to see things differently."

"I see plenty. More than I've ever wanted to, trust me." I swallowed back the sorrow, but it still came.

Pity rolled over Bo's face. He was fresh out of ways to fix me. And I was finished being told how wrong I was. I was standing there ready to explode, and the sky did it for me. A thunderous clap above our heads eased the tension between us. Bo's shoulders fell back. The clap of noise shook us both.

"I missed you the last couple of days," he said with less tension. "The garden misses you too. You should see your lilies." He tried to relay a lighter note. "Every day there's a new set of blooms." His attempt at changing the subject only made my heart ache more.

The garden was nothing but a colorful distraction. I hated it and everything about the Ross home. I bit my tongue. Bo would hear no more derision from me. He'd hear no more complaints about the way things were. We'd set our paths, two separate directions.

He blew out a small whistle, not sure what else he could say. "I'm glad you stood up for Ruby. Really, it was the right thing to do. Miss Tilda will get over whatever's up her craw. Just be your lovable self."

"Oh, right . . . that's me, lovable." I watched the group behind him enjoying themselves.

"You are," he said. He kept his eyes turned down.

When I looked back, Bo was already gone, joining in on the clapping while a couple danced arm in arm around in circles.

It was time to say goodbye. The two little orphan children who played in the fields holding hands no longer existed.

37

Sorrow

I returned to the mansion and went straight to the kitchen, ravenous. It was late enough that no one would be there. I saw a plate filled with bread and jam left over from earlier in the day. Trying to avoid Tilda by not eating supper most nights, I'd come to eat anything I could find. I rolled my finger in the jam and spread a bit on the next bite of bread. I took a seat at the table and continued filling my jaws.

"Looks like someone's starving," Cleo said, coming into the kitchen holding a tray. "You'd think you was the one nursing little Lizzy." It was a friendly tone, something I'd missed.

I had trouble swallowing quickly enough to respond. I was so shocked she was no longer ignoring me. She set a cup of warm milk in front of me. I eyed it with suspicion. But I was also thirsty. I drank, swallowed, chewed, and swallowed some more. "Thank you, Cleo."

Cleo poured steaming water from the kettle into the teapot. She dropped brown sugar lumps onto the small plate, then packed up the other half of bread I hadn't gotten to.

"This is for Miss Tilda. She don't come down for supper. Masta Ryland neither."

No one's having supper. This was news. I'd thought Tilda and Ryland had been reveling in their time alone without the pampered, ungrateful outsider.

"Leaves a lot of food at the end of the evening. I take it down to the quarters. Tonight's supper, pork belly and mashed potatoes. Want some before I take it down?"

I grabbed my stomach full of bread. "No." I stood still as she moved about before leaving with the tray. Whatever had softened Cleo I did not want to ruin.

I approached the hallway after Cleo had visited Tilda. I saw that she'd left the tea tray at Tilda's closed door. Had I splintered Ryland and Tilda's relationship to the point that no one was speaking to each other? As much as I wanted Tilda to stop placating her eldest son, I never wished to come between them. I could hear Bo in my head telling me this was the aftermath of my storm.

I attempted to rap my knuckles on the oak panel, only to stop myself. This wasn't the door I should be at.

I moved away. I told myself to not be afraid. My right arm lifted with a dedicated fist, only to stop midway. This was hard for me. But it was for the best. In my quest to take responsibility, I would be more open to understanding that all fights were not to be won but sometimes merely a lesson to be learned.

I knocked with renewed dedication to my mission. The door swung open. It was dark inside, with mustiness hanging in the air. Ryland stood unsteadily holding a silver flask with the initials RR boldly engraved on the front. He tilted it up, draining what was left. He stuck his head out the entryway as if expecting someone else.

"Sister Lily, beloved wife of my beloved brother." He stuck his neck out the door again. "She's 'posed to bring me another bottle."

I pushed him back. "Ryland, you've had enough to drink."

He took ahold of my wrist. "I was wondering when you were going to come."

I easily peeled his fingers away. "We need to talk about your mother. She's angry with us both." I tapped his face and grasped his chin and jaw with both hands. The jolt shook him. "Ryland, tomorrow we will be at the table as a family. Do you understand?" I couldn't be responsible for ruining their bond. After the chastisement from Bo about interfering, I didn't want to hurt anyone else around me. Tilda and Ryland were mother and son. Regardless of what I felt for either of them, I didn't want to see them torn apart.

He nodded. "I'm sorry," he said. His half smile came and went. "I'm so profoundly sorry. Do you think she forgives me?" he asked.

Who? Was he speaking about Maggie?

I stood there wanting the words to come. "Maggie forgives you." I backed away and hurried off down the hall. I wanted to forgive as well. With the loss of Maggie, the birth of Lizzy, and the saving grace of Ruby, all I wanted to do now was let go of the past and focus on what was ahead.

Ryland kept his word the next evening, though Tilda refused to come. We met at the table for supper, just the two of us. We sat across from each other with dread and very few words. Ryland inquired about Lizzy and I said, "Growing."

Neither of us spoke of Timothy. He'd been gone for weeks without a word. If Ryland had heard from him, he hadn't shared it with me. That was all right. It was the first time I wasn't concerned about Timothy or when he'd come to take me away with him.

I had Lizzy. She was my secret joy. Each time her eyes opened, and her sweet smile followed, I was made whole again.

It was Tilda I felt sorry for. For every day she held on to her grudge with me and Ryland, she missed out on holding Lizzy.

The next day, I slipped a note under her door, a sincere letter of apology documenting my faults and wishes for reconciliation. I sank as low as asking Cleo to spy, which wasn't much different from what she did on a normal basis. What was Tilda eating? Did she look ill? Had she bothered to bathe or wash her hair?

"Miss Tilda is fine," Cleo responded.

"Well, did she at least read my letter?"

"I wouldn't know nothing about that." The dart of her eyes said otherwise. Cleo knew everything going on in the Ross household. What we ate and drank, and when. She knew every detail of our comings and goings.

"I will tell you one thing." Cleo waited until she had bent close enough to my ear while plumping my pillows. "She asked me to lay out one of her finer dresses this morning."

This was the tiniest bit of information, but full of presumption. Miss Tilda wouldn't request a fine dress be laid out and prepared unless she planned on being seen, on making an appearance, an evening appearance.

I approached the dining parlor at precisely six o'clock, the Ross supper hour, with anticipation, expecting to finally see her sitting at the head of the table.

"Welcome," Ryland said with a nod. He watched as I approached, then quickly stood. "You're looking lovely." He rose and pulled out my chair, then went back around to the other side across from me. His face was shaven and his clothes fit square on his shoulders.

"Your mother?" I looked to her empty chair.

"Still no sign of Mum. But I did happen to catch her on the veranda at sunrise." Ryland shyly kept his gaze downward. "She thought no one else would be up that early. When I came to sit beside her, she conveniently took to her room."

Cleo entered, wearing a white shirt tucked into a black skirt and apron. Her usual scarf was gone, replaced by a white bonnet. She donned the formal serving attire only for special occasions. "Master Ryland, shall I begin service?"

"Yes. Please do," Ryland answered, snapping his linen open to place under his chin. "Can't wait for the soup. An old favorite of mine, pea and pork," he bragged, as if he'd been in the kitchen all afternoon and couldn't wait for others to taste his handiwork.

I could see what was happening. The candles should've been my first clue. The softly lit wax burned in an array of sizes around the room instead of in the oil lanterns. Flowers sat in a cream vase. The table setting was for two, though I'd been told of Tilda arriving in her finest dress attire. I'd done the same, wearing a green silk dress with a beaded appliqué and ruby earrings, a wedding gift from Timothy.

How could Cleo have done this? She'd helped him pull off this ridiculous farce of a poetic setting.

Ryland folded his hands neatly in front of him. "You don't look happy. You haven't even tasted the soup."

I didn't respond right away. I counted down. It was something Mother Rose had constantly instilled in Annabelle and Leslie. *Think before you speak. Count backward from five. Whatever you say afterward will hold far more value.* Perhaps it was better to say nothing at all.

"When will you ever stop tormenting me?" I pleaded.

Cleo moved quickly out of the room. I was determined to follow right behind her. I rose, nearly knocking over the chair, stumbling, nearly falling. Before I went backward, Ryland gripped my wrist, pulling me up to stand straight.

"You're upset about a nice presentation? A wonderfully prepared supper, and this bothers you?" he huffed, out of breath from the extra work of keeping me upright. He let me go without a struggle. "I spoke to Mum directly and told her I was having a special meal prepared in her honor. She slammed the door in my face. I figured, why not enjoy ourselves? We could enjoy a lovely evening instead of facing each other with grim expressions all night. I see you sitting in the nursery, staring into oblivion while holding on to Lizzy, and it scares me. I fear that you're slipping into a dark place. I figured you needed some cheering, a reason to get out of those drab clothes."

"A dark place?" I cleared my throat. I kept in mind that it was he who'd helped put me there. The "dark place" was filled with the memory of his blatant attack, and now this. "You used Cleo to trick me."

"If she hadn't told you something about Tilda, you wouldn't have shown up. I threw the dress part in to inspire you. Cleo is not to blame. I know the two of you speak regularly. I used her. My apologies. But if it's going to be just the two of us, we should enjoy some part of the day with a pleasant dining experience." He hunched his shoulders. "If you want to leave, I understand."

He'd tried his hand at changing the gloomy air around here. Taking a day off from one more dreary evening—there was no wrong in that. I swallowed my pride.

I nodded toward my chair. He pulled it forward from where it had been pushed back during my great escape. I sat down.

A relieved expression broke through before Ryland took his seat. "I'm sure Mum will see reason eventually."

"For now, she'll continue to hate me." I grabbed the spoon and took a generous sip of the soup Cleo had prepared.

"Do you like it?" Ryland asked. Before I could answer, Cleo returned, obviously having been listening and ready to bring the second course. A good fight worked up an appetite. She presented a full bird, browned to perfection. Savory spices wafted with each slice served.

"This all looks wonderful, Cleo," I said, determined to offer praise where praise was deserved.

When she went to pour wine, Ryland put his hand over his glass. "None for me." Ryland saw my expression, questioning. "You're welcome to indulge. As for me, I'm in need of a rest." He took a sip of tea instead as if it were the most delicious thing he'd ever tasted.

Cleo left for the kitchen. The door swung forward, then back before settling closed.

It was just Ryland and me in our utter aloneness. Unlike before, I did not fear him or wish for his death in a thousand different ways. We sipped our soup. We ate our bird. And by the end of the evening, we had exchanged just enough pleasantries.

"Thank you for the pleasure of your company, once more," Ryland said, dabbing the edges of his mouth. "I should be getting to bed. I have an early ride in the morning." He stood, folding his napkin to leave it neatly on his empty plate. "Have you ever gone riding before? I have a gentle horse, one perfect for you. Would you like to ride tomorrow?" he continued without pause. "We'll go slowly. You'll enjoy the freedom, the air, and sun hitting your face. The tranquility is unmatched."

The kindness in Ryland's voice I'd heard only once before, when he held Lizzy for the first time. I didn't believe he was being genuine then. I still wasn't sure now.

I shook my head no. I braced myself, expecting his worst behavior to surface. "I don't think riding together is appropriate."

"Why not? I think it's very appropriate. Learning to ride a horse is quite acceptable, and necessary." He thought about what to say next. "I'm not . . . I wasn't in my right mind those times before. I'm doing my best to make you see that. You have every right to fear me or hate me. But I wish you didn't."

His tone dropped. "I'm not proposing anything besides a pleasant ride. No different than having supper together, which you have to admit was much more enjoyable than eating alone." He paused on the word, letting it sink in as if he knew it was my weakness. "But that also is inappropriate, I see." He looked down. "Maybe we should not have dinner together, or be seen anywhere near each other. You're probably right. It's what I deserve."

"No. I don't want that—to eat alone. It's just that I don't understand."

"There's no explanation for what I did, but you have my word, it will never happen again. If I could change time and go back, I would."

It wasn't a difficult decision. I briefly thought of Timothy, who'd left me at a moment's notice, and Bo, who'd shown we were too different to be friends again. "I'll see you in the morning," I answered.

Ryland escorted me slowly to the hall stairway. "I'll make sure you have the proper attire. Good night."

Instead of going straight to my room, I turned in to the nursery. The moon illuminated the room, showing my way to the bassinet. Lizzy slept soundly. She moved her lips, suckling air, taking a pause every few seconds, resting her soft cheeks. I went to my knees before settling to a sitting position. I lingered, waiting for her sweet scent of innocence to rise, a combination of nursing milk and the rose water used to gently wash her newborn skin. I defied the urge to pick her up. If I woke her, she wouldn't go back to sleep without nursing at Essie's breast. I quietly slipped out of the nursery as easily as I'd come.

By the time the sun had risen, I felt I'd rested only a few minutes. But then the question arose, when had the stack of folded clothing been placed on the chair a few feet away? Pants. A shirt. A belt. These were men's clothing—Ryland's, I assumed—for me to wear for the ride.

The clothes were far too large. Still, I'd rather be wearing oversized men's clothing than the corsets that cut off my air.

A light knock on the door came just as I figured out the proper way to cinch and clasp a belt. Cleo entered and stopped, giving my new attire a hard stare. She'd come without tea or breakfast, only herself standing in the middle of the room. "Miss Lily, I need to speak with you."

"Of course." I sat on the bed but continued with the process of getting prepared for my riding lesson. I slipped my foot into one leather half boot, then the other. "Go on, Cleo."

"Well, last night, I shouldn't of let you go to supper all gussied up like that. It was cruel. I realize that now. I'm sorry."

"You have nothing to be sorry for. In fact, everything turned out fine. I enjoyed the evening, and the food you prepared. Thank you."

"I don't expect no praise, Miss Lily." She moved in front of me. Her fingers looped the leather bands of my ankle boots two sizes too large. "These folks won't change they minds about how they feel about us. I know you mean good. You want everyone to see through your eyes, but your eyes ain't like the rest. They'll never see us as nothing but mules. We're nothing to them. And you'd best decide where you belong, which side you want to be on, and stay there."

Cleo wasn't done. She'd thought long and hard about what she wanted to say. She pulled and tied the last knot. "Don't be afraid to be who you need to be," she continued. "That Negro blood in you is strong. It'll give you strength to survive where you didn't think you could, but it'll also get you hurt, killed, even. Choose where you want to be, Miss Lily, and stay there. No one's judging."

She was wrong. I was being judged, constantly, by everyone, and worst of all I judged myself. I didn't want to tell her I'd lost any hope of belonging. I did my best to swallow the lesson she was trying to teach. This was the first Cleo and I had had an honest talk since Lizzy was born. We hadn't talked about what happened that night with Maggie dying. Or what happened to Ruby. I blinked fast and hard to dry the tears threatening to well and fall.

"Please don't cry, Miss Lily." She let her hand rest on my knee.

"No. It's all right. I'm glad we talked."

I thought about that night Lizzy was born. I'd seen the telegram on Tilda's desk, the talk of ending slavery. I doubted Cleo would believe me, but I wanted to tell her she would see freedom. I prayed for freedom all the time. For me as well. I was just as afraid as she was. Each day I woke up terrified, wondering if this was the moment I would be pulled into a wagon, sent back to the Holt plantation, and forced to make amends for running away.

She pulled out a clean linen from her apron pocket, handing it to me. "I mean you no harm."

"And I mean you no harm. I'm just doing the best I can with the situation I'm in."

"We all are," Cleo said, standing now. "You can't change anything. Best you worry about yourself." She left, closing the door behind her.

The message was delivered and received. I had my own issues. Starting with the fact that I was about to rendezvous with the man who'd tried to have his way with me. The man who'd stashed money under his bed that he'd acquired by unscrupulous means. Yet here I was, set to ride off with him, willingly. I was indeed worried about myself. There was no doubt about that.

38

Ride

Ryland stood at the foot of the stairs, waiting. I took careful steps with the pants feeling too wide, the belt holding them up too heavy, and the boots too loose on my feet. Every step I took felt like I was going to tumble forward.

He put out his hand. "Relax. You're fine." He was dressed in a casual riding coat and brown pants tucked into high boots.

"I'm sorry I'm late. It took me a while to get dressed. Did you visit with Lizzy this morning?"

"I'm glad everything fits." His eyes shifted downward, landing on the bulky leather strap holding up the gathered fabric of my pants. He ignored the subject of Lizzy.

I was doing my best to slay my habit of meddling, so I didn't push further. "This belt is heavier than I am."

"Good thing the horse won't care." He pointed toward the dining parlor. "A bit of food now? You should eat something for your strength. Riding takes effort."

"I'm fine, really."

"Where are you two headed off to?" The sound of Tilda's voice sent a shiver down my spine. She'd been unwavering in keeping herself hidden. Now she stood pale like a ghost, wearing a white housedress that blended in with her graying hair.

"Mum. It's good to see you up and about." Ryland moved swiftly toward her, leaning in. He kissed her lightly on the cheek.

"Good morning, Tilda. Ryland has offered to teach me how to ride," I added, as if the questioning concern on her face had anything to do with my appearance.

"The two of you?" she asked pointedly. The new alliance before her was unlikely. I understood her discomfort. I felt the same, strange and out of sorts. But I was determined to listen to Cleo's advice, to move inside this space and stay there. I had no choice. The otherness, the not belonging, had pulled me down a hole of staggering loneliness.

"Yes. It will be just the two of us. Unless you'd like to join us," Ryland offered.

"Ryland, I'd like to speak with you when you return." Tilda's voice was harsh and weighted with all that she wanted to say but could not. She glided off, then stopped abruptly as if she'd forgotten something. "I would like to speak with you alone."

"Yes. I understand, Mum. See you in a few hours," he said solemnly.

We headed out into the bright morning light. Ryland and I walked at a steady pace toward the stable. Bo would be there tending to the horses. I wasn't looking forward to him seeing me with Ryland. Though I was only doing what Bo, and now Cleo, had suggested.

I'd chosen a side.

I glanced over at Ryland's profile while he chatted about having a British upbringing, significantly different from one in America, he assumed. I could no longer say I hated him. By continuing to hate him, I was only making myself fear him. He'd been polite and even humble. I couldn't assume the worst. I still had no idea who'd attacked Bo in the horse stable.

"Am I boring you?" he asked.

"Not at all," I answered. If I wanted to make the best of my situation, there had to be forgiveness.

"Are you all right? We can slow down." Ryland stopped. "Really, there's no hurry. I was so busy dogmatizing about my youth, I hadn't noticed how hard you were trying to keep up."

"I'm fine."

"Next time we'll have sufficient riding clothes." He tugged on the extra fabric hanging from my shoulder. We began again, taking much slower steps. "Maybe it was all my rehashing of the past. You must think it's awful of me to speak of my childhood without mentioning Timothy. Seven years of difference in age. Almost a lifetime in child-rearing. We managed to stay close because of hardships."

"By hardships, you mean whatever caused you to steal that money?"

Ryland looked away. "I'm not proud of that. You've met our aunt. She would easily have us living on the side of the road without a second care."

"So you only did it the one time?"

"Yes. I wouldn't say it was something I'd like to make a habit. And since Timothy is no longer here—"

"What is that supposed to mean? Is there something you want to tell me? Is this why you brought me out here?" I asked, knowing I didn't want to hear much more.

He took off his hat and wiped his brow. "All right, let me be honest. I haven't heard from him directly. No one's heard a word. I sent a telegram at Mum's request, telling him about Maggie's death—which as you know was weeks ago—and he has yet to respond. He has absolutely no regard for anyone but himself. I'm quite done saving him."

I nervously swayed to and fro. "Saving him?"

"Drink. Have some water. This is what happens when you get a late start. The afternoon heat has set in."

We continued on the trail. "What did you mean about saving him?"

"We came up with the plan together, to give us more time to stay here. Timothy and I had been planning it for months. That was the day. Then out of nowhere you appeared. Surely Timothy has told you everything?" He glanced over. "Well, maybe not. Timothy is complicated. We were about to go through with it, and then you turned up. He saw the chance to back out. Saving the young lady in distress and all. So, he's told you none of this? Even with his deception, you remain loyal?" He posed the statement as a question.

"He is my husband," was my answer. My only answer.

"I know you miss him. I miss Maggie as well."

"Timothy isn't dead."

"No. You're right. Timothy is not dead. Far from it. He's alive and well."

"Timothy has been running all over the place looking for financial backing. Does he know you went through with it, that you have the money?"

"He knows I have the money. He also knows I refuse to give it to him. After he left me in limbo to chase after you, I decided then and there I wouldn't give him a cent of it. I risked my life to steal that money, and what did I get in return?"

I stayed quiet. *What did he get in return?* Did he expect me to be his reward? And why not? I was the cause of everyone's troubles, it seemed. I licked my dry lips. I was getting nervous again.

"I've soured the mood, haven't I?" Ryland inquired after a few more steps of silence.

"No, I'm fine."

As we approached the stables, I slowed. There was Bo standing between two horses instead of holding only one. He'd known I was coming. I wondered when Ryland had told him of our ride together, when the invitation was only offered the previous evening.

Bo dropped his gaze, not bothering to look my way. "Both saddled and ready to go, masta-sir. Miss Lily," he said without looking up.

"All right. Lily, you take Berth. She's gentle and always in good spirits." Ryland gave the horse a soft scratch under the ear. The horse blinked her big brown eyes with approval.

"Sir . . ." Bo held the horse steady. "Berth here is holding a foal. She ain't really in her right mind. Prolly not the best time for a new rider, masta-sir."

"To the contrary, Berth is the gentlest of all the horses. That's why Lily shall ride her. She will be slow going in her current state, without any sudden outbursts."

"Excuse me, Bo. I'll be fine," I interrupted. I knew the rules now. I didn't want the lines crossed. From here on, we looked out for ourselves. We stayed out of each other's way. I pressed my foot in the stirrup and waited for Ryland to lift me up.

Once I'd mounted the horse, I looked down at the distance to the dirt and tried not to think of falling. The rough edges on the leather saddle dug past the fabric of my pants as I nervously adjusted myself in the seat.

"Best to stay calm," Bo said politely. He handed me the leather straps, still warm from his grip.

"You look like a natural. Are you sure you've never ridden before, Lily?" Ryland asked, easily straddling the other horse.

"Never," I said, though Bo was there to witness my lie. He'd surely gotten used to me bending, even desecrating, the truth by now.

Ryland offered his first bit of tutoring while he led the way out. "Gently but firmly squeeze the horse's sides to keep a steady pace. If you want to stop, pull back your straps slowly."

Berth began moving at a slow gait. Bo watched, his eyes steadfast on my grip. I didn't want him to worry. He was free to live his life as I was going to live mine. Isn't that what we'd agreed to?

Bo knew it was a bad idea, Dahlia riding a pregnant Berth. A horse in that condition was unstable, no different from a woman.

He leaned over the horses' trough and splashed water on his face to cool down. At least the flat terrain would make it an easy ride. The green stretch of land turned endless and open at the bottom of the hill.

He wasn't going to worry about Dahlia. She'd obviously made her choice of who she wanted to be. That's what he tried to tell himself.

Dahlia. Miss Lily. Whatever the case, she wasn't Bo's problem.

He pushed his entire face into the horses' trough and stayed there until he couldn't hold his breath any longer. He rose up, used his sleeve to wipe the drips off his face.

He could blame the bash to his head for the constant noise and spinning. But this other thing, rage, piled in the back of his throat. The thought of Master Ryland and Dahlia, those two riding off together. He wanted to destroy something with his bare hands.

This is what Essie must have felt when she wanted to lash out. No reasoning to it. No understanding. Only rage. The ringing in his ears got louder. He stuck his face back in the cool water to drown out the high-pitched churning.

He stood, gasped for air, and took a few breaths to calm down. Try as he might, he couldn't stop the wheel of anger rolling around in his head.

"Look-a-here, if it ain't Mister Bo."

Bo turned around to see Abel. He had no business on this side of the hill. Behind him was another body. There was Preach. Bo expanded his chest and held it there.

"What can I do for you, gentlemen?" Bo asked.

"We're here to ask a polite favor," Preach said. "Since you been among us, there's been malaise and misfortune. It wasn't like we were living on heaven's wings before you came, but young sir, the days have gotten dark with you in our midst."

"I can't say I've heard any such thing," Bo said. "You the first."

"Well, that's because we're a kindly bunch," Preach said. "No one likes hurt feelings around here." He pushed his thumbs through his suspenders. "Abel here believes you treaded on his territory, disrespectfully, carrying on with Miss Essie the way you have. She belonged to him before you came."

Bo chuckled.

"There something funny, young sir?"

"No. Well, yeah. I believe Essie has a firm mind of her own. She's not likely to believe she belong to Abel or anybody else."

Abel took a large step forward. His big toe stuck halfway out of his leather shoe. "You ain't nothing but a thief and a coward."

"I'm sorry, Abel. I apologize. I didn't know you was with Essie." Bo let out the breath he'd held for too long. "You and me don't have no trouble. I'll tell Essie. I'll tell her about this visit and what I did wrong. You won't have no trouble out of me."

"I told ya he was a coward," Abel said, his fist balled, ready for a fight.

Bo lifted his hands in surrender. After he'd worked himself up about Dahlia, he simply had no strength left to deal with these two men. He didn't care what name calling came next. He wasn't in any condition to fight big Abel. He'd let Essie handle that all on her own. Bo wondered if Abel knew Essie at all. She was a fighter. She wasn't likely going to take the news well.

He put out a hand to shake with Preach as if a deal had been struck. "Sir?"

"I knew you'd be reasonable, young sir." Preach shook his hand good and firm.

"That I am," Bo said.

Next, he put out his palm to Abel. After holding it there an unbearable minute, Bo let his arm fall to his side.

The two men walked off. He watched until they disappeared down the hill. Bo sighed relief and fought the urge to crawl into the space where he'd found Ruby a few weeks ago. He wanted to rest and hide. He was a horse trainer, a breeder. He wished he could write. He'd make a sign. *Here for the horses. That's all.*

39

Lessons

"Is this as fast as we're planning to go?" I asked.

"Look at you. Ready to go galloping down the lane already?"

"Yes. I'd like to go faster." I wanted to feel the wind in my face, freedom.

Ryland slowed even more. "You're not ready. We still have a few lessons yet."

"Lessons? There's nothing else to learn. I'm balanced. I have control of the reins. I know how to slow her down, to turn, to stop. What else do I need to know?"

"It's about you and your horse, understanding without speaking, so to speak. Connected. Besides, this was the very reason I chose Berth for you, to keep you from galloping off."

"I can't be more connected, can I?" I let out an exasperated sigh. "I'm here. We're here together, aren't we, girl?" I gave her mane a soft brush of my hand.

"All right, fine. You seem to know it all. I hope you can keep up," Ryland said, snapping his heels at his horse's sides. He began at a trotting pace, then faster. He suddenly rode off.

I mimicked his gesture, using my legs to kick slightly against Berth's sides, only to remain still. "Let's go, girl," I said, giving her another soft jolt, remembering she was with child. "Come on, girl, let's go," I whispered near her ear. Still nothing. "Ryland," I called into the air at barely a note higher than a whisper. I didn't want to frighten her by screaming. But I felt like doing just that.

I sat completely alone under the stillness of the blue sky. The horse simply stood immobile. I rubbed my hand over her head and leaned close to her ear again. "Hey, sweet girl, it's all right. We'll wait till you're ready. We are connected," I said clearly for her to hear.

She shook her head and let out a neigh, indicating she would not fall for my placating. I couldn't imagine what I'd done to insult her. I swatted at the flying bugs having found Berth and me as the perfect resting spot. The one thing I couldn't protect us from was the sun. The burning heat became relentless. I reached around for the bag like the one Ryland had on his saddle, only to find I had nothing of the sort in the way of supplies. My mouth was already dry from panic and getting worse with every second I sat there.

I wiped the sweat away before it dripped and burned my eyes. My head swirled from the heat. It was best to climb down voluntarily before I fainted. The last thing I wanted was for Ryland to return and find me on my back, unable to get up. If I cried, all the worse.

As I gripped the saddle, my feet hung, searching for ground below. I eased myself down. Once secure, with dirt under my feet, I could breathe.

Berth was relieved as well. She gave her head a nod and shake before suddenly sprinting off in the direction Ryland had gone, trotting merrily in the wind with her full belly in tow. I stood there bewildered. The distance back was farther than I'd ever ventured on foot. I wasn't sure if I was on the Ross land or if we'd set out past the property line. I began my walk back. I would have to pass the stable eventually to get home. I'd see Bo. He'd see my shame and embarrassment.

"Are you lost, ma'am?" The man's voice was familiar. I narrowed my eyes from the glare of the sun to see a silhouette sitting on a mule. A beaten hat that flopped at the sides also kept his face from being visible completely, but I knew it was him, the overseer, the one who'd held Ruby by her neck as she hobbled on one foot. He remained easily still while perched on his mule, with no hurry or destination.

"I promise I don't bite." His mule stepped lazily to the side, close enough for the overseer to show a set of yellowed teeth. "Mort Holder at your service. Everyone around here calls me Mo." He leaned forward, putting out a weathered hand for a shake.

"Lily Ross." I didn't take his hand, instead pointing in the distance. "I need to get back to the house. Am I going in the right direction?"

"Yes, ma'am. I'd be happy to give you a ride back. Not safe out here for young ladies such as yourself. These fields are full of dangerous snakes, the kind you least expect." He took off his hat for a second to use it as a fan. "If the snakes don't get ya, the heat will."

"I'm fine, thank you."

"Oh, really? Don't look fine to me." He gave silence a try for a few moments before he picked up again. "The problem is, you never know when one of them snakes is going to snap out. No warning, just out of nowhere. Next thing you know, they got their fangs sunk into your flesh."

I began to walk, making a sweep of the ground with my eyes before each step. I thought I heard something in the brush ahead and stopped altogether.

The overseer and his mule were a few paces behind. "Me and my family came with the property when these Ross folks bought the land. We been keeping order and making sure those fields turn ground for the past ten years. Nice to see some new blood put into the dirt. Good land. Safer place than most, but I wouldn't go walking off like you did."

"My horse trotted off and left me, so I had to start walking. It wasn't voluntary."

"Just saying, best not to go wandering off on a plantation. These men are plain animals out here. Got no conscience. One of 'em get ahold of you, not going to be good."

"You're talking about people, not animals, Mister Mo."

His body tensed. He adjusted the shotgun he carried strapped across his shoulder. "Oh, right. I remember you now. You the one speaking up for that Ruby gal after she killed one of your own."

"Ruby didn't kill anyone."

"What're you, one of them troublemakers from the North? Those people been coming around talking about the moral sins of slavery. What they don't know is that the slaves depend on us. We give them discipline and God. Without those two things, you got nothing but chaos."

"If you don't mind, I can walk alone. Thank you." I increased my pace.

"You're too young to understand. But you will." He persisted with his lesson. "This is the Christian way. We taking care of these people, as you want to call them, on the cause of they can't take care of themselves."

"As I said, I can walk alone." I turned when I heard a set of galloping hooves approaching. Ryland had gotten ahold of Berth by the reins and kept her alongside as he made his way toward us.

"Looks like Mister Ryland found your horse. Be seeing you around," the overseer sneered. He slowly rode away on his mule.

"Drink," Ryland said, leaning down to hand me the canteen of water. He pulled both horses off to the side, tied them to a branch, then marched back to me. I continued to guzzle the water. "You're welcome," he said, to the fact I hadn't thanked him.

"How could you leave me out here? I don't know why I ever trusted you. I don't know why I thought you'd suddenly turned a new leaf."

"And here I thought I was your knight in shining armor."

"You're hardly anyone's knight."

"No?" He let out a smug chuckle. "I know about you and I've told no one. I did a bit of digging. I found out where you were from, who set the bounty. You and the horse trainer are from the same land. He is your friend; that's why you wanted Timothy to purchase him. You see, I know everything. I've protected you from an examination that surely would've revealed the mark down your back. When will you and I get past the animosity? I think I've earned some absolution."

"You never would've known about the mark if you weren't attacking me. Pulling at my clothes like an animal. You wouldn't know any of this."

He closed up his water. "How did you get that mark? Did someone do that to you? Were you beaten?"

"It's none of your business."

He backed away. "Understood."

For a moment he stayed quiet. His acceptance of things didn't last long. He spoke in a low voice with barely enough energy to spark fear, and yet there was something ominous on the horizon. "Sometimes, it's the simple truth that hurts. Hardly anything I've done. You don't want to admit that you made a mistake that day, latching onto my brother. Whatever your plan was, you hadn't imagined that you were the one being used. And now you're angry for it. What you feel has very little to do with me."

"It has everything to do with you. Your threats. Your attacks."

"I shouldn't have acted that way. Demons have a way of releasing themselves. We can admit that no one's perfect, can't we? The same way you are not who you say you are." He adjusted his hat and slipped his riding gloves on. He offered the reins of Berth. "Shall we go?"

I wasn't through yet. "This is no different from you advising Timothy that I needed to be loved . . . that I deserved love, so it would be best if he let me go. I know how you plant these seeds of doubt and let them work, but not on me, Ryland."

"So you don't need love, or joy, or to be touched?" he asked with his familiar smirk. "Are you riding or walking?"

Bo saw the two horses coming over the ridge. The ride had taken much longer than it should have. As the silhouettes got closer, he could see that only one of the horses carried someone. Wild fear struck him directly in the ribs. The ache made him unsteady on his feet. This was what he'd feared the most. Dahlia was still out there. He searched around for what he'd need. Regardless of how many times he'd been told not to ride the horses, he knew how. After Master Ryland returned, he'd ride out and find her—and then they'd keep going.

The horses and Master Ryland were only minutes away. This time when he looked, he saw a small figure, legs covered in trousers, poking out behind Master Ryland's wider body.

She was riding on his horse, tucked behind him. Bo was relieved and angered at the same time, sick and tired of being scared to death, always wondering when it was going to happen, when she'd finally get herself too low in the mud to come out.

He pushed the stable doors open wide to prepare for their arrival. Something told him the horses weren't the only ones who would need tending.

They were still a ways out. He had time to straighten his shirt, put himself back together. He saw it in Dahlia's face, her concern. He didn't like her pity. That's not what he wanted at all, no more than she wanted his. He looked out to see how much farther they had to come. When Bo didn't see them, he stepped out further, only to be startled by Essie. His heart skipped a beat or two.

"What're you doing here?" He looked past her. "You got to go. Master Ryland is coming. He right outside this place, Essie."

"I couldn't come earlier. Your Miss Lily lady didn't stay to watch the baby like she normally do. I missed you." She threw her arms around his neck and tried to kiss him.

His breath caught in his chest. "You can't be here." He gave her a light push in the right direction. She stumbled but caught herself before a fall.

"Bowman Carter, you sent me away once, and now you sending me away again? What's wrong with you?"

"Just go!" he yelled, though it came out hardly above a whisper. He didn't have time to explain. If Master Ryland still didn't know the truth about *Lily*, he couldn't have Essie running into them. Who knows what she might say given the chance.

She sulked away. He didn't know if she kept going or hid in her usual place behind a stack of hay.

He went outside and surveyed the area. They were nowhere to be found. The horses, Master Ryland, and Dahlia were gone. They must've kept going on to the mansion. He let out the breath he'd been holding and went back inside.

"Essie, you can come out. Nobody's coming." He was relieved when all he heard was the steady breathing of himself and the horses.

40

Pride

The gold pendulum on the clock swung back and forth. I counted the seconds, then the minutes. Half past eight, ten before nine. I watched from where I lay in bed, fighting the morning light as it broke through the curtains. I had to get up. Lizzy needed me. I'd already missed holding her a full day, choosing to ride off with Ryland instead. The entire day away from her had weathered my mind, body, and heart.

I tried to rise but the pain all over my body gave me a jolt. I sat back down and inspected the red blisters the size of silver coins on the sides of my feet. The ill-fitting boots had worn against my skin when I'd attempted to walk the distance back to the house.

I took a few awkward steps like a child learning to walk, reaching the washbasin and wetting a towel to wrap around my feet. I needed to get myself together to get to Lizzy. She ate and slept, the full extent of a baby's day, and I wanted to at least see her eyes open for a brief moment before she fell back to slumber.

I dressed and took the painful, slow walk down the hall. I heard voices coming from the nursery before reaching the doorway. A man's voice. Then two. I stepped to the door and saw a man wearing a uniform, gray and heavy. The double-breasted jacket had yellow braided accents around the neck and sleeves. The gold buttons were large with an embossed flag. Every detail was excellently performed. It took me a second or two to realize it was Timothy. He stood regal and straight, talking to Ryland as they stood over the bassinet.

"You've finally done something right, mate."

Ryland nodded. "This is all Maggie's beautiful work."

Timothy looked up. "My darling Lily."

I stood stiff when he approached. He wrapped his arms around me. I couldn't bear to meet eyes with Ryland as he watched. I didn't want him to see how all the things we'd talked about had affected me, my feelings toward Timothy.

How there was one more lie between us. I'd counted each and every day of disregard. Nine months from the day I'd arrived on the Ross land.

"My goodness, are you the captain of a ship?" I asked snidely when he pulled way. He could feel my mood, my shudder against his chest.

"Captain Ross to you." He saluted with a whimsical hand. "This is my uniform. I'm a soldier. Meanwhile, look at this beautiful little one. You are a lucky man, brother." He rested a firm hand on Ryland's shoulder.

"I should leave you two alone." Ryland moved toward the door. He didn't want to be a part of whatever Timothy was about to share. The look on his face said that this time, it wasn't his doing.

"I'll meet you in the library," Timothy called out to him as he passed. Ryland didn't answer and kept walking.

"The uniform, Timothy?"

"Come, sit, darling."

"I do not need to sit." I walked over to Lizzy's bassinet where she slept easy. "Your mother no longer can stand the sight of me. Your brother . . ." I trailed off, holding my tongue. "Whatever this uniform means, I cannot stay here," I said, shaking my head. "I won't. You promised we'd leave together. The promise to work for Mr. Yates. What's happened with your plan to work for Mr. Yates in the capital?"

Timothy came toward me. He brushed my hair behind my shoulders. "I hear Lizzy's offered you a great deal of solace."

I snatched his hands away. "My answer will be the same. Whatever this uniform means . . . I can't stay here."

"I've already spoken to Ryland. He will be here protecting you and Mum."

"Ryland?" I said, shaking my head. "He's bent on destroying any semblance of peace around here. From day one, he's poked and prodded at my resolve."

"Your resolve?"

I searched my mind quickly to assign new meaning to the word. "Yes, any shred of hope I have to be happy. He doesn't want me to be happy. I don't understand why," I said quickly.

"Yes, he can be difficult. But Lily, he does not wish you any harm. I'll talk to him."

"Don't bother. Please." I'd done my share of damage to this family. From the day we met, it seemed, I'd come between them. If it hadn't been for me, Timothy would've gone with his brother to commit a robbery. They would've been unified in their crime.

"A war is about to begin," he said almost cheerfully. "Our livelihood, everything I have sacrificed to start over, is at risk. We will have nothing left if the abolitionists succeed. There'll be no more second chances. I've told you, Lily, everything about our history. That's what will happen here, if this government is successful. Our livelihood . . ."

"I know, your livelihood, your livelihood," I said, sick of hearing about what was at stake for him, for his family.

Timothy took a sharp breath. He stood straight and official in his uniform, as if he'd practiced his speech, this very moment, and was disappointed that he'd been interrupted.

"Our state wants no part in Lincoln's absurdity. We will claim our own president. We'll maintain our own laws. Owning our property will continue. Our land, our wealth, everything will continue. It's purely evil to debase a man's private property, a man who has paid good money and sacrificed for his stock, to turn it over with nothing in return.

"Lincoln, this man, has no idea of the work and dedication others have put into growing their land, the hard work required to maintain a life, to provide for the people you love. The confrontation shouldn't take more than six months, possibly a year. Once we've defeated them and sent them back to their brick mansions, we'll be free to live our lives again."

He only paused when Lizzy let out a delicate but long yawn.

"Darling." Timothy smiled. "This is far more pressing. Why is that so difficult for you to understand?"

"What happened to the dignity, respect, and love all humans deserve? Don't you remember saying those things to me? You'll be fighting for slavery. Why is it so difficult for *you* to understand?" My throat felt hoarse and I'd only spoken a few words.

"For now, we will agree to disagree." He was tired of the argument. "Surely you can stay vigilant during this time. Besides, you have nowhere else to go." Timothy made this declaration, and it was true.

I had nowhere else to go.

I bit my lip deliberately so as not to speak. There was a fragile distance between what I was truly feeling and what Timothy wanted to hear. When I said the truth, I was punished. When I lied, the result was no different—only delayed retribution and, inevitably, consequences not far behind.

"I may not have anywhere to go, but it's never really stopped me," I said between gritted teeth. "It won't stop me now."

Timothy gripped my shoulders, surprising me with his impatience. "I need to know you will be here, waiting for me. I have to know. Simple as that. The position that I have gained—once all this is over—requires that I have a wife. Politicians of stature must have a fine wife by their side. Do you understand?"

"Yes," I said quietly, swallowing my pride at once. "I understand."

"I promise, darling, when this is all over, you'll have all the comforts you've grown accustomed to. You'll be free to have your own home and garden, just like the one you've made here. It's beautiful, by the way."

There was anger in my blood, roaming, looking for something to set ablaze.

"It won't be long, my darling Lily. I promise."

Tilda's favorite son had returned in a uniform. What could be more honorable? She came back to life instantly. Her first order of business was to throw an extravagant celebration. He deserved a proper send-off to war, for fighting and for preserving their freedoms. She invited prestigious families from the southern regions, some she'd met and most she'd never seen. People with a common fight in the reign of human bondage necessary for the safekeeping of their estates.

"A party during this dire time would appear flippant and trite," Timothy protested.

"To the contrary," Tilda scoffed, "you are to be celebrated for your heroism. I'm asking guests to bring a donation to help fund the Confederacy. This party will not be in vain."

Once Tilda decided her position, there was no turning back. Preparation required every able set of hands to be involved. Cleo had assembled her team—four cooks, six butlers, and five cleaners. The house windows were opened. Dusting, beating of curtains, and sweeping proceeded. In one room, a seamstress worked with a steady hum of her machine cranking to complete the additional staff's white jackets and black trousers.

Now, with one day left before the extravagant affair, linens were freshly pressed and laid on tables adorned with silver candleholders erect and ready to be lit.

"We'll need flowers," Tilda said. She stared straight above my head.

This was the first time she'd spoken directly to me since I disagreed with her version of Ruby's actions.

"I would be happy to provide whatever blooms are available. But it's been weeks since I've checked the garden. The nights have been cool—"

"I've inspected your garden. There are yellow lilies and roses. Those will do fine. I've had the vases set out. I prefer to arrange them myself. Keep the stems long," she said before skirting off.

"I will," I said, though she had gone.

Bo cut the roses and laid them on the spread cloth so they could be bundled delicately when carried. He had his orders to gather flowers for Miss Tilda. He worked quietly at a steady pace. He'd been grateful when Cleo delivered a message that Dahlia wanted to meet at the garden. He hadn't talked to her since the night at the commons. He'd said some things that hurt her feelings. He hated to see her heart ache that way, but he had to say what he'd said. Next thing he knew, she was going off horse riding with Master Ryland. More to worry about. But he wouldn't say a thing about any of it. He promised himself, *not a word.*

"Ryland knows the truth about me," Dahlia blurted when she arrived. "That's all there is to it. We have an agreement of sorts. I know something about him too."

"I never said nothing about you and Ryland," he said, though she must've read his mind.

"I know what you're thinking, so . . ."

He bundled the roses carefully, smothering the thorns so she wouldn't get pricked when carrying them back.

"Say something, Bo."

"It's dangerous, having these men fighting for you." He shook his head, angry with himself for betraying his promise. *Why can't you stay quiet?*

"Nobody's fighting over me. Ryland knows where I come from, who I really am. Timothy doesn't know, but he doesn't care one way or the other."

Bo stood up. "You're worth fighting for. Whether you a slave or free, you gotta know that. You're worth fighting for," he said. Hadn't he run into a burning house for her? He hated to admit it, but he'd do it again and again. Best not to add to her feelings. She was lost and trying to find herself in the center of two men. He didn't want to be the third.

She pushed back the loose hair stuck to the moist skin around her face and swallowed what might be a wave of tears. "Doesn't matter now anyway. There's a war coming. Timothy is fighting in the war to keep their precious lives intact. So, you see, that's what they truly love: money, freedom to own slaves, to own—to own everything. I can't stand this house." She swallowed again as if there was a terrible taste on her tongue. "I'm leaving. I'm serious this time. No turning back. I've thought about it long and hard."

He hunched his shoulders. "I've been thinking too."

"Good. I've been practicing my writing. I plan to make you freedom papers. That way when we leave, no one will question it. You're my driver. I'm the mistress of the Ross Manor. We're riding to Washington, DC, and no one will stop us."

He went to say what he'd meant to say before she'd interrupted. "That bounty man already been here looking. He's not likely to come back. But out there, no telling—"

She cut him off. "There's going to be ugliness and danger here too. Mother Rose used to talk about the governments fighting when she was a child. Shooting, killings, and maiming. War is the end of all things. Nothing will be left standing. I want to go to Washington where the president is. If you come with me, no one will hurt you or me. They don't allow slaves there, in Washington, DC."

"Slaves everywhere, Dah—Lily," Bo muttered under his breath. "No place is free."

"No. I read a telegram. Holding people enslaved could end with the new president. We can go there and be free together."

Something awakened in Bo, then quickly went dark.

"I know you blame me for uprooting your life, but what if all this was supposed to happen? Maybe we were meant to be here, so we can leave, together. Be free together."

"What about that baby? You gon' just leave that baby?"

"What? Lizzy isn't mine to have. She's the sweetest thing. I'd take her with me if I could. She deserves more than what Tilda will make of her. I know you don't trust me with all my going back and forth, but not this time. I have it all planned out—"

Before she could continue with her grand scheme, boot steps were heard coming their way.

"Enough of this playing in mud, boy. I got some real work for you." The young overseer's wide straw hat blocked a bit of the sun over them. Bo stood straight for a stretch, then hunched down before Overseer Junior got the impression he was trying to stand too tall. Nobody liked an uppity Negro. Papa Sap used to warn him, *Best to always behave half of yourself or they'll cut you down to make it so.*

"Now get going, ya hear?"

"Where are you taking him that's more important than the duties I've ordered?" She spoke with such audacity, Bo flinched. He'd never heard a slave, or someone like her, speak that way to an overseer. To talk back and not be slapped or beat for it.

The young overseer cocked his head and shifted his eyes toward Bo. "You gotta problem doing what I ask, boy?"

"No, sir, I do whatever you need me to do, masta-sir."

"Excuse me, I will decide what needs to be done," she said, not backing down.

He gripped his rifle like a comforting blanket. "I don't believe you have any say here."

"I beg your pardon?"

"My daddy says I only listen to the Ross men, the misters of the household. You don't look like no mister to me."

"I'm Lily Ross. I have plenty say around here and you'll do what you're told."

The little overseer stood straight. "Ma'am. I'm sorry, but I was told this boy here needs to help clear the road, a clean path to the gate for the party guests."

"When he's finished with his duties here, I will send him on his way."

"Yes, ma'am. I guess that'd be all right."

Once he'd moved out of earshot, Bo whispered, "All right, then."

"You see, Bowman Carter, you can trust me." She touched his hand. "I can fool them all. We'll ride right out of here. You'll be the carriage driver of Missus Lily Ross," she said with conviction.

Bo's chest rose and fell breathing in the possibility.

"I'll tell Cleo to bring you into the big house for the party tomorrow. That way you can get your fancy clothes all ready. Just don't give 'em back. Ball everything up and hide it for the day when we leave. You're going to need those clothes as my driver. I'll write out the pass. Then I'll plan when we leave."

"When?" Bo asked. "I got some things to say to some folks." Guilt surrounded his shoulders. Leaving others behind wasn't easy.

"I have to figure out the best time," she said calmly. "Please don't change your mind, Bo. This is important. We can do this together."

"I'm not scared," he said, calmer too. "Well, maybe a little."

"Bo, was that a smile?"

"Nah. A bug got on my face, is all."

41

Sisters

The afternoon began with a barrage of carriage wheels squeaking onto the property. One after the other, guests stepped down after their long rides and were escorted up the stairs to the sprawling Ross foyer where Tilda stood, full of exuberance, to celebrate her son going off to war. Her spirits were as high as her voice as she welcomed her guests.

"I'm Tilda Ross. Thank you for coming. Oh, you look lovely." Tilda looked exceptional herself. Bright emerald and diamond earrings dangled at her lobes, matching a gown that fit her thin frame. Her hair was smoothed and polished, pinned in a twisted chignon. Her smile was rehearsed, but undoubtedly the act of smiling alone injected life into her veins. She was a proud and happy mother with a rising social status with every salutation. "Welcome to my home."

The other ladies came through the foyer with coiffed hair and unfettered gowns. The men wore bow ties and tails. A few were already dressed in their uniforms, heavy gray coats with bars signifying a hierarchy that had yet to be established.

We were the next greeters. Timothy and I stood together shaking the hands of the guests, some of whom I recognized from our wedding. Timothy wore his uniform and opaque white gloves. I wore a pair of lace gloves I'd chosen only because working in the garden had shaded my skin unevenly. My gold brocade dress shimmered with beige embossed trim.

As anxiety chilled my bones, I nodded hello to everyone. A wealthy woman with snow-white hair and spectacles at the edge of her nose spoke. "Such a lovely ensemble, dear."

"Thank you. Welcome to our home. I'm Lily Ross."

"Henrietta Henry," she offered. "Good to meet you."

I smiled. Henrietta. I liked her name. It made me think of Lizzy and Maggie all at once.

"Lieutenant Ross, of the Confederate Army," Timothy announced with a bow of his head over her hand, a traditional greeting of respect, barely grazing his nose to the translucent skin of her knuckles. A lock of dark hair fell over his eye before he pushed it back. "Thank you for coming."

"I wouldn't miss this evening. I wish you much success, Lieutenant Ross. May the hand of God guide you to victory."

"I thought you were a captain," I whispered over his shoulder.

"Not yet. It sounded better at the time."

Once the introductions were over, we began mingling, rolling from one group to another with the sole purpose of selling our cause. Tilda had given strict instructions to move on to the next guest with rehearsed statements. "A man has the obligation to do what is necessary to feed his family. Inalienable rights. God's law. We are the righteous. We are the chosen. Money raised for support of our troops could make the difference between life and death."

"I need something to drink. All this talking," I said to Timothy, waving a hand at my throat. I couldn't take another minute. "Please excuse me."

He gave me a harsh look. "We haven't gone around to all the guests yet."

"I'll be back," I said, determined to fall away, to drift in the crowd. I ambled through the standing guests, burrowing forward with no destination.

I landed squarely into a woman's back, knocking her off balance.

She spun around, her dress covered with red wine from the crystal glass she was holding. "Look at this, it's ruined." Her hand swiped against her bodice in sweeping motions where the stain was already setting.

Something as simple as a hand gesture, and I recognized her from all those years of serving her tea. All the times I'd watched her count the brown lumps of sugar as she plopped them in, with her pinched fingers, one at a time. I held my breath waiting for her to scream my name. I kept my head down.

"I'm so sorry," I said.

"Oh my." Tilda had rushed over, a face of concern, yet it was clear that underneath she was in no mood for any of my escapades. Seeing the red splash on the front of Annabelle's dress sent her in a panic. "What's going on? Lily, what's happened?"

"I'm fine, really," Annabelle said calmly, dabbing at the stain with her hands. She still hadn't looked up. She still hadn't seen me. There was time. I could escape. But I was hemmed in, staring at Tilda's brilliant emerald earrings on one side and Annabelle on the other.

Too late.

A slight gasp. Annabelle closed her lips. She was quick to recover from her shock. She stayed silent, letting her eyes do the work for her. *Dahlia?*

"Surely we have something you can change into." Tilda faced me. "Fetch Cleo. She can show her upstairs. You have more dresses than you know what to do with, don't you? The two of you look the same size," Tilda said. She made the reference harmlessly, but the comment made Annabelle wince. She'd heard it enough over the years. She wanted nothing to do with any comparisons, even slightly, to a Negro slave.

"What's happened?" The soft voice belonged to Leslie. It took everything for me not to reach out and pull her into my arms. *Oh, how I've missed you.* It took her a beat longer to realize it was me. Not like Annabelle, who saw right away. "Dah . . . ?" She pulled back when Annabelle dug her nails into her arm.

"I can show her upstairs. I'm sorry, I didn't get your name." I tilted my head pleasantly at the two of them.

"Annabelle," she said with a tight line across her lips. "And this is my sister, Leslie."

"Pleased to make your acquaintance," I said. "Preferably under better circumstances. No need to wait for Cleo," I offered. I peered around to see who else had come. I hoped for a glimpse of Mother Rose. A reunion would've been welcome. I wanted to run into my grandmother's arms and tell her about my adventure. I wanted her to see that I was the granddaughter who'd listened, paid attention to her teachings. I'd seized my moment and lived it. Married. A garden of my own. A baby, lovely Lizzy. Pretty dresses. But she wasn't there, and none of it had been real anyway.

"Yes, please," Annabelle said. "I'd like to change out of this damp dress immediately."

"I'll come too," Leslie offered.

Annabelle looked disappointed. She wanted to have me all to herself. She was going to enjoy this.

So was I.

I felt Annabelle's arm slide against mine. Linked together, we walked with haste away from the others. I felt Timothy and Tilda watching the three of us together, maybe noticing the likeness, the uncanny resemblance.

I led them through the hall, out the back, and down the stairs to the courtyard. I didn't want Annabelle anywhere near my dresses. Or anywhere near Lizzy, who slept peacefully a few doors down in the nursery. Neither she nor Leslie questioned the misdirection. We made our way through the maze of boxwood bushes, only high enough to cover our shoulders. The sun was beginning to set over the trees. Onward they followed, past my garden, what was left of it anyway. Nearly every bloom had been hacked down for the party vases. Green headless stems greeted us as we passed by.

Once we were a good distance from anyone who might've heard our conversation, I stopped and faced them.

Annabelle's hunched body posture spoke of her shock. She kept her hands crossed at her chest, ashamed of the stain, even if it was only Leslie and me who saw it. "So, this is where you've run off to, Dahlia. Here, right under our noses. Just one town away."

"I'm sorry. You must have mistaken me for someone else," I uttered. "My name is Lily Ross. My husband is Lieutenant Ross of the Confederate Army. You just met him inside."

Astonishment washed over Annabelle's face, followed by a giggle from Leslie, who'd been unable to stop herself. Her full cheeks turned blush pink to match her dress. "You look beautiful, Mrs. Lily Ross. Pleased to make your acquaintance." She stuck out her hand.

Annabelle slapped it away. "Don't be ridiculous. Are you insane?" Her anger had risen to its rightful place. The lines on her forehead deepened. "You can play dress-up all you like, but you're still the same house girl, property of Lewis Holt."

"I really have no idea what you're talking about," I replied under my mask of politeness. "By the way, you look beautiful too," I told Leslie. It was true. She'd blossomed. I'd missed her soft smile and gentle tone. "I love your dress."

"Thank you." Leslie smiled and did a brisk bend of her knees. "I love yours too. Did you make it?"

"Stop this nonsense," Annabelle shrieked. "You will not make a fool of me twice."

"Perhaps I can get you some water. You don't look well."

"I'm married now . . . Annabelle LeBeau. Merris LeBeau is my husband. He's downstairs, also wearing a uniform, preparing to fight in this war." She followed up with this information as if it would make the ground more stable between us.

"Well, Missus LeBeau, I'm pleased to make your acquaintance." I put out my hand. When she didn't take it, I smiled pleasantly. Underneath the smile lay my desperate hope that she wouldn't make a scene. Even away from the other guests, Annabelle had a voice that could carry past hedges and pierce through walls.

She took a seat on the stone bench on the cobble path and said nothing. Leslie sat next to her watching with enthralled interest. How would this settle out? Who would be the victor?

"Fine, suit yourself. It was good to meet you. Maybe our paths will cross again in the future." I turned to leave. My heart raced. *Please don't come after me.*

"Do not walk away from me." Annabelle stood and grabbed my arm in a pinching hold. I yanked it back. That was the line she'd crossed, handling me as if she had every right to. The many times she'd slapped me, pinched me, and pulled my hair while screaming her demands.

No more.

I put my head close to hers. "Don't you ever touch me again." This was what I hadn't wanted to happen. My newfound will to survive, to fight back, learned while living in the Ross home, might be dangerous for Annabelle. She saw it too and removed her hand.

"You see, no different than you've always been. Such a child." Annabelle hurled the words as an insult.

Deep inside, I was a child. One who never got to be lucky or happy or assume good things were coming my way. I quickly made a sweep of the grounds to make sure no one witnessed our heads knotted together. From a distance, I was sure we appeared as two women of substance with a fondness for each other, sharing a secret, a new answer to an old problem. No one would suspect Annabelle had relished treating me poorly, making it a daily goal to see how much lower she could push me before breaking my spirit. But on closer inspection, one would hear the jealousy built up over the years, our disdain for each other. Here I stood. I'd risen past her hate, and I was enjoying every moment of it.

"You can't get away with this, Dahlia. You're breaking the law. There's a bounty on you. One snap of my finger and you will be in chains."

I let out a deep sigh. I had so much to say. The charade was over. When, if ever again, would I have a chance to speak frankly?

"I'm an heir to Lewis Holt, no different from you. We have the same father, Annabelle. I'm expected to be your slave for the rest of my life?"

"Having the same father does not give you birthright. Your mother was a slave. That makes you a slave. Besides, we've always treated you with the highest regard, haven't we, Leslie?"

A laugh trickled from my throat. "I'm sorry, but as you can see, I've made a life for myself, just as I deserve, just as anyone deserves. You have no claim to me. No more than I have claim to you. We've intermingled ourselves to the point of no difference at all." I held out my wrists. "Same blood, Annabelle."

"We are nothing alike. You're a daughter of a whore, and I am a lady. You're a slave, and I am your rightful owner."

"You can't hear me because you're simply evil," I said, raising my voice.

"I'm not evil. My family is not evil. Neither are the people here tonight supporting our soldiers. You are the evil one, to play this dreadful charade on such a loyal man and his family." She stood entirely too close. "While we're here to honor your husband for his dedication to the Confederacy, you're making a mockery of him and all that he stands for."

"Fine, tell him. Walk in there with your stained dress and accuse a man's wife of being a slave. You can't prove anything. Besides, I haven't hurt anyone."

"Your very existence hurts everyone," she spat.

I'd had enough of Annabelle and her determination to kill what was left of me. "And how will it look that you and I resemble each other? You and I are not all that different. Have you ever met your mother? Seen a picture? Have you ever looked through our father's birth journal? The one that lists his rightful property? Annabelle Holt. Born May second, 1840. Your name, listed right there with all his other children born from his Negro property. Slaves." I said the word and watched her squirm.

Her eyes lowered. "You saw the book? Who else did you tell?"

"You're just like me, living in the house your father built. Swept up from the quarters at birth and moved in before anyone could know the truth. I saw it with my own eyes. Was it you who scratched out your name and Leslie's right beside it?"

"Stop it." Annabelle looked like she might be ill. She covered her mouth and darted her eyes toward Leslie.

"What is she saying?" Leslie asked. A simple question, but Annabelle was busy searching for an answer.

"Don't believe her. Don't listen to her," Annabelle said to Leslie, who'd gone blank staring at her palms.

"Dahlia, is my name in the book?" Leslie asked.

I didn't want Annabelle to ever see me cry again. I nodded yes. My tears fell anyway. "It's gone now. The night of the fire, it burned in Holt's library. But it's true. I'm sorry if this hurts you, Leslie."

Leslie stood up, swallowing back her tears.

"Sit down," Annabelle spat. "None of this is true. She's a liar. She's always been a liar."

"Mother Rose and Daddy always said our mother was a missionary. She died helping people in Africa. I heard him say this. Over and over, I heard the same story. None of it was true?" Leslie said at barely a whisper. Then she screamed, "Answer me!"

Annabelle flinched, caught off guard by Leslie's outburst. "No. None of it was true. Daddy was never married, not to anyone. Our mother's name was Lucy," she screamed. "She was a slave, a Negro born on our land." She'd spoken too quickly to take it back. Instead, she covered her mouth and closed her eyes, as if it was the worst thing she could endure. But it wasn't. She had more to say. "She was Daddy's own half-sister. That book was a constant reminder of who and what we are," she said with disgust.

Leslie came toward me, ignoring Annabelle's plea to keep her distance. "I hate that all this time you were treated so horribly. When all the while, we were no different at all." She faced Annabelle. "How could you let this go on?"

"Because she cares more about herself than anything," I answered for her.

"That's not true. I care about my sister, my only sister. Leslie, I never wanted you to hear any of this, for your own protection. I tried to end it. I tried to get rid of that book so no one would ever know. It told our story, plain and simple. Do you remember the night of the fire? I went down to Daddy's library and stared at it for the last time. I wanted to protect us. I poured oil over it and lit a match. Before I could get the heavy thing into the fireplace, it fell from my hands. I couldn't put out the fire."

Leslie gasped. "We almost died, Annabelle."

"No. No, I pulled you up, remember? I grabbed your hand and led you out, then we woke up Daddy and Mother Rose."

"But not me," I said. This was the part Annabelle didn't find as easy to admit. She'd awakened everyone but me. "I heard you whispering. I watched your bare feet move about the room. When I sat up, you told me to go back to sleep. I went back to sleep. Then there was nothing but smoke."

"But . . . you told me Dahlia was already outside," Leslie said.

Annabelle, unsteady on her feet, sat down again. "Our father was growing to love her. I saw it in his eyes. I was afraid he might reconsider his promise of keeping it all a secret. If he was willing to welcome her with open arms equally, then questions would start. How does one go from being a slave to his legitimate daughter? Then everyone would begin to look at us, Leslie, and wonder about us too . . . I was afraid."

Annabelle looked at me. She genuinely looked remorseful. "I'm sorry for all the cruel behavior toward you. You didn't ask for any of this."

"It doesn't matter now. None of it matters."

"I will be better. I will do better," Annabelle continued. "When you return home, you'll see. Our father and Mother Rose miss you. They'll be so relieved to have you back, and I promise, we will all make it up to you."

She'd said *our father*. I wiped at the tears I fought against and stared out at the maze of hedges. I was still afraid to trust her. How much had she hated me, that she would've let me die in that fire? If it weren't for Bo, I wouldn't be here now.

I brushed my hands down my skirt and adjusted the hem. "I'm going back inside, Annabelle. You're welcome to any of my dresses. All of them will fit you nicely." I paused for a moment. "All I ever wanted was for you to see me. To see me as your sister. For our father to see me as his daughter, just as much as you and Leslie."

Leslie reached out. "When we return, I'm going to talk to Father about this. You deserve—"

"I don't want anything from him. Not anymore."

Leslie still held my hand. "Mother Rose really does miss you. She talks about you all the time. I miss you dearly too. Come home."

"I'm married now," I said, as if it meant anything. "Please tell Mother Rose I think of her often. I can't return. I just . . . I think it would be best if I found my footing. I don't want to go back to—I've grown so much. I can't chance that Holt—*our father* will treat me fairly. He hired a bounty hunter, a slave catcher . . ." I trailed off, fighting the next wave of tears. "I just can't go back there."

Annabelle took in the moment, noticeably lingering on my hand in Leslie's. "What about Bo? He misses you," she announced. "Don't you want to see him again?"

Why would she say this? I was stunned to silence. And here I thought we were—*Smile.* I took a deep breath. "How is Bo?" I wiped at my face. It was clear now what Annabelle was up to.

Leslie was the only one in the dark. She couldn't hide her questioning glare. She faced Annabelle for answers.

"Bo will be happy to have you home." Annabelle spoke quickly, hoping Leslie would take her cue. Silence. "The two of you can be together again."

I fought the tremble of my lip. Whatever her plot, I wanted this to end. "I'd like to see Bo again. Yes," I said, playing along. I exhaled the breath I was holding.

Annabelle was happy to hear this. "Good. I think it's best for you to return to the Vesterville discreetly. You shouldn't tell anyone. Let's keep this between ourselves. We wouldn't want any rumors moving about our circle. It's safer for you to return home voluntarily. If the bounty hunter that Daddy hired catches you, it might cause quite a stir if you tell this story, this tale of who you think you are, to save yourself. Questions might arise about me and Leslie," she said. "The entire Holt name will be defamed. Leslie, can you see how important it is that none of this gets out? Our reputations are important to maintain."

Leslie's eyes shifted down. Soon she would need to find a husband as well. This wouldn't happen if she were deemed to be the daughter of a slave, now, would it? Clearly this was the message Annabelle wanted her to understand; it wasn't too late to save their reputations.

She kept her eyes down, unsure of what she was supposed to do now.

I let go of her hand. I wouldn't make it hard for her. "I'll need time. I . . . I just have to explain somehow, why I'm leaving. A week, one week will do, enough time for me to say my goodbyes."

"Wonderful," Annabelle said. "I can't wait to have you home. I'm sure the Ross family will miss you. However, they're not to be trusted with any of this. You can't tell them a word of your relation to me, to us." Annabelle had resorted back to feeling her noble self. "Now, how about showing me all your pretty dresses?"

I didn't pay much attention to what else was said after that. My mind spun in a blur of planning, too far ahead to remain in the moment.

Annabelle walked ahead, leading the way back, though she didn't know where she was going. She believed she'd won, so it didn't matter.

We walked back to the house silently. I helped Annabelle change into a new dress, just like old times, and we parted ways in the parlor. Annabelle did not want to be seen too close to me.

42

North

I marched swiftly to the kitchen, where the staff scurried with poured drinks and prepared round trays to serve.

Bo stood regally in his handsome white coat and gloves, getting ready to go out the door with a tray on his shoulder. He saw me too, noticed immediately the panic in my eyes. He set the tray down before leaning into the ear of another server. The tray was transferred to new hands without delay.

Bo wasted no time. "Miss Lily, anything I can help you with?"

"Yes. Please follow me."

The added servers barely noticed us. Cleo shifted a glance in our direction, one that said she had a kitchen to run, a party to facilitate. If there was going to be trouble, she preferred it be taken elsewhere.

I opened a door into a dark stairwell. Only the slaves used this steep, narrow staircase instead of the main one in the center of the house. We were alone, but that wasn't good enough. I led Bo down the stairs to the basement. We could barely see each other in the darkness. I kept ahold of his sleeve.

"Annabelle and Leslie are here. They've already seen me. We had words. They can't see you. Annabelle lied to me and said you were still at the Vesterville. I went along with it, but if she sees you, there's no telling what she will do."

His face twisted in disbelief. "Here? What about Holt and Miss Rose?"

"No. Just Annabelle and Leslie. We're lucky they're not here too. Annabelle said she'd give me a chance to return myself to the Holt plantation. I promised I would. She said she won't tell anyone here who I am. She doesn't want anyone to know about me because she's afraid I'll tell the truth about her."

"About her?"

"And Leslie. Their mama was a Negro slave," I said now. There was no reason to worry about who knew anymore. It wasn't my secret to keep.

Bo's eyes grew wide with confusion. "Wait a minute. What?"

"Annabelle started the fire to burn the birth book because she didn't want anyone to ever know." I knew this wasn't the time to explain. "We have to leave now. If Annabelle sees you, she's going to sound the bell, make accusations, the kind that will get you killed. I don't trust her. I don't know what she's capable of anymore. We have to go right now. With all the carriages out front, no one will notice if one more rides out of here tonight."

"What about papers? I can't leave here without a pass, Dahlia. If I get caught—"

"I took care of it," I whispered. "If anyone stops us, I'll be below in the carriage, a lady of a manor traveling with her driver. Bo, we can't stay here."

"I don't know," he said, shaking his head.

I didn't have time to convince him all over again. "We have to leave together. You're already dressed—Bowman Carter, chauffeur to Missus Timothy Ross. Please, Bo." I tiptoed to rise up for a conciliatory hug. With our hearts pressed against each other, we made a silent promise that we could do this. With Bo's strong arms wrapped around me tight, I wanted to stay there. But we had to go.

We crept back up the stairs, aware of each step as the wood sang underneath our feet. When we arrived at the top, Bo peeked out first, making sure the hallway was clear. The presence of fear had a distinct smell on both of us, in our skin, on our breath. If anything would give us away, it would be the telltale signs of not believing our own story.

Voices of joyful drunk guests echoed a few feet away. Bo put out his hand to help me up the final step, which was steeper than the rest. My hand in his, that's where Essie found us. She'd come down the back stairwell.

The puzzled look on her face quickly went to a suspicious stare. "What's going on?" she asked. "Bo?"

"We leaving," he told her.

Essie's hand went to the fullness of her belly. She cradled the roundness. Because she was still nursing her own little one, I'd assumed she was carrying the weight of a newborn.

I touched Bo's arm. "A baby? I didn't know, Bo. I would've never asked—"

"You mean you going with her? Answer me. You running off with her?"

His mouth fixed to speak, but whatever it was he wanted to say was slow in coming. The way Essie's eyes filled with glossy exactness said she didn't plan to lose him without a fight.

"Can't you see she's using you? You saw what happened to Ruby out there. It's not safe. She ain't been no good ever since. Can't walk straight, can't put words out her mouth without spit and stuttering. Her," she shouted, pointing her finger. "She's the cause of it all."

"Ruby was on foot," Bo answered. "We're not running through rivers and high grass."

"What about our baby we having?"

"You gon' keep with this, Essie?"

Essie opened her mouth to speak, but nothing came out.

Bo continued. "I waited for you to tell me the truth. I wouldn't have cared whose seed you were carrying. I just needed you to tell me the truth. Instead you stayed busy trying to shame me into believing a lie."

"Everything about her is a lie," Essie shouted, then shushed herself. "She been lying since the day she got here."

"At least I know who she is," Bo whispered.

"I know who she is too. She the reason that lady died. Then she let Ruby take the blame. She think she better than all of us. She think she can get away with anything just 'cause she look like a white woman. It ain't right."

"She got no control of what she look like, no more than you, or me. We born the way we born. You a day in the sun darker than her. There ain't no difference."

"Then why she trying to be something she ain't? I'm telling Miss Tilda. I'm telling everybody."

"You do what you have to do," Bo said, turning to leave.

"You choosing her over me?" Essie asked in disbelief. "You really leaving me here?"

"I'm not choosing her over you. I'm choosing me. What I want, for the first time."

"Then take me with you," Essie pleaded, stepping closer to Bo. "We can go right now, together. We don't need her."

"Essie, them boys need you."

"What difference do it make? My boys gon' die anyway. Sold, shot, hung . . . either way, they gon' die. I shoulda hit you harder with that shovel. I was trying to knock some sense into you. But you ain't got none. Go! Nobody want you here." Essie's shrill voice carried through the hall.

"You. I didn't want to believe it." Bo's sickly expression made it clear how he felt.

I stood beside him, unable to move. *Essie hit Bo.* The thought sent shivers through me.

Cleo came out of the kitchen. "What y'all fussing about?" She put a finger to her lips, shushing us before any of us could answer.

I touched Cleo and kissed her cheek. "I'm leaving. Me and Bo are leaving together."

She wrapped her arms around me and held on tight. "You gon' be fine. Go. God bless. Just go."

Bo slowly stepped toward the door, unsure of what Essie might do.

"You won't get far," Essie said. "I promise you that."

Cleo held Essie. "You gon' get us all hurt if you interrupt this party. Miss Tilda will not be happy."

I rushed up the stairs while Cleo did her best to keep peace.

Inside the nursery, I went straight to the bassinet. I picked up Lizzy and held her against my heart. I inhaled her sweet baby breath and kissed her cheeks. *I could take her with me.* I closed my eyes. I didn't want to leave her. But taking her would mean they'd never stop looking. "Oh, my sweet baby."

There were so many regrets. The decision to leave Lizzy was the worst pain of all. I could only pray that Cleo and Tilda kept her safe.

After I put her back in her bassinet, desperation took over. I went to my room, grabbed the book with the hidden money and the bag I'd already packed longing for this day. I was ready to go.

I heard someone behind me. I kept the bag close to my chest and tried not to fall apart.

"Miss Lily, Master Timothy is looking for you." Pico waited at the door.

"Tell him I'll be there shortly." I stood still, waiting to hear him walk away.

"I'm to return with you, or not return at all," he murmured.

I turned and faced him. "Please, Pico, tell him I'm ill. Unable to return."

His eyes fell on the bag. Then back to me. He nodded and backed away.

"Thank you." I moved down the hall, to the hidden stairway, and out the side door.

Bo was waiting outside. "That one," he said. He pointed to the carriage and horses that belonged to Ryland.

He sat up top. I jumped into the covered seating and watched the door of the Ross mansion, praying no one was behind us. I watched until it was small in the distance.

Our plan was to use the train tracks as our guide into the capital. The carriage flowed along, with him perched high in the driver's seat and me below. After a while, we slowed down. Better to not look like we were running.

In my aloneness I watched the curtains wave open every now and again, showing the brilliant sunset of the countryside. By now, Tilda's party would have ended. Tilda, Timothy, and Ryland would have said their goodbyes to their guests.

Annabelle would have noticed that I'd done it again—walked off, disappeared. Because she feared her own secret would be exposed, she'd say nothing until she arrived home to tell our father.

Essie was the one I worried about. She'd tell anyone willing to listen. I was sorry for her wanting Bo and for coming between them. Having someone you could call your own was no small honor. Something both of us only dreamt of having.

The rhythmic gallop of the horses, along with the easy sway of the carriage, took the storm out of me. I dozed in and out of sleep, as much as I tried to fight it. Eventually sleep won. When the ride stopped, I sat up, confused and disoriented, not sure how long I'd been asleep. I tried not to panic, telling myself to remain calm. I poked my head out to see darkness. Bo had climbed down and was standing in front of the horses, soothing them with his touch.

He saw me poke my head out and came around to the side, crunching the underbrush with his solid boots. "Too dark to see where I'm going. We'll be safe to rest up here."

The wooded area was dark and shaded. Barely any moonlight glowed through the dense great oak trees. What little light there was came from the reflection off a river not far away.

"Come inside, then. You can rest in here." I reached over, pulled the lever to open the carriage door.

Bo stood by, hesitant. "I probably should stay out here. If someone sees us, they'll know something's strange. I can't be caught in there with you."

"You just said it was safe, no one would see us. You need to sleep for a little while. I'll keep watch. If I hear anything, I'll wake you." I took his hand and pulled, not letting go until he had no choice but to take the step forward or fall over. His weight shifted the carriage once he was inside.

The interior of the carriage seated four people comfortably. Ash wood paneling covered the floor and sides.

Bo ran both of his hands across the cushions as though he'd never been inside. His body stretched along the panel. He finally released the breath he'd been holding. He unbuttoned his vest and unfastened the collar of his white shirt, the attire for the party.

I handed him the flask of water. He'd been the smart one to grab the water and bread from the kitchen before we left. I gave him a couple of dinner rolls. It didn't take but a few seconds for his hands to be empty, not even a crumb left. He took another gulp of water. I tried to offer him another roll. He lifted up a hand to say he'd had enough.

"Might be a long trip. I don't want to eat up everything."

"How much farther do you think we have to go? Are we going in the right direction?"

"North," he answered. "Everybody knows how to go north."

On the contrary, I had no idea how to go north. I only knew that was where all the free men and women ended their journey.

"What you plan to do when you get there?" he asked.

I shrugged my shoulders. "I don't know. I guess find a way to make a life for myself, for us."

"I'm not talking about that far down the road. I'm talking about when we land on the city streets. Then what? You got money? Them boarding places don't take pretty smiles for payment." Bo forced a grin. "I don't think the North is that kind of free."

"I have money." I reached inside my purse and pulled out the folded wad of bills I'd taken from Ryland's stash.

His face lit up. "That real?"

"Yes, and if this runs out, I have jewelry to sell. Timothy gave me ruby earrings and a matching necklace for my wedding gift." I was struck with a moment of sadness. My wedding day had turned out to be hurtful and embarrassing. I hadn't told Bo the story. In his mind I'd been childish, a child bride full of myself, wanting what I wanted, demanding what I'd been promised. He didn't know about the emptiness. Money and jewelry couldn't fill the emptiness. I shoved the bounty back in my bag. "There's also a note-paying system, like when Mother Rose and Master Holt would sign their names and they'd get anything they wanted."

"What name would you be signing, exactly?"

"A white woman's name is unimportant. What matters is that she's white."

"Works for me," Bo said, throwing back his head, ready to finally rest.

"You don't trust me. Still, after all this time, you don't believe anything I have to say?"

He opened his eyes to heaven and sent up a prayer, mouthing the words *Why me, Lord?*

"Say it. Just say it, Bo. Why'd you even come with me if you think I'm leading you to slaughter?"

He reached over and took my hand. "We have a lot to figure out, that's all. Best not to rush into making promises we can't keep. We'll figure it out along the way."

"I heard you, Bo, when you said to Essie that at least you know who I am. Were you trying to say I'm just one big bag of tricks, but that's okay, 'cause at least you know what to expect? Is that what you meant? When we get to Washington, you plan on ditching me, like you did Essie?" Bitterness brewed in my throat. I regretted saying it the second it left my lips. "I didn't mean that, Bo."

"All I'm trying to do is keep the truth between us. I don't want to dream or pretend. We have to do whatever we need to. That's all."

I reached inside my satchel and pulled out a folded paper. "I took the liberty of granting you your freedom, Mr. Henry Rossman."

Bo was lost in confusion. "What're you saying?"

"Nothing matters but what's on paper. If I say you're a free man, then you're a free man. Edgar P. Rossman, your past owner, has granted you your freedom. I'm Mrs. Henrietta Rossman, his loving widowed wife. Pleased to make your acquaintance, good sir." I bowed my head out of respect. As I looked up, Bo was still speechless. "I practiced for days. I wrote until my hands were sore. I wanted it to be perfect. I got the seal from Timothy's drawer. The R in the red wax makes it look official."

I read out loud. "On this day, September fourth, 1860, know ye that I declare Henry Rossman, a Negro man of about twenty years of age, with strong build and brown eyes, has earned this declaration of freedom from work in worth of payment of four hundred dollars for his right to live pursuant to the laws of the nation. I, Edgar P. Rossman, a free person and resident of the State of Virginia, entitled to be respected accordingly in Person and Property at all times and places, and due full lawful esteem, do hereby acknowledge this note as official."

Bo finally cleared his throat. "How? How did you know what to say?"

"I saw a letter Master Holt had written for Papa Sap," I admitted. "He was getting up in age and could hardly do any more work. The least Holt could do was grant him his freedom. But Papa Sap didn't want to leave. He didn't want to leave you or any of us he'd helped raise. Besides, where was he going to go?"

Bo swallowed the lump in his throat. "I wonder all the time how he's doing, even if he's still alive. He cried when they took me away in chains. I'd never seen him cry."

"He loved you. He loved all of us like we were his own. I know he'd be proud of us. He'd say we were doing the right thing. He'd say, 'Ain't nobody going to save you, so you got to save yourself.' Remember that? Remember how he used to say that whenever you'd fall or get hurt?"

Bo smiled and nodded. "Henry Rossman, huh?"

"I had to use the R. I couldn't think of another name to start with R."

He picked up my hand. "Thank you, miss. I do kindly appreciate my freedom."

"That way, Bo, when we get north, you can leave and be on your way."

"That's not what I meant."

"It's all right. Get some rest." I whispered to keep my voice steady. I didn't want him to know how much the thought scared me, us not having each other.

It didn't take long. A cadence of locusts chirping into the night lulled him like a baby to sleep. I took off my shawl and wrapped it over his chest and shoulders, letting him relax for a change. Seeing him sleep brought me peace.

A low growl passed from his throat. The grunt of snores that followed made his exhaustion only more apparent. I remained alert, sitting up straight, keeping watch. I took my duty seriously and would not let anything happen. I watched his fluttering eyelids and hoped he was having dreams of freedom. That much he deserved.

43

Lake

He jumped. Startled. The scream could've been part of his nightmare. He and Dahlia chased by the man in the field. Always the same dream. This time he was caught. Beaten within an inch of his life with the dreaded cattail.

Run!

Dahlia kept on running.

Now that he was awake, his back hurt as if he'd received each stroke of the whip seen in his nightmare. Knowing the pain came from the awkward position he'd slept in didn't conquer the fear. He could count his blessings that he'd never been beaten harshly, but he'd been a witness to folks being whipped for what felt like an eternity. Lashes cut deep into the skin that bled endlessly. The dream had to be a premonition of what was awaiting him in Washington, DC.

There it was again—not really a scream at all, but more like a howl of pain. He nudged the curtain aside. Panic closed around his throat when he realized the sun was up. How long had he slept? He followed the sound, along with a dirt path through the trees.

As much as he wanted to call Dahlia's name, he stayed as quiet as possible. He slowed and tiptoed so as not to crack a single leaf. The moist brush underfoot gave him silence.

He saw a shimmering reflection of the morning sun bouncing off a bed of water and immediately thought the worst. He rushed, stripping down as he went. By the time he reached the lake's edge, determined to dive in and save her, she stood just fine. She was naked. The shallow water stopped at her waist. Her full breasts bobbed up and down in the fresh cool circles around her. Every dip caused her to sing out with a shiver.

When she popped back up, she noticed him.

"About time you woke up, sleepyhead." She glided over to where he stood at the water's edge.

"I thought you were drowning out here. I heard you screaming from way over there. What if someone heard you?"

"There's no one out here but us . . . you, me, and the fishes." She scooped water into both hands and tossed it up. Just enough to splash coldness at his feet and legs. "Come on in, Bo. Water feels wonderful."

"It's too cold. It's freezing. Get out of there. Might be snakes."

"When did you become such a stick-in-the-mud, Bowman Carter? You are no fun. Now, I demand you jump in." She splashed him a second time, not bothering to cover herself.

She floated away backward. Her soft breasts rose to the sun. He felt the stiffness of his nature rising as he watched the water caress every part of her naked body. Before he could cross his hands to cover himself, she lifted her head to speak. Bo took only a second to consider his options. He took a small running start, jumping into the water before she could witness his indignity.

"That-a-boy!" she cheered, laughing with his heavy splash. The cold water solved his problem quickly. His body quaked in shock. His teeth locked into an uncontrollable chatter. If he could have spoken, he'd have told her a thing or two.

"You poor thing. You're so cold." She swam closer with the sun behind her back while he shivered.

Her graceful shoulders disappeared into the bluish-green hue of the lake. She kept coming, and he wanted to tell her not to come any further. He felt himself growing again, defying the coldness, warmth taking over his entire body. She giggled lightly, gliding closer. Her bare shoulders shined with moistness. He imagined kissing those shoulders. Kissing all of her.

Even as he saw her coming, her touch still took him by surprise. Her breasts pushed into his chest, her stomach to his. She pulled him forward until her full cool lips, sweet and dewy from the lake, touched his.

"We can't, Dahlia."

"Why? You and me, Bo. It's always been us. We're all grown up." She kissed him again, this time wrapping herself around him.

He no longer knew or remembered what coldness felt like, with her this close. This was the one time he wished a moment could last forever. Her warmth made him want to melt as he breathed her in. Her touch fired his desire. Her embrace washed over him.

He was supposed to protect her. How could he do that if he was lost? Lost in her touch.

Before he could talk himself out of it, he cradled her, carrying her up the slope. He slipped a couple of times before climbing out. She held on.

When they got to the straight landing, she held his hand even after they were safely out of danger. She was shivering now. Her cool body tensed when he traced her shoulders. He kissed her mouth, her neck, and back to her lips. He stopped himself there. What he wanted was so much more. The thought of them together, then him losing her, was too much to bear. And yet he was sick of being afraid.

He let his caressing fingertips fall away from her face. He squeezed her close, leaving no space between them. They slowly moved to the ground. *Whatever may come doesn't matter . . . there is only now,* he thought. All they had was now. He gripped her wet limbs and pulled her against him. He looked at the beauty of her face in the warmth of the sun and had a feeling of oneness. No separation between them.

She gripped his face and searched his eyes. "I love you, Bo."

He'd never heard those words before. His mouth pushed against hers. He paused long and hard to try and understand if he felt the same way. If it meant he would die without her, then he was telling the truth. So he said it over and over again. "I love you, Dahlia." *I love you.*

Her breath in his ear and the strong sun at his back sent a powerful jolt through his entire being. They locked onto each other's eyes. They were no longer hiding. Unafraid. This was true freedom.

He kissed her head to toe until there were no parts he hadn't touched. Afterward, they stared up at the blue sky with her head resting on his shoulder. The rest didn't last long. It all began again and nothing could've made him happier.

"I think we need to get back in and wash off," Dahlia finally said, standing up. She brushed the mud off her thighs then reached out for his hand. "Last one in is a rotten egg." She squealed with delight, leaping in, sending a cascade of water overhead. Bo jumped in right behind her. The water wasn't so cold this time. They played and splashed, laughing between accidental gulps of air and water.

44

Safe

"A man," Mother Rose once said in her proper tone, "wants attention, a hot meal, a bed to sleep in at night with a woman by his side. As for a woman, she is only required to feel safe. If she feels safe, there's no limit to her happiness."

I knew that feeling for the first time with Bo's hand in mine. By his side was the safest place in the world. We'd been friends as children. It was something else now, something rich and full. When I breathed, it hurt a little, just the thought of us not being together.

"You can't sit here," he warned when I climbed up on the perch next to him. He still smelled like the lake, fresh and clean. "I already told you. Someone sees you sitting here beside me, that'll be the end, the end of everything."

"For a little while?"

"No." He faced me, leaving a kiss on my forehead. "We'll get there soon enough."

I stayed, stubborn, with my arms folded over my chest.

He let out a sigh followed by another kiss. "Remember the time you wanted to ride that big horse and you just wouldn't take no for an answer? You were no match for that mare. You had to try anyway. The first step that horse took, you slid right off her backside and landed on yours."

This trip down memory lane was intended to remind me of what was at stake. I didn't like to listen, to follow anyone's advice or orders, a nasty habit. I wouldn't just land on my backside. Our lives were at stake if we were caught.

I took my place below in the carriage. I attempted to push the heavy velvet curtains back from the small window and the rod snapped, falling, exposing the full view outside. I tried hanging it back up. It wouldn't stay. I tossed the curtain and the rod out of the way and stuck my face out the window. I inhaled the jasmine-scented air and watched lush woods as we rode. Every now and then a cool breeze rushed inside the moving cabin.

All that mattered was that I could breathe again, the same way I'd felt in the lake. Alive.

I was still afraid of what we would face in Washington. I'd made the story sound believable to Bo when in fact I had no idea if freedom awaited us.

The time when the horses slowed came earlier than expected. Bo called the horses to a final stop. The carriage shifted as he climbed down. From my open view, I saw him walk into the covering of the woods. I needed to relieve myself as well. We'd drunk up all the lake water we could hold. I stepped down and went behind a grove of trees. I moved quickly. I didn't like the idea of leaving Bo alone, not for a second. I was his protector, just as he was mine.

I walked back to the road. The horses remained at the ready, shiny and well managed. My heart skipped erratically as I got closer. I moved around, fully checking the carriage before sticking my head in for a peek. Bo wasn't there.

"Got us some berries," he said from behind me.

"You scared me."

"I got stabbed by prickly bushes for you, woman."

I took the handful of blackberries. "Thank you, kind sir. But can we make a promise to always tell the other of our whereabouts? Always."

He nodded. "I'm sorry I scared you."

"And . . ."

"I don't like making promises I'm not sure I can keep, Dahlia, that's all." He kept his dark lashes down, avoiding me and the potential for getting into another disagreement. We had both been through enough—resentments and betrayals—before now. It felt better to be direct and honest.

"I respect that. I just want you to know . . . I don't want to lose you," I told him.

"I'm not planning on letting you out of my sight either." He held my hand, guiding me back inside the carriage.

Another full day passed and we were in Washington, arriving smoothly without so much as a dip in the road. We'd made the trip. I shrieked with excitement. Onlookers walking in the city street peered briefly in our direction. We slowed to a stop in front of a tall building. It was a risk, but we were prepared to take it.

Checking into a hotel was only right for Mrs. Henrietta Rossman. Bo took on his chauffeur role, grabbing the bag I'd packed with clothes, and stayed a few steps behind as I walked into the hotel.

"Good day, madam. Welcome to the Willard Hotel. Will you be staying with us?" The desk clerk wore glasses and a neatly trimmed mustache. He opened up a large signature book without waiting for the answer to his question.

"Yes, I will be staying two nights. I'll also need accommodations for my driver."

"Absolutely. We have special accommodations for the service help. Please fill out your name here. Your room is four dollars per night."

I was almost too giddy for words. I had four dollars and so much more. I dug into my bag and pulled out the wad of bills.

"You pay when you check out, madam." I wanted to turn around and say to Bo, *You see, I told you so.*

Relief and delight all at the same time tingled from my fingertips. I signed *Henrietta Rossman,* just as I'd practiced. Two days would give us plenty of time to sell the jewelry too. We'd have money to spare. Our plans were in motion.

The clerk slipped a finger onto the page. "And here, your driver's name."

"Yes, of course. And exactly where will he be staying?" I asked, as I wrote Bo's new name. Henry Rossman.

"We have quarters downstairs, madam. Very accommodating," he chimed before hitting the bell on his counter. "You'll be in suite 402. I'll have someone escort you to your room and carry your bag. If you need your driver, we'll have him summoned. Here is your key. Please enjoy your stay." The clerk's cordial manner almost went beyond reasonable. Then again, what else did I expect? This was a place where service and kindness were important. And I was Henrietta Rossman—why wouldn't I expect kindness and respect?

I turned to leave the desk. The anxiety of separating from Bo kicked in. I faced him, nervous. "Henry, I'll be needing a ride directly in the morning. Eight o'clock sharp." I wanted to grasp his hand, touch his skin. Instead, I kept my wrists clasped and crossed against each other. "Thank you. That will be all."

Bo gave me a nod to ease my mind. "Yes, ma'am." He blinked wearily, tired from the long ride. Stress and fear had gotten the best of him, of us both. But we'd made it.

The bellman went to take my small bag but I pulled it close to my chest. "Not this one." I would not let the purse with the money and jewels out of my sight. I'd learned at least that much from Ryland. Keep what you cared about most closest to you.

The bellman took the other satchel, of dresses Timothy had given me, as many as I could shove inside. I followed him through the lobby, turning back to get a last glance at Bo. He was already gone.

I followed the bellman up the polished stairwell, so many steps, I was sure we'd reached heaven.

When we finally stopped, I was out of breath and slightly dizzy. The number 402 was painted in gold on the door. I stopped at the entrance as the bellman held the door open.

"After you, ma'am." He waited off to the side.

The room was breathtaking. I took the first step inside and was greeted by opulence. Gold satin appliques covered the wall to the ceiling edge. Dark blue velvet curtains hung over the paned windows, as beautiful as any dress I'd seen. I couldn't resist rushing to the window to see the view of the city street. High aboveground, I could see the horse carriages. People below milling about looked small and fragile.

"Ma'am, may I get you anything else?"

"I'm fine. Thank you." I fought to control my excitement. This room with the flowered walls and framed art was all mine, at least for the night. The bellman remained standing at attention, even after I'd told him he was no longer needed. "You can go," I said, unsure of any other way of telling him. He left with a shrug.

I sat on the smooth bed and rubbed my hands across the floral appliques. There was a table with a small vase and flowers as well as a bowl of fruit. A basin sat in the corner with an oval mirror attached. Ornately framed art hung on the walls. There was nothing more I could ask for, except to have Bo here by my side to share it.

45

Henrietta

I stared at the paper I'd made for Bo with the signature of Edgar P. Rossman.

I should've given the freedom certificate to Bo to keep in his possession in case someone questioned him while I wasn't around. I carefully folded it and put it with my other valuables, then went downstairs and asked the clerk to call Bo.

I sat to have morning tea. I'd easily become a blur, a swirl of nothingness blending in with petticoats and muted conversations. I ate a single piece of bread with jam. I'd been up since sunrise, waiting for eight o'clock, when Bo and I were supposed to meet.

Large white columns blocked my view of the other side of the lobby, so I moved seats. Then moved again when my view still wasn't clear enough.

"More tea, madam?" The waiter stood at the ready to pour. His red vest was stained with various drippings, but his gloves were spotless white.

"Please, thank you. Do you happen to know the time?"

He pulled out a pocket watch and eyed it closely. "A quarter to eight, madam."

"Thank you." I pushed on the heavy bun of hair I'd pinned, making sure it wasn't falling down. Henrietta Rossman would never be caught with a hair out of place. I listened to the chitchat of the ladies at the next table.

"The *Post* reported battles in the field could begin any day now. All of this to end the slave trade, which has nothing to do with us. Why should our sons and husbands be responsible for their lives?"

I stood abruptly, knocking into the table, spilling tea over the white tablecloth. Silver forks and spoons jangled to the floor. The waiter rushed to offer assistance.

"I'm fine." I grabbed my shawl and went to the desk clerk. "Hello, sir, have you summoned my driver, Henry?" The soft-waxed floor underneath my feet felt slippery. I tried to relax when I realized I was grabbing the clerk's counter with a death grip.

"Yes, madam. He's been summoned."

"He isn't here."

"He's most likely waiting at your coach, madam?"

I made my way toward the exit. The doorman in his red coat and black pants stepped aside, opening the door wide.

There was no urgency besides wanting to see Bo's face and cure the jitters in my stomach. I slowed my gait, breathed in and out gently, and made myself believe Bo would be standing outside with the carriage, when in truth something, a needling stab in my side, had already told me he would not.

I stepped out into the bright sunlight. The city street was littered with muddled piles of filth and horse droppings I hadn't seen before.

On our arrival, I'd been too excited to notice the litter and imperfection. I'd imagined heaven here in the capital. But it was the paper, the notices flapping in the wind, that mostly caught my attention. One landed underneath my foot: *Runaway*. For a second, I panicked. But the picture was of a man who looked like every captured soul, as far as the artist was concerned: wide nose, heavy forehead, and full lips. I kicked it away, then turned my attention up and down the block. There was a line of carriages. None of them was accompanied by Bo.

"Would you like me to summon your driver, ma'am?" the doorman asked patiently. I'd been standing there, unable to move. "Which one is yours, miss?" He nodded toward the line of carriages, where men sat on their stations, at the ready. None of them was Bo.

The longer I stood there, the more I was convinced something had gone wrong. A surge of fear exploded in my chest as I replayed Lewis Holt's stories of slave kidnappings, free men as well, taken and sold. The hairs on my arms stood up with the thought of Bo in chains again.

I began walking, checking the horses and the buggies that all now looked alike. The only thing I knew for sure was that *our* horses, the ones we'd taken from Ryland, had been clean and well kept. Bo cared for those horses better than he cared for himself. I spied a healthy-looking horse, brown, a shiny coat, across the street, then saw the carriage with the curtain missing. I picked up my skirt to save my hem from the dusty filth in the road and began in that direction.

Dahlia!

Was the calling of my name just my imagination? Bo wasn't where the carriage sat. I searched, spinning, my view landing on two men approaching. Men I didn't recognize. Men I had never laid eyes on before this day, and yet they knew my name.

"Good day, Miss Holt," one of them said, as earnestly as any gentleman.

I turned away, determined not to panic.

"Miss Dahlia Holt." I felt the tap on my shoulder, then a full-on grip, hot around my neck.

I gasped and struggled to get away. "What're you doing? Get your hands off me."

He whipped me around to face him. He was a big man with an orange beard. "How do you do? You mind having a word with me, Miss Holt?" His polite words didn't match the spite in his eyes.

"You must have mistaken me for someone else."

The thin, taller man took a step closer, waving a piece of paper. "This telegram says to check the base of her neck for a scar. A long scar, goes all the way to her buttocks."

"Do you mind if we go somewhere to examine your back, Miss Holt?" The orange hair of the other man's whiskers turned up in a sly smile. He looked almost embarrassed to ask, and yet I knew he felt nothing but empowered.

"My name is Henrietta Rossman." Caught between them, I attempted to move past his sturdy frame.

He pushed himself closer. "If you're not Miss Holt, you can go on your way. This will only take a moment, I promise." He grabbed at my collar.

"Let us see your back then, *Henrietta*," the thin man said smugly. He tugged and pulled until I heard a rip.

"Help! Please, get off me."

"What're you doing accosting this woman? I'll have the police on you. Back away now." A man with glasses and a satchel approached.

"Sir, this here is a runaway slave. Dahlia Holt."

His bright blue eyes brimmed with shock. "A slave? This is a white woman. Let go of her." He attempted to put out a hand.

The thin man slid in front of him. He held up his notice. "We can prove it. She's got a scar down her back. See this notice, here?" He held up the sketch. "Dahlia Holt, property of Lewis Holt of Hampton, Virginia."

The larger, orange-bearded man reached for the weapon hiding underneath his jacket. "She's not a woman. She's a slave. I suggest you mind your business." The shiny pistol was long and menacing.

I held my breath, afraid my rescuer was about to be shot because of me.

The man backed away slowly. "I'll call the authorities, miss," he said before turning to a trot. He looked back, unsure, holding his hat and satchel, and turned the corner.

I struggled between the two men with no way out. I'd been caught. I only hoped and prayed they hadn't taken Bo too.

46

Underground

The hotel workers all shared a dark, cool space where cots were set out in three long rows, putting all these grown men in one space, no different than slave quarters. And here he'd thought he was free.

"So, where you from?" one of the men asked Bo when he first arrived in the basement.

"Not too far, down the road a bit," was Bo's standard answer. He didn't like questions. More so since he and Dahlia were on the run.

"Caleb." The man put out a rugged hand. "I'm a driver, sometimes a cook, a doorman, whatever they need me to be." He chuckled to himself. "I give full honest days of work and still can't afford to be nowhere but here."

Bo nodded. He could see now. It wasn't going to be easy. Making his own way, making a living, would be hard.

"You look like this might be new to you." Caleb shuffled a set of playing cards thick and bent on every edge, proof that the men had nothing else to do on their off hours.

"I'm tired is all," Bo answered.

Caleb set down a folded blanket and pillow. "I know a newly freed man when I see one. Let me give you some advice. Don't ever think you got something to say. Don't matter who you think you are. They got black doctors, teachers, bankers, right here in this town. Still, nothing's changed. A white man can still pull out his pistol and shoot you where you stand and ain't nobody going to bat an eye. So don't go around feeling cocky about yourself."

"Then what's the point of being a free man?" Bo countered.

"Those few hours when you don't have to say *yes sir*, *no sir*, you can dream. You can hope. Couldn't do that before now, could you?"

There wasn't really a time when Bo had stopped dreaming. He could admit that now. He admired Dahlia for actually doing more than dream. She was a doer, a chance-taker, and now he was too. This trip had been the boldest thing he'd done in his life.

He replayed every single moment. Afraid as he was of being caught, he still had never been happier. And now he wanted to see where things would go, what kind of life they could have—together. He was willing to do whatever it took as long as he could be with Dahlia.

The next morning the men woke up and ate where they slept. Bo dressed quickly in his pants and white shirt, with plenty of time before he and Dahlia were supposed to meet up.

He watered and fed the horses with what should've been Bo's breakfast, toast and mashed oats with honey. Master Ryland's horses weren't used to nothing but the best.

Just as he reached underneath to check the bolt that attached the carriage to the horses, he heard the men. He sank deeper to peer at their scrambling feet. Boots. White men.

"RR stands for Ryland Ross," one of the voices said. "When we find the coach, we find the runaway." There were two of them checking the horses, looking for brand markings.

Bo's heart tried to leap from his chest. He stayed still, fighting to keep his balance. He lost, falling backward. A horse-led carriage barely missed him before he flipped himself over and crawled out of harm's way.

He stayed low, hunched, and moved fast as possible until he was far enough down the street to not be seen. He circled back and ran to the hotel. He had to warn Dahlia. *RR. Ryland Ross.* He'd sent men to find her.

"Hey there, brother, looks like someone fell in the horse pit." Caleb stood in front of Bo, taking in the mess he'd made of his shirt from rolling in the filth.

"Yeah," Bo breathed out. He didn't have time to explain. He was trying to get back through the side door of the hotel. *Warn Dahlia. Save Dahlia.*

"I got a shirt I can let you borrow," Caleb said, blocking his entry. "You can't go in like that."

When Bo glanced back in the direction of the carriage, he saw her hurrying across the street. The two men were on the other side of the carriage where she was headed. She wouldn't have seen them.

"Dahlia, no!" He was about to chase her down when he felt the grip on his shoulder. Caleb's hands were all over him, yanking him backward.

"Let go of me." Bo struggled. He felt himself being dragged. Not just by Caleb—there were others, men from the basement, gripping him until he could barely move, let alone see.

"Whatever it is, you better off alive than dead."

"Hold him down," one of the others ordered.

Bo kept up his struggle. They didn't understand. He had to protect her. All he ever wanted to do was protect her.

"We can't let you go, brother, until you calm down."

"All right, then, I'm good," he said, waiting for the chance to break free.

Caleb outweighed him, and the other men were pure muscle, tightly pinning Bo to the ground. "Tell us what's going on. You see, we don't like anyone bringing attention to the group. You make trouble—next thing you know they busting through the roost house with a noose, and any one of us will do. Now what'd you do to get yourself up in this mess?"

Bo was far too angry to talk calmly. *Dahlia. Bounty hunters.* He relaxed long enough to be believable. As soon as he felt their weight lift, he fought harder, swinging his legs around, twisting himself out of their grip. He broke loose but the place where the carriage and horses had been sitting was an empty space.

Dahlia was gone.

He bolted without a clue as to which direction they'd taken her. He ran with no idea where he was running to. It was as if the blue sky had opened up and swallowed her whole. Gone from existence. When he couldn't take another step from exhaustion, he found himself at a crossroads, confused, not sure which way to turn. He panted for air. Sucked in dust from an open field and wondered how he'd gotten there.

He fell to his knees and wept, cursing the devil and God all in one breath. Where had they taken her? His delirious thoughts relayed back and forth to what the men were saying. *Branding marks. RR.* They were looking to take her back to the Ross land.

Even if it took the rest of his life, he swore he would get her back.

47

Run

I struggled against the rope that bound my hands behind my back. I couldn't see with the dusty burlap sack over my head. The rattle of wheels was the only sound besides my heart pounding a tumultuous drum in my ears.

"Please, can anyone hear me? I can't breathe."

The motion of the carriage caused my stomach to swell until I could no longer hold on to the tea and bread I'd had earlier, waiting for Bo. Did they have Bo too? I prayed he'd gotten away. The horses came to a halt. There was silence. The most I could hope for was to be taken back to the Holt plantation.

I was led out to stand. The burlap sack was yanked away. My hands remained tied. I could see the silhouette in front of me. I blinked until I'd adjusted to the brightness.

"Miss Dahlia Holt?" The silhouette slowly revealed the face I knew would match the voice. Ryland stood with his arms folded over his chest. He leaned in close. "I thought we were having such fun and off you go, leaving me, without notice." He turned to the men. "You can leave."

"Ryland." My throat burned from the bile I'd pushed up. Fear turned into a bitter paste on my tongue. "You hired them?"

"Lizzy's wet nurse couldn't wait to tell me your plan to run off with your friend Bo." He sighed. "Essie, that one, she doesn't like you much."

He offered his flask against my lips. I gulped, desperate for each swallow of water.

The men waited patiently until Ryland was finished. One was already on the horse he'd ridden while the other had manned the stolen carriage. "We'll take what you owe us and be on our way," the stocky orange one said. He stepped toward us.

I shrank away.

"You don't have to be afraid. I'm here to protect you, Lily." Ryland pulled a coarse package from his breast pocket and handed it over. "There's a bonus in there for returning the horses as well. Good work."

The men plodded away on a shared horse. We were left alone in a wooded area.

"Now," Ryland said, "it's just you and I."

I closed my eyes. I wouldn't cry. I was done crying. "I'm not going back."

"You have no choice. There's a bounty on you. Everyone knows the truth now. But I will protect you. You, me, and Lizzy, we can be a family." He dangled Lizzy's name like forbidden fruit. I wanted to hold her and be with her. She'd given me life when I thought there was nothing much to live for.

"I didn't want to leave Lizzy."

He saw a break. "You don't have to. Me, you, and Lizzy, together? Why not? Timothy and Tilda will understand. They will have to, won't they?"

I couldn't speak. I knew there was no right answer. When he leaned in I turned my head. He pulled my face toward him. "I think we can agree that you don't have a lot of choices here, Lily. I've been patient with you. More than kind, even while everyone else in the house has been against you. You don't want this life," he said, rushing his words. "To be chased, hunted, always looking over your shoulder. I will make sure you stay free. And your friend, Bo. I promise no more running for either of you."

"You have Bo?" I forced myself to speak though the dryness was cutting at my throat.

"Yes. Yes, I do."

"Where is he? Where?" I'd always blame myself. I was the one who talked Bo into leaving with promises of freedom. And look what I'd done.

"He's safe," Ryland said, offering no more details.

"Where?" I demanded. My hands twisted against the rope still tied around my wrists.

"He'll be at the house when we arrive, Lily. Don't worry. He's safe, unharmed, and just as worried about you as you are about him."

"What about his fever? He was burning hot when I left him," I lied. Bo wasn't sick and he didn't have a fever. The mark down my back prickled with heat. I waited for his answer.

Ryland paused. "He's being treated by a doctor. Trust me, he'll be fine."

In that moment I changed. I wasn't frightened anymore. I wasn't unsure about Ryland and who he truly was. I wasn't unsure about who I was. I knew in my heart I was going to see Bo again, and Ryland was not going to get the better of me. I closed my eyes, this time falling against him. "Thank you."

"All right, then," Ryland said, with his usual confidence. He reached to the side of his belt and pulled out a sharp blade. He turned me around. The dull side of the knife wedged against my skin. The rope fell away from my wrists. The blood immediately rushed to my tingling fingertips.

"You deserve to be happy." He took my hands and brought them to his lips. "You have to understand. Being with me is the best thing for you. You understand me, right?"

I nodded my head. *Yes.* The only answer I could give. Unbearable dread washed over me.

Ryland took my arm and escorted me to the carriage. I was hitched upward to the bench. I sat trembling. This was where Bo had sat as we rode away to escape the Ross home.

After Ryland tied his horse to the back of the carriage, he came and sat next to me, still silent. He snapped the reins. We began the ride. I recognized the path, the same one Bo and I had taken into the city, only now going the opposite direction.

Washington, DC, wasn't far away. Bo might still be there. Ryland didn't have him, that much I knew for sure.

"I'd much rather take our time, Ryland." I leaned on his shoulder and caressed his arm.

His body tensed. He immediately stopped the coach. He leaned forward and cupped my face with his gloved hands. "Lily."

I kissed him lightly. The knife strapped to his waist was a reach away. I stayed in the kiss, willing myself to reach for it. I could feel the blood nervously coursing through my veins, plotting my getaway. I didn't think I could stab him with a knife and mortally wound him, but if I could hurt him, just enough to escape . . .

He took my hand and led me down the steps of the perch.

He pulled and I followed into a hidden dry area. The squawk of a bird announced our arrival. My heart raced while he cleared a flat landing of any sticks or rocks. He kneeled, stroked the ground, then held out his hand as if a formal invitation made it a fair fight.

I came and kneeled beside him. I was running out of time.

Knife. Belt. Knife. Rock. There was one rock, large and jagged, far too big for one hand. It would require two. Now that his body was pinning me down on one side, I wouldn't be able to grab it. There was another rock behind the bigger one. While he nuzzled at my neck, I could see it just a grasp away. That one would fit in one grip. The right size to be lifted, and jagged enough to come down on Ryland's head with damaging force.

I stared up at the sky, the shift of leaves allowing glimpses of the sun. I could do this.

I lifted and swung, only grazing the back of his head but enough to shock him.

He grabbed my wrist before I could connect with my second attempt. The rock thudded to the ground. We both contemplated what to do next. We both came to the same conclusion. Utter amazement and horror washed over his face. Shock had turned to disbelief over how I could betray him. He slapped my hand away from the knife at his waist and rolled over, releasing me from his weight.

I scrambled to my feet to put distance between us. He rose to his feet, paced a few steps, then came back.

"Stay away from me!"

"You think I'd hit you, beat you?" He shook his head, still moving back and forth. "You realize I could have anyone. Anyone." His voice rose, hitting an arc of disgust. "I chose you."

"You can't have anyone, because you can't have me," I screamed. "That's what this is about. You're so used to having whatever you want. What is not given, you take. You rob. You steal," I panted. "You had Maggie and you still wanted more."

"What is this nonsense? You have no choice, do you understand?" he nearly screamed back.

"I have a choice. I won't go. Why are you doing this, Ryland? You have everything and more, is all you know. Where were you the night Lizzy was born? You were gone for three days. Where were you? Is that what you were apologizing for? You asked me if she forgave you? Well, what do you think? Do you think she would forgive you now, for what you're doing?"

I sank to my knees. I couldn't have stood any longer even if I'd wanted to. "I have nothing but myself, and you want to take that too. When is enough enough for you, Ryland? Why can't you let me go?"

He leaned forward, breathing hard. He was angry. Or something else, hurt. "Enough, then," he whispered, his voice hoarse. "Now. Now is indeed enough." He yanked me to my feet. He led me back to the carriage. We rode together in silence, with all the fight drained from both of us.

48

Heaven

The road became wider. We passed buggies and carriages coming and going. A sign swung sideways from a tree where it had once been secured: *Welcome to The Capital.* It could still be a trap. Ryland had decided to bring me back to the street where I'd first been dragged away. The carriage pulled to a stop. I was a step away from the hotel. I checked around for men with more guns.

Ryland stared straight ahead as I climbed down from the carriage. I should've counted my blessings and run, but I stood there until he looked at me. I swallowed back the urge to put out my hand. "Thank you."

"You deserve to have a chance, Lily." He began to say something else, then stopped. He let out a defeated sigh.

"I will never forget this kindness."

He signaled for the two horses to move, pulling away slowly. When he and the carriage turned the corner, I breathed relief and forced myself to take one step at a time toward the entrance of the hotel. I approached cautiously, aware I could be manhandled and scooped up at any turn. Master Holt had put out his own bounty. John Browder wouldn't stop looking. Just as Ryland had said, I'd always be looking over my shoulder.

The doorman shifted noticeably when he saw me coming. He took a straight stance, folding his gloved hands in front of him instead of opening the door. There were no patrons of color allowed. Staff and servants were to go through the side entry. I braced myself to be turned away.

Surely he'd witnessed the commotion, seen the men dragging me away like so many others who'd stood by helpless. My secret would be flowing in whispers among the staff.

"Ma'am," the doorman said. "Yo' driver been searching for you since this morning, ma'am." He swung the door open. "Welcome back. Good to see you fine and well." He stole a quick glance directly to my eyes. He knew. Though I was hardly fine and well. I could feel scratches swelling around my neck. The knot at the side of my head pulsed with pain. Between fighting with the men on the street and grappling with Ryland, I was surely a sight.

I slipped inside, grateful to be on the other side of the door. "If you see my driver again, could you summon me? I'll be in my room."

"Yes, ma'am." He tipped his tall hat.

As much as I wanted to rush and hide in the hotel room, I was more afraid of never seeing Bo again. I stepped to the clerk at the front desk. "My driver. Henry?"

The clerk looked me over, my disheveled state, and paused. "No, madam. In the meantime, are you in need of assistance?" His eyes lingered on the torn threads at the neck of my dress, where the men had torn at my back. I pushed loose strands of hair behind my ears.

"Can you notify me when he's found?" I said with the confidence of Henrietta Rossman, disheveled or not.

"Of course," he said.

I headed up the many stairs to my room. I stopped several times to catch my breath and focus on what I had to do. One, two, three more steps . . . *keep moving*.

I'd been slowed, tripped, and pushed down, but I'd never given up, and I wasn't going to give up now.

When I opened the door of suite 402 I foolishly imagined Bo standing there.

Instead, emptiness. I locked the door behind me, rushed over to the bed, fell to my knees, and reached underneath. Panic struck as I felt around. I reached further before my hand found the satchel. I pulled it open. The money. The jewelry. *Thank God.*

The hotel would be my sanctuary. There was enough money. If Bo showed up he would know where to find me.

The next day, I left my room, down the four flights of stairs, only to ask if anyone had seen Henry Rossman. My driver. Henry. I'd even uttered the name Bowman Carter in case he'd divulged his truth to one of the other servers or stewards on the hotel staff.

On the second day, I sat down to have my tea and remained there until my legs were numb. When I couldn't take it any longer, I moved slowly to stand. The servers in the parlor of the hotel had grown used to me. One rushed over. "Ma'am, you all right?"

"Yes. Thank you." I reached out and touched his arm. "Have you seen a driver named Henry?"

The man kindly shook his head no. "We all know you looking for him, ma'am. If we see him, we'll tell you fast and in a hurry. My name is Caleb. Anything you need, ask for me."

The next day was the same.

I watched the door open and close as the staff arrived for work. When evening came, I retired to bed. In the morning, I returned again. Every so often one of the butlers would ask if they could bring me something to eat. I replied with a no, thank you. They poured more tea. They all knew I was looking, waiting, for a man, my driver, Henry Rossman, and every so often I'd ask about someone named Bowman Carter. Then would come the shift of their eyes followed by silence.

"Ma'am, can I offer you assistance?"

"No . . . no, thank you," I said, turning to face the server to make my usual inquiry.

"Dahlia. Don't look. Turn away."

I fought the urge to scream his name and leap into his arms. "I thought I'd never see you again," I whispered.

I couldn't bear not to look. He kept his eyes down and moved the sugar bowl around on the table for effect. There was a bruise over his left eye.

"How did you get that?" I asked, fighting the lump in my throat. "Are you hurt?"

"Nah, not anymore," he said. "Before seeing you, I thought I might as well die. I was out there looking—I didn't know." He choked up. "How'd you get away?"

"Ryland. He wanted me to go back with him. We came to an understanding."

He pulled out a rag and wiped the table next to mine. "An understanding? Is he waiting for you?" He stopped moving the rag. He straightened up and stood with his back to me.

"No. I couldn't go back there. I couldn't go with him and leave you, Bo." I grabbed his hand, looped my fingers through his. "I'm sick of running. I'm tired of pretending."

To anyone who bothered to look our way—his hand wrapped around mine, even in the great capital where every man was entitled to his freedom—we were wrong. It was dangerous. We weren't free enough to announce our love for each other in a public space. Our hands separated. But only for the moment. We'd have our own moments after that.

"I have enough money to buy train passes," I said. "We can go somewhere no one will ever look for us. Further north."

"And what's after that?" he asked, finally turning around.

"Heaven. I don't know," I said, shaking my head. "I wouldn't care as long as I was with you."

"And all this time, turns out you really are an angel."

On a cool spring day, I walked off, becoming a free woman in more ways than one.

ACKNOWLEDGMENTS

Dahlia Holt became more than a historical truth, she became my child, my daughter. I wanted to see her make it to safety and freedom. I'm thankful to the Library of Congress for the wealth of information and documents accessible for research and study. When I came across a picture of three little girls, sisters who were enslaved, I saw my story, the one I wanted to tell. Delving into the history of separating families is not easy. There is an overwhelming feeling of loss that must be dealt with on the page and in the heart and mind. I experienced the emotions in each step of my character's journey. I'm so thankful to Cameron Thomas and Gail Ragen for caring about Dahlia's story and for the countless re-reads. Having these two in my corner makes me feel like I have wings. I appreciated the truly honest and loving feedback. I'm immensely grateful to Claudia Cross and Jeff Kleinman, who worked tirelessly to find a home for this story. I especially want to thank Jodi Warshaw for loving Dahlia and Bo as much as I do and for giving them a soft place to land.

ABOUT THE AUTHOR

Photo © 2005 Kristen Mary Potts

Trisha R. Thomas has been featured in *O, The Oprah Magazine*'s Books That Made a Difference. Her work has been featured and reviewed in *Cosmopolitan*, the *Washington Post, Publishers Weekly, Kirkus Reviews, Essence,* and the *Seattle Post-Intelligencer.* Her debut novel, *Nappily Ever After,* is now a popular Netflix original film. She is also a reviewer for the *Los Angeles Review of Books.* Trisha is a recipient of the Literary Lion Award from the King County Library System Foundation, was a finalist for an NAACP Image Award for Outstanding Literary Work, and was voted Best New Writer by the Black Writers Collective. For more information visit www.trisharthomas.com.